A REIGN OF EMERALD FIRE

A YARN SPUN FROM THE LORE OF UPRYNENOS: 1

A REIGN OF EMERALD FIRE

MATTHEW J TURNER

Dedication:

To Kelsey, the epitome of patience, understanding and tolerance for dealing with all my idiotic tomfoolery. For Rowan & Theodore, who hopefully won't put me in a home.

Acknowledgment:

To my father, Colin Turner, who raised me regardless of how painful the experience must have been. Children – not even once. To the British Educational System, for giving me something to prove. To my friends; CJ, Graham, Ben, Simon and Guy, Danny & Brandon for the memories, the ale and the banter. I also wish to raise a toast to all those who aided me in transitioning from my ex-publisher to self-publishing. It's been a long road, but we all found freedom in the end.

THE KINGDOM OF UPRYNENOS

Chapter One

A Caravan Getaway

Awakening with an exaggerated stretch, the sun peeked over the horizon. Its dazzling rays spread across the land, glazing the desert with a warming glow, announcing the beginning of its glorious ascent.

The new day's light glaring rudely into her eyes, Yilonia emitted a rueful sigh, her huff lost in the hubbub of hundreds of weary folk starting their day with an obnoxious disregard to her weariness. She'd awoken in an uncomfortable state. Relentless fatigue sent a shiver down her spine, despite the oppressive heat. Her back, slick with sweat, screamed in agony from hours of hunching in positions a contortionist would struggle to master. A persistent ache in her neck rendered the typically simple task of lifting her head a significant challenge, leaving her almost as crooked as some of her shadier companions on this journey of the damned.

Haggard in appearance, together they shared the many trials and tribulations of travelling in a cramped vegetable cart, living through each bone-crunching bump of the road in grudging solidarity. Each traveller selflessly endured the dislodging of every splinter with their arses without complaint, which Yilonia believed was a true show of camaraderie. Sadly, life as a human pincushion wasn't as glamorous as it sounded. Riding in such a rundown old thing, still marked by a few stubborn beetroot stains, and emitting a pungent rotten-cabbage smell no amount of scrubbing could get rid of, hardly filled Yilonia with enthusiasm. The prospect of rolling through another long and arduous day – a day that was once again lacking the faintest hint of a breeze – was becoming less appealing by the second.

After a fruitless period of tossing and turning, Yilonia reluctantly abandoned all hope of falling back to sleep. She attempted a series of complex manoeuvres to free her arms and stretch her body. Unhappy with the orange-tinted dawn, she turned the air from amber to blue with a string of harsh curses, cringing as every muscle in her back unknotted itself.

The sun rose early this time of year. Only two of the nine travellers who journeyed with Yilonia in the shoddy little cart were awake; neither of them seemed any happier than her at being so.

Slouching against the opposite corner was a tall, withered old man with dark olive skin. According to rumour, he was the rightful lord of some hovel down south. He now spent his days as a bitter outcast, after his younger brother usurped him of his lands and title.

Sitting across from Yilonia, waving his wide-brimmed hat as a makeshift fan, grumbled a dwarf. Owing to a disastrous combination of scalding heat, bright ginger hair and pasty white skin, he'd been left looking not so much sun-kissed but sun-open-mouth-snogged-with-tongue. To make matters worse, he had one of the strangest accents Yilonia had ever come across. She'd tried to offer him some blight oil to help with his sores, but he'd waved his big fluffy hat and shouted at her in a voice akin to an enraged goat's.

There's just no helping some people, she mused.

Admittedly, dwarfs were not, stereotypically, the most accommodating people at the best of times, and much like Yilonia, he was presumably getting sick of trundling along endlessly, day after day, night after night.

Morning wore on. The caravan rumbled along the ancient road, coarse sand crumpling under its wheels, leaving nothing to show for their long journey but a faint trail. Apt, as no fool traipsed this far out into the desert without hoping to become nothing more than a fading stain on history.

Droughlyke – the perfect spot for anyone desperate to leave their past behind and escape to the edge of the known world. To most, being slowly roasted alive under the scorching desert sun wasn't particularly desirable. Yet safe havens were tough to come by, so enjoying relative safety in exchange for back-breaking, unappreciated and utterly pointless labour in intolerable conditions was as good of a deal as you could get. Thankfully, running away this far north, you would've had to have committed regicide for anyone to bother coming after you.

Coincidentally, Yilonia hadn't broken any real laws. At least not the King's Law. She'd simply indulged in one of those basic human rights that had, once upon a time, attracted the vindictiveness of some fool who'd held wildly fanatical views and wielded far too much power. Through fear of their own persecution, precipitated by an effective regime of hardship, torture, and unrepentant cruelty, the masses had accepted it as just another law. An unwritten one, but a law nonetheless.

Yilonia huffed then coughed as the rickety cart swayed along in the vast caravan of the Val Company. The dust-filled air turned each breath into a lungful of grit and her underwear into sandpaper. Flies swarmed both ends of the monstrous oxen that'd eaten, sweat and shat their way through the last six hundred miles or so. For Yilonia, much as for the oxen, sustenance was essential to surviving the scorching bleakness of the north. So why must she suffer dried meat for breakfast again? Dried fucking meat! Her tongue already tasted like it'd licked the arsehole of a sand-serpent.

Against all better judgment, and with much resistance from her jaw, Yilonia forced her portion down. Attempting to ignore the hunger pangs in her stomach, she made her way carefully to the edge of the cart. She slipped off to settle her affairs before her journey's end.

Striding past cart after cart, with the glaring sun on her back, Yilonia struggled to comprehend the sheer magnitude of the landscape spread out before her. The sight always remained the same – the seemingly-endless caravan stretching off into the golden horizon – yet each wagon she passed brought new sensations. The whiff of ox shit, for example, was a fragrance she knew all too well. However, some things would always seem out of place. To Yilonia's ears, the laughter of playing children had become un-nerving.

Val's caravan seemed to comprise a whole city, passing through a perpet-ual blaze of sun and sand, passing from settlement to settlement, making trades for goods or gold before returning to the road. Dozens of families, hundreds of exiles, and countless ordinary folk trying to make an honest living. Never staying, never home. A whole patchwork of people, each striving towards a purpose. Maybe they'd shaken off the shackles of orderly existence and feudal obligation a long time ago. No fields to till or crops to reap ... or fathers to please.

Even the lowliest scum here have their fleas to confide in, friends to share a cup with, family to care for, she thought. Such things left her feeling like an outsider, flailing hopelessly in an ocean of unachievable freedom.

She was snapped away from the ravaging jaws of self-pity by a familiar, joyful cry.

'Loni, Loni!' she heard from a few carriages behind, followed by the distinctive thud of a small child crashing down from a cart, with the grace only little Lysio Lightfingers could possess.

A thin smile formed on Yilonia's face. Slowing pace, she pretended not to hear the shouts of the oncoming child until the very last moment, when she swung round, grabbed Lysio under the arms and threw her into the air.

Lysio's laughter rang through the desert, washing away Yilonia's doubts and sorrows, as if a calming wave had reached her from the ocean a thousand miles away.

'Put me down! Put me down!' Lysio cried, forcing each word through her wheezing laughter. 'I've got something for you. *Please* put me down!'

After throwing and catching Lysio thrice more, Yilonia gave in to the ache in her arms and plonked the girl back down, ruffling her short yet remarkably knotted brown hair.

'Lysio, never doubt my appreciation of your ... talents,' Yilonia said, 'but I think you should return whatever you have to its rightful owner, don't you?'

Lysio looked down to her bare feet. Her toes wiggled, digging a tunnel in the sand, fidgeting with feigned shyness.

'Whaddya mean?' She beamed up at Yilonia, with a flutter of her lashes that would've melted the caravan's entire supply of butter, if the desert sun hadn't done so first.

Yilonia huffed. 'You know exactly what I mean. I don't want to be involved in another argument with some Lundinian bastard who says the lovely new veil you gave me belongs to his wife!'

Yilonia hadn't long recovered from the last embarrassing encounter and wasn't willing to let herself be drawn into another any time soon. Little Lysio Lightfingers was sweet as freshly drawn honeycomb and precious as gold leaf, and she damn well knew it. Yet disguised behind her innocent facade was one of the finest pickpockets in all the wide north. Since she'd been old enough to grasp things in her tiny hands, she and her inadequate wretch of a father had travelled together in Val's ever-shifting caravan, selling supplies and trinkets to anyone shady enough to ask no questions. Which was quite a significant percentage of the population.

'Cor, you do something once and get tarred with the same brush for the rest of your life!' Lysio exclaimed, throwing her arms up in the air. She gave Yilonia a crooked smile. 'Didn't turn away the little silver pendant I stole for you, though, did ya?'

'That was different – it was mine to begin with!'

'And I got it back for you, so fair's fair. By the way, you never did say thanks for that,' said Lysio, clearly trying to sound hurt as she plopped down with a pout.

'What? Er ... thank you, I guess.'

'You're welcome.' Lysio beamed. 'Anyway, it was a win-win in the end – me and Pa got some coins, and you got your pendant back. I don't see what the problem is.'

Yilonia was about to argue, but she caught sight of Lysio's eyes staring deep into hers and buckled.

That's my argument soundly defeated, she thought.

'Come on. If you're just going to get up to no good, you can help me find Mascal,' she said, hoping the girl would be humble in victory.

Lysio's face, however, soon bore the sly yet enchanting smile of a child relishing in one-upping an elder. She sprung up, hugged Yilonia's legs, then shot off, kicking up a storm of sand as she went.

'Let's go, slowcoach! Catch me if you can!'

Rubbing the grit from her eyes, Yilonia watched Lysio run off along the caravan, sighed at the whimsy of youth, then shouted and chased after her.

By the time Yilonia had caught up, she was wheezing uncontrollably, feeling as if a white-hot gauntlet had seized her lungs and clawed searing nails deep into her soft pink flesh. She hadn't ever considered herself out of shape. However, kneeling there, gasping for each precious lungful of air as Lysio frolicked around her, Yilonia conceded how decrepit she must look.

Eventually, she regained enough strength to stand and continue on. *Must be all this time riding in the back of that sodding cart,* she thought, panting like a dog. She resolved to put more effort into keeping herself fit. *I've never heard of an exile being 'on the brisk walk' before. If I can't go twenty feet without coughing up a lung, I've got no chance.*

'Hurry up. It'll be supper by the time we find Mascal at this rate!'

Lysio took Yilonia's hand, dragging her along. For a while, Yilonia carried the young girl on her shoulders to save her legs. However, before too long, Lysio jumped down and zoomed off like a crossbow bolt, leaving Yilonia wondering why she'd bothered carrying her in the first place. She smiled at Lysio's antics all the same.

After being delayed by some distractions, including wolf-whistles from a few scumbags in a passing cart – one of whom earned himself a black eye from a good shot with an apple core – and an elderly elven couple who needed help fitting a new wheel to their broken carriage, they came upon Val Mascal.

In an age gone by, Val Mascal had been a strong but elegant tower of a man. A man gifted with a silver tongue, whose words had been honest as the reflection in a mirror. Sadly, as the decades passed, those words had become tarnished, the silver tongue pawned off for wine. Years of trailing the caravan, watching the world change around him and failing to evolve with the times had left Mascal lonely and pitiful but undoubtedly rich.

When Yilonia and Lysio approached, he was arguing with a frail elven woman, in a cart bearing a tattered sign: *Heleaif's Antique Trinkets of Mystical Magic and Wondrous Witchcraft.* Peering at the wares, Yilonia noticed all sorts of odds and sods, some of which looked quite dangerous, especially since the Cull of Magic.

Unsurprisingly, there appeared to be some disagreement over money that the old woman, who must've been Heleaif, owed Mascal. Pleading hysterically, eyes awash with tears, the elf professed the small pouch of coins she held in her trembling hands to be all she had.

Val Mascal sat shirtless. His bulbous belly dripped with sweat as he stroked his chin with one heavily ringed hand. He may have been more imposing if he'd had a beard, rather than flaps of loose skin hanging from his cheekbones. To Heleaif, however, he must've cut a forcible figure. He barked a string of insults, wagging a large sausage of a finger in her face, before snatching the pouch of coins and jumping down from the cart.

'Ah, if it isn't my favourite little puppy!' he boomed, with enough volume that the arse-end of the caravan probably rocked from the shockwave. With all the grace of a disorientated lamb strolling onto an icy lake, he'd landed only an inch or two from Yilonia's face. 'Maybe puppy isn't a strong enough term – I think *bitch* might be more fitting. Anyway, come to pay your debts, have you? Don't think old Mascal has forgotten about your imminent departure!'

Lysio's ears perked up.

'Oh, and what do we have here?' he said. 'Blimey, she's a little one, isn't she? You surprise even me, Yilonia.' He knelt to whisper to Lysio, loud enough for everyone within arrowshot to hear. 'I'd be careful around this one, if I were you. She's been known to get up to *all sorts*.'

Yilonia couldn't resist imagining gelding him with a blunt cheese knife.

'How could I forget?' she said curtly. 'I've been religiously counting down the days.'

'Well, I'm glad to hear you haven't totally disowned the old ways. We faithful followers know every sinner shall face punishment within the cleansing Flame once the Eternal Shuffler comes to claim their souls, and I think we can all agree *your* sins, my dear, are wholly certain.' Mascal smiled, baring a mix of gold and rotten teeth.

'Let me worry about my sins, and you can worry about yours,' Yilonia said, with a smile just as scornful. 'And yes, as a matter of fact, that's why I'm here.' She tossed a small pouch at Mascal, which he snapped out of the air with a reflex belying his age and size. 'There's my full payment for a one-way trip from Stunheath to Droughlyke.'

Mascal looked up from the gold coins he'd poured out from the pouch.

'You're short,' he said.

'Well, that's a miraculous observation, Val. I blame my mother. She was one-eighth dwarf.'

'That's not what I meant, and you know it!' he thundered.

'It's the amount we agreed on,' Yilonia said. She'd expected some form of extortion and prepared for it appropriately.

'That was for Stunheath to Droughlyke in six months. It's been eight and half!'

'That's your fault, not mine.'

'You still need to pay for the extra resources you've used.'

'I'll pay you what we agreed, and nothing else,' snapped Yilonia.

He's damn lucky to be getting what he is! she raged. The conditions were significantly worse than Mascal had led her to believe. Besides, she'd looked after herself for most of the journey, so his talk of 'extra resources' was utter bullshit.

'You feral clam-shucker!' Mascal exclaimed. 'It's all you filth ever do! Play up to the strings of good, honest men, such as myself, just to turn around once you've got what you want and screw us over – and not even in the way we like! I've always said you can't trust women, especially ones who ...' Mascal paused to gaze around him. 'Hey, why aren't the carts moving?' he shouted to no one in particular.

'Don't know, Val Mal,' a dishevelled dwarf called from the nearest cart. 'Looks like something up front is blocking the way.'

'Why aren't they going around it, then? Flame and ashes, I suppose I'll have to go and fix everything, like sodding normal! And for the love of the gods above, put some blight oil on, man. I've seen healthier things in the privy bucket!'

Mascal threw one last spiteful look over to Yilonia, then made his way towards the head of the caravan. With nothing better to do, Yilonia and Lysio followed.

'Oh! Fatty just reminded me,' Lysio said. 'I was meant to give you something!' She dived into her ratty brown satchel and pulled out a small dagger.

'Wow, I hadn't realised you'd moved up to that kind of theft.'

'What? No, no, no. It's a gift.' Lysio beamed. 'I bought it for you.'

'You bought it?' Yilonia asked, both astonished and relieved. 'Why? I mean, I'm touched, but ...'

'Well, I know you're leaving soon, and I know what kinda place you're walking into.' Lysio took Yilonia's hand. 'You're the closest thing to a big sister I've ever had, and it'll be two or three long years before we're back up this way, so I just wanted to say thank you.'

'Aww, Lysio.' Yilonia scooped her up and gave her a spinning hug. 'You've brought me so much joy on this journey. Thank you so much – I promise to keep it with me always.'

'And the hilt's engraved with two rings linked together. That's us. Friends forever!'

'It's beautiful, little one. Just like you.' Yilonia hugged her again, before putting her down and tucking the dagger away.

'That's not all. Look,' Lysio said, as she held up an ornate gold ring. 'It's Fatty's.'

Yilonia burst out laughing, grabbed the young girl and ruffled her hair wildly.

'Oh, Lightfingers, you're a wonder to behold!'

***

The head of the great caravan was tremendously crowded. Everyone from the first mile of carriages must've come to see what was causing the ruckus, and every one of them was fighting their way forward, attempting to get a better glimpse of the action. Yilonia could see Val Mascal in the centre of the crowd, bellowing orders from his camel, glancing down at something on the ground. Whatever it was, it'd spooked him.

Yilonia picked Lysio up and tried to work her way through the braying mob. As she shoved her way forward, various mutterings of what had happened spread through the crowd. Most stories she heard were as crazy as they were different, but all were worrisome.

Yilonia could hear the wailing of an old woman close to the front, and occasional shouts of fear, yet she needed to see with her own eyes what had stopped the never-ending journey of the Val Company caravan. When she finally fought her way through, she struggled to understand what lay before her.

A crumbled mess of cinders slumped on the parched earth. A whiff of stale smoke drifted through the air.

What creature from above – or, more likely, from the abyss below – could've done this?

A whole host of possibilities ran through her mind, as she stood gazing down at the scorched, blackened bones of a horse and rider, fused together in a twisted wreck.

Chapter Two

A Stroll Through the Forest

'   and *the early bird catches the worm* – my father always used to say that, too. Which seemed strange to me, as he was never up before midday. He was a man of sage advice, though, was my old dad. He would always say to me, *Smiggly, my young lad, it'll be the ...*'

'If you don't tell that lad to shut up soon, I'll be forced to provide the *early birds* with another kind of worm, if you get my drift, sir,' Ivein whispered into Stánwilte's ear.

'Yes, point taken,' Stánwilte whispered back, before raising his voice. 'I think that's enough of your father's wise words, thank you, Smiggly.'

'Oh, righty-o, sir.' Smiggly pouted and kicked a patch of dead leaves, looking all his thirteen years of age, before his eyes lit up with renewed excitement. 'My mother, now there's a wonderful lady! Do you know what she used to say to me when I was a wee lad? She'd say, *Smiggly, my boy ...*'

Blimey, he's a simple one.

Stánwilte's weary thought drifted away as if caught in the forest breeze, likely joining a choir of similar musings from the other men in his patrol, which manifested in a crushing silence that finally caused Smiggly to cease his storytelling.

Cutting through the uneasy silence, the cold wind continued to blow, whistling from the gloomy depths of the clustered trees.

I hate this fucking place, Stánwilte grumbled to himself. No one else would want to listen to his complaining, so he decided he might as well try to cheer himself up by cursing in the blessed solitude of his mind. Alas, it didn't work.

It was a damp and sullen evening. The kind that makes a man want to be lazing by a roaring fire, a horn full of mead in one hand, the other resting on a belly full of bread and boar. Yet here Stánwilte was, trudging through the forest, feet squelching on the dead leaves littering the rain-sodden ground, wasting his time on another fruitless patrol. He wouldn't mind so much if what waited for him at the watch house was more than a cup of watered-down wine and the last scraps of Mistress Roslyn's meatloaf, which had been a stodgy wedge of fat and gristle when it was cooked a week ago.

Stánwilte's mood soured further as his mind drifted to times gone by. He'd once guarded kings and queens, watched over the royal palace and stood proudly as Commander of the King's First Legion. The finest smiths in all Uprynenos had crafted his sword and armour. As right-hand man to the throne, he'd worn the gold and blue of the King's First, along with the royal coat of arms – the spire rising against a flaming sky. His blade had been polished to such a shine that a man could see his terrified reflection before Stánwilte rammed it through his skull.

That'd been five years ago. Five punishing years of regret eating away at his soul, piece by bloody piece. These days, Stánwilte was lucky if his sword was sharp enough to slice his ration of stale bread, let alone pierce the flesh of his foes.

No. For all the perks of quaint country life, Stánwilte still couldn't get used to being Captain of the Watch in a small western town.

Peplyshaw was not, in all honesty, a bad place to be. It had solid defensive walls, a long-established trade in exotic treasures, and a lush, well-stocked forest. Most of its population took every opportunity to boast that it was the most peaceful town in the kingdom. To the fresh-faced recruit, or the ageing, war-wounded soldier, it was perfect. To Stánwilte, however, it was a living hell.

Stánwilte had built his name through great deeds in the face of nigh-impossible odds. What of his name now, after he'd been publicly banished by his own king? Here he was, pussyfooting around, hundreds of leagues from any real action. Captain of the idlest town watch in history, keeper of a peace that was hardly ever threatened. It was hardly fair to the good people of Uprynenos that the hero of the Siege of Bracknol was unable to protect them, unable to lead the king's army into glorious battle against invasion from across the sea.

No matter how charming and picturesque it seemed to everyone else, Peplyshaw was never going to feel like home.

***

Finally, the rain appeared to have stopped, although it didn't make of a difference to Stánwilte. Thousands of tiny droplets still fell upon him, blown from their sanctuaries in the ancient ash trees by harsh gusts of wind.

He'd sent his men back to the watch house to be alone with his thoughts, which now, after being soaked to the core, mostly consisted of cursing the fact that his clothes and boots would still be damp in the morning, even if he hung them by the fire all night.

Reaching the edge of the forest, he stood under the silvery moonlight, finally free to see that the storm had indeed passed. Now that the heavy clouds had cleared from the darkened heavens above, it seemed it wasn't going to be such a terrible evening after all. He wiped the last of the rainwater from his brow, tucked his damp cloak closer around himself, and made his way towards the town gates.

Trudging along the dirt track that served as Peplyshaw's main trading route with Minland in the west, Stánwilte soon caught sight of the town's stone walls standing cold and unyielding in the distance before him. As he approached, he saw the wisp of a single flame, glimmering wildly from side to side, fighting to stay alight in the harsh winds. The man holding the torch was standing under the minuscule cover offered by the gate's archway, wrapped up snugly within his thick cloak.

Whoever the waiting man was, he must've seen Stánwilte approaching through the veil of darkness. He rose sharply from his slouch. This show of respect eased Stánwilte's mind, as it showed that the waiting man was likely a member of the Watch. Well, either that, or someone had gone for the cut-rate choice when hiring an assassin to take him out ... again.

'I was wondering when you'd be returning to us, sir. I didn't think you'd be out for so long on a harsh night like this,' spoke a tired and trembling voice, as the man offered a leather-gloved hand in greeting.

Stánwilte smiled. He took the man's hand, wrenched him in and embraced him as if he were a long-lost brother. As intended, Stánwilte got the poor soul, who'd been doing a reasonable job at keeping dry, considerably damp.

'Bæwylm, you old dog, you'll catch your death hanging around out here!'

'Well, I *was* doing a bloody good job of avoiding it until you came back. What took you so long, anyway?'

'I just thought I'd give the forest a proper look-over. We both know people wait for angry nights like this to smuggle goods into town.'

'Aye, you have a point. But as far as I'm concerned, crooks and bandits can wait until morning. I'm far too old – and *we* are far too busy – to be poking around in the rain. Besides, I have a nip of Lundinian whisky waiting to help me sort through next week's roster.'

Bæwylm was right about the amount of work that needed to be seen to, but he was wrong about being *too old*. At sixty-four, he was as fit and healthy as most people half his age. Although he was more than a few inches short of an imposing height, his greying beard, assertive posture, and astoundingly muscular arms commanded respect.

Bæwylm often kept himself busy with the real running of the Watch, while Stánwilte, a man of thirty-six, had the simple duties of strolling around to inspect the men, nodding his head and giving the occasional order.

Stánwilte knew this to be a great injustice. Bæwylm had spent forty-one years in the Peplyshaw Watch. He should have, and *would* have, been its captain, if Stánwilte hadn't been exiled there. However, Bæwylm never held it against him, even if some of the other men did.

Stánwilte gave the old man a mighty slap on the back, put an arm around his hulking shoulders and started to lead him back towards the great hall.

'I'm glad one of us is on the ball,' Stánwilte said. 'I trust the men are keeping vigilant as ever, and Brolo has completed the inventory for tomorrow's supply trip?'

'Not really, sir.' Bæwylm stopped and scratched the back of his neck. 'Brolo's teaching the men how to play cards in the hall.'

'You mean he's trying to win all their wages again?' Stánwilte asked, his voice rising.

'You say turnips, I say neeps.'

'By the sodding Flame!' Stánwilte cursed under his breath.

Stánwilte was as far removed from religion as anyone who'd witnessed the horrors of the world, so the Dragonian curses he'd picked up were something of an annoyance to him. He'd grown up in the rich and cultured east of the kingdom, where the old belief system had long been abandoned by the noble class. Instead, they followed the Circle, which was far less harsh on life's more disreputable pleasures. Stánwilte also thought the idea of worshipping dragons absurd, especially as they hadn't been seen alive in the kingdom for centuries. Yet the kings of Uprynenos still annually sacrificed livestock to the church, as well as vast amounts from the royal purse. Acts born from fear of a peasant uprising. Apparently, you could take a person's land, force them to work in god-awful conditions and give them only the most basic of human rights without hearing so much as a peep. However, if you tried to mess with the funding of their millennia-old fire-breathing reptile religion, the masses would be marching with torches and pitchforks faster than you could say *'All this gold? Horrible stuff, if I'm honest. Here – you sweet-scented, merciful peasants can have the lot.'*

'I've warned Brolo before about playing card games!' Stánwilte said. 'I explicitly told him to get the inventory done by the time I returned. Bloody dwelf!'

Stánwilte's chief problem with Brolo was that he and a significant portion of Peplyshaw's population were constantly locked in petty disputes. Which wouldn't exist, as Stánwilte was tired of pointing out, if Brolo simply gave the odd apology. However, he seemed determined to maintain all grievances against him, leading to his reputation as one of the most contemptuous runts in all Uprynenos.

'Ah, we all know what he's like,' Bæwylm said. 'He's happy to do anything for the Watch, as long as it doesn't involve paperwork, manual labour or, well ... watching.'

'You don't have to defend him every time he's in the wrong. I don't need excuses – I just need him to do what he's told.' Stánwilte sighed, tired of the same old argument rearing its head.

'He's independent is all, sir. If you'd had the childhood he did, you'd probably be the same.'

'Yes, yes. Mixed-race bastard abandoned by his father immediately after conception, lost his mother not long ago, blah, blah, blah. I've heard it all before. Look, I like the lad at times, but if he doesn't get his sodding act together, I'll have to reconsider his place here. Understood?'

'Understood. I'll have a word with him.'

'Good. Thank you.' Stánwilte smiled. 'Come on, old man, let's get you in the warmth. We'll break up this little social night, then see if we can find something nice to eat, eh?'

'Just Mistress Roslyn's meatloaf left, I'm afraid,' Bæwylm said, sounding as if he were giving a mother the news of her son's passing.

'I suppose two out of three ain't bad,' muttered Stánwilte, as he contemplated another night of cramps from Roslyn's *speciality dish*.

Chapter Three

Don't Forget to Flush

It was quiet. Almost too quiet. Only a few faint whispers echoed through the ancient stone hall of the Peplyshaw Watch. A cold wind hurried the death of the fire, left abandoned like a scorned lover in the great hearth. Darkness had consumed the room, save for the flicker of candlelight from the lone occupied table in its centre. This table had captured the attention of the hearth's supposed attendee, Mistress Roslyn, along with all the off-duty watchmen and some of the on-duty sluggards, too. All drawn like fleas to a mangy mutt.

Seated at the table were the three remaining players of what had started as a friendly game of poker between esteemed colleges, but had quickly escalated into a high-stakes, all-or-nothing battle royale between the conniving, the daring and the reckless.

Wilkhelm Cormorant, fourth son of the Lord of Arbour Vale, and Igelf *'The Wall'* Rocksnor faced Brolo the dwelf as he skimmed over his cards with a cautious eye. All summoned an iron strength of will to withhold the slightest iota of expression from forming on their faces. All except Igelf, who had the poker face of a five-year-old and was easy to read as a raised middle finger. Despite stroke after stroke of pure ineptitude, beginner's luck had kept the Wall still in the game. However, it didn't take a wizard's magic twenty-cube to see Lady Luck was watching over Wilkhelm's shoulders this night, as he sat smirking with a vast quantity of gold stacked neatly on his side of the table.

Being the fourth and youngest son, Wilkhelm didn't stand to receive his father's title, any of his expansive land, or much of his wealth. Adding insult to injury, Wilkhelm's father had also failed to provide the extensive tutoring bestowed upon his two eldest brothers. Nor had he learnt the basic household management skills his third brother had been fortunate enough to master. Instead, he'd been forced to serve Peplyshaw as a member of the town watch. Despite all of this, he still found it within himself to act as regal as the Queen of Uprynenos.

The Wall, though, was a completely different beast.

Igelf had a long history of proudly boasting that he'd earned his nickname from being as steadfast and unconquerable as the Aqulinoc Wall – a vast structure that had stood for almost eight hundred years. Truth be told, he'd earned it because conversation with him usually left you wanting to bang your head against the nearest mass of stone.

Playing Igelf wasn't too different from playing Wilkhelm. In Brolo's eyes, both men were as thick as Mistress Roslyn's potato consommé, which often doubled as wallpaper paste. However, where Wilkhelm's arrogance indicated a hapless fool with more money than sense, Igelf's mild comprehension of the rules could lead him to play a rather unpredictable game. With his tall, muscular body, trunk-like neck, and strangely rectangular head, the Wall cut an unnerving figure. Untamed black hair hung over his face, hiding the raisin-like eyes that sat above his bulbous nose. His hazy gaze gave the impression of a man deep in contemplation of life's great mysteries, such as *if I buttered both sides of my toast and dropped it, would anyone mind if I still ate it?*

A cold gust of wind blew through the hall, reminding everyone of the unseasonably harsh weather outside, and almost blowing out the room's only light source. Some of the onlookers shuffled, breaking the hall's silence with a few muttered obscenities. Brolo, though, with the warm orange candlelight shimmering in his jet-black eyes, kept focused on the two men seated across from him. The majority of his attention remained on Wilkhelm, as he'd deduced from Igelf's sweaty palms and defeatist slouch that he would be folding very soon. Unless, of course, he was even stupider than Brolo thought.

Brolo's hand wasn't perfect either – a straight. Fighting his nerves, he let his eyes flicker to the ante piled in the centre of the table. The sight of the coin he'd already placed down was too tempting a gamble. Besides, backing down would cost just as much again in the loss of face and pride.

It would take a miracle for that bumbling bastard to get a winning hand anyway, Brolo mused. *He couldn't pull a thorn from his backside, let alone pull off a victory.*

In a surprising change of pace, considering the last half hour had mostly consisted of the three of them firing distrustful glares at each other, Wilkhelm grabbed his cup of weak ale and rose from his seat. Grinning, he duly implemented the unorthodox yet characteristic tactic of goading his opponents.

'If I may, gentlemen. As much as I enjoy Brolo staring at me lovingly, I would like some time to enjoy my night off. I fully intend to spend some of my forthcoming fortune at the closest tavern, so could we dispense with all the scowling and get this over and done with, eh?'

Wilkhelm radiated confidence as he sat back down. If Igelf had looked on edge before, he now possessed the countenance of a man who'd ridden his horse backwards off a cliff.

Brolo reached for his horn. He took a deep gulp of the stale water inside, trying his hardest to imagine the taste of the robust brown ale he loved so much. Tossing the drained cup aside, he stroked his scruffy blond beard, which was crudely braided in the dwarfish fashion, as he tried to assess his next move. After twenty seconds of intense consideration of every way his play could go horribly wrong, he decided to roll the dice, so to speak, and play Wilkhelm at his own game.

Without uttering a single word, Brolo placed his cards facedown on the table, jumped down from his seat, and turned towards the small door that led to the Watch's living quarters.

'Just where do you think you're going, dwelf?' came Igelf's lumbering, disturbingly hollow voice.

Brolo stopped.

'Why, my good man, to make this interesting,' he replied, with a flicker of a smile, then opened the door and left.

A few minutes later, he returned carrying a large wooden trunk. The hall fell silent once again. After Igelf helpfully cleared a space on the table, Brolo sat the trunk down, placed a tiny black key into the rusted keyhole and unlocked it.

Ever so slowly, he lifted the lid, taking extra care not to break the frail hinges holding the chest together. He removed a tightly-packed layer of straw, producing a large linen-wrapped item, and gently placed it upon the table. He began to unwrap the faded green-and-gold linen, as delicately as if he were pruning a bush of elven ice roses. Once he'd fully exposed the only heirloom bequeathed to him by his father, he held it up, showing it off to the watchful eyes in the hall. The sight of it brought gasps from Igelf and the assembled crowd, but Wilkhelm only arched an eyebrow.

'It's called Lawgismirin, the Gavel of the Justice Bringer,' said Brolo, raising the great war hammer above his head. 'My father left it to me, as his father before left it to him, and so on through the ages.'

'Is this the same noble father who left when you weren't even halfway formed of your mother's belly?' asked Wilkhelm. 'Or should I say *malformed*? It must've been hard enough for a dwarf to get a fine, intelligent elven girl into bed – only to vamoose before his bastard was born? Legendary! A stellar example of knowing when to cut your losses, and perhaps one you should follow. Alas, dwelf, I'm afraid sentimental value has no place on the poker table.'

There was no denying Brolo had to bite his tongue, both physically and metaphorically. As he still held the war hammer aloft, the thought of caving in the side of Wilkhelm's skull proved tantalising. However, he instead let a sliver of a grin form on his face and placed Lawgismirin gently down onto the table.

'South-Rimmien steel, sourced from ancient dwarfish mines. The haft is expertly carved from Nimudian red sproak – the toughest tree this side of the frontier, which has also been extinct for around four hundred years.'

Brolo grabbed the hammer and smashed it against the wall, leaving a great chip in the sturdy stone and a ringing in the ears of all present.

'I think you'll have also noticed the fine pieces of mammoth ivory and golden inlay adorning her as well.' Calmly, Brolo placed the hammer down and sat back on his chair, staring straight into Wilkhelm's big green eyes. 'This hammer has fought countless battles, endured innumerable blows, passed through the hands of some of this land's greatest warriors, outlived the reign of many kings and crushed more skulls than all those combined! Such value cannot be denied to such an ancient piece of dwarfish lore. So, you can joke and jeer as much as you wish, but I'm betting you don't have the balls to match me now.'

Brolo's heart raced in his chest, just one side effect of placing such a monumental bet against unsure odds. Another being that his genitalia felt like they'd made the conscious decision to retreat from whence they came.

The Wall sat silently, looking gormless as always, but Wilkhelm just smirked up at the ceiling as if he didn't have a care in the world.

Conqueror's bollocks to what Wilkhelm thinks of the hammer! raged a voice at the back of Brolo's mind. *This bastard can play the part of arrogant fuck if he so wishes, but he walks alone! To every other chump in this room, Lawgismirin's value is plain.*

A long huff echoed through the hall as Wilkhelm blew his cheeks in feigned contemplation.

'Well, well, well. I'm not sure if you're trying to act brave or desperate. Either way, this puts me in a rather difficult position. On one hand, I could accept your hammer as valid, and hope it proves to be as precious as you claim. Or, more tantalisingly, I could renounce this novelty egg cracker as worthless and force you to find something of a more *solid* value. Although, let it not be said that I'm an ungracious man. As long as our dear friend Igelf here also agrees to—'

'I'm out.'

A symphony of coughs, gasps and splutters filled the room. Brolo himself had to mop the spilt water dribbling down his chin.

'Ah, so the Wall has crumbled,' Wilkhelm said. 'I've never taken you for a cautious fellow. But if you're sure...'

'I'm sure as stone. I've lost much today, and I can see where this game is heading. I want no part of it.'

Many failed to keep the shock from showing on their faces. The fact that Igelf, a man with a tendency for making astoundingly bad choices, had uncharacteristically come to a sound decision was exceedingly surprising. However, this was not something one should openly say in front of the

Wall. The last person who made such a mistake ended up hosting an impromptu meeting between his face and rectum.

'Well then, Brolo. We should see this through to the end, don't you think? Tell you what – just to make things interesting, I'll accept your hammer to the full value of all my gold.' Wilkhelm pushed the remainder of his coin to the centre of the table.

Regardless of how many times Brolo imagined the oncoming events, the results kept becoming progressively worse. He knew he'd been playing a risky game, letting his cockiness get the better of him, especially as the odds had been stacked against him for much of the evening. He forced himself to draw inspiration from the fable of Brodin – the ancient dwarfish god of camaraderie, mischief and boozing. Brolo's favourite tale as a child had been that of the god's magical eight-legged horse.

Legend said Brodin had challenged the greatest horseman in the mortal realm to a race against his divine steed in a one-on-one steeplechase. Upon race day, as expected, Brodin's steed had blazed ahead, galloping on all eight legs around the track, effortlessly leaping the wide ditches and high fences. Right until a few feet shy of the finish line, when, alas, the horse had slowed, cantered sluggishly for a few moments, and fallen asleep. The trick of entering a narcoleptic horse into an otherwise assured race had netted Brodin – the only person to place bets against himself – immense riches and earned the napping horse the name Sleep-Near.

'I must say,' Brolo said, 'this is a most gracious offer. The contents of your lordly father's sock drawer!' A murmur of laughter fluttered around the hall, as a bead of sweat ran down his face. 'I think we both know who's really making a sacrifice here. Hard cash isn't all you care about, Wilkhelm, so you can feign it all night, but I'm no idiot. I see through your game. Nonetheless, I agree to these terms, by my honour as an elf, and my honour as a dwarf.'

Brolo's sense of honour had been his undoing before. If anything, it'd brought him more harm over the years than good. He'd cursed the hot-headedness his dwarfish heritage had bestowed upon him plenty of times, almost as many times as he'd damned the elven set of principles his mother had whipped into him as a child. Sadly, he'd come too far to back down now, but his stomach churned at the sight of Wilkhelm sitting cocksure, caressing his cards, displaying all the vanity of a peacock in a house of mirrors.

'You do like to babble on, don't you?' Wilkhelm asked. 'It's almost like you want to delay the inevitable. Why don't you have the honour of placing your cards first?'

Brolo had been worried Wilkhelm would make such a suggestion. He'd known the arrogant bastard wouldn't be able to resist the chance to make a show of playing his winning hand.

Sod this. If he wants to be so damn dramatic, then I may as well let him simmer under the pressure a little while longer!

With rapidly draining confidence in his chances, he decided to play his hand one card at a time. Even if all it achieved was to annoy Wilkhelm a tad, it was worth the effort.

Brolo, hand trembling, laid down a six of hearts. Nothing so much as an intake of breath from Wilkhelm, or the assembled crowd. No more than Brolo had expected, if he was honest. Next came an eight of hearts. This time, Wilkhelm let slip a slightly raised left eyebrow. The crowd's excitement was a little more obvious, with a flurry of spirited murmuring, and the discreet exchanging of cash.

It would seem there was more than one game being played this evening.

Brolo's spirit took a much-needed boost from this sudden uneasiness. He prayed his next card would miraculously cause Wilkhelm's poker face to dissipate altogether.

Biting his lip, he picked the card and placed it on the table, ready for the big reveal. Then a hand fell heavily upon his right shoulder.

'Well now, what's all this?' came Stánwilte's voice.

'Fuck,' Brolo said.

'Fuck,' echoed Wilkhelm.

The word rippled around the hall, as if someone had dropped a pebble into a calm lake of obscenities.

'That's a big collection of gold you have sitting there, Wilkhelm,' Stánwilte said. 'A very fine stack indeed. However, I wouldn't want to show it off to everyone out here. You couldn't trust this lot as far as you could chuck them. Well, maybe Igelf could toss 'em further, but that's beside the point.'

A nervous chuckle rolled across the hall, swiftly deflated by a sharp look from Bæwylm, who stood with a disapproving scowl at his captain's side. Stánwilte brushed some dust from Brolo's shoulder, ruffled his hair, then started to pace around the table.

All eyes were on Stánwilte as he strolled with the casually predatory aura of a peckish lion, gazing at everything on display. Somehow, he managed this while also patting backs, shaking hands, and generally mingling with the off-duty men in assembly, and firing icy-cold stares at the few who sure as hell weren't being paid to gawk about.

Abruptly, Stánwilte came to a halt, stopping dead between the two players. He leant upon the table, squinted at them both, then began stroking his greying beard.

'So, Brolo, I hadn't realised it was that time already.'

'What do you mean, sir?' he said cautiously.

'It must be much later in the evening than I thought it was. Otherwise, you'd still be out on your watch.'

'Well, the thing is ...'

'You wouldn't be sitting in here drinking, merrymaking, and having a little round of show-and-tell if you were on duty, would you?'

'The thing is ...' Brolo's brain violently stalled. 'Show-and-tell, sir?'

'Yes, show-and-tell. Unless I'm mistaken about what's going on here? I mean, Wilkhelm is obviously being a pompous git and flashing off his family's wealth again. Which, I must say, is not very becoming of a gentleman, so we'll be having words about this in the near future.'

Stánwilte snapped a look in Wilkhelm's direction, which suggested words weren't all he'd be receiving.

'Ah, and dear Brolo here seems to be showing off the family heirlooms. Although, I don't believe his mother would've been too pleased about this, do you?' he asked Bæwylm, who nodded, aiming a long, stern glare at the dwelf.

Brolo wasn't sure what Stánwilte was up to. Whatever it was, it wasn't going to be pleasant. Undoubtedly, he'd crossed the line when he'd skipped his duties to play games, and he should probably be punished for it, yet he was determined to try his damned hardest to avoid the consequences.

'Oh, and what a highly detailed pack of cards,' Stánwilte said. 'Though they can't be worth much now, all soaked in sweat and booze. Belong to you as well, do they, Brolo?'

'Yes, they do. Why? Is that important?'

'Not really, no. I just wanted to make sure the rightful owner packs them away properly. Speaking of which, as it's getting far too late for you all to be hanging around in here, I recommend you do it now.'

'But, sir, he can't,' Wilkhelm said, standing abruptly. 'We've not finished our ga—'

'Your *what*, Wilkhelm?' barked Stánwilte. 'What *exactly* have you not yet finished? Because if you're about to do something as drastically stupid as admit there's been illegal gambling going on here tonight, then you'll both spend the next four weeks in a cell! So again – and I warn you to think very carefully before answering me, boy – what were you about to finish?'

Wilkhelm fell back in his chair, deflated.

'Nothing, sir,' he said. 'Nothing beyond loitering around a little, enjoying some light-hearted gossiping with those lucky enough to be off duty.'

'No harm done, then.' Stánwilte smiled. 'So, grab your things and go enjoy your night off, Cormorant. That goes for the rest of you as well!' he shouted to the mumbling crowd. 'And a friendly note to those of you who are currently meant to be working. You'd better pray your mothers have recently knitted a long enough skirt for you to hide behind, because if I catch the slightest glimpse of you again before the evening's out ...'

The first half of his threat had barely finished echoing around the hall by the time it had drained of the majority of its occupants.

'Except for you, Brolo,' Stánwilte said, turning back to him. 'You stay here and help Mistress Roslyn tidy up this mess. Of course, by *help out*, I obviously mean you can do it all, while she puts her feet up, enjoys her book and has a nice hot drink.'

'But ... Captain,' Wilkhelm once again protested.

'What now?' snapped Stánwilte, fixing him with a scowl that could've flayed a man at twenty paces. Wilkhelm grumbled, slammed his cards onto the table and stood up once more.

'I'm sorry, sir. Nothing. I'll be leaving now.' He levelled a cold, suspicious stare at Brolo, then headed for the door.

'Right then, I'm off to bed,' Stánwilte said. 'It's been a long day, and tomorrow doesn't promise to be any shorter. I'll be leaving this one in your care, Rozza.'

Mistress Roslyn had already sat herself down, with her now-shoeless feet twinkling in the air, and her long, arched nose buried deeply into one of the romance books she loved so much.

'Hm? Oh, right you are, Captain. Be seeing you for breakfast in the morn, I hope?'

'Not if my taste buds can help it,' Stánwilte said, clearly aware the old crow was hardly paying attention.

'Good, see you at half-seven,' she muttered, waving vaguely in his direction.

Stánwilte dropped his forced smile and turned to Brolo.

'Now, I expect this place to be so clean I can see my reflection in the tables when I come down to inspect your work in the morning.'

'But the tables are made of old wood, sir. Like, terribly ancient wood.'

'Then you'd best get polishing, hadn't you? Also, as you seem to have had this little unscheduled night off, you can pull a double shift tomorrow.'

'Now, hang on! I've got things to be doing tomorrow.'

'You're damn right you do,' said Stánwilte. 'Not only do you have the stock check to finish off, but you've also got the count of supplies coming in to look forward to.'

'Come on, sir,' was all the argument Brolo could muster.

'I suggest you just start tidying here now, lad. Make it easier on yourself,' said Bæwylm, stepping between captain and guard. 'Save your energy for tomorrow.'

Sombrely, Brolo watched Stánwilte and Bæwylm leave, laughing about something as they walked through the door – no doubt at his expense. After cursing under his breath for a few moments, a spark of realisation ignited in the dark recesses of his brain.

I can look at Wilkhelm's cards!

It took all his restraint to stop himself from rushing to the table like a ravenous jackal chasing its lunch. He instead attempted to approach it with an inconspicuous glide.

Hands in pockets, gazing around the hall as if he hadn't a care in the world, Brolo began to slide his way over to the table. He succeeded so well in his portrayal of an unobservant ignoramus that he was caught unawares by one of the chairs left lying in the hall.

'For fuck's sake!' Brolo shouted, as he fell with a crash.

He lay sprawled out in a crumpled mess for a few moments, swearing through gritted teeth and rubbing his grazed knee, when he suddenly remembered himself and shot up to peer at Mistress Roslyn. She still sat reading, apparently undisturbed. She even went as far as licking her finger to turn a page, displaying how little attention she'd paid to his ruckus.

Pride and knee wounded, he gave up on pretence and hobbled the rest of his way to the table. He plonked himself down onto Wilkhelm's chair and looked upon his cards.

Do I really want to know if I beat him or not? a little voice whispered at the back of his mind. *Finding out what Stánwilte really cost me would surely make things worse.*

So much had been at stake here, beyond mere gold. At no point had Brolo's victory been assured, but the chance to see Wilkhelm's face as he laid down his winning card had simply been too enticing to pass up. Yet it had all been for nothing, thanks to that callous meddler Stánwilte.

Finally, after stoking his emotions into a rage sufficient to obscure all rationality, Brolo took hold of Wilkhelm's cards.

You'd better be praying, Stánwilte, because if there's one thing a dwarf hates more than losing, it's being cheated. You can be damn well sure I'll find a way to get back what you owe … oh.

He took a long, hard look at the cards in his hands, checking them over and over to make sure he'd read them correctly. No matter how intensely he gazed upon them, they didn't change. In his hands were a five of hearts, a five of clubs, a five of spades, a jack of clubs, and a jack of spades – a full house.

Stánwilte had saved his bacon. Saved it from being stuck between two heavily buttered slices of bread, slathered in a thick brown sauce and scoffed up for a hangover-curing breakfast.

Brolo made sure no one was watching as he rapidly packed away the cards, so he alone would keep the secret of Wilkhelm's winning hand.

Chapter Four

The Flaming Aftermath

Dying was all Yilonia had left. She desired nothing more than to give in. To let her inevitable death wash over her, consume her body in a furious tide and drag her down into the murky depths of the Eternal Shuffler's domain.

Even in death, all I think of is water, she thought, unsure whether to laugh or cry. Then she decided she probably didn't have enough liquid left within her to shed tears. Smiling would only cause her cracked lips to split and bleed.

The sun shone above her, broiling the ground, which in turn scorched the flesh of her hands and knees as she dragged herself along the endless sands. The pain, dehydration, exhaustion and inexorably grim fate lying before her shredded any scraps of survivor's guilt she may have otherwise harboured.

As if half those bastards deserved the quick death they so fortunately received, while I suffer alone. None of them endured this kind of drawn-out torture. I have no tears left for them; they should be feeling sorry for me!

Each time Yilonia shut her eyes, images flashed through her waning consciousness. Eventually, her eyes would open again, removing her from the dungeon of her mind and returning her to the wandering hell in which she existed.

I should've trusted my instincts and turned around after we came upon that...incinerated wretch, she told herself for the thousandth time.

Hindsight was a bitch like that.

***

The moment Yilonia saw the charred remains of some unfortunate soldier, scout or traveller lying in a heap like the abandoned remains of a spit-roasted hen, she knew there was something more than a little amiss. Val Mascal was in fine fettle, traipsing around the blackened corpses of man and beast, making jest after jest at their expense. The gathered mob, however, rapidly grew antsy.

Men with families to feed began to call for the caravan to turn back. Men with egos to feed began to claim they could fight off whatever beast had caused such destruction. Shouts declaring some men craven and other men reckless were flung around the crowd. Petty arguments broke out, until the horde was squawking like a murder of crows fighting over a morsel of flesh. In the end, Val Mascal decided for them.

'Right!' he bellowed. 'Back to your carts and carriages, you lot. Nothing special to see here – just some fool who couldn't use a flint and steel unsupervised!'

A few folks happily trundled off, but most of the mob weren't appeased by this summation of events.

'Flint and steel? Pull the other one, Val. Look, he's landed under his horse, for the Uniter's sake!' a well-to-do merchant shouted, to the prattling agreement of his posse.

'So?' Mascal retorted. 'What does that prove?'

'For a start, it shows he was still on his horse when he died!'

'And that proves?' Mascal asked, obviously knowing the answer, but remaining steadfastly belligerent.

'The poor sod's hardly going to be lighting a fire while he's riding a bloody horse, is he?' the merchant said, with the crowd rallying behind him.

'He could've been trying to light his horse's farts to make it go faster, for all the Golden Swans I give!' Mascal shouted. 'But let me make one thing clear – you can pack up, turn around and make your own ways back to whatever shitholes you crawled out from if you're too chicken to continue, but I'm taking the caravan on! Let's see how far you make it before you get hungry, thirsty or buggered by bandits!'

Mascal's rant decided it. They all saddled up and carried on with their journey up to Droughlyke, a few days' ride ahead, without another word of argument. However, as she and Lysio walked back to their respective wagons, Yilonia's heartbeat worked itself up into a frenzy, her pulse thumping in her ear.

***

If Val Mascal had appeared confident when he'd strolled around the mysteriously burnt corpse of the rider, he could do nothing now but let that facade melt away like hot wax running from a candle.

By all the Flames… I know he's a good talker, but I'd like to see him explain this one away, thought Yilonia, reeling at the devastation lying before her. As the realisation of what must've happened dawned, bile rose in the back of her throat.

Droughlyke was in ruins. The once-bustling hive of activity had been reduced to a smoky, lifeless husk. From a distance, nothing disconcerting had shown itself to the outriders of the Val Company caravan; everyone had assumed the thin wisps of smoke rising into the pale blue sky had come from open cook fires, or perhaps from smith's yards. However, as they'd drawn closer to Droughlyke, the true source had become apparent.

The vast wall of stone running the perimeter of the town had been reduced to a stack of blackened rock, the clear aftermath of an unfathomably intense flame. The dwellings lying beyond had fared just as horribly. Some of the stone buildings remained standing, but they were little more than charred shells. Of the dozens of wooden buildings that had once housed the poorer population, nothing remained but ash, still-glowing embers, and bone.

A few of the braver members of the caravan, including Yilonia, decided to mount a proper search for survivors, or at least some kind of clue as to what had happened. Some of the more callously astute merchants used the opportunity to look for any treasure they could steal from the still-cold – or, in this case, warm – fingers of the dead.

Slowly, they passed through the giant archway that would've once housed the heavy oaken gate into the town. They worked with no sound but the whispers of the wind, digging through fragments of scorched timber and rock, finding nothing to reward their efforts. Each corner they turned merely offered street after street of smouldering wrecks – homes turned funeral pyres, businesses in crumbling ruins, places of worship obliterated to sacrifices of stone and cinder.

The search for survivors came to nothing. The search for clues yielded little more. Only those hunting for spoils came away with any kind of results – a few rings and coins pried from whatever they'd melted onto. A poor showing by anyone's standard, but silver was silver.

Back outside Droughlyke's walls, hundreds of travellers and merchants had gathered like flies around a freshly-felled corpse. Every member of the caravan was desperately afraid for their life, and for the lives of their loved ones. Every member except Val Mascal.

Tears trickled down his blotchy red cheeks. He knelt in the sand, glaring at the place where the gate into Droughlyke had once stood.

'Gone,' he muttered. 'They're all gone.'

'Aye, skipper. Such death is a terrible thing. The poor souls,' said a trader, placing a gentle hand on his shoulder.

'Souls?' Mascal barked, shoving the hand off. 'It's not their bleeding *souls* I care about, you inbred goat herder!' He rose to tower over the trader. 'You think a few people's souls bother me? No, I care about the fact we've travelled hundreds of leagues out from the last settlement, through godforsaken lands and unbearable heat, for nothing! Absolutely nothing! This is going to break me, you know?' He was now shouting wildly at everyone who'd gathered around the town gates. 'Droughlyke was my best spot! Its trade kept this route viable – without it, heading out north is worthless! And what are we going to do with all this?' He pointed to the carts laden with spices, wine and preserved meats. 'It'll be spoilt by time we make it back to civilisation!'

Despite his rather admirable show of thoughtlessness and greed, Mascal wasn't wrong. Traders who'd only feared for their lives now faced the dire realisation that they also stood to lose their homes, their jobs, and probably the clothes off their backs if they didn't get back to the towns of the south and sell their goods post-haste.

For Yilonia, and the other vagabonds like her, the future looked just as bleak. Most had come to make Droughlyke their new home and had paid Mascal all they owned to make it there. For many, going back was far from a practical option. Turning round to face the very jaws of justice you'd run away from wasn't exactly an outlaw's idea of a picnic ... although you'd have needed to be a few pork pies short of one to flee this far north in the first place.

***

The remainder of the day withered slowly away, as Val Mascal held a forum to deliberate what to do next. The fugitives received no say in the decision-making, which ruffled the feathers of those who disliked the idea of being led straight back into the lion's den. Yilonia, however, just sat in the meagre shade of a carriage, reflecting on the day's events.

Such utter destruction, such complete carnage. Only one thing could've caused this ... but it can't be, can it?

'Hey, Loni!' Lysio plonked herself down next to Yilonia, shattering her thoughts. 'It's a right mess here, ain't it?'

'Aye,' Yilonia said, putting an arm around the young girl. 'Indeed it is, sweetling.'

'What will you do now? Head back south with us? Hey, at least this means we can spend more time together! Big Jon taught me a new game, it's called Ox Pat Sandals. What you do is—'

'I think I can guess the rules.' Yilonia nudged her playfully. 'But yes, if Val isn't monster enough to leave us to die up here, I'll be coming back with you. As to where I'll end up, I'm not sure.'

'You could stay with us?' Lysio said, with hope in her eyes. Yilonia smiled ruefully.

'Ha! Your dad would love that, I'm sure. I can just imagine how he'd want me to pay my way.'

'What're you blabbing about?'

'Don't you worry. Anyway, how's he taken all this in?'

'Okay, I think. It's not like he pays much for his wares, so he hasn't lost a great deal. He's happy enough to make his way south.'

The prospect of travelling with Lysio sounded sweet enough to Yilonia, especially considering her other options, yet she knew she'd have to avoid Stunheath.

'We'll see,' she said. 'Maybe I'll change my mind on the way back.'

Yilonia didn't truly believe she would, but she enjoyed making Lysio smile.

***

The sun was hanging low in the sky when the Val Company caravan finally decided to pack up and head home. As the carts swayed to life, many looked wistfully back at the remains of Droughlyke. Yilonia, having seen the wanton destruction that'd befallen the place firsthand, was all too happy to leave.

Darkness came. Yilonia lay wearily in her humble vegetable cart. Above the guttural snoring of her companions and the creaking of the convoy, silence drifted. Yet her fear didn't abate. Regret and sorrow overwhelmed her; questions and suspicions kept her awake.

An hour passed before she heard it – in the distance, a flutter of wind. It almost soothed her to sleep. Drifting in and out of dreams, she listened to the breeze cut through the desert, swishing gently in the night.

It grew louder, and louder still.

Along the meandering length of the caravan, cries echoed through the dark, until they were swallowed up by the thunderous gust sweeping rapidly closer. Yilonia rose to peer over the side of her cart. Cold dread washed over her, as sand flew into the air with each monstrous thump.

A hollow thud beat above her. Bursting like a shockwave, a gale tossed Yilonia across the cart, smashing her into her fellow passengers. The very earth below seemed to have come alive. A beast filling its lungs with air and exhaling in mighty blasts, belching up vast mounds of sand.

Yilonia grimaced, every single one of her bones quivering in absolute terror.

Ripping through the once-serene desert, the screaming began.

The sky lit up with a blinding flare of light. A roar trumpeted through the darkness as a great gust swept over Yilonia's cart, almost tipping it over.

No ... this can't be real.

A trail of flame engulfed the cart next to hers, knocking the breath from her lungs.

Everyone in her cart jumped up in a blind panic. Her vision burnt red and black, flickering from fire to darkness. Blindly, she pushed her way through her panicking companions, falling out of the cart as it teetered over.

Yilonia lay for a few moments, eyes shut, refusing to believe what was happening, until the howling fire flew overhead and awakened her to reality. She pushed herself up. Screams pounded her skull, and she almost fell again. Out of the darkness came another ball of liquid flame, blazing along the caravan, burning everything in its path. A cart exploded, shooting flaming splinters in all directions.

Another earth-shattering roar echoed through the world. The beast swept down and smashed through a row of burning wagons, rising with two men in its clutches, who screamed until they were torn to pieces.

Yilonia could do nothing to save them. She could do nothing but survive.

She ran. She ran as fast as her legs could carry her, along with hundreds of others. They knocked her to the ground, stampeding over her like pigs late to the trough, leaving her to die.

The law of *every man for himself* now ruled.

As she struggled to rise, Yilonia spotted her saviour – one of the very few horses taken north.

She ran to it. The horse was extremely distressed, thrashing around and almost kicking Yilonia's head to a pulp, but she was able to calm it enough to mount. It hadn't been intended for riding, so she had to make do without a saddle, but she wasn't about to stay and look for one. She used the dagger Lysio had given her to cut the crude harness connecting the horse to its wagon and galloped away from the carnage.

Lysio!

Without thinking, Yilonia turned back the way she'd come, trampling everything and everyone in her path. The beast flew down behind her and immolated a score of people in white-hot flame. Their screams echoed out to her, only to fade into whimpers as she rode away.

I should be dead, she thought. *I should be dead twice over by now.* Still she rode, determination driving her on until she reached Lysio's wagon, where all heart drifted away from her like a twig floating down a stream.

Yilonia could not bring herself to utter a single word.

She closed her eyes. For a moment, the fire and death ceased to exist, until someone tried to steal her horse. She veered it up and trampled him, squishing his skull into a paste beneath its hooves, then turned and sped away.

***

Two days had passed before she'd gained the courage to look behind her. She'd seen nothing but sand and sky. After another day and a half, her horse had collapsed and died of exhaustion. Now here she was, a day later, facing her own death.

She reached out an arm, pulled herself along a tiny fraction, then reached out the other arm to do the same, over and over until she was unable to carry on. She whimpered and sprawled on her back, refusing to go on. The sun was shining in her eyes, yet she was too exhausted to close them. Her breathing was slow. Her madness had once again set in, as she could hear galloping in the distance.

Here comes the Eternal Shuffler to claim me. He's late. Yilonia let a grimace splinter her chapped lips.

As if a host of storm clouds had swept over the horizon, the world around her dulled. A shadowy figure loomed over her, and another, and another. She couldn't see their faces, yet she knew their cold, dead eyes stared hungrily at her soul.

'She alive?' one asked, kicking her gently with his boot.

'Don't know. If so, she doesn't look like she'll live much longer,' said another, also giving her a kick. 'What d'you think, Sahar?'

Sahar? That doesn't sound like the sort of name a harvester of souls would have. Oh well, that's what happens when you go crazy, I suppose …

'She's muttering to herself, so she's got some fight left in her. I say we carry her back to camp and let the captain deal with her.'

Camp? Captain? Nothing made sense. Everything her mother had told her about death was wrong.

She found herself hefted up and slung unceremoniously over the back of a horse. It took an hour or so of riding for her to work it out.

I … I … I think I'm being rescued!

The thought danced around her head like a bumblebee on ice, yet all her body could manage was a weak smile.

I must get back, she told herself. *I can't let myself die now. The Radiants preserve us – dragons fly again!*

Chapter Five

Skipping Breakfast

Stánwilte awoke to a beam of light streaming through his window, the shimmering glow suggesting divine greatness, or that it was merely sunny outside for a change, depending on how one looked at these things.

Lifting his hands to block the worst of the light, a ghastly figure loomed over him as he lay helpless in bed. A ghoul from his deepest nightmares, reaching to strangle the very life out of him. Although, strange behaviour as it was for a murderous beast, Stánwilte found himself being stripped naked from the waist up. Truthfully, he would have preferred evisceration.

'Morning, sir,' said Mistress Roslyn, pulling Stánwilte's nightshirt over his head. 'Don't mind me. Just getting the morning washing done.'

'Oh, burn me! Every single bloody day!' Stánwilte cried, as he came to his senses. 'Mistress Roslyn, can you please shut those sodding curtains? I can't see a thing. Right, we need to have a very serious talk about boundaries ...'

'I've run you a bath, and I've got your breakfast on the go,' Mistress Roslyn added quickly. 'By the time you've had a ...' —she shuddered, her voice dropping disturbingly in pitch— 'a lovely, *hot* soak ... I shall have your clothes for the day folded and waiting for you, sir.'

Stánwilte rolled out of bed, red-faced and soundly defeated before breakfast, as he was most mornings.

'And will I be changing in peace this time, or will you be forgetting something else that just cannot wait until I'm dressed? It was a sock yesterday, wasn't it?'

'You wouldn't want to be left with odd socks now, would you, ducky?' Mistress Roslyn smiled innocently. Well, as innocently as an old witch could look.

She had a kind heart, though, for a witch. One of the deciding factors in her banishment from her coven had been her staunch refusal to use a puppy's tail as an active ingredient. The other had been the minor detail of her inability to brew potions without blowing up everything within a two-league radius. Hence why she'd become the cook of the Peplyshaw Watch – to keep a public menace and erstwhile student of illegal magic from accidently committing genocide at the local soup kitchen, while keeping a watchful eye on her. A noble policy of rehabilitation for which the Watch had gained notoriety since Stánwilte came up with the idea soon after his arrival.

However, there was a downside. Much to the suffering of Stánwilte and the other diligent members of the Watch, Roslyn still couldn't identify a cauldron from a capon. Regardless, Stánwilte decided to bite the arrow and inquire as to what the disgusting concoction slopped in the bowl sitting upon his bedside table was. It was always difficult to guess, as Roslyn's cooking never seemed to possess any discernible feature other than being grey.

'So, what delectable delicacy do I have the good fortune to be dining on this morning, Roz?'

'Barley porridge,' she replied, whistling away while pointlessly folding dirty clothes into a wash basket.

'And?' Stánwilte pushed.

'With a hint of ginger, sir. To give it a bit of a twang.'

Stánwilte started to believe he was still dreaming. He had to pinch himself to check.

'*And?*' he asked again.

'*And* a great, big dollop of honey for sweetness. Just the way you like it.'

Stánwilte was ready to start floating. He always preferred the dreams where he could fly.

'And nothing else?' he said.

'No, sir!' said Roslyn, hefting up the basket of clothing and heading for the door. 'Well, apart from a healthy dose of pig's liver … you know, for texture.' Quick as a flash, she darted out of the room, and Stánwilte's heart fell right to the pit of his stomach, which was now going to go hungry.

I hate being right. At least the liver explains why it's so darn grey.

After his bath, Stánwilte dressed himself in the clothes Mistress Roslyn had left for him, giving the steaming bowl of porridge a wide berth, and made his way down to the great hall to debrief the previous night's watchmen.

The six guards who stood waiting for him looked, as always, quite ridiculous. Lined up, shoulder to shoulder, they made a pitiful sight when engulfed by the sheer enormity of the place, appearing like teeny-tiny krill in the stomach of a humongous stone whale.

Each guard in turn made his report of the night's events, spinning tedious yarns of petty bar fights and a brothel implementing an illegal two-for-the-price-of-one offer, which had drawn very stern complaints from its competitors. Three men had slept off hangovers in the cells after a scuffle in the streets, and a letter of warning had been written to some local youths causing mischief. Stánwilte nodded dutifully through each dull tale and sent the guards off to rest.

He ventured out into the courtyard for a breath of the cool spring air. The sun shone brightly for the first time this year, the wind was surprisingly mild, and the air was crisp with the herbal smell of cut grass and blooming flowers. The courtyard rang with the sweet symphony of steel on steel as Bæwylm conducted an active demonstration with the newest recruits. If they were lucky, the old man would be using blunted swords.

Stánwilte watched as Bæwylm parried swing after swing, ducking and swaying as the two lads attempted to work a two-pronged attack against him, hacking away from each side. Yet Bæwylm displayed all the strength of a man half his age, as well as the full skill and experience of his sixty-four years. After disembowelling them both at least half a dozen times, decapitating them thrice, and leaving them beaten, bruised and cowering on their knees, Bæwylm sent the two boys to clean the Watch's armoury.

'Bravo! Encore, encore!' Stánwilte shouted, which earned him a two-finger salute from Bæwylm as he walked off, smiling.

A loud *hurmmmmmmmmmph* bellowed from the watchtower by the eastern gate, signalling that some sod was speeding down the ancient Qhondik road.

Intrigued, Stánwilte took the short walk through the town, stepping through puddles left by last night's storm and skipping over mounds of pig shit left by the local livestock market. Reaching the gate, he climbed up the ladder to look for himself. The watchman in the tower blew his horn again as Stánwilte climbed through the hatch, blasting another *hurmmmmm-mmmmmph* into the air. His blaring heralded the band of horse-drawn carts hastily approaching Peplyshaw and earned himself a slap round the head from Stánwilte.

Recognising the carts as Glendor returning from his supply run, Stánwilte signalled for his men to raise the portcullis and open the gates, then climbed back down to meet the returning band. As the carts rolled through the narrow stone arch, Glendor jumped down from his seat.

'Captain! Urgent,' he said, wheezing, winded from the short jog over to Stánwilte. 'News from the north! Destroyed, sir. All dead!'

Stánwilte struggled to make sense of Glendor's jabbering. He was bent over to catch his breath, slurping in vast gasps of air as if he were trying to swallow a link of sausages whole.

'What's destroyed, man? Who's dead?'

'We should go somewhere more private, sir. Too many ears around here,' said Glendor.

Nodding, Stánwilte finished watching the supply carts rolling in. Then, to save himself from bearing the brunt of another coughing fit, he guided Glendor onto the last wagon to enter Peplyshaw. When they arrived at the garrison, he summoned a steward to count the supply carts, asked him to send up a cask of mead as soon as he checked one in, and reminded him to fetch Brolo so he could take part in the count.

After Stánwilte had discharged his responsibilities, he led Glendor to his solar up in the High Tower. Once he'd found a seat sturdy enough to bear Glendor's weight, he sat him down with a horn of water, waited for him to recover, then asked for his story.

'It's all over the countryside, sir. Got people all fired up and the likes, most with fear. The small folk are flocking to the capital in their thousands. Preachers taking up shop all over the city, plaguing it with their incessant nattering ... it's not good, I tell you.'

Glendor took a deep draught of water and carried on. Stánwilte noticed his hands were trembling.

'About a month ago, the royal palace received a raven. Then, a little over three days later, the story was flooding the city, causing all sorts of panic. Large bonfires set ablaze within the Square of Purification, Circle priests pelted with rotten fruit, peasants flooding into the city to hear mass at the steps of the Cathedral of Fire – I've never seen people jump into hysteria so quickly. The king has since made a decree to the nobles. I think it's safe to assume it was never intended to be public knowledge, but somehow it got out.'

'Come on, man! Out with it already!' said Stánwilte, rubbing at his temples to calm a looming headache.

'Not to understate it, but the word is …' Glendor leant in closer to whisper, 'Droughlyke, Captain – it's been obliterated.'

'What do you mean, *obliterated?*'

'I mean *totally sodding wiped out in a blazing flash of white-hot flame and death*, sir. And that's not all. Apparently, the Third Royal Legion of Scouts found a young girl wandering the desert. Near death she was, poor thing, but they got the story from her. If she's to be believed, a whole trade caravan was destroyed as well. She said she escaped on horseback, but she appears to have been the only one.'

'The desert? Why was there a legion of scouts so far north? Ánad is a barren wasteland – no one lives out there, other than the few scraps of scum huddled within Droughlyke.'

'That's just it. If the girl isn't telling porkies, something else is roaming around up in that desert.'

'What do you mean?' Stánwilte asked, almost fearing the answer.

'A dragon, sir. The young lass claims a dragon put Droughlyke to the flame and burnt the caravan to ashes.'

Stánwilte almost laughed. Almost.

'Don't be ridiculous. Dragons haven't existed for hundreds of years, if they ever truly did! What did the king have to say about all this rubbish, then?'

Glendor looked abashed.

'After word got out, he apparently blessed us with some typically stirring message about having nothing to fear. *The royal army shall protect the people of the kingdom*, and so on. His men shall find the truth of this tale, and no harm shall come to the beast if found safely in the north.'

As would be right. If there really *was* a dragon, it would, constituently, be the king's overlord.

'You say people are heading to the Cathedral of Fire in their droves – any word from His Eminence?'

'No, sir. High-Keeper Relfread has been rather quiet on the matter, the last I heard.'

That was surprising. Normally, the man wouldn't shut up about anything. It was always *blasphemer* this and *nonbeliever* that.

'It was good of you to bring me this news, Glendor. Let's hope the issue resolves itself, eh?'

'Sir, there's just one more thing. On the day the king gave his less-than-rousing address, three ravens were seen leaving the palace in the dead of night.'

'Three? Only three?' said Stánwilte, more to himself than to Glendor.

'Aye. And there's only one place those ravens could be flying to.'

'Oh, I know, Glendor,' he said, turning to gaze out his window. 'They're heading to the Lords of Uprynenos.'

CHAPTER SIX

THIRSTY WORK

Water trickled down the moss-coated ceiling and pattered into a puddle. Each forlorn drip echoed along the narrow corridors, bouncing off the damp stone walls and pounded away at Brolo's skull, leaving him to question if a lost child sat blubbering somewhere in the yawning abyss of the cellars.

Drip ... drip ... drop ... plop ...

Brolo lost count for the sixth time.

I'm going to go mad down here, he thought. *Between the water and the bloody cheese, I may very well turn crackers.*

Wheel after wheel of hard brown cheese, a speciality of the Blemish Islands, sat maturing on the dusty old shelves, lying alongside sacks of oats, barley, wheat and corn; barrels of pickled vegetables and preserved foods; casks of ale, wine and mead. Hanging above Brolo in the profuse darkness were smoked garlic, dried fruit and herbs, and various kinds of hams and bacons.

Ignoring the vast barrels of curing pork, Brolo himself couldn't help being a tad salty about the fine bounty lying before him like the plump farmer's daughter had after last year's harvest festival. He understood the Watch sold most of the cured meats it produced to subsidise its running costs, but it would've been nice, for a change, to sample something other than Mistress Roslyn's woeful slop.

With a huff, Brolo started his count again, even trying to make a game of it. It didn't last very long, however. Something at the back of his mind, right around where his inner bastard was currently giving his self-confidence a damn good hiding, left him suspecting that even in a game with a player of one, he would still come out the loser.

Drip ... drip ... drop ... plop ...

Brolo had hoped beyond hope that his punishment for neglecting his duties would've been swiftly forgotten by Stánwilte, so he could lie back and enjoy some time off. Alas, as sure as finding a lack of privy shells only after you've sat down to go about your business, Brolo had been woken up at the crack of midday and sequestered away into the bowels of Peplyshaw to count the vast stocks lying within.

Drip ... drip ... drop ... plop ...

Brolo shuddered, his heart pulsing in his ear. *Never mind the cells, this is where the real punishment takes place.*

His torch flickered lower and lower as he worked, until a breath of wind blew down the stone corridor, rushed through the small gap beneath the stockroom door, and snuffed out its remaining life, coating Brolo in complete darkness.

Well, dare I say, this couldn't get much worse, he thought.

Drip ... drop ... plop ... drip ...

'What?' he shouted, spinning around in a blind fury. 'What in the Eternal Shuffler's creaky balls do you call that? It's *drip, drip, drop, plop.* Not *drip, drop, plop, drip!* Don't you go changing now!'

Then came the brazen reply:

Drip ... drip ... drop ... splat ...

'Oh, bollocks to this shit!' Brolo barked, scrunching up his tally and throwing it away into the shadows. 'This is too bloody intolerable by half!'

He marched straight for what he thought was the exit, instead connecting face first with a wall, which only served to irritate him further.

Clutching his now-bloody nose, Brolo pulled himself along the rough stone floor, feeling his way out into freedom. It took him the best part of an hour to find it. As distant sunlight finally beckoned him towards the exit, he salivated at the thought of enjoying a nice cup of ale and a warm breeze against his face in the garden of The Crone's Wimple. The inn was perfectly placed beside the bank of the Flewsa, giving a picturesque view of its sapphire waters as it trickled past the old mill. When Brolo emerged into the Watch's yard, however, he was greeted by the smell of horse shit and the first droplets of rain falling from the grey clouds above.

Most of the folk who'd been busying themselves in the yard evaporated almost immediately, probably to avoid the rain. Yet, watching his fellow watchmen shoot off like rodents catching the first notes of a merry tune, Brolo couldn't help feeling he was the one being avoided. Sighing, he started crossing the barren yard. Barren except for Glendor, who was lying across the seat of a wagon, eating an apple.

'Oi, you finished inventory already?' he said, through a mouthful of pulpy apple. 'You've only been down there a couple hours.'

'Yes, I've made the executive decision that the Watch, and indeed Peplyshaw, has enough cheese down in those horrid cellars to last us all thrice over until the Penultimate Moment. So, I'm off to the pub, if you don't mind?'

'I doubt Stánwilte will share your sentiment.'

'Stánwilte can go suck a long, hard co—'

'He's not here, anyway,' Glendor quickly interrupted. 'He left for Craginhall no more than fifteen minutes ago.'

The tubby pillock's revelation roused Brolo's interest. *Off to see Cormorant, then? Probably to inform him what a conniving little shite his son is.*

'Therefore, he won't have any problem with me being excused from my duties, will he? It is my day off, after all.' Brolo turned to walk away, but Glendor dropped off the cart to block his path.

'Just one more thing before you go off gallivanting,' said Glendor. 'Don't think you can hide behind Bæwylm's skirts every time you get in trouble. I've heard talk of last night, and the rumour is you set things up so the captain and Bæwylm would save your arse from losing.'

'That rumour holds as much water as someone with dysentery,' said Brolo with a scoff.

'So, you say, dwelf, but I'd watch my back if I were you. You two weren't the only ones gambling last night, and if people find out you caused them to lose their coin unfairly ... well, let's just say you weren't very popular to begin with.'

'I'm hurt to hear that. In fact, I now feel the need to go and drown my sorrows with ale. Tears over lost friendships can bring such a terrible thirst.'

'Your arrogance will be your undoing, lad.'

It's not arrogance if I've got the brains to back it up.

'And sausages will be yours,' Brolo said, rubbing Glendor's jiggly stomach. 'Now you must excuse me, I've got a foaming mug with my name on it. So, I bid thee a good day, sir.'

He squeezed past Glendor's bulk, leaving him to choke on his apple core.

***

The rain was positively streaming down now, sending everyone in the streets carting off in search of shelter.

So much for sitting on the banks of the Flewsa and dreaming the world by, thought Brolo. Even though the town was virtually empty, he didn't want to risk bumping into any patrolling watchmen, who would likely dob him in to Stánwilte for getting out of work early.

Taking the short route over walls and through gardens saved him some time, but splashing through muddy water, rotting compost and soggy pig shit did nothing good for his boots. By the time he reached The Crone's Wimple, he was plastered from the knees down in reeking brown muck. Entering the smoky haze of the inn, he was surprised to find it practically empty, save for a table of a shady-looking dwarfs hunching over a map, an elderly couple nursing drinks by the fire, and a trio of elves arguing loudly. The smells of sour ale, stale urine and the dung used as fuel in the fireplace gave the place an odour about as welcoming as the beer mats on every table, which read *'Drink up and fuck off!'*

Prying his feet from the notoriously sticky floor, Brolo made for the bar to trade barbs with its proprietor, Nora Vlump.

'Afternoon, my sweet,' he said. 'How are you on this dazzling day? It's almost as delightful and warm as you are, if you don't mind my saying so.'

'Only as dazzling as your fucking witticisms, boy. The usual, is it?' said Nora, pouring an ale without turning to face him.

'Ah, you're my kind of woman, Nora. I love 'em with a bit of fire.'

His words rang with mockery. The only reason 'Bloody' Nora would carry a torch for anyone would be to light their funeral pyre – she may have once been a pretty lass, but years of grafting hard behind a bar, squeezing out and raising six children effectively on her own, and possessing a penchant for dealing with fights with a *'fists first, ask questions never'* policy had left her far beyond the border of attractiveness, stranded without a map.

'Coincidentally, I'd say you're my kind of lad, too.'

'Oh, yeah? How's that, then?' asked Brolo, intrigued.

'You're the kind whose measly balls I could easily crush into a pulp,' she said, plonking a pot of ale down in front of him, sloshing a good half of it all over the bar.

'Point made. I'll just go sit in the corner, shall I?'

'Probably for the best,' Nora said. 'Unless you really think you can have another go?'

Brolo wasn't drunk enough for *that*, so he paid and made his way to a table, dodging pools of spilt wine, which disturbingly appeared to be growing skins, along the way.

***

Brolo's brain swam in and out of awareness, blocking out the putrid aroma of the bar and blurring the loud carousing of those around him. He wanted nothing more than to lay his head down on the table and have a little shut-eye, but even he wasn't drunk enough for that. His face would be glued to the sticky residue of many long years' build-up of spilt drinks, and he'd lose a layer of skin when he tried to sit up. He'd seen it happen before, and it wasn't pleasant.

He knew it was time to leave when Nora started to look attractive. It was dangerous to interpret their repartee as flirtatious, especially after last time. As he rose, the door swung open with a burst of rowdy new revellers. The sudden whiff of fresh air had bile rising in the back of his throat, and he slumped back down into his seat, fighting a losing battle to remain conscious. Laughter echoed through his skull. The world around him melted, falling away into a dark void, and he found himself engulfed in a circle of dancing horrors.

He stood helpless yet captivated by the singing of faces weeping flesh and blood. They revolved around him and, one by one, caught fire. As their skin seared and their eyes bubbled and burst, still they danced, drawing closer with every turn. Before he could do anything to stop it, he was swallowed by a ring of flames, catching in his hair and consuming his body in a blaze of vivid green.

Brolo woke to a pot of cold water splashing over his face.

'Come on, you. I'm closing up. It's time you went home,' boomed Bloody Nora, in a tone almost as horrifying as his nightmare had been.

His head pounded like someone within was smashing at it with a sledge-hammer, trying to escape, and he'd vomited over himself at some point.

'Stone me, Nora, you should market your sodding beer for its hallucinogenic properties. How long have I been out?'

'There ain't nothing wrong with my beer, boy; you just need to learn to handle your drink,' she said. 'You've been twisting and turning for about three hours. I had a bloody good mind to throw you out, but it got so busy I just left you to it.'

'Thanks for the kind hospitality,' said Brolo, with as much sarcasm as he could muster in his current condition. 'I'm just glad I didn't spoil the atmosphere. I trust I didn't miss anything too spectacular?'

'Not really. Just a group of drunkards from the capital spouting nonsense, as you booze hounds have a habit of doing. Bunch of fairy-tale rubbish if you ask me. Anyway, I wanna get to bed, so get up and be gone with you,' she said, picking up his empty pot.

'Okay, okay, I'm going. Sorry about the sick.'

'That's fine, the dogs will clear it all up by morning.'

With that pleasant image branded into his mind, Brolo stumbled out into the dark streets of Peplyshaw, threw up in the gutter, and began to make the long way back to his lodgings, putting the torturous day behind him.

CHAPTER SEVEN

A LITTLE BIRDIE TOLD ME …

Stánwilte had been waiting outside Lord Cormorant's audience chamber for almost an hour. Hands behind his head, he leant back, eyes closed, settled in comfortably for the long haul. Sucking in all the sounds and smells of the western shoreline – the intoxicating salty air of the Arbour Vale coast, the faint lullaby of waves crashing into the Maiden Cliffs, and the irritating songs of the various seabirds inhabiting the windswept rocks.

He'd spent many long and peaceful afternoons in this antiquated obligger wood chair. It was a comrade he knew intimately, remaining as close as two things could only be after a whole married life together – or after merely one campaign of war, where everything short of your undergarments was shared. Lucky, if you were, to still have some. For any newcomer, however, she was indeed a wild beast to tame. It took many hours of uncomfortable shifting to find the one sweet spot where your arse-cheeks wouldn't turn to stone after fifteen minutes.

Cormorant, Stánwilte knew, was a busy man. Patience wasn't just appreciated when meeting with him; it was necessary.

During Stánwilte's first visit, shortly after he'd been named Captain of the Peplyshaw Watch, he'd paced up and down the corridor for a mere forty minutes, wearing out his shoes and patience, before he'd stormed off. Thankfully, his temper had mellowed since those bitter days. Now that he knew the protocol for dealing with Lord Cormorant, the endurance waiting wasn't half as frustrating.

It was after one of Stánwilte's piss breaks that he first took notice of the tapestry hanging on the opposite wall. He was sure it'd been there on every other trip he'd made to Craginhall, but this was the first time he'd ever really *seen* it. Its colours had clearly faded over many years, to the point that they'd failed to grasp his attention before now. It was astonishingly large, stretching almost the entire length of the corridor, which was around two hundred feet long.

Stánwilte studied it closely. It seemed to tell the tale of Arnheld of Schwartz, the Uniter, showing in intricate detail how his whole family had been massacred on the western shores of what was now Arbour Vale, before he'd been beaten and left for dead by the invading Ohmen forces. As the old legend went, after discovering his near-lifeless body, local peasants had nursed him back to health. Once recovered, he'd slipped off to travel the kingdoms, emerging many years later to fight a guerrilla war against the Archduke of Ohmendy. A large portion of the tapestry depicted the great forest gathering of the three remaining kings, who'd pledged their swords and lives to Arnheld. They'd sworn to join as one kingdom, putting aside all former quarrels to defeat the greater threat, naming Arnheld as their lord and the first king of what had later become known as Uprynenos. Stánwilte was just about to reach the epic battle scene when he felt a tap on his shoulder.

'Captain Stánwilte Stángefeall, His Lordship will see you now,' came the familiar brisk tone of Cormorant's steward, Rimuir.

Rimuir was a frail old twig of a man, with a mouth permanently puckered and ready to kiss the nearest noble backside, who'd served both the former and current Lord of Arbour Vale in almost every aspect of their governance. He was draped in rather exuberant robes of violet silk laced with gold thread. Not Stánwilte's idea of appropriate garb, but old age did funny things to people, and at least it drew attention away from his scabby, bald scalp.

'I do wish you wouldn't call me that,' said Stánwilte.

'I mean no offence, Captain, but of all the names that precede you, Stángefeall seems least ... offensive. I do beg your pardon,' he said, with a smile that Stánwilte took to mean he begged nothing at all.

'How about you simply call me Stánwilte from now on, eh? Can you manage that, or will your spongy old brain let it slip like your breakfast down the front of your robes? Now take me to Cormorant, I've waited enough. Thank you.'

Rimuir took a moment to brush the crumbs from his garish robes, then sombrely led Stánwilte down the corridor.

'You know, many mistakenly believe this to be a tapestry, when it's actually an ancient piece of embroidery that has been in the Cormorant family for generations,' said Rimuir, his smugness wafting through the air.

'If I'd wanted the grand tour, I would've bought a ticket at the door.'

While Stánwilte found the titbit interesting, he didn't want to engage with the steward any more than was strictly necessary. With an indignant huff, Rimuir guided him to Lord Thrielf Cormorant's audience chamber, muttering obscenities under his breath all the way.

In stark contrast to his steward's extravagant sense of style, Lord Cormorant's audience chamber, and indeed the man himself, paled in comparison to the lavish fashions of the other lords of Uprynenos. The chamber was circular, and topped with a cracked dome, which let in a large streak of light that shone almost directly onto Lord Cormorant's desk. A crimson carpet must've once run like an imposing stream of blood from the entrance, past a few rows of empty stone seats, and along to where Cormorant sat, but it was now dusty and strewn with muddy footprints. There was little in the way of decoration; only a few bookshelves, a faded mural on the wall behind the desk, and two snarling boar heads mounted on pillars flanking Cormorant, their wild, dead eyes poised straight at anyone entering the room.

As Rimuir led Stánwilte down the aisle, a cool breeze rushed in through an open window, filling Stánwilte's nose with the sharp, salty twang of the sea that crashed thunderously into the rocks below.

'Captain Stánwilte of the Peplyshaw Watch to see you, my lord,' announced Rimuir, spouting a fine mist of spittle.

'Ah, Captain,' said Cormorant, in a tone that displayed, with all the subtlety of a crossbow bolt to the chest, the distaste he felt at Stánwilte's presence. 'Take a seat. May I interest you in some wine or ale to quench your thirst?'

'Just some water would be fine, thank you, my lord,' said Stánwilte, as he sat.

'Most unlike you, but please yourself. Rimuir, please fetch the captain some ... water.' Cormorant gave a wry chuckle, dismissing the old man with a wave. 'Let's get straight to it, shall we? How fares my peaceful jewel? Still suffering under a crime wave of scrumping pigs? Has old Nora been caught putting slop back into the fresh barrels again? As I told you last time, speak to Mayor Jur before coming to me with every trivial problem.'

'No, my lord, it's not about those. Although I still haven't the foggiest idea how those thieving swine managed to find their way into O'Brio's orchid,' said Stánwilte, with probing sarcasm.

'Oh, really?' Cormorant said, not even bothering to look up as he scrawled away on a piece of parchment. 'This should be good. Let's hear it, then.'

'My lord, I've come to hear *it* from you – what news was so pressing for our king to hasten a message to Craginhall, that is.'

This time, Cormorant paused. Dropping his quill with a splatter of ink, he met Stánwilte's stare, scrawny eyes pulsing as if painstakingly calculating everything they took in.

'What is said between His Majesty and me is for our own knowledge, not for that of the common folk,' said Cormorant, his words chopping like an unsharpened butcher's cleaver before he realised his mistake. He picked up his quill and carried on scribbling. 'How did you know I'd received a message?' he asked, finally.

'Half the bloody capital saw three ravens fly off from the Palace of the United in the middle of the night. It doesn't take a wizard to figure it out.'

The chamber fell silent, save for the scratching of Cormorant's quill and the crashing of the relentless waves. Both men spent a few moments measuring each other.

Cormorant was a sharp and calculated man. However, he'd been known to take risks when the situation called for it. He was a commanding lord, and loyal to the king, with good reason. As the king had no surviving issue, upon his death, the lords of Uprynenos would hold a moot to decide his successor. Having strong blood ties to the royal family, and being from a house with a noble past, Cormorant stood a very good chance of elevation. Stánwilte intended to take full advantage of his lofty ambitions.

'I would hope not,' Cormorant said. 'You know as well as I do what the penalty for wizardry is these days. Besides, my receiving a Raven's Call doesn't explain your presence here. The matters of the realm have nothing to do with the petty captain of a town watch, I assure you. So, pray, what did you hope to accomplish by coming to Craginhall?'

'That depends on whether the rumours pouring all over the kingdom are true,' Stánwilte said flatly. The time for graciousness was past.

'I wasn't aware that the once great and noble Stánwilte had taken such an interest in the idle chit-chat of the common peasantry.'

'And *I* wasn't aware that the illustrious and powerful lord of Arbour Vale could be so naive. In the years of my service to the Crown, and since my unjust downfall and exile, I've learnt that the *common peasantry* poses a far greater threat to the kingdom's stability than any invasion, civil war or supposed fire-breathing beast.'

Rimuir returned to the chamber with a flagon of water, bowed to Cormorant, and poured Stánwilte a cup. A most fortuitous arrival – the tense atmosphere had started to make Stánwilte a little hot under the collar.

'That's where you and the king agree,' said Cormorant. 'If you must know, then yes, the stories seem to be true. Dragons have returned to Uprynenos.' He beckoned Rimuir to pour him a glass of wine. 'Well, at least *one* dragon, which has blessedly remained far from the kingdom's borders, but the point remains. The court first heard of such tales a year ago, when whispers of travellers going missing in the far north began to flutter around Lundinia. Nothing too worrisome, at first; people disappear in the barren wilds of Ánad almost every week. There was no reason to bother the king with such issues.' Cormorant gave Stánwilte a look rich with the implication he should learn the same courtesy. 'Yet these latest events cannot be ignored, especially with the rumours of a survivor who bore witness to them.'

'The king, I presume, has ordered that the beast not be harmed?'

'Yes, that's the official declaration from His Majesty, though my letter states otherwise.'

It wasn't difficult for Stánwilte to work out why. In fact, before he'd left Peplyshaw, he'd already suspected how the state of royal affairs would lie. It was a legal predicament he was counting on.

'The Dragona?' he asked, using experience from his many years at court to conceal the fact that he already knew the answer.

'Exactly,' Cormorant said, as if speaking to a slow child. 'They're bonded tightly to the Crown – constitutionally, politically, and financially. The Dragona have prophesied that dragons would return to these lands for hundreds of years. Still, over the last few centuries, the faith has been dwindling, with many converting to the Circle. But now?' He took a deep gulp of wine. 'Their following has increased exponentially, seemingly overnight, and it's not confined to the capital. Pilgrims from all over Uprynenos have flocked to the Cathedral of Fire. His Eminence Relfread has been gracious enough to hold mass for them every night, praising the return of the realm's true protectors.'

'You speak as if His Majesty is displeased by this prophecy,' said Stánwilte, fishing.

'Yes, of course he is! You know the legends, I'm sure. The world was forged from the fires of the Great Serpent, and for many thousands of years the beast's offspring ruled the skies and land, until man came along and put a stick in the spokes. When Arnheld of Schwartz united the five kingdoms against the Ohmen forces, he did so with gifts granted to him by the last dragon, Byrnegona. It is said the dragon bequeathed him a serpent's glamour to woo the lords of the land, brute strength to fight valiantly in battle, and a mighty sword of screaming fire to wield in combat. Arnheld also gained the ancient wisdom of dragons. All he had to do was give up his sight in one eye and, rather peculiarly, hang upside down from a tree for a weekend. Scholars aren't sure if that part of the story is true.'

'And to thank Byrnegona, Arnheld promised to pay penance for man's crimes against the dragons, naming them rightful rulers of the known world, and founding the Dragona in their honour,' finished Stánwilte. 'Surely no one takes that rubbish seriously.'

'Worryingly enough, many do. The most fanatical believers have already started rallying at the royal palace gates, calling for His Circle-Following Majesty to renounce the throne in favour of a Dragonian vassal.'

'And how do they believe a *dragon* can justly rule a kingdom?'

'Peasants don't have the capacity to think about this kind of thing. They simply catch the whiff of a prophecy and start lining up like lambs to the slaughter. The beast has no interest in ruling them, only in dining on them.'

Stánwilte dwelt on that thought for a moment, imaging a few choice people in the capital who deserved roasting by a winged serpent.

'So, the king wants the matter dealt with discreetly, I take it?'

'He's requested that each lord send their best knights north, to kill this beast as quickly and quietly as possible. If the peasants are content with making pilgrimage to the capital, all the better for its economy. Let them believe their empty-headed prophecy. Trying to explain logic to rustics with nothing but wool between their ears is a futile task– they'll never cotton on to what's best for them.'

Stánwilte knew what he must do. He didn't doubt for one moment the folly of the task ahead of him. Yet it was the only way to gain what he truly desired.

This is going to be painful. Not just to ask, but quite possibly on the 'not being eaten alive by a mythological creature' side of things.

'My lord, I wish to go,' he said, as humbly as he could manage.

Cormorant sat back with a grin forming on his tight lips, fingering the stem of his goblet.

'You, Stánwilte?' He paused for a moment, perhaps to allow the muscles of his face, which had long since withered away, to strain with the intolerable weight of pulling his grin up wider. 'You're far too old for such nonsense. You of all people must be aware that such a task is tantamount to suicide. Let the younger men ride off hunting the glory they so desperately crave. Why risk yourself?'

'The reward from the king ... it would be quite substantial, would it not?' he replied.

'Ah, so that's it!' Cormorant said. 'You want to make it back into the king's good graces. Well, the prize for bringing him the dragon's head is three thousand Gold Swans, and the promise of vast tracts of land confiscated during the Cull of Magic. A fine reward, no doubt, but this is not your finest idea. The king would see you hang before he ever accepted you back into his service.'

Stánwilte was aware of how he fared in the opinion of the king, but he still had to try.

'Nonetheless, I need to right the wrongs of the past, my lord. Not just for myself, but for the memory of Prince Auldalin.'

'I think you've already done enough for the prince, don't you?'

Those words stung more than any blow Stánwilte had ever received in a combat. They always did.

'I was loyal to the prince and the king throughout all my years of service. The prince was young, bold ... careless.'

'And you let him die.'

'No!' he shouted, louder than he'd intended. Without realising it, he'd bolted up from his seat, and now leant over the desk with both fists clenched. He mopped his brow with his sleeve, sitting back down. 'Forgive me, my lord. I forgot myself.'

'You've forgotten yourself far too many times this afternoon,' Cormorant snapped back.

'Indeed, I'm sorry. However, my lord, please let me put it another way. If I go in search of the beast, with a small group of volunteers from the Watch – if we track it, kill it, and return to receive our thanks from the king – forgiveness is all I want, and whether I receive it or not, I will place all other glory at your feet. I'm your man, my lord. You will receive more praise than I.'

Stánwilte needed to reel his last point in gently to land his catch, subtly enough not to scare it away.

'And when the sad day comes of our noble king's passing ... what man could be more highly regarded, deemed more worthy as successor, than the one who killed the dragon?'

Chapter Eight

The Highest Room in the Tallest Tower

Drifting in and out of consciousness, Yilonia's mind spiraled for what seemed an eternity. From time to time, she would wake to gape inanely at the sky scrolling past above her, only to close her eyes and tumble back into the pit of nightmares like a rag doll dropped into a well.

Sometimes voices called to her through the veil, as unintelligible as they were ominous. Occasionally, a whisper she could understand would break through the baleful chorus.

'My feet hurt,' one ghostly echo complained.

'What's your name?' she heard often.

'Keep her cool, don't let her dehydrate,' boomed another voice.

None of it made sense. Yilonia felt like she was a young girl again, and comprehension was a beautiful butterfly she was trying her hardest to catch, but her net was torn and full of holes.

As she'd grown up, many dark and gruesome images of what the Pit of Iros was like had been painted onto her impressionable mind. An old woman had once told her it was all fire and brimstone, with hulking great demons flaying the skin from sinners' backs. Someone else had explained that the underworld was other people, which at the time had been utterly believable – but now, Yilonia knew that neither of those could possibly be what waited for sinners in death. *They*, no matter how painful and terrifying, still had constants, and a true nightmare of eternal torment would be an underworld unbound by constants.

Time shifted. The world was shapeless, totally devoid of form or matter, existing as an unremitting whirlwind of fear, blurring the lines between what *was* and what *could* be.

***

Yilonia awoke under what appeared to be a starless, dull grey sky. The calm of night was a blessed change from the whirlpool of horrors she'd previously occupied. Still, the all-consuming darkness worried her. She was drenched head-to-toe in sweat, yet the breeze flowing around her was brisk and fresh, and she realised she was lying in a bed – an actual, feather-pillowed, four-poster bed.

What's a bed doing outside, and how did I get in it? she wondered sluggishly.

Her eyes took a while to focus. She wanted to believe she'd only been asleep for one evening, but the weariness of her body suggested otherwise. Besides, after such vivid dreams, she couldn't trust this place to be reality. It could just as easily be the beginnings of a new nightmare. She lay as still as possible, peering at the hazy sky above her, awaiting any signs of normality or delusion.

As her sight adjusted, Yilonia realised the sky she'd been gawking at was in fact a high stone ceiling, and the chill breeze brushing against her face was coming through two large open doors that appeared to lead out onto a balcony.

So ... I'm not outside? thought Yilonia, completely bewildered. *Then where in all the kingdom's crannies am I?*

She sat up and swept her legs round to stand, but as soon as she tried to force them to bear her weight, they gave out, and she collapsed to the cold stone floor.

The feeble mound known as Yilonia lay crumpled for a while. She'd cracked her knees violently in her fall, and they pulsed in agony. Wiping away her tears, she built up the courage to try again, using a small table beside the bed for extra support. The effort left her woozy to the pit of her stomach, but she resisted the urge to give up and forced herself to try a step.

The appalling state of her balance was unnerving, yet what really shocked her into the reality of her situation came when she crept trembling past a large mirror and caught sight of the deathly figure staring back at her.

Substantial weight loss had taken its toll on Yilonia. The outline of her skull seemed to be fighting its way out from beneath her skin. Days shrivelling away under the sun had changed her hair from a luscious brunette to the dusty yellow of baked straw, which was almost as brittle to the touch. She cupped her head in her hands, refusing to believe the image facing her was her own, but as she rubbed at her blurry eyes, she noticed how skeletal her fingers had become.

Why am I alive? she thought. Tears ran down her cheeks in a steady flow, falling to the cold, hard floor.

'No!' she shouted suddenly, her harsh voice echoing around the dark room.

I'm alive – that's all that matters, she thought. *So many died, yet I somehow lived. No matter what has happened, I must be thankful for it. Lysio ...*

She almost lapsed back into despair, but she forced herself to rally, at least until she could find out what had happened to her.

As she drew closer to the balcony doors, she closed her eyes, fearing the worst.

Am I back home? Maybe some bounty hunters found me lying at the Eternal Shuffler's door and took me back to Father for a few pieces of gold.

She shook away the thought. This room, as bare as it was, was far too large for her father's castle. And the scent of the breeze made it clear she hadn't been transported home. Stunheath was surrounded by dense woodlands, pastures, and farms, stretching to the imposing mountains beyond. The heavenly aromas of lavender, meadowsweet, lily-of-the-valley, and honeysuckle that blanketed the town each morn supposedly had regenerative qualities, which drove hordes of the elderly and infirm to take up residence there for a few months each year. However, the brisk wind rushing through the balcony doors carried an altogether more communal pong about it.

Yilonia could hear the feverish buzzing of civilisation below, despite the deep purple sky, which suggested it was still an hour or so before sunrise. She took a step out onto the balcony, wrapping her thin arms around herself for warmth, and gazed upon the world lying before her.

Spires. Hundreds of them. They rose out of the murky streets, winding from the shadows of the houses below and striving ever upwards, leaving the common architecture to bask in their glory. Each spire seemed to be reaching up and over the others in an unyielding scuffle to be the closest to the heavens, like a field of sunflowers growing taller and taller as they wrestled for the lion's share of sunlight.

Breathless, Yilonia stood towering above them all.

The realisation of where she was winded her like a gauntleted punch to the stomach. She'd visited only once before, a few years back, when she came with her father to mark the eighteenth birthday of the man history would remember as the Lost Prince. Nevertheless, she could still remember the names of all the landmarks her father had pointed out as she'd strolled starry-eyed through the city, part of a celebratory procession in the prince's honour.

The Hookfield meat market, a gory grotto of anything and everything fleshy – all the meaty delicacies you could ever want, hung for twenty-eight days, whether they were supposed to be or not. The Great Library of Uprynenos, which housed the only handwritten copy of *Ohmen Invasion – My Account of the Uniting of the Land* by Wigtree Hefindoren, chronicler of the attempted Ohmen conquest and advisor to Arnheld of Schwartz. Almost as popular as the library was its adjoining elixir-house, where bitter beverages with revitalising qualities were brewed, and which had become one of the primary employers of wizard graduates soon after magic was outlawed five years ago.

Their names all came flooding back to Yilonia in a pleasant wave of nostalgia. All except the Cathedral of Fire, which stood in the centre of the city.

The cathedral was a brutish monster of masonry. Yilonia recalled how its four gargantuan belltowers had tolled, how their rumbling cries had shattered the clouds. The imposing walls of black granite were plagued with crumbling chimeras and corroded gargoyles. Tooth-shaped merlons lined the gabled roof. A dozen flying buttresses ran along its length, like the legs of a demonic insect, giving it the appearance of a beast that had lain dormant for many centuries, ready to rise again at any moment. Yet, as ghastly as the cathedral was, it was dwindling into Yilonia's memories of simpler times.

Spyrata – I'm in Spyrata!

Yilonia stood amazed as the sun rose, spreading light across the land below.

I must be in the royal palace. Way up high on the Hill of the Last Stand rests the Palace of the United and the Five Towers of the Crown. From the look of this view, I'm in the highest room in the tallest tower ... how original, she thought, with the first smile she'd cracked in days.

***

An hour or so passed before Yilonia heard the door to her room open, followed by a panicked murmur and the clamour of something smashing against the ground. Whoever had entered must've seen her empty bed and fled before she had a chance to reveal herself from out on the balcony. Suspecting they'd scarpered off to alert someone to her supposed disappearance, Yilonia decided she'd best wait patiently for the answers to her questions.

She tided the mess by the door, which appeared to have been a jug of water. Afterwards, she sat herself as calmly as she could on the bed, wishing the water had made it to her bedside so she could quench her thirst.

Before too long, four guards clad in shining gold-and-blue armour came bursting through the heavy oaken door, followed by a huffing old crow of a woman. When her beady little eyes clocked Yilonia, her bottom lip flapped like a banner caught in a strong wind.

'I thought you said she'd vanished, Briwetta?' said the guard leading the pack.

'Well, I ... her bed ...'

'You stupid bat, she's sitting right there!' said the second guard.

'Yeah, you should get your eyes checked,' said the third, before the other men gave him disapproving glances. 'Um ... you old hag.'

'Get her bathed and dressed, ready to see Master Findu. And try not to lose her this time!' the first guard barked as Briwetta waddled past him, earning a wave of sniggers from his men.

'Wait, please!' called Yilonia, standing as the troop of men turned to leave. 'Please, tell me – how did I get here? Why *am* I here?'

'I'm afraid I can't divulge such information,' said the lead guard, as sympathetically as a guard could get, which wasn't very. 'But Master Findu, the king's personal physician, will tell you all you need to know soon enough.'

'But how long have I been here? Spyrata, I mean. A few days? A week or two?'

A brief shadow of silence fell over the room. The guard leader shook his head as he strode over to her. He put a cold gauntleted hand on her shoulder and gently sat her down.

'A month and a half,' he said, then walked away without another word.

A month and a sodding half! Yilonia felt a sudden surge of nausea. *A month and a half, wasting away here! And Spyrata's at least another two months travel from Ánad. I can't have been out that long, surely ... can I?*

Yilonia sat cradling herself, staring out into nothing. Briwetta began to undress and wash her, wiping more than three months of sleep away from her eyes, as tears welled to replace it.

Chapter 9
Hungover at Dawn

The last four days had drifted by for Brolo. Well, not so much *drifted*, more *dragged by a chain around his neck as he forced the kicking and screaming earth to continue its journey around the sun.* He'd spent each morning begging for salvation before the privy, as if it were a shrine to the deity of misguided drinkers, praying it would grant him sweet mercy.

Getting back to work had been a greater trial than he'd envisioned. He'd led himself to believe that the fresh, open air would do him a world of good – would rejuvenate him out of his rut of vomiting and dodgy bowel movements.

Sadly, this theory had proven to be as reliable as an old wives' tale. Walking the beat through Peplyshaw's excrement-splattered streets was a traumatic experience, especially when in a delicate, alcohol-induced state. His senses of taste, sight and hearing had all become dysfunctional, due to his screaming headaches and bunged-up sinuses; however, his sense of smell had heightened to a degree where even the sweet aroma wafting from the window of Boggin's Pie Shoppe had caused him to keel over and trade chunks with the nearest gutter.

Waking on the fifth day, Brolo was relieved to find that the worst of his headache had subsided, and that he was able to keep his breakfast down. His mind was hazy, his stomach gurgled like a hog drowning in mud, and it would be a fair while before he trusted a fart again, but he was glad to put the trial of the last few days behind him.

Unlike most members of the Watch, he shunned the free accommodation offered within the garrison, only staying on the nights he was on shift. Peplyshaw was an inescapable void of mundanity as it was. Imprisoning himself within his place of work would only serve to suffocate him further. To enjoy at least some sense of freedom, he occupied a small room nestled between a tannery and an abandoned Church of Flame – which had been left to ruin after a rather ironic fire – lodging with a sweet if slightly forgetful old lady named Yivon Dwimm.

The constant reek of urine and dung wafting from the tannery was bearable once you got used to it. Harder to deal with was the old-lady smell clinging to everything in the place, which was cluttered with a lifetime's worth of hoarded crap. Still, the rent was cheap, and most weeks Brolo was able to convince Mrs Dwimm he'd already paid it.

Donning his uniform, but carrying his well-worn boots, Brolo crept through the house. He tried his best to navigate the treacherous assault course of creaky floorboards and precariously placed vases, so not to wake Mrs Dwimm, and eventually snuck out into the mist of the early morn.

Even in the hazy darkness of six o'clock in the morning, with the brisk spring air biting deep, the town was brimming with activity. Smoke rose in soft plumes from the chimneys of Mr and Mrs Drossop's bakery as they worked to provide Peplyshaw with its daily bread. Priests of the Circle stood wrapped in thick, woollen robes, singing prayers before a crowd gathered on the town green. Greengrocers, butchers, smiths, and pedlars set up shop, ready to display all sorts of fine wares from around Uprynenos.

Yet as one world awakened, one must fall to sleep. While Lady Lace N'Strap's brothel closed its doors, the last few revellers from the various pubs and inns found themselves unceremoniously tossed out into the gutter and left to stumble their way home.

Taking the short route through the town's graveyard, Brolo arrived at the ludicrously oversized Watch house. The two men guarding the main gate waved him through, trying to hide their grins, then broke into girlish giggles as soon as he was supposedly out of earshot. Although Brolo ignored their mockery, he added their faces to his mental list of those he'd like to cave in one day.

In the courtyard, men were rushing around like worker ants. Some were fulfilling morning chores, such as feeding the people in the cells, mucking out slop buckets and honing weapons. Others were busying themselves with training, practicing their swordsmanship and exercise drills, while the guards who'd returned from an evening on duty waited sluggishly to hand over their shifts so they could get to bed.

Inside was similarly chaotic. Men were rushing to breakfast; Mistress Roslyn's army of helpers were dishing out stacks of her oatcakes, which were often used in training as replacement bucklers; overnight prisoners were lining up for processing; and Bæwylm was pinning something to the Watch noticeboard, which probably assigned duties for the day. Deciding to spare his teeth the agony of breakfast, Brolo headed over to see what his tasks were to be.

Most likely goods inspection duty at the gate ... again.

However, on closer inspection, he found that he hadn't been assigned anything for today. Nobody had. The only message on the board was addressed to all members of the Watch, commanding them to be at the great hall by eight o'clock sharp. The note bore the swirly signature that marked it as an order from Captain Stánwilte.

So, he was back. He must've ridden hard to get to and from Craginhall so quickly.

'And you won't be sneaking off this time, Brolo,' came Bæwylm's stern voice from behind. 'I hope you weren't stupid enough to think Stánwilte wouldn't find out about your little excursion.'

'Oh, come on, I've already suffered enough. I really don't need to deal with you trying to make me feel ashamed.'

'You've already accomplished that yourself, from what I've heard,' Bæwylm said, shaking his head. 'I've tried my hardest with you, lad. Your mother would—'

'My mother's dead,' Brolo said bluntly. 'My mother's dead, my father left before I was even born, and I'm stuck in this pothole of a town. I've no friends, no family and no future, except for stopping the occasional theft of cabbage from a market stall.'

'Maybe so,' Bæwylm conceded. 'But before your mother died, I promised her I'd look after you, and I'll be damned to the Flame if I let you waste your life like you've been doing. You need to stop drinking, Brolo.'

'What I do in my own time is my business, old man. I'm not a child anymore, so you can stop with this bullshit about what you promised my mother. It's my life, and I'll do with it as I please.'

Having said his piece, Brolo turned and stormed off towards the great hall, leaving a rather red-faced Bæwylm fuming behind him.

It's always the same with that bastard. 'Don't do this. Your mother wouldn't approve that.' It's like he wants me to rot in this pestilently mind-numbing hovel! Brolo's footsteps slapped angrily, echoing around the corridors as he went. *Let's go see what Stánwilte wants, then.*

He probably has some form of public humiliation lined up for me. Yeah, that'll be it, the rancid cocksnout!

Brolo shoved the heavy doors to the great hall open with a long-buried strength that almost pushed them off their hinges and stepped boldly through.

Silence greeted him. He was the first to arrive.

Oh, fan-bloody-tastic, more time alone. There's nothing quite like berating myself for being an utterly intolerable waste of space. As if I haven't listened to that lecture a hundred times already!

Brolo leant against the jagged stone wall to await the arrival of other watchmen. The great hall whined with the faint death knell of the winds trapped and left to die within its vast emptiness, far from the rolling hillsides they yearned to sweep across.

Brolo was under no illusion that he was destined for greatness. Nor did he believe he stood above anybody else in Peplyshaw, in either a figurative or literal sense. He did nurse a small belief that after all the shit he'd endured thus far, the world owed him a break at some point, but he highly doubted he'd be earning a knighthood, royal patronage, or burial in a vast shrine. What he didn't want, however, was to end his days in a shallow pit in the same graveyard he walked through on his way to work every day.

The stories Mother used to tell me when I was a boy ... they painted a world overflowing with wondrous experiences and places. All those nights, she would speak of Father, of his exploits around the kingdom and across the seas, gallivanting in unexplored lands. How, truly, could anyone exposed to such visions be expected to content themselves with wasting away in the cradle?

Bæwylm had taken him in as a kindness to his mother, who'd used her vast knowledge of medicine to ease the suffering of Bæwylm's beloved wife, Ellana, during her own prolonged illness and death. Yet his generous deed didn't give him the right to force Brolo to become the child he and Ellana had never had.

As the doors to the great hall screeched open, Brolo let out a sigh, resigning himself to the comedic character he was supposed to portray. The *himself* he allowed others to see. He wielded his quick wit like a sword, his sarcasm like a bow, and his jovial nature like a set of full plate armour, in case he needed extra cover from anyone who broke through his primary defences.

A few of the entering watchmen wafted their hands in front of their noses as they passed Brolo, laughing to themselves. Brolo smiled and matched them with a hand gesture, signalling they could go fuck themselves, which they met with even more laughter.

For now, at least, this was his life. He could only pray it wouldn't be so for much longer.

CHAPTER TEN

CALL TO ARMS, LEGS, KNEES OR TOES ... ANYTHING!

Abead of sweat dripped from Stánwilte's wrinkled brow as he strode down the narrow corridor, passing various unused storage rooms and eventually coming to the door of the great hall. Despite his best efforts, he couldn't shake the insatiable parasite of doubt that had sunk icy teeth deep into his mind, sending shivers down his usually rigid spine.

Everything about his plan had seemed so flawless back in Craginhall, when he and Cormorant had ironed out the fine details, yet now he saw it teetering on a knife's edge. His task was to convince a host of glorified farmers' sons armed with rusty swords that a treacherous journey through hostile and lawless lands, fending off bandits, thieves, wild animals and a literal *dragon* was, all in all, a good idea.

Stánwilte scuffed his boots against the rough stone floor as he waited by the doors. Knowing what to say to persuade the men to join him was a task almost as tough as the one he'd be asking them to take on. Lord Cormorant, however, had been all too willing to volunteer Wilkhelm.

'If you insist on going on this suicide mission,' he'd said, *'feel free to take that brat of mine with you. With luck, you might get rid of him for me, or*

toughen him up a bit ... though I know which outcome I'm staking my coin on.'

Stánwilte still failed to grasp how a man could show such disregard for the well-being of his son, though he was willing to acknowledge that Wilkhelm wasn't exactly the kind of man who'd make a father proud. If anything, that intolerable princess was exactly the sort of useless turd Stánwilte had hoped wouldn't tag along on his journey northwards.

Nevertheless, Stánwilte had to make do with the meagre scraps fate felt obliged to offer him. He'd decided to be as honest about the dangers of the quest as he could, while giving away as few details as possible. He was the only fool who stood to gain from all this. If anyone got hurt, the blame would belong at his feet alone. He already knew how it felt to bear the chains of guilt for another's death; he didn't expect them to sit any easier if it actually *was* his fault this time.

In his rush to prepare, Stánwilte hadn't even had time to explain any of his plans to Bæwylm. Regretfully, he featured in them little. While having the old dog's sword at his side would've made Stánwilte feel infinitely more comfortable about facing off against a fire-breathing dragon, he knew Bæwylm's place was in Peplyshaw, commanding the Watch.

Through the oaken door, Stánwilte could hear the assembled men of the Watch causing an almighty ruckus, in the sadly customary fashion of pigs at feeding time, until a horn boomed across the hall. As the wave of mutterings drew to a still, he took a deep breath and reluctantly entered.

All fifty-seven men of the Watch turned to face him as the old door screeched on its hinges. He made his way to the makeshift dais where Bæwylm stood, one hundred and thirteen eyeballs following his progress. The one hundred and fourteenth eyeball stared to the left of the hall – poor Trivour Googily's lazy eye always lagged behind.

Five years, and out of fifty-seven, only four would bother to step around my corpse if I were to drop dead here and now.

'Men of the Watch,' he began, 'I thank you for coming on such short notice, but the matter at hand is too important for us to waste any time. Before we begin, I must be honest with you all: the charge we face is for the greater good of the kingdom, and not an official duty of the Peplyshaw Watch, so none of you are obligated to stay here – except you, Wilkhelm. Your father has ordered that you partake in this task. However—'

Relieved sighs echoed throughout the hall as the first handful of men made a hasty exit. Wilkhelm also began to bleat loudly about his forced involvement, demanding to speak to his father.

By the Uniter's sack! Categorically not the reaction I was hoping for, but at least thirty or so men are loyal enough to stick around.

Undeterred, Stánwilte continued.

'However … I know you all as proud men, good men, dutiful and brave. I know deep down, in your heart of hearts, none of you would stand idly by while you had blood and steel within you to fight. Not one of you could bear to see your kingdom fall, crumbling feebly before the unspeakable horrors that assail it. The time to make your mark is now!'

Raising his fist triumphantly into the air, Stánwilte faced a wall of backs as an even larger group left the room.

Twelve men remained – a pitiful showing. Stánwilte turned for support from Bæwylm, but the old man simply shrugged. From here, Stánwilte knew he had a mountain to climb. Despite all past grievances, and against his better judgment, he left his pride behind and rallied himself.

'Alright, if this is how you're going to be, then I'll bite. Forget all that glory crap, you'll find none here. The pages of the great tomes of history are brimming with the fables of forgotten men. Some were otherwise unremarkable and humble, some were mighty figures of their age. All, I can assure you, died in some shit way or another. Yet if you look beyond, gaze deeper into the grand scheme of things, you'll see that the world is bigger than the glory of any one man. It isn't the tale of a hero's epic fight for honour and glory that lives on forever as a testament to his greatness, but the security of the kingdom he serves! Each brick that forms the vast towers, spires and walls of a kingdom has been paid for dearly by the blood of a hundred thousand fallen heroes. Their names may not be remembered in any annal or poem. Yet, for as long as the sun continues to rise over their precious lands, their stories shall live on. This, my friends, is what I can offer you!'

Stánwilte was almost proud of the heart he'd given his speech, yet he couldn't help wishing more people had stayed to hear it. Other than Wilkhelm, of the fifty-seven men who'd occupied the hall when Stánwilte had begun his recruitment drive, only two others were left standing awkwardly before him.

What have I done? Going at it alone would surely be better than travelling with these three.

A great dopey grin spread wide over Smiggly Jenkins's acne-riddled face. The young lad stood as straight-backed, wide-eyed and bushy-tailed as a human could be, yet his suicidal enthusiasm couldn't offset the petty whining of Wilkhelm, or the conflicted stare of the party's only other volunteer, Brolo.

Stánwilte felt a light tap on his shoulder as Bæwylm leant in to whisper in his ear.

'I'm sorry, sir. I can't say I expected young Brolo to sign himself up, but if he can do it, so can the others. I'll have another word with them later. Offer some encouragement, give an incentive, perhaps a thick-ear or two. A few stern words and a couple of disappointed looks should get at least a few more men to join.'

'No, all is fine, Bæwylm. We've got very little time to lose, and if we're to be gone as soon as possible, then we'll have to finish briefing these … fine recruits.' Turning to face his far-from-bountiful harvest of men, Stánwilte feebly attempted to mask his disappointment as he beckoned them all to follow him. 'Come on then, you lot. We'll discuss the details of this little task in my solar.'

As Stánwilte stepped down wearily from the dais, Wilkhelm attempted to pounce on him, demanding to send a message home to Craginhall. However, he flat-out ignored the boy. Only when he reached the behemoth of a door did he realise his odd procession was already a man down.

'Come on, lad,' bellowed Bæwylm. 'Captain Stánwilte hasn't got all day, y'know!'

Brolo stood still for a few moments, as the echoes of Bæwylm's call bounced around the hall. Finally, he uncrossed his arms and strolled across to catch up. A tortuous foreboding in the pit of Stánwilte's stomach told him that he'd end up wishing Brolo had refused to budge from his spot – that, or Mistress Roslyn's breakfast was finally starting to take effect.

CHAPTER ELEVEN

ALWAYS INN TROUBLE

Brolo suffered from a desperate craving. An intoxicating beverage – frothy, malty and dark – would certainly take the edge off, but he'd gratefully gulp down a mug of distilled tripe juice after *that* briefing. Maybe two.

In the grand scheme of things, I'd probably get a quicker death if I wrestled a grizzly bear while smeared in delectable salmon guts!

Brolo was not the only one to voice concern once the full details of the matter were disclosed. Wilkhelm flat-out refused to believe his father would neglect him so, until Stánwilte handed him a letter with Lord Cormorant's wax skua seal left unbroken. Seeing the young lordling's face drop had been worth a chuckle or four. Sneaking a peek over Wilkhelm's shoulder, Brolo had been able to catch a few choice passages.

'Be the proud bannerman of our noble family in this great and honourable quest!' was a fantastic use of family pride. Altogether more hilarious, however, was *'If you don't go, I'll make damn sure you'll regret you didn't end your existence as a stain on the back of your mother's dress!'*

Brolo had to give it to Lord Cormorant – he made one hell of a motivational writer. Alas, as much as it gave Brolo pleasure to see Wilkhelm squirm, *he* at least hadn't done something as profoundly stupid as volunteer.

Eternal Shuffler, give me rest … or a flame-retardant tunic. A dragon!

The thought grasped Brolo with a mix of terror and wonder. If he was honest, he'd been hoping for some words of comfort after the first utterance of dragons had been casually slipped into conversation. However, he'd been left bitterly disappointed. Even Captain Stánwilte had lacked his usual steely confidence as he'd talked them though the journey ahead, sipping on more than a few glasses of whisky.

A fire-breathing dragon!

In fact, the only one who seemed eager to mount a horse and hit the road was Smiggly.

I doubt Young Master Dopey will end up as anything more than dragon-fodder, Brolo thought, as he took another deep gulp of ale. *Perhaps we all will.*

Stánwilte had given them the rest of the day to tie up their affairs, purchase provisions, and make any last-minute preparations for the journey ahead. He'd forgotten, however, to ban Brolo from getting pissed at the nearest tavern. It would be remiss of him to forgo one last night of merrymaking before months of being cold, wet, and saddle-sore, simply to end up as dwelf jerky in the talons of a dragon.

Putting his looming death aside, Brolo's evening had been very profitable thus far, thanks in no small part to his future endeavours.

As soon as he'd hopped over the passed-out dwarf blocking the door to The Crone's Wimple, Brolo had made no attempt to hide his up-and-coming adventures to any patron who'd give him an ear. Which was rather fortunate, as the flea-bitten down-and-outs who frequented this shithole were always entranced by farfetched anecdotes, desperate for anything to liven up their wasted days. Tossing in a few added heroics – a truth-tweaking story of how he'd demanded Stánwilte let him join the noble quest, and a flat-out lie about it having been his idea in the first place – had resulted in drinks coming his way all night, foamy, fast, and free.

Handy, because I've hardly got a Duck to my name ... which reminds me, are we even getting paid for—

Brolo's trail of thought ended abruptly as he received a hearty slap on the back, causing him to choke on his ale. The sharp breath of pickled eggs and sour booze wafting over his shoulder was enough to tell Brolo that Pete – or Old Wee Pete, as he was known around town – had come to trade witty banter with him. Sadly, when it came to Pete, the conversational conversion rate was always terrible.

'I hear, m'lad, I hear that you'll be heading out soon, riding off on an epic journey, I say, travelling out into the big bad world. All hush-hush, I hear. All very cape-and-shiv stuff, with not a word to anyone, so I've heard. I must say, you have my soft old brain tingling, say buzzing, *brimming* with excitement for you. When I was your age, I would've loved gallivanting across the kingdom on a brave quest. Not that I'm saying you're going on a quest! It's all hush-hush, I hear ...'

'Here, Pete, have a drink on me!' said Brolo, hastily reaching over the bar while Nora's back was turned, grabbing the nearest bottle and passing it to Pete. 'Get this down your gob. Oh, look! Is that Stefan? He seems to be immersed in a spell of storytelling, why don't you go interrupt him?'

Pete's eyes lit up like hooch hurled into a fireplace.

'Oh, thank you, laddie,' he said, as he struggled to bite the cork out from the bottle. 'Thank you kindly indeed. Here's to you and your safety on your travels. I pray the fires of Byrnegona keep you warm at night!' The senile old git raised the bottle in toast and took a deep draft, spilling a fair share of the green-tinged liquid down his shirt, before stumbling off to bore some other poor soul half to death.

From the far corner of the inn, an accordion began to drone through the drunken crowd, some of whom joined in, singing along to the sombre tune. Acrid smoke drifted in thick plumes, as various revellers toked away on their pipes. The smog amassing above Brolo's head began to make his eyes water. He returned to an uncomfortable slouch on the sticky bar, face buried in his arms, as he mulled over the ominous words with which Pete had departed.

May her fires warm me, indeed! If I didn't know better, I'd say I've been flapping my gob more than I should ...

An unusual heaviness gripped Brolo's stomach, preceding a screechy scolding from a voice burrowed deep in the back of his mind, which he suspected could be his conscience. An attempt to drown his woes was thwarted by the revelation that his horn had become bereft of booze, and a peek up the bar showed that Nora's attention was now fully on him. She stood polishing glasses with a suspicious look in her eyes, suggesting she'd noticed something was missing. With no more than a Copper Chick left to his name, and a will to survive the night, Brolo decided it would probably be best to head on home. As he made to hop off his stool, another figure pushed him back down with confident ease and took the seat to his right.

'Two ales, please, Nora. Naturally, take one for yourself, too,' said Bæwylm.

'Oh, yes, Master Bæwylm, sir. Coming right up,' Nora said, scuttling off with an obedience Brolo had never seen before.

'You must've given her pantry a right good old-fashioned dusting at some point for her to serve you so bloody fast,' Brolo said. 'I've shifted my own fair share of cobwebs, yet it still takes me the best part of twenty minutes to get a fucking drink.'

He flinched as Bæwylm laid a heavy, leather-gloved hand upon his shoulder.

'It's called respect, Brolo. I can't say I'm surprised you haven't heard of it; you've got a long road ahead before you can earn any for yourself.'

Nora slopped two great foaming mugs of ale down onto the bar, spilling half their contents in the process. With a broad smile from behind his fuzzy grey beard, Bæwylm handed her an exceedingly generous Silver Goose and requested some peace. After eyeing the coin in her meaty talons, Nora bowed and slid over to the other side of the bar to continue her polishing.

'I've been looking for you,' was all Bæwylm said, once she was out of earshot.

'Undoubtedly. I didn't truly believe this was the kind of place you'd frequent in your downtime.' Brolo grasped his mug of ale and took a hearty swig.

'Sarcasm is the lowest form of wit, boy. How many times must I clip you round the ear before you remember that? What I meant was that I shouldn't have needed to go looking for you. You should be at home, packing.'

'You know me – I never like to be predictable.'

'I popped round to talk about … well, you know, and to drop something important off for you. Yet, lo and behold, dear old Mrs Dwimm hadn't seen or heard from you all day. So, if you weren't at home preparing – despite those being your orders – the sodding town simpleton could've guessed where you'd be.' Bæwylm took a mouthful of his own ale, then winced.

'I *am* preparing. If you'd been scheduled to meet the same fate as I, I'm damn sure you'd be in here doing the same thing.'

'I wish you'd stop trying to act the martyr for once in your bloody life,' Bæwylm said. 'It may have slipped you by, but you're not a child anymore. You volunteered for this, so it's high time you grow up and accept your responsibilities like the proud son of a dwarf should.'

It was hard to ignore the disappointment in Bæwylm's voice. His brow, hair, and jowl sagged with the weariness of his many years, yet his steely-blue eyes glared at Brolo with all the piercing fire of a man half his age.

'That's hardly fair. Yes, I volunteered, but it's not like I knew what I was signing up for, now, did I? If I'd even had the faintest whiff of a clue about the fiery task at hand, I would've been the first to tell that git Stánwilte to shove it where the sun doesn't shine! I mean, a fucking *dra*—'

Like a shot, Bæwylm's slapped across Brolo's mouth.

'—gon,' he mumbled through Bæwylm's fingers.

'You've got a mouth far too big for your own good, lad. Remember your orders, for fuck's sake!'

Slowly, Bæwylm removed his hand and took a drink, gazing around the bar for anyone who might've been listening in.

'Why did you stay, then?' he asked. 'That's what I don't understand! As you said yourself, I expected you to be the first to leave. What are you up to?'

'Me? Absolutely bloody nothing. Why would I be up to anything?'

Bæwylm's grey eyebrows rose like spears ready to thrust themselves off his face, while his sunken eyes blazed white-hot.

'Okay, okay, fine! Yes, I was childishly seeking to even the tally with Stánwilte. Are you happy now? I was seething about him treating us like brats the other night, and assumed I was going to end up in the shit for ditching my last punishment. When he started banging on about *honour* and *glory*, I rather rashly decided involving myself would get me out of having my knuckles rapped, while letting me make his life a bloody nightmare. Well, that backfired quite spectacularly!'

'I knew something was amiss. I wanted to believe you'd finally spouted a set of stones and taken some responsibility for your life, but you couldn't do that without turning it into some petty scheme.' Bæwylm shook his head. 'I hope this will be a lesson learnt, lad. I honestly don't know why you hold this foolish vendetta against Captain Stánwilte.'

'And *I* can't understand why you're happy to be his loyal, slobbering bitch.'

Bæwylm pointed a gnarled finger into his face. 'Watch your tongue. You're not too old for me to give you a boxed ear!'

'Oh, come on, we both know you should be in command of the Watch. You're popular with the men, mostly because you truly give a damn about what they have to say and don't simply pretend to do so. They couldn't give a rat's fart for Stánwilte and all his graces and glories, I can tell you that!' Brolo spat upon the ground with a sneer. 'You've worked your arse off for this shitty little town. Year upon year of loyal service, and when it comes time to give you the break you deserve, they bestow the captaincy on some pompous Spyratan git. Worst of all, you accepted it like a compliant pup! You should've shown some balls – pissed in his boots, chewed the furniture, dragged your arse along the carpets until he tired of your shenanigans and fucked off! A bad metaphor, I grant you, but you understand my meaning.'

Bæwylm rose, placed his now-empty mug onto the bar and laid a hand on Brolo's shoulder. He shrunk under the combined weight of the old man's hold and gaze.

'You don't need to worry about my problems, Brolo. You have more than enough of your own to deal with.' Bæwylm turned to make his leave, stopped, stood awkwardly for a few moments, and spoke one last time. 'I follow Captain Stánwilte's orders not just because of the role he holds now, but also for the one he held before. He's spent more time in battles than everyone else in the Watch has spent sitting around with their thumbs up their arses. Yes, he has his faults, and maybe at the beginning I too felt a little cheated, but I've never regretted the fact he's here.' His back straightened, his shoulders rising. 'One day, this town will face a shitstorm. I don't know when, and I don't know how, but it will come. When it does, my lad, I'll be glad Stánwilte is around to lead us.' Very slightly, his voice softened. 'I bid you a safe journey. I hope you take in what I've told you, and that you'll come back to us with pride in your heart.'

This time, he left for good, without so much as a glance over his shoulder.

'And I hope I just come back,' Brolo whispered. No more than a second after the door closed behind Bæwylm, Bloody Nora scuttled over to Brolo's end of the bar and began the ever-so-subtle brand of inquisition unique to women in small communities.

'By heck, he left in a bit of a fluff, didn't he?' she said casually, polishing the same cup she had been for the last five minutes. 'Wouldn't be surprised if it were your fault again. I suppose it's none of my business, though. That said, he's always been far too proud for his own good, that one. Stresses of the job will weigh on anyone's shoulders eventually.'

'Oh, bugger off, Nora. I'm heading home.'

'See what I mean? Bæwylm wouldn't speak to a lady like that. He knows how to treat a woman proper-like. I should know.' She raised a suggestive eyebrow.

'That saucy old dog. I knew it! *Respect*, my pointy bloody ears!' Brolo's initial reaction, however, soon soured as a horrific afterthought hit. 'Gods, please tell me this foul deed took place way before I was born. Why do I have to be right all the time? And I thought today couldn't get any worse!'

'What's the matter, lad? Jealous of the idea?'

'Don't flatter yourself. I simply cannot fathom Bæwylm dabbling in sullied merchandise – least of goods of a physical nature. Not that the concept of you two sharing a tumble in the rushes is *natural* in any way, shape or form.'

The contents of his stomach swiftly approaching the need to be spewed across the floor, Brolo stumbled his way out of The Crone's Wimple, dodging steaming puddles of vomit and spilt ale, grasping for the doorhandle like a blind man feeling his way around a brothel. As he stepped outside, the evening's brisk chill gave him a mighty slap across both cheeks, stinging his face red-raw. Thankfully, it helped calm his stomach and his nausea soon dissipated.

For a lowly midweek eve in early spring, the streets of Peplyshaw were teeming with activity. Groups of raggedy men, fresh from working on farms all day, staggered from tavern to inn, from inn to pub, laughing and arguing at the same time, hurling the kind of abuse only shared amongst the closest of friends. Wagons brimming with goods trundled along, entering the town after a tiresome journey from the outlying villages of Arbour Vale, or quite possibly further afield. Yawning merchants rode by in their carriages, looking eagerly for stables. The few who rather optimistically inquired with Brolo about their chances of finding a bed for the night rolled away with an air of disappointment. Children ran along the cobbled street, knocking on doors to see if anyone was home. If no one answered, the rapscallions would smear what appeared to be shit on the doorhandle and run away. Harmless enough, right up until the occupants retuned after an evening's merriment. Brolo giggled at the thought of the surprise awaiting the poor saps, especially considering the drunken instinct would likely be giving their hands an inquisitive sniff to work out what the warm gloop was.

Despite the hustle and bustle of the world around him, Brolo resigned himself to his duties and made his way home through the crooked streets. The looming night stretched its hand across the shimmering starlit sky, its heavy shadow creeping through the twists and turns of Peplyshaw and draping them in darkness. The echoes of laughter soon dwindled into a distant memory, making way for a rattling almost-silence. Dread and drink played tricks on him. He heard the lumbering clunk of an unseen stalker's footsteps following closely behind, the rustle of leaves helplessly caught in wailing winds, the clatter of unknown creatures scuttling in the shadows. The Church of Flame stooped in the spectral gloom, decaying brick by brick, dying a slow death over a hundred ages as it crumbled to dust from within.

An overwhelming paranoia gripped Brolo's mind, constricting until he began to run for the safety of home, sprinting as fast as his legs could carry him. Once he finally reached the door to Mrs Dwimm's house, he spared no thought for slamming it behind him with a mighty thwack.

He was still panting shallowly when he finally lifted his weight from the door. As always, several tallow candles had been left burning overnight, giving the shadowy confines of the house a warm, gentle glow. Despite the number of times Brolo had warned the old bint about the dangers of unattended candles, tonight he was thankful for the light.

Silence permeated the house. Walking through the living room and into the kitchen area, Brolo found a note, written in Mrs Dwimm's crude scratch, waiting for him on the rickety dining table.

'A young friend of yours popped round to drop something off for you. I let him take it upstairs as I dare say it would be far too hefty for my frail arms to carry. He seemed like a nice boy, so I hope you don't get all huffy over him going in your room. He also gave me four Gold Swans – said it's your rent for the next year! Hope it wasn't your birthday and you didn't tell me! Left you some pie on the table. Don't forget to clear up your mess. Nighty nights.'

The only thing more baffling to Brolo than what Bæwylm might've brought was how ancient Mrs Dwimm must really be if she referred to him as a *nice boy*.

He set the world to rights by pouring a nightcap of Mrs Dwimm's homemade sloe gin, serving himself a generous slice of apple and rhubarb pie, and devouring both. Afterwards, he washed up his plate and crept upstairs to his room, taking one of the candles with him. Avoiding the creaky floorboards and muting the whine of his bedroom door by sliding in through the narrowest opening possible, Brolo set the candle down on the battered chest of drawers underneath his window, and stared at the wooden trunk sitting on his bed.

Chapter Twelve

An Invitation to Breakfast

The torrential rainfall was truly a sight to behold. Practically within touching distance of the dark heavens, Yilonia watched as millions upon millions of liquid pearls cascaded to the tune of the booming thunder, crashing down into the sodden streets far below. Streaks of lightning split the sky, each monstrous cloud hurling a barrage of fiery-orange arrows at its neighbour in a savage fight for power, illuminating the whole of Spyrata.

A chill crept up Yilonia's spine. Wrapping her fur gown tighter around herself, she walked to the small fireplace in the corner of the room, chucking another log onto the dwindling flames. As they came back to life, kissing her face with their tender glow, she wished for nothing more than to sit back in a comfy chair and relax. Alas, it was not to be.

The room was the same one she'd woken in a little over three weeks ago. A room in one of the imposing Towers of the Crown, belonging to the royal Palace of the United. She'd seen little else. When she'd questioned the guard posted outside her room, she'd been informed she wasn't a prisoner. Yet whenever she asked if she could leave, the same reply always came back. *'No!'*

Not that she was left wanting – far from it. Despite her being common as pig shit as far as anyone knew, the guards tended to her needs and fulfilled her requests without hesitation. All except for granting her freedom, of course. She'd left her room a few times, but implying they'd been pleasant experiences would be a pie so porky it would unquestionably oink.

The first opportunity had come on the day she'd awoken from her coma, when she'd been taken to a kindly royal physician, one Lord Findu, who'd given her a thorough once-over. Yet the other two times, she'd opened her blurry eyes to find a half dozen guards leering in the darkness over her bed, waiting to march her out for rigorous questioning from four armed men in a dank room.

The interrogations had been subtle. None of the traditional methods of torture had been implemented, and nor had her interrogators ever raised their voices. They'd merely asked her the same questions over and over until her tongue had been ready to drop to the floor.

'What's your name? Where did you come from? Who are your family? Why were you in Ánad? What happened? What was the last thing you saw?'

Tired and confused, Yilonia had given her answers as honestly as she could – all except those about her parents. During the first interrogation, she'd told the four men the truth about being born in Stunheath. However, she'd subsequently implied that her father was a local blacksmith with the surname Risúe and that she'd journeyed north with the supply caravan to sell his wares. Her tale had seemed to fly well enough; they hadn't probed any deeper into her story, at least. Yet the stress of the experience had soon reared its unsightly head. When she'd returned to her room and crashed wearily onto her bed, she'd had trouble falling asleep. Alas, after her second trip to the cold, claustrophobic room, sleep had abandoned her completely.

That interrogation had been no fiercer than the first. The four men hadn't pressed any harder than they'd needed to, but something puzzling had caught her eye. Something she'd only just noticed about the men who'd interrogated her, something so baffling it'd kept slumber at bay every night thereafter.

They had not been the king's men.

That such a glaring detail had slipped her by the first time disturbed her almost as much as the fact itself. She had – naively, as was now abundantly clear – assumed that since she resided within the chief royal palace, her interrogations had been at the king's behest. Despite her misgivings about her confinement, she acknowledged that someone found beyond the kingdom's borders blabbering about surviving an encounter with a dragon would be suspected to hold some important information. What had befuddled her brain as she'd sat on a wooden stool in the cramped interrogation room, surrounded by three burly men in shoddy brown tunics, was why the fourth man, who'd been garbed in official attire and obviously of a higher status, had borne an emblem of two monstrous golden wings flanking a crown of flames.

Such a gloomy crest didn't belong to any of the offices of state she was aware of, least of all within the king's own palace. Nor was it an emblem of any noble house. So, her continued presence in the royal castle had begun to prey on her mind.

If the king isn't the one keeping me here, who is?

***

Overnight, the pounding rain eased to a barely noticeable spittle. Up above the swirling sludge of the sea, the sun finally began to peer through a crack in the bulging clouds, sending a fine ray of light shimmering down into the bay. Perhaps it was a divine sign that the worst of the weather had passed, although Yilonia wasn't inclined to believe in such fancies.

As she did every morning, she waited patiently on the side of her bed for Briwetta to arrive, supposedly to wake her up and bring her breakfast. Neither of which was required, as she was always awake and rarely hungry. An absurd wish, which she nevertheless crossed her fingers for daily, was that Briwetta would bring some fresh clothes for Yilonia to wear after she'd helped her bathe.

Regardless of her hope, Yilonia dreaded each morning spent with the stooped old woman. She'd come to assume, by the savage way her back was scrubbed, that Briwetta still harboured a grudge for her disappearing act on the day she'd awoken. Thus, Yilonia gave a sigh of relief when the door to her room slammed open, and rather than Mrs Rough-Sponge, in slithered her interrogator with the mysterious insignia. Alone.

Her guard closed the door behind him, followed by the clunk of the bar falling into place. The sunshine sheened his pasty skin as he stood staring at Yilonia. He was a tall man, and unnervingly snakelike – slender, agile, and blessed with the habitual sneer of a true bastard.

Yilonia suspected that underneath his black doublet, he bore the scarring and muscle of a life of hard living and even harder fighting. However, she was convinced he was no common crust-sword. He presented himself as formally as any of the lords of the kingdom. When he spoke, his voice flowed like the whisper of a storm on the wind, brushed with the edge of danger yet to come ... although his speech carried an accent he could not conceal.

'You are to ready yourself in the appropriate fashion and come with me,' he said, a command rather than a request. 'Now.'

Yilonia was tempted to resist, purely to test how far he'd go before using force. Whoever his master may be, he'd obviously been instructed to cause her no harm, hence the rather placid interrogations. But how far would his leash stretch?

Compliance might buy her the answers she wanted, however, so she grudgingly decided to obey. Though not without partaking in a quick game of jabbing the serpent.

'Ah, bugger,' she sighed. 'Your timing's a shame, it really is. You see, I've got an urgent appointment to gaze blankly out of my bedroom window for three hours, then I've got to pick at the grime under my fingernails for a while. Then, after all that, I must count how many tiles make up the ceiling for the hundredth time. Consequently, as you can see, my diary is exceedingly full today. You'll just have to try again tomorrow.'

The man wiped a strand of his slick dark hair back into place, before crossing his arms.

'Would you like me to drag you out myself?' he said, in a tone honeyed with the utmost elegance. 'Giving you time to ready yourself is a courtesy that can be withdrawn.'

Yilonia screwed her nose up at his utter lack of humour.

'Fine, fine. Don't get your braies in a knot. It would be nice to know where I'm going, is all. I need to choose what I'll wear.'

'A servant will be in shortly to run your bath. She will lay out an appropriate dress for you, but you are to say nothing to her, just as she has been ordered to say nothing to you. I hope I've made myself clear.'

'Crystal,' replied Yilonia, with mock dutifulness. 'You still circle around my question, however. Where *exactly* am I to be taken?'

He bared a brief flash of a frown and rapped on the door. A scrambled ruffle of keys preceded the sound of the door unlocking. As it began to creak open, he nodded to Yilonia and made to depart. Yet after he stepped out, he paused and turned back.

'To breakfast,' he said, before the door slammed shut behind him.

'I wish people would stop doing that,' Yilonia said wistfully.

***

As instructed, Yilonia prepared in silence. The young servant girl who served her in Briwetta's stead ran her bath, scrubbed her back and brushed her hair without making a peep. At one stage, the girl tugged too hard, attempting to untangle a knot in Yilonia's dusty-straw hair, and pulled out a sizeable clump. Her panic at Yilonia's yelp was upsettingly telling of what she'd been threatened with if caught in conversation. She cowered behind Yilonia's back, staring at the door as if the Eternal Shuffler himself were about to burst through, and only returned to brushing Yilonia's hair after the door failed to open.

Waiting upon Yilonia's bed was a flowing dress of leaf-green velvet embroidered with garish orange roses across the waist and neckline. It was far too sickening for her simple taste. To her annoyance, when she tried to wordlessly convey this, the lass once again waved her arms in panic while backing towards the exit.

Resigning herself to her situation, Yilonia put the horrid dress on, alone. Undeniably appearing far more ridiculous than she had on her thirteenth birthday, when her father had demanded she wear a comparably cringe-worthy garment, she knocked on the door to inform the guard she was ready.

Not one but four brightly armoured men greeted her, all draped in cumbersome blue cloaks and carrying shields emblazoned with the king's royal coat of arms. With a nod to the other three, one guard took the lead down the long, narrow stairwell.

What was waiting for her, Yilonia could only speculate, but they'd gone to so much trouble that she had to assume it was something grim.

When they reached the bottom of the stairs, the guards swept into a diamond formation around her, blocking her view of the surrounding splendour. Peeking over their shoulders, she could only manage the odd glimpse of the magnificent tapestries and paintings adorning the Palace of the United. The faces of old kings and queens captured in time for all eternity, or the historic events portrayed by the seemingly magical power of paint or thread, were spectacles beyond her own admittedly privileged upbringing. Even the ceiling, way up high above her head, displayed the power and wealth of the throne. It housed a fresco of epic scale, which told the tale of the forest meeting between the remaining kings of Uprynenos, where the one kingdom had been forged in all its glory.

More than once, Yilonia bumped into the guard in front, or had her heels trodden on by the one behind. They marched for what must've been miles through cavernous corridors, up and down twisting staircases, turning corner after corner of endless majesty. All the way, they passed through hordes of servants buzzing around like bees, completing early-morning errands.

Just as she resigned herself to her endless tour through every nook and cranny of the palace, Yilonia's face cracked against the polished cuirass of the guard in front of her, the troupe having come to an abrupt halt outside an unassuming door a few blows shy of collapsing into splinters.

The lead guardsman knocked three times, waited five seconds, knocked a further four times, then stood ramrod straight as he waited for a reply. Sure enough, the door eventually creaked open, though only by an inch. A brief exchange took place, before the door opened properly. The lead guard stood aside as the other three rushed her through, then he slammed the door shut behind them.

The room was spacious, yet notably dull. Apart from a few candles dotted about, the only decorations were a long dining table set with cutlery and glassware, and the extravagant chair of blackened wood at its head. A less-than-welcoming pair occupied the ebon chair and the markedly plainer seat beside it.

'I'm so glad you could join us for breakfast, my dear Yilonia. Please, help yourself to some toast. It's nice and burnt, exactly how I like it.'

Drifting like a thick plume of smoke, the voice of the man in the throne-like chair shrouded her mind in a haze of confusion.

The black-clad interrogator stood and spread his arms.

'Sit, girl. Don't you know it's rude to refuse an invitation from His Eminence?'

Chapter Thirteen

Keeping Stable

They hadn't even left yet, and Brolo was already fed up. The yawning sun peeked over the horizon, stretching its orange rays of light across the farmlands of Peplyshaw, shaking loose the cobwebs of a long night's rest and, like all selfish early risers, making as much effort as possible to wake up everyone else.

The bastard, Brolo thought glumly.

He'd spent much of the night packing his bags for the journey ahead: clothes, money, tools, Lawgismirin … the essentials. Food wasn't necessary. Stánwilte had insisted that provisions from the Watch's amply stocked cellars – he'd cast a stern eye in Brolo's direction at that point – would keep them fed until they reached the next settlement. From then on, they'd stock up as they went. Brolo had told him that was a stupendously short-sighted idea that would see them all starve. Stánwilte had countered with the fact that they had a long journey ahead, through hot, dry and torturous terrain. Any food they packed would spoil by the time they needed it.

'Better to carry light and make haste early on. Once we hit Ánad, we'll have all the time in the world to be sick of dried strips of beef, don't you worry.'

Brolo hadn't been able to fault the logic there, so he'd kept silent, much to his own surprise.

Having finished all the preparations he'd possessed the energy to make, Brolo had slumped onto his bed and tried to grab a wink or two. Ruefully, sleep had eluded him. After counting more sheep than existed in the whole of Arbor Vale, and failing miserably to catch flies, he'd jumped up, grabbed his things, and taken off into darkness of Peplyshaw.

The night that had seemed so fraught with danger just a few short hours ago now seemed sleepy and quaint. Trees swung in unison with signs above shop doors, stirred by a brisk wind, while all the creatures from the surrounding forest crooned their merry songs. It was all romanticised, ridiculously chirpy bollocks, but Brolo was chided by the foolishness of his own paranoia as he trundled through the town in which he'd been raised, possibly for the last time.

Their meeting place was the Watch's stables, nestled inside the main gate of the garrison. Unsurprisingly, Brolo was the first to arrive of the four who'd be departing Peplyshaw. As he approached the stable doors, lamplight flickered faintly from the crack underneath, along with a tunefully whistled rendition of the song *She Had a Nice Big Drum and Two Great Honking Horns*.

After rapping gently on the door, Brolo winced at the clatter of many heavy-sounding items crashing violently to the ground, succeeded by a barrage of language so coarse it would've made Lady Lace N'Strap blush.

'Oof, my bloody toe!' roared Huereld Blurkop, the Watch's old dwarfish stable master. 'Who in the blue blazes of buggery is that at this hour? I hope you've got a ruddy good reason for making an old man jump! Oh, Brolo, it's you,' he said, upon swinging open the stable door. 'What can I do for you, then? Are you part of Captain Stánwilte's group? He mentioned he wanted the horses ready to go nice and early, but I didn't expect him to mean *this* early. By my mother's beard, I've still got plenty to do!'

'No ... I mean, yes,' said Brolo. 'I am part of the captain's group, but we're not leaving right now. I just couldn't sleep, so I thought I'd come down early and wait here, if it's all the same to you.'

Huereld fixed Brolo with an inquisitive stare, his eyes like little peas above his wide snout of a nose. 'You'd best be coming in then,' he said, beckoning Brolo over the threshold. 'First things first, you can help me clear this mess up, seeing as it's your fault.'

'Beg your pardon? That's hardly fair!' protested Brolo.

'Aye, your fault,' Huereld snapped. He was clearly used to playing judge, jury and executioner. 'And I hope you've shod a horse before, laddie. If not, you can muck out instead. No point in you sitting around like a bag of oats when there's work to be doing.'

From there on, Brolo's budding morning grew progressively worse, as Huereld saddled him with a string of menial tasks. When Stánwilte finally arrived two and a half hours later, Brolo smelt no better than a mare's backside. Considering the amount of dung and straw stuck to his clothes, he probably appeared about as alluring as one, too. Sapped of his last piddly puddle of strength, he courageously resisted the urge to swipe the smug grin off Stánwilte's face.

'Well, well, well. Look what we have here. I wasn't aware you were so fond of horses, Brolo. Hey, I've got an *equestrian* for you – what are you doing here so early?'

After that remark, the urge to wallop Stánwilte across the mush with a shovel became almost too much to bear. Brolo was far too tired to be dealing with wretched puns. In the end, he had to content himself with mentally replaying the image of his brutal shovel-based assault a few times.

No point fighting now. There will plenty of time for that on the road, he mused, a smile discreetly forming on his lips.

Huereld shuffled over to Stánwilte as gracefully as he could manage while hopping on one stumpy leg. 'Being nothing but a bloody nuisance, that's what, Skipper. Sneaking up on an old man in the middle of the night, scaring him half to death, then lounging around like a bloody harlot on a street corner. Spending as much time on his back as one, too. Nothing but a lazy sod, he is.'

'What happened to dwarfs sticking by each other?' Brolo asked, giving up all pretence of bravado and leaning wearily on his shovel.

'Show me a dwarf, lad, and I'll support him on my broad shoulders till the end of days,' Huereld said through gritted teeth, fixing Brolo with a glower that screamed the *'Bastard!'* he dared not speak before Stánwilte. Brushing Brolo aside as easily as the piss-soaked straw strewn about the stable floor, he began debriefing Stánwilte on his finished duties, most of which he'd discharged to Brolo. 'All your horses are ready to go, Skipper. They're fed, shod, groomed and saddled. They ain't gonna win any jousts, sir, but they'll do you no disservice. Oh, yes, rest assured – these fine beasts of burden are the best the Watch owns.'

'But as of yesterday evening, the Watch only owned three horses,' said Stánwilte, with all the feigned awe of a grown man humouring a child. 'Where in the entire sodding kingdom did you find another horse on such short notice?'

Huereld slid his thumbs through his braces and rocked back on the balls of his feet, proud as punch. Which was, coincidently, exactly what Brolo would've liked to do to him.

'See here, there's just one thing you need to learn about us dwarfs – no matter how short we are, we can pull almost anything out of our arses.'

As Huereld beamed with utmost pride at the rather sickening image he'd created, Stánwilte gave him a pat on the back for his efforts, then glanced over to Brolo with a strangely awkward grin.

'I'll remember that from now on,' was all he said. Supposedly to Huereld, but Brolo had the grim feeling it was meant for him too.

I don't like where this going, Brolo thought. *Right off the bat, I had bad puns clogging up my ears, and now it's dodgy smiles and smarmy words! This won't end well at all.*

Twenty minutes later, Wilkhelm finally trudged in, pouting like a toddler who'd been slapped on the arse for stealing another child's toys. From what Brolo had heard, he'd tried everything to worm his way out of this quest. Bargaining, bribing, and finally pleading Stánwilte to let him stay behind. All to no avail. Apparently, he'd even sent a raven to his father. It wouldn't arrive in time, of course, but Brolo would've loved to see the anger on Lord Cormorant's face once it did.

Wilkhelm dumped his belongings next to a couple of feed sacks without so much as a word to anyone, but cold, spiteful stares for everyone.

Another hour ticked slowly by. After finishing their last-minute preparations and becoming acquainted with their horses, the three men of the Watch were left standing around, waiting. Judging by the precious few avenues of witless small talk already exhausted, Brolo decided that being dragged naked over a mile of broken glass by a horse with diarrhoea would've been a more enjoyable prospect than the journey ahead.

The only interruptions to the blanket of total silence were the swear-laden mutterings of Huereld as he went about his work, throwing in the odd curse at the scruffy layabouts who littered his stables and occasionally tipping an entirely imaginary hat to Stánwilte.

When even the least punctual cockerel was cock-a-doodle-done with its only task for the day, and the lingering veil of darkness had all but vanished, Smiggly Jenkins finally arrived – unsurprisingly, with his mother in tow. He was evidently embarrassed by the presence of his dear old mum; his chubby cheeks were reddened either by humiliation, or by the amount of slobbery kisses Mrs Jenkins had planted upon them. However, no matter how beetroot his face became, it was overshadowed by his garish crimson tunic.

'Smiggly, what in the name of bloody inconspicuousness are you wearing?' Stánwilte said, as he dropped his head into his hands.

'Hi, chaps! Sorry for being late, but Ma had to finish knitting this for me— whoa!'

A high-pitched meow screeched out from the black cat whose tail Smiggly had inadvertently stood on, as it scarpered across the stables like a greased hog from an abattoir.

'Oi, watch it,' barked Huereld. 'That's my best mouse-catcher you just trod on, you lumbering oaf!'

The shock of this lambasting smacked the wavering Smiggly across the bonce, throwing his already-bungling balance off completely. He stumbled backwards through a ladder that led up into the hayloft, crashing into an ill-placed mirror that just so happened to be lying around the stables gathering dust.

As Smiggly landed with a symphony of shattering glass, Mrs Jenkins hobbled over to him as quickly as she could, smothering him with kisses and doting reassurances that it wasn't his fault.

'Will you get that boy out of my bleeding stables, please?' Huereld screamed at no one in particular. 'And that silly old woman while you're at it, too! This is too much to deal with so early in the day!' He cast his pitchfork down and stormed off, muttering curses.

Stánwilte heaved a weary sigh. 'Yes, I think it's long past time we go. You two,' he said, pointing at Brolo and Wilkhelm, 'help him up, will you? I'll go clear the air with Huereld. We leave in five.' With a shake of his head, he turned and left, following in the wake of the stable master.

Wilkhelm, who was slouching against a large sack, doing a fine impression of being asleep, must've sensed Brolo's scornful gaze through his closed eyelids. He raised a hand slightly and waved in the direction of Mrs Jenkins, who was still struggling to get her son up onto his feet.

Being too tired to argue, Brolo sighed and went over to help.

'Come on, let's get you up,' he said, as he slung one of Smiggly's arms over his shoulder.

'Oh, dear, I hope the poor puss-puss is alright … ouchie! I think I've hurt my back, Ma.'

'My poor Smiggly,' said Mrs Jenkins, as she caressed her son. 'You can always come with me to the market. I'll let you choose your favourite pie fillings, and we'll head on home once we're done. I'll get cracking with the pastry while you put your feet up. Before long, I'll be serving up a nice big slice of my special pie. How does that sound?'

Smiggly's face lit up with a sappy grin, as he seemed to recover instantaneously from his fall. Yet after a moment, he took a long look at Brolo and Wilkhelm with a bold, glassy sheen in his eyes, and stood to face his mother with his back straight and proud.

'No, Mummy … er, Mother,' he said, putting on a deeper voice and placing a hand on her shoulder. 'I gave Captain Stánwilte and the boys my word, and I shall stand by it.'

The old woman's eyes welled with tears. She pulled out a grubby handkerchief and dabbed at her cheeks.

'You're a good boy. A good, foolish boy.' She threw her arms around him, then turned to Brolo. 'You'll keep a close eye on him, won't you?'

Brolo hoped either Stánwilte or Wilkhelm were standing behind him. They weren't.

'Um, yeah ... sure I will. I won't let him out of my sight,' Brolo said. *Here we go, something else to make this bloody trip just that little bit worse – babysitting!*

'Oh, thank you!' she cried, springing at Brolo with both eyes and nose running, crushing him in an almighty hug. 'I don't know what I'd do if my baby didn't come back home to me.'

Smiggly gave Brolo a chirpy grin. Brolo glowered back.

After Smiggly and his mother had finished saying their goodbyes, and she had finally left for home, Brolo walked over to where Wilkhelm still pretended to sleep and gave him a good hard kick in the shins.

'Time to mount up, you arse-breathed goat,' shouted Brolo at the top of his lungs, as he kicked Wilkhelm again for good measure.

Wilkhelm rose with all the fury of a wasps' nest knocked down by the stones of playing children. A growl buzzed in his throat, building until a snarl spouted from his mouth, which was embarrassingly kitten-like after all the build-up.

'How dare you! I am the son of your noble lord, dwelf, and I shall be treated with all the respect your betters deserve!' Wilkhelm screamed, jabbing a finger into Brolo's chest. 'And, I'll have you know, I chew mint leaves like your whore of a mother chewed your father's dwarfish sausage, so my breath is as fresh as a spring dawn, thank you very much!'

Having expected such a response, Brolo had little trouble keeping his nerve. He wiped the spittle from his face and gave a gleaming, innocent smile.

'Really? Well, if it's not your breath that smells like the runny droppings of a mule, then it must be that mound of horse shit you've being sitting on.'

'Wait, what? Oh, for the love of ...'

Brolo swung around and marched off to find his horse, listening to the sweet tune of Wilkhelm's disgusted moans as he tried to wipe away the smelly mess that had spread up the back of his erstwhile white shirt. Thankfully, it wasn't long before Stánwilte returned and gave the order to mount up.

Of the four horses, Brolo had been assigned the rather small, grizzled chestnut gelding that had only fallen into the Watch's ownership a few hours beforehand. The haggard old beast looked ripe for the knacker's yard. It had a weary glaze to its large black eyes that suggested it would sooner trot in and hand over its own hooves than be ridden for a lengthy journey.

Bloody great. I'll be lucky to make it past the town gate on the back of this old milksop, Brolo thought, as he gave the horse a sympathetic pat.

Mounted and all set to go, Stánwilte rode over on his own larger and decisively grander horse. 'Come on,' he said. 'It's high time we were off.' He gave Brolo a pleading look. Pointedly, Brolo ignored it.

'Time we were off? You can't expect me to ride this poor bastard, can you? I've seen blind, three-legged lambs with surer footing. It's okay for you – that thing you're on looks fancy enough for a sodding royal parade.' Stánwilte's horse whinnied, as if in appreciation of the praise. 'This old guy, however, appears ready to canter on over to the great paddock in the sky, if you get my drift.' Brolo whispered the last part, to avoid upsetting the gelding.

'He was all Huereld was able to get a hold of. However, I must admit,' Stánwilte said, checking over the horse with his eyebrows raised, 'I do hope the coper didn't fleece him too much, or I'll be forced to take it up with the town *mare*.'

He dared crack a smile, before returning swiftly to a serious tone. 'I'm sorry, Brolo, but the other horses are simply too big for you to ride ...'

Clearly realising the offensiveness of his reasoning, he trailed off, clearing his throat. 'Maybe we can trade him for a better horse in the next town,' he offered sheepishly, before trotting off without another glance.

Watching his captain traipse gracefully towards the stable doors, Brolo could do nothing but grumble to himself and mount up. Climbing clumsily into the saddle, he wobbled as the gelding wavered under his modest weight. By the time he'd adjusted his feet into the stirrups, the poor beast's legs looked close to buckling out from underneath him.

With nary a neigh, the gelding shuffled out of his stall, knocking over an empty bucket as if in half-hearted protest.

'Don't forget to give him a name, lad,' called Huereld, as he swept the stable floor. 'It's bad luck to have a horse with no name, especially up in the desert where you're going. Trust me, you'll be needing as much luck as you can get.'

'Thanks,' said Brolo through gritted teeth. *You shit-shovelling bastard.* He gave a curt wave, then rode out to join the other watchmen as they headed through the waking town of Peplyshaw. They passed houses with soft plumes of smoke rising like puffy snores from their crooked chimneys, barren streets of closed shops, and packed-up market stalls that would soon be bustling with townsfolk hoping to make a steal, or, in some cases, just to steal.

Leaving without so much as a single piece of colourful bunting to acknowledge his departure hurt more deeply than Brolo had expected. With an air of *good riddance* wafting from every cow pat they passed, they trundled out of the town gates. Wilkhelm and Smiggly followed Stánwilte closely, leaving Brolo to lag behind as they headed north along the sloppy dirt road, onwards towards their fate.

CHAPTER FOURTEEN

BITTER RECOLLECTIONS

Stánwilte gazed upon the lush landscape rolling out from his horse's hooves, ending in a distant horizon of craggy peaks. Before him sprawled gently sloping fields, bordered by hedgerows and ditches, peppered with the little white specks of sheep.

He didn't see the need to hide his grin as he crested yet another of the sweeping hills that dominated the lands of Arbour Vale. Listening to the gentle sway of trees blowing in the breeze, the calming clip-clopping of hooves upon the road, the buzzing of bees and the chirping of birds was enough to soothe even the grouchiest of souls.

My, how I've missed this! Riding league upon breathtaking league, with nothing but the brisk wind in my hair and the sturdy ride of a good horse between my legs. It's been years since I've been blessed with a troop of men who'll trade banter with me, will share exciting stories and a skinful of wine around a campfire ... and, most of all, will follow my every word without question. Stánwilte glanced behind briefly, but it was enough to wipe the smile from his face. *Why the hell is two out of three the norm these days?*

Following distantly behind him, Brolo and Wilkhelm rode next to each other, both trying to pull out in front. Regretfully, this was a game that often rendered Brolo's pitiful excuse for a horse staggering and gasping as if it might collapse from exhaustion and die in the middle of the road.

They'd bickered like children for the entire twelve miles from Peplyshaw, mouths flapping away, arms flailing around, pointing and pushing to emphasise the words spilling from their lips. Stánwilte couldn't make out what they were saying, and doubted he wanted to know, but could guarantee it wasn't complimentary. Never mind fatigue, hunger, dehydration, bandits or a bloody dragon – he'd be lucky if one of those two didn't stick a knife in the other's back by nightfall.

Smiggly, too, had begun to wear him down faster than he'd anticipated. Now, the lad rode at a pitiful pace, head down, in that rarest of all things – complete silence.

Stánwilte shuffled about uncomfortably in his saddle, his conscience chafing away at him. He hadn't meant to upset the boy so, but his resolve had been worn to breaking point by the lad's seemingly endless prattle about anything and everything he saw.

Why couldn't someone able to consider anything more complex than their next meal have agreed to come? He'd known he'd be asking a lot, and not all the men respected him as they should, but he'd thought a few had started to come around. For a start, he'd assumed Ivein would come. Maybe he should've let Bæwylm come, too. The Watch would've been fine looking after itself for a while. *Let's face it,* he thought, *I could put a horse in charge, and things would run as smoothly as ever.*

Stánwilte's horse bridled as if it'd been reading his mind and took umbrage at this insult to equine intelligence. He brushed its mane and leant forward to whisper a few soothing words into its ear.

From the position of the sun, it was long past noon, which meant they were already behind schedule. Stánwilte had hoped to reach the tiny village of Ryoksham by sundown, intending to find rooms at the local inn and indulge in a little morale-boosting first-night feast. Sadly, with two of the group focusing most of their energy on petty arguments and another sulking like a child, the reality was that they'd be camping out under the stars tonight. And if they uttered one damn word of complaint, he'd be sure to let them know whose fault it was.

Slowly, the hours passed, as surely as the miles drifted by. Despite the trials to come, Stánwilte found himself sitting with his back straight, one arm resting on the pommel of his sword and the other keeping a firm hold on the reins. For the first time in years, he rode like a real soldier.

Closing his eyes to the sights around him, Stánwilte let the cool highland breeze wash over him, taking him back to days long past.

***

The night was shrill and stark. An unholy torrent hammered the labyrinth of bogs and head-height reeds that formed the Hoghamny salt marsh on the southeast coast of Kasindra. Yet, in the Royal Army's encampment atop an overlooking hill, it was hot, muggy, and cloudless, with only a dusting of stars twinkling in the sky above. The unnaturally focused downpour and the ominous emerald glow looming over the swamp would usually be quite remarkable. Nonetheless, Stánwilte, studying the brooding sky, flanked by his fellow officers, knew the cause full well.

'Blasted wizards,' muttered Sir Nuthain Haynes of Bhunheld for the umpteenth time. A rather forced look of disgust glistened on his chubby face. 'We should charge down and smoke them out like the rats they are!'

Stánwilte couldn't fault the young cavalry sergeant's attitude towards his duties, but his stupidity, rashness and complete ignorance of battle tactics left a lot to desire. Stánwilte couldn't stomach idiots leading men, most likely to their deaths. Thankfully, another officer piped up first to point out the staggering ridiculousness of Sir Nuthain's plan.

'Have you ever been through a marshland, boy? Are you truly so dense?' barked Deguro Flay.

The man was an infantry officer who, while uncouth and lacking the noble birth to warrant him unearned respect, was a battle-hardened warrior. He'd survived more brushes with the pointy end of a sword than he'd had wet farts, which, considering the shit fed to infantrymen, was substantial. After earning himself a brutal reputation, he'd been bestowed the charge of his own troop and had since won copious battles in often ludicrous circumstances. Under his leadership, Stánwilte had faced his first skirmish, back when he'd been a fresh-faced recruit. There was no doubt Flay should've been knighted by now, but everyone dreaded the thought of what bile could slip from his tongue in the presence of the king, so the honour had been delayed thus far.

'You try charging into that there marsh, you'll be chest-deep in bog-water, leeches, frogspawn, and gods know what other kinds of filth before you even reach a gallop,' Flay snapped. 'And that's if you're lucky enough to still be on the beast's bloody back! Well, it's not really a question of luck, more of stupidity, but something tells me you've got it in you to try.'

Sir Nuthain wagged his gauntleted finger in Flay's direction.

'I don't have to stand here and be lectured on warfare by some jumped-up peasant,' he said boldly, but was soon hushed by the warning stares of the other commanders.

Trotting over to where Sir Nuthain sat upon his horse, Flay studied him with the look of a man trying and failing to find the faintest speck of beauty in a sun-baked turd.

'Oh, don't mind me, sonny. Here I was, thinking we'd all like to go back to the capital alive and well, with our fucking nutsacks still hanging where they're supposed to and our insides not magically turned into our outsides. How foolish! The bright idea to mark all bright ideas has been sitting right in front of us all along – march the whole army to its death! How I didn't think of it, I'll never know. Quick, go tell the men the good news. It being their last night alive, they'd probably want to make the most of it. I hope you're handy with a spade, Sir Nuthain, because you'll have a lot of graves to dig by tomorrow night. I'd say a good three thousand should cover it.'

Sir Nuthain gawked for a moment, then rallied.

'An exaggeration, surely. It's only a few wizards, after all.'

'*Five* wizards!' said Flay. 'Five very bloody angry, highly powerful wizards! They aren't stupid, boy. They know what they're doing. Just look at the sky yonder.' He pointed to the pendulous green clouds looming above the swamp. 'Look at what great lengths they're going to, simply to keep us away. Now, I want you to imagine what they'll have waiting for us *inside* that marshland.'

Sir Nuthain's face turned milky white.

Flay was right, of course – three thousand men to find five wizards may have seemed a little extreme, but any attempt to enter the boggy expanse would be catastrophic.

From behind came the heavy thudding of seven horsemen approaching in some haste, while still managing to maintain a dignified canter. Six rode protectively around one boxed in the middle, with the two in front carrying the royal standard of the Prince of Uprynenos, which flapped savagely in the high wind, threatening to be whipped away.

'Shit, here we go,' Flay muttered rather too loudly, earning himself some stiff glares from the other officers.

Stánwilte, despite his oath to lay down his life as Commander of the King's First, the elite unit charged with protecting the royal family, couldn't help sharing in Flay's dejection at the arrival of the young prince.

Auldalin sat straight in his saddle, looking elegant in his gleaming plate armour and sumptuous purple cloak. Yet, despite all his grandeur, his posture hinted at his discomfort. For as long as Stánwilte had known him – which was since the boy had been old enough to hold a sword – he'd watched with a heavy heart how the burden of his title weighed upon him. Auldalin was a remarkably handsome young man, blessed with a razor-sharp wit, an overwhelming arrogance towards people he considered below him and a healthy dash of royal charm. Sadly, however, he lacked the discipline to learn either the sword or hunting bow – both essential attributes for any young lord, let alone a prince. He spent far more time drinking with his lordly friends than he did on any of his royal duties. He was even nervous around horses, due to a childhood incident where he'd snuck into the palace stables and accidentally spooked a horse from behind, which had kicked out and broken his shoulder.

All his faults had been kept well-hidden from the public throughout his adolescence, but now that he'd reached maturity, his father had decided it was high time he learnt what it meant to rule, to lead, to experience life out on campaign. He hadn't taken to it as well as the king may have hoped.

'Well met, good sirs. I hope I'm not disrupting you from taking in this rather stark view, but I do believe we have some wizards to hunt.'

Flay huffed, which once again earned him more than a few uncomfortable glances from his fellow officers. Prince Auldalin, however, wasn't one to let such things drop.

'Ah, Flay. I believe you have something you wish to say?'

'You must be mistaken, my noble prince. You'll not hear a peep from my lips. Absolutely nothing at all. I just found the notion that we still had anything to discuss here amusing.'

Auldalin gave Flay a derisive look.

'Right,' Auldalin said. 'I just want to make sure I understand. You've discussed your plans and come to what I'm sure you think is the best tactical decision, all without consulting me. Am I correct?'

An elderly lord of an astoundingly portly stature, considering how easily his horse seemed to carry him, piped up to explain himself, unwittingly taking the metaphorical arrow for the group.

'We're sorry, my most gracious prince, but you were nowhere to be found within the camp. Decisions had to be made, and rather hastily—'

'So, it's *my* fault you didn't follow the commands of my fa— your king, is it?' said Auldalin, who'd begun to finger the hilt of his sword after his voice broke partway through, daring someone to point it out. 'He specifically ordered that all meetings of council, all plans involving the tracking of these wizards, or concerning the resulting engagements, were to be made in my presence, and executed only with my full consent!'

'My prince,' said Stánwilte, 'I'm sorry for any offence caused, but let me assure you, no plans have been finalised. With your whereabouts unknown to us, and nightfall looming, we decided a tactical briefing was the sage step forward. However, all agreed that nothing would be confirmed until you could honour us with your presence.' His words weren't strictly truthful. Petty bickering had delayed any plans being made, but it was a fine excuse all the same.

'Yes, well, if you had true command of your men, Lord *Commander* Stánwilte, you would've been informed that I'd ordered a visit to Yre to curry favour for my father in the southern reaches of his realm.' This comment blew the wind out from Stánwilte's sails, leaving his face hot with embarrassment and anger. Flippantly, Auldalin moved on. 'Sir Nuthain, how would you suggest we proceed?'

Some of the officers of higher status scoffed silently at the prince for deferring to the wholly inexperienced Sir Nuthain, but Stánwilte had remembered why he'd been promoted to sergeant in the first place – he was Auldalin's childhood friend.

'Well, um … my original thought, my prince, was an all-out mounted charge into the heart of the marshland, early in the morning, in the hope of catching those vile wizards off-guard.' Even Sir Nuthain appeared to now understand how stupid of an idea that was, having found the good grace to abandon his former cocksureness. 'But Sir Stánwilte and—'

'Sir Stánwilte does not hold the power to dictate a military assault, Sir Nuthain. That is your charge. Sir Stánwilte's decisions are limited to choosing who puts my tent up and who is to cook and serve my food. Show some ruddy conviction, man.'

'With all due respect, Stánwilte has—' began Flay.

'With all due respect, *my prince,*' hissed Auldalin.

'With all due respect, my prince, Stánwilte's life has been nothing but warfare since before either of you two had finished slurping your mothers' teats dry. I'd not so easily dismiss his advice … nor mine, for that matter.'

Auldalin rode over to stand in front of Flay and Stánwilte.

'You've been given the charge to find and arrest, or kill if needs be, five wizards who stole holy Dragonian artefacts of unknown power from the royal collection. My father tasked me to learn how to command and lead an army. Neither of us will accomplish those orders by hanging about on the crest of a hill all day. I want this over and done with quickly. *Decisiveness is the mark of courage* – that is how I shall lead.'

Huzzahs piped out from a select few of the gathered men, while the rest gazed at each other nervously. None trusted the prince's logic. Nor did any have the balls to argue with it, except one.

'More like *rashness is the mark of a dead man,* my prince,' snapped Flay. 'I cannot stand idly by while two boys greener than spring plan to lead three thousand good men to their deaths!'

'Fine, then, you may take your leave,' said Auldalin, transferring his cold stare from Flay to Stánwilte. 'Both of you. When you cowards reach the capital, be sure to let my father know how you deserted after refusing to follow my orders. I'm sure he'll be sympathetic.'

'On the contrary, boy, it'll be me having to offer my sympathy to the king.'

With that, Deguro Flay turned his horse and rode away, leaving Stánwilte in the foreboding shadow of his parting words.

***

'Sir? Are you feeling alright, sir? Captain Stánwilte!'

Stánwilte snapped back to the present with the nauseating sensation of the earth trembling violently beneath him. After a brief period of blind panic, he was relieved to find it was Brolo riding beside him, shaking his shoulder.

'It's getting dark, and none of us know where we are,' Brolo said. 'Shall we make camp for the night?'

Stánwilte looked about himself, attempting to regain his bearings. To his surprise, a familiar patch of woodland to the east, which was heavily carpeted with bluebells, meant they were just shy of a league from Ryoksham.

It would seem we quickened the pace while I daydreamed. I would strive to do it more often, if it didn't leave such a foul taste at the back of my throat, Stánwilte thought glumly.

'No, we'll keep on riding,' he said. 'Give it an hour or so, and we'll be warming ourselves in front of a big fire with a mug of ale.'

The news appeared to perk up Brolo's spirits, but Stánwilte himself could manage little more than a flicker of a smile.

'Great, I'll tell those other two planks to get a bloody move on then. Um ... are you okay, Captain?' Brolo asked tentatively. 'If you're feeling like heading home already, I wouldn't blame you. We had a pretty good run.'

'What? No, I'm fine, Brolo. It's just ... do you ever feel like you can't escape your past mistakes? Like you're being forced to relive them over and over again, knowing what you did wrong, but powerless to prevent them from repeating?'

Brolo gave Stánwilte a funny look.

'I don't, sir, but only because I'm living mine right now.'

Plopping this scathing remark in Stánwilte's lap like cold soup, Brolo dropped back to tell the others to quicken their pace, leaving Stánwilte on his own again, sullenly shaking his head.

CHAPTER FIFTEEN

ONE BAD EGG

'My backside has never throbbed as it did last night!' exclaimed Wilkhelm, plonking himself down at the communal table, which was lushly adorned with fresh bread, spicy Kasindran sausages, rashers of smoky bacon and hardboiled duck eggs. So many tantalising delights, all spread out in a spacious room across the hall from the bustling kitchen of The Stoned Wizard inn. 'I may have to purchase myself a more comfortable saddle before we move on,' he continued, winking at Brolo as he scoffed a whole egg in two bites.

Wilkhelm had every excuse to be cocky. Against Stánwilte's strict instructions, he'd packed a reasonably-sized pouch of Gold Swans and a flock of lesser coinage, which he could afford to spend lavishly on items of luxury, such as a saddle that didn't leave his arse feeling sorer than a hog with a hangover. Brolo hadn't been surprised to find out Wilkhelm had packed for comfort rather than practicality. The throttling he'd almost received from Stánwilte when he'd insisted they turn back to retrieve his favourite handkerchief still brought a sweet grin to Brolo's face.

The memory soured, however, as he listened to Wilkhelm boast of the peaceful night's sleep he'd procured by paying to stay in the inn's finest room. Even the jam on Brolo's bread began to taste bitter after a few minutes of his self-centred rambling.

Brolo's bed had been rough, hard and teeming with lice. In the end, he'd spent most of the night on the floor, which had sadly been far more comfortable.

I shouldn't complain, really. It's the last time I'll be sleeping under a roof for a while, he thought.

From what Stánwilte had told them yesterday, as they'd sat by the fireplace in the inn's common room, they would be spending the next few nights underneath the stars before they reached another settlement.

'And then keeping on until we cross the border into the barren north,' said Wilkhelm, waving a knife speared with a chunk of sausage, seemingly finishing Brolo's thought. 'I mean, there has to be a quicker way.'

Smiggly sat silently, squashed between two burly men who appeared to be brothers. Both wore eyepatches, with a plethora of scars and burns upon their faces, leaving their complexions worse than the crispy bacon they were gorging on. With a plate of food sitting untouched in front of him, Smiggly radiated all the sheer, helpless terror of a little lost lamb breaking bread with some very hungry wolves. Wilkhelm paid no attention to this, of course.

'Will you just shut up and eat your breakfast in silence, you fat, loose-lipped bastard?' said Brolo through gritted teeth, trying not to draw the attention of any of the others stuffing their faces around the table. 'Don't tell me you've forgotten what Stánwilte told us about tickling the interest of strangers, because the only detail you've *not* shared of our journey is the part about the ... big, winged fire-breathing thing.' He took a moment to admire the hypocrisy of his warning, especially considering his last night in Peplyshaw. However, with Stánwilte still not down for the breakfast he'd paid for, Brolo took it upon himself to keep Wilkhelm's mouth in check. It was a position he felt fit him like a tailor-made glove.

'Not everyone is half-elf,' said Wilkhelm, through a mouthful of heavily buttered toast. 'We aren't all blessed with being naturally slender, yet grotesquely squat. Anyway, you might as well bulk your bony rump up now. Once we hit the north, you'll be sweating the weight away like a hooker entertaining a group of sailors. Ah, sorry, Brolo – didn't mean to mention your mother again.'

Before Wilkhelm had even swallowed his mouthful, Brolo lunged across the table, scattering cups and plates, knocking him off his chair and pressing a jam-smeared breadknife against his throat as he pinned him to the floor.

'If you so much as mention my mother again, I swear by the Eternal Shuffler's creaky balls that I'll jam Lawgismirin so far up your arse, you'll scream and whimper all the way back to Craginhall like the gutless fuck you are! Just like the time you got caught smooching that warty young tavern wench and shat yourself while pleading her father not to disembowel you with his pitchfork. Not that you had much left in your bowels!'

The two loutish men flanking Smiggly snorted with laughter, spitting chunks of half-chewed egg across the table, earning a few glares from the trio of elves watching the whole altercation with thinly-veiled disgust.

'You two!' came a mountainous bellow from behind Brolo as he grappled with Wilkhelm on the floor. 'Stop this fucking embarrassment of a fight right this instant, or I'll sell both of your bloody horses and you can walk the rest of the way north!'

Stánwilte loomed in the doorway of the dining room, dressed in a set of full plate armour Brolo had never seen before. Even marred by the odd scratch and in dire need of a polish, it still made him stand out rather impressively from the common rabble – as did the volcanic tide of anger brimming on his face.

Grudgingly, Brolo released Wilkhelm, whose head cracked against the floor with a hollow thud. Tossing the knife to the ground, Brolo bolted to his feet.

'Where in all the Fires do you think you're going? I want a word with you, now!'

Stopping dead in his tracks, Brolo carefully weighed the benefits of obeying the order against telling Stánwilte to shove it down his piss-hole. In the end, he decided he'd listen to his captain. For the moment, at least.

'Whatever you say, sir,' said Brolo with mock enthusiasm, marching past Stánwilte and into the hallway. Glancing back, he saw Smiggly rise from his chair to follow suit, before Stánwilte put a hand up to halt him.

'Take care of that one, will you, Smiggly?' he said, pointing at the crumpled heap on the floor, which they occasionally called Wilkhelm when trying to be polite. 'I'm sure his lord father would be disappointed to see him carted home so soon.'

Smiggly struck an awkward salute and bounced on over to Wilkhelm's side, smiling far too broadly for someone comforting an injured man. Shaking his head, Stánwilte apologised to the other patrons of the dining room for the scene they'd witnessed and left them to return to their breakfast.

'The thing is, Captain,' Brolo said, before Stánwilte silenced him with a cold stare and slammed the dining room door shut.

'Before you even begin your excuses, I'm telling you now, I don't want to hear it. I won't put myself through your petty squabbling anymore. I'm bloody sick to death of you imbeciles, and it's been less than two days! I'm not your nanny. I'm not here to look after you, clean up your messes, or keep you out of trouble. I've done that job before and I'm sure not going to be doing it again!'

Stánwilte closed his eyes and took a deep breath, his shoulders slumping wearily.

So many more miles still to ride, and he's fracturing already, Brolo thought. *He may have all that armour to shield him from a dragon, but what's going to save him from himself? With his past, there's no surprise he has something plaguing his mind. I could almost feel sorry for him. Almost.*

Brolo sensed the stares of The Stoned Wizard's cook and her staff of serving girls as they pretended to busy themselves with their assorted tasks, while keeping a good eye on him and Stánwilte. And what an unusual sight they must have made – a man long past his prime, clunking around in a suit of dented armour, giving a young dwelf quite the earful. Brolo almost wished he were in the serving girls' shoes.

'What do you want me to say?' Brolo asked. 'I'm sorry? Well, I *am* sorry to let you down again, but I'm not sorry for what I did to him! That prick deserves everything he's got coming. I honestly hope that if we somehow ever actually make it to Ánad, I'll survive long enough to see his eyes bubble and burst from dragon flame. I want to see the beast use his entrails to dislodge the bits between its teeth! To use his testicles as a chew toy! To turn his—'

'Yes, yes. I get it. You don't like him,' groaned Stánwilte, rubbing his forehead. 'This may come as a surprise, but Wilkhelm was the one person I wanted to tag along less than I wanted you. If it weren't for his accursed father, I'd never have put myself in the position of dealing with his bull-dung. However, if there's one thing my past has taught me, it's to shut up and deal with the hindrances that crop up in life – so that's exactly what I'm trying to do with you two.'

'Fine, if we're such a burden to you, we'll happily leave. I'm sure you and Smiggly will have a *smashing* time together on your way north,' said Brolo, with a wolfish grin.

All the colour drained from Stánwilte's cheeks. A few more leagues with only Smiggly for company, and he'd be smashing the poor lad's head against a rock to shut him up. He was in a corner, and Brolo knew it.

Putting an arm around Brolo's shoulders, Stánwilte led him away from the watchful eyes of the kitchen and down to the privacy of the common room. At this early time of day, it only contained a few dedicated patrons sipping weak ale and nursing hangovers from the night before.

'Truth be told, Brolo, I need you. I need all three of you boys, in fact.' Judging by the expression that gripped Stánwilte's face, admitting such a fact appeared to inflict more anguish than any wound Brolo had ever seen. 'We all need to work together if we ever expect to make it back to Peplyshaw alive. The more time we spend at each other's throats, the higher the chance something or someone unexpected catches us out and splits our skulls like boiled eggs at breakfast.'

Brolo's stomach churned. He wished Stánwilte had used a metaphor from a meal not still in his belly.

'Why are you telling me all of this, Captain? It should be Goat-Turd-For-Brains getting an earful, not me!'

'Because you're surprisingly capable of being a sharp, rational, and level-headed bastard when you put the effort in, that's why. I still haven't the faintest idea why you of all people would've volunteered for this, and I suspect from your behaviour since, nor do you. Yet, despite everything, Bæwylm trusts you. I respect that man above all others, and he cares for you as if you were his own, regardless of your constant attempts to drive him from your life. So, when Bæwylm tells me something, I take it for fact. Before we left, he assured me that you would, sooner or later, show yourself to be a dwarf your father would be proud of and the elf your mother was sure you'd become.'

As much as Brolo wished he could believe those words – and, to Stánwilte's credit, they were delivered with the utmost conviction – he sensed a snake hiding amongst the patchy grass of Stánwilte's goodwill. However, there was some wisdom in his appeal. Two days in, and Brolo was already beginning to tire of his constant squabbling with Wilkhelm, even if he did revel in publicly humiliating him. Perhaps he could put his talents to better use elsewhere.

If harmony is what he wants, then harmony he shall have ... but there's nothing to say I can't try and make a bit of profit from it, is there? As they say, peace sells, he thought, with a sly grin.

Casually, he sat at an empty table, next to a window that looked out upon the Ryoksham village green and the gargantuan yew tree adorning it. He waved to the lass cleaning mugs behind the bar, gesturing for her to bring over a couple of drinks. Joining him at the table, Stánwilte took the full brunt of the sun glaring through the cracked glass, an annoyance Brolo had carefully considered before choosing his own seat.

'I want a raise,' he said bluntly, before Stánwilte's arse had even fully clapped down upon his chair. 'And I want a promotion. No more inventorying the cellars, no more dealing with grubby farmers at the town gates on market day. I want a cushy position, something that has a nice ring to it – like the Official Peplyshaw Ale-Conner, or something to that effect.'

Stánwilte shuffled violently, as if he'd attempted to bolt to his feet, but had been kept in his seat by the weight of his armour.

'I don't know what you think gives you the right to—'

'Or I'm going back home to Peplyshaw, leaving you to deal with Wilkhelm and Smiggly on your own. It's your call.'

Brolo astounded even himself with how'd he managed to turn events around. One moment, he was being scolded by his captain for fighting, the next he was bargaining for promotion! It hadn't been his original intention, but it would suit him quite nicely for now.

Stánwilte gawked at him like a big dumb hound that had chased a cat down a dark alley, only to find twenty of its close chums waiting with bared teeth.

'Well, there's the dwarf your father would be proud of,' he grumbled, as the serving girl sloshed two mugs of ale on to the table. Giving Brolo a wink as he tipped her a generous Silver Goose, she curtsied sweetly, sweeping her skirt as she spun away to carry on with her work.

Stánwilte took a large gulp of ale, keeping a firm gaze on Brolo over the brim of his mug. 'Fine,' he barked once he'd finally put it down. 'You can have your sodding raise. However, I want no word of this getting to the other lads until ... *if* ... we make it back home. Agreed?'

'Agreed,' said Brolo. 'Actually, speaking of ifs and buts, I have one final request – a new saddle for my horse.'

'You know I don't have the gold to waste on such trivial purchases. You'll have to make do with what you have.'

'Conveniently, I anticipated your financial concerns,' said Brolo smugly, tossing a leather pouch upon the table.

Stánwilte pulled the cord to peek inside, then winced.

'And where did you bloody well get this?'

'Wilkhelm's room,' Brolo said. 'I took it after he went down for breakfast, then trashed both of our rooms to make it seem like we were robbed. Of course, I had nothing worth stealing.'

'You *are* a devious little shit, aren't you?' growled Stánwilte. 'I should drag you back to Peplyshaw by your elven ears and stick you in a cell! But ...' He stroked his chin, as a smile formed on his face. 'I suppose this was given to Wilkhelm by our dear Lord Cormorant. And this quest was ordered by him personally, so this money could be considered part of the official funds.'

'Some of which could be used to buy us new saddles?'

'Most definitely. We should purchase Wilkhelm one, too. He might need the boost after he discovers his room has been ransacked.'

Stánwilte raised his mug in toast. Brolo met it with his own, clashing them together with a hearty clonk that slopped thick brown ale all over the table.

'Who'd travel with a bloody dwarf, eh? They're nothing but trouble,' said Stánwilte, shaking his head as he rose from his seat.

'I'm just half-dwarf, remember? Imagine traipsing across the land with, say, thirteen of us.'

Stánwilte's face turned to stone.

'Don't even joke about such things,' he said, before chuckling and slapping Brolo on the back. 'Who'd be that stupid?'

From upstairs came the sound of high-pitched screaming.

'Ah ... Wilkhelm's made it back to his room,' said Brolo, with a grin.

***

It took a few solid hours of stroppy tantrums before Wilkhelm was finally persuaded to leave Ryoksham, The Stoned Wizard, and his lost gold behind them. Upon discovering his ransacked room and stolen purse, Wilkhelm had laid the blame rather accurately at Brolo's feet. Thankfully, once he'd discovered Brolo's room had also supposedly been burgled, he'd set his sights elsewhere. He'd ranted and raved, threatening to round up everybody in the inn, and even in the entire village if needed, to interrogate them one by one.

The innkeeper had apologised profusely for the break-in, proclaiming her staff to be innocent and trustworthy people who wouldn't dream of stealing from a guest. After some protests from a rather guilty-looking Stánwilte, they'd ridden away from The Stoned Wizard without paying even a Copper Chick for their rooms.

So, thanks to me, as things stand, we're currently in profit from this trip! Ha! Let it no longer be said that I'm frivolous with money! Brolo thought, as his sluggish horse P'va ambled across a narrow stone bridge, crossing the shallow stream that marked Ryoksham's boundary.

In stark contrast to the previous path, which had strolled across a stirring landscape of rolling hills and fertile fields, the crumbling track before them trailed off endlessly into the north, with barely a change in incline or scenery. Regardless of the flatter road, only a trickle of time passed before Brolo's arse again began to grow sore. Sadly, the purchasing of new saddles had needed to wait until they reached the next pocket of civilisation, courtesy of Wilkhelm's overblown reaction.

Smiggly had spent most of the day trying to console Wilkhelm. However, his lack of tact and grating cheerfulness had only served to fan the flames of Wilkhelm's short fuse. After sensing he was a few short stories away from a swift garrotting with his own bootlaces, Brolo had suggested it would be best if Stánwilte sent the lad to scout ahead until he hit a junction in the road.

'And from there on, it's a long stretch east for us,' Stánwilte had said, with an air of relief.

Forgoing a few minor hiccups here or there, Brolo could see a confidence budding within the group. Even Stánwilte whistled a faint yet chirpy tune … right up until they rode past of a row of dilapidated buildings. Vines had consumed them, hulking tendrils splitting through their stone walls, their ceilings sitting in a heap of splintered wood. A vast network of weeds, their roots tinged a disturbingly bright green – pulsing with life, like the veins of a reanimated corpse – grasped out from the ruins, extending to the road's edge.

'An abandoned wizard's dwelling,' Stánwilte muttered.

For a while, they carried on in silence. It wasn't until they'd trundled a mile further through the lifeless countryside that a seemingly obvious thought occurred to Brolo.

'Um, Captain ... far be it from me to question your judgment—'

'Bollocks! You're always questioning him, over everything,' said Wilkhelm.

'At times like these, you should be bloody grateful I do, fuckwit!' Brolo snapped back.

'Brolo!' barked Stánwilte. 'It hasn't even been two hours – don't tell me you've forgotten our little conversation already. Just tell me your problem and shut up, the pair of you.'

Deflating once again, Wilkhelm let his horse drop behind the other two, muttering curses under his breath.

'Well, Captain, if we are making our way to Ánad, shouldn't we be, y'know, heading north?'

Stánwilte appeared to consider the question for a few moments, rolling his tongue around the inside of his mouth.

'That's a good point. Well posed and seemingly well observed, aside for the simple fact that we aren't travelling to Ánad.'

'What? Oh, huzzah!' said Wilkhelm, with all the enthusiasm of a condemned man pardoned just as the noose was tied around his neck.

'Where in the sodding kingdom are we going, then?' asked Brolo.

Stánwilte smiled. 'Spyrata, of course.'

Chapter Sixteen

Behind Door Number One

Yilonia walked back to her room in total silence, focused on deciphering the hidden meaning behind each word spoken to her over breakfast. In contrast to her previous trip through the winding hallways of the Palace of the United, rather than being accompanied by a retinue of heavily armed guards, she was guided back to her quarters by a talkative elf, a boy a year or so younger than herself.

He was admittedly polite for his age, well-versed in the graces of elven nobility. However, he radiated the nauseating aura of confidence that personified privileged males of a certain age, earned by the thump of serving girls tripping in their wake. Naively, they began to saunter around with a swagger to their step, unaware that the clinking of their coin purses held all the real attraction. The elf's method of slipping on the charm was therefore about as elegant as a crusty old sock. He spoke far too quickly, details scrambling into each other as he sought to give Yilonia an in-depth description of every item they passed.

Had it been under any other circumstances, Yilonia would've been equally as passionate about the histories of the various antiquities gracing the palace. Thankfully, elves weren't renowned for their flirting, so the boy – whose name she'd been told, but had completely forgotten – had immersed himself far too deeply in his own stories to notice that Yilonia had long stopped paying attention.

Freed, just like that, she thought. *Essentially, at least. With nothing more than a snap of his fingers.*

High-Keeper Relfread undoubtedly hid some ulterior motive behind granting her freedom of the palace. Nonetheless, she was happy to take his generosity at face value, for now. She was also glad to have hopefully seen the last of her serpentine interrogator. She still had no name to put to him, but she did have his title – Inquisitor.

Uprynenos hadn't been under the shadow of a Dragona Inquisition for well over two hundred years. Why would the king suddenly order one, when the royal family had unofficially converted to the Circle a long time ago?

'And this extravagant portrait is of King Petyier's aunt, Princess Ursula Bon Gella. Hers is a most interesting tale. You see, Lady Bon Gella married into the royal family as part of an accord with her parents, who owned vast salt pans in the south and agreed to supply the king and his army with an almost limitless supply of salt, useful in the preservation of food and other such essentials. As part of the negotiations, King Wrentyew the Fourth – King Petyier's grandfather – proposed the union of his third son, Prince Phormly the Gnome, and the Bon Gellas' oldest but most dentally challenged daughter. As you may have guessed, this portrait is exceedingly complimentary. In all honesty, Lady Ursula had a ... unique smile, and a laugh akin to a horse suffering a giggling fit after its lips have been pinned back to its ears. The prince, however, was no catch himself. You don't earn the cognomen *the Gnome* by being a strapping young prince worthy of the tales of yore, do you?'

The elf stopped and waited, grinning, for a compliment that would never come. A few awkward seconds went by before Yilonia's glassy eyes flickered over to him, then a few more before she noticed he was staring at her expectantly.

'What? Oh, yes! It truly is a splendid sculpture. Completely captures, um ... the thing. Yes,' Yilonia finished, rather abashed at her feeble attempt to cover her lack of attention.

'Lady Risúe, excuse my prying, but does something trouble you?'

Panic flickered briefly within Yilonia's chest.

'Call me Yilonia. And let me assure you, I am no lady,' she said, flustered.

'My apologies, Miss ... Yilonia. Nevertheless, you are a guest within the palace. And I merely assumed that one who dresses so radiant and fair must be of noble birth.'

Damn it! I'd forgotten I was in this stupid dress!

Creepy passes aside, the boy had a point. Was it so obvious? What if Relfread and the Inquisitor learned who she really was? She still didn't know what they wanted from her. What if they turned to her family for answers, forcibly or not? If they found out about—

Yilonia grappled with the defiant stallion of her thoughts, reining it in before she fell to blind panic. It simply wasn't possible that they'd stumbled upon the truth of who she was. The High-Keeper had no reason to doubt what she'd told him. Although ... would they ever stop trying to weed answers out of her, even now she was supposedly free?

A new thought occurred to Yilonia. As a sense of dread crept up on her, she began to back away from the elf, taking subtle steps to fool the unobservant eye into believing she was as close as she'd always been.

'How did you come to be in the High-Keeper's service, um ... Júvion?' She'd pulled the name out of thin air; she hoped it was close enough not to offend, but far enough to keep him talking.

'Júvion?' He laughed innocently. 'My name is Inajiff, of House Ye. My family has held the Barony of Hoghamny – and its surrounding marshlands – for centuries. If it troubles you to think so, I am not in His Eminence's service. However, my family are indebted to him for his support in maintaining our standing during and after the Wizards' Rebellion. You see, many nobles accused us of harbouring renegade wizards in our lands, supplying them with provisions to fend against King Petyier's forces – accusations made simply because we are elven. It was typical for the ignorant dwarf lords and menfolk to assume any misuse of magic was from an elven source. To hear how some tell the story, we caused the whole mess in the first place! As if the outlawing of magic was beneficial to us in any way—hey, where are you going?' Inajiff spluttered, as Yilonia bolted away from him mid-rant.

Scrambling round corners and pushing past bystanders, Yilonia held the hem of her ugly, cumbersome dress and ran. She had no idea where she was going and didn't particularly care.

I can't trust anyone, not in this place, she thought, scuttling like a crab down the narrow corridors of the Palace of the United. She bounded into wall after wall, knocking figurines, vases and candlesticks of unfathomable value off tables and into the hands of servants who dived to catch them. She could only imagine the premonitions flashing before their eyes, foretelling the punishments laid upon them for allowing large sections of the palace to become a ceramic graveyard.

Eventually, after turning many more corners and rushing up and down a ludicrous number of stairs, Yilonia's lungs and legs finally gave up. She slumped over, exhausted, against the only door in the corridor. Its rough, woodworm-ravaged panels gave the impression that there was nothing held within of any serious worth or importance.

Gasping heavily, with a deluge of sweat running under her much-maligned dress, Yilonia sat against the splinter-riddled door with her face buried in her palms.

Look at me, running away from my problems again! Oh, how Father would chuckle if he could see me now.

Yilonia sat on the cold stone floor for some time, laughing at her own idiotic bout of despair. Wiping away the stray tear running down her cheek – one of amusement or sorrow, she couldn't tell – with the sleeve of her horrid dress, she pushed herself up to stand.

Only then did she notice the silence around her. The heavy, breathless silence.

Barely the faintest resonance of a raised voice barking orders at some poor servant came echoing to her ears. There was no heavy thud of footsteps approaching or passing by. Even the distant clatter of people hard at work within the palace could not be heard through the thick walls of ancient stone.

Something strange gripped her, some aura of an unseen presence – or perhaps it was the lack of one. A cool breeze swept in through the row of narrow windows adorning the stark corridor, sending the threadbare curtains flapping haplessly. For the first time since she'd been found shrivelled as a sultana, lying half-dead and delirious in the desert of the Ánad, Yilonia was alone. Truly alone.

While she'd smashed through wave after wearisome wave during her countless weeks spent drifting aboard the good ship *Tedium*, locked in a comfortably large yet undeniably confining cell, Yilonia had known every move she made was secretly being watched. She had no proof. It was, in all honesty, only a feeling. A feeling akin to the one she tingled with now: an uncomfortable icy sweat that tickled the hairs in places she wished there really weren't any.

Yilonia couldn't be sure her paranoia wasn't teasing her, yet it had dogged her thoughts each sleepless night she'd spent pacing up and down her room. Everything added up. A creaking here, a whisper there, the all-too familiar feeling of unseen eyes piercing through the darkness. She'd once found peepholes in the walls of her bedchamber back home in her father's castle, hidden behind her collection of dolls nestled in the corner of the room. The servant responsible had been caught watching her dress one morning and was blinded and gelded for his trouble.

Yilonia had searched her prison for such spyholes and found nothing, yet she was sure they were there. Although the dreaded Inquisitor had appeared satisfied with her answers, she was certain his curiosity hadn't ended in the confines of that dank room in which he'd questioned her. Here, in what appeared to be one of the older parts of the palace, undisturbed for years by a servant's duster, the utter calm almost overwhelmed her. The ever-watchful eye that had entombed her under its gaze had briefly let her slip from its sight. Now, she could taste freedom again.

Freedom. So wonderful and sweet, especially within the relative safety of the palace. Ever since she'd left Stunheath under the veil of darkness, alone and frightened, the only security she'd enjoyed had come when she'd had no one else to rely on, when the only one able to betray her had been herself. More than once on her travels north, someone had tried to subdue her and drag her home to claim the bounty her cursed father had placed. Such encounters had rendered her unable to trust anyone as far as she could throw them – except for that one dwarf, whom Yilonia had found she could toss a quite considerable distance, proving that there was always an exception to a rule. Regrettably, each rare occasion she'd let her guard down had always ended in tragedy.

'Oh, Lysio,' Yilonia muttered to herself.

Shaking off her bad memories, she crossed the corridor to look out from the windows, attempting to gauge where in the sprawling Palace of the United she stood. When she braced her elbows on the windowsill, her breath was taken by a gust of salty air. It brought more than a few stinging tears to her eyes as she took in the steep drop to the craggy shoreline below.

The sky was a crisp, summery blue. Nary a cloud dared blot the golden orb of the sun, which sat in all its crowning glory, reflecting onto the waters of the Atrinoc coast. Seabirds squawked as waves crashed into the rocks on which they perched, occasionally taking flight to dive into the ocean, either in search of food or in vicious yet futile revenge for being splashed.

Yilonia's wandering eyes caught on the row of rusty, cobweb-strewn lanterns dotted along the cracked walls of the corridor. They were all adorned with fresh tallow candles. If this section of the palace was as unused as it would appear, why would anyone go to the trouble of keeping it lit?

Yilonia squinted at the battered door to the corridor's only room. When it failed to snap off its own hinges and run for a safe place to hide, she slid over and gave its knob a firm twist. It didn't budge.

She gave the lock a heavy kick, sending it swinging open and snapping the heel off the extravagant shoe she'd forgotten she was wearing. She cursed herself for the mishap, not because she liked the shoes – far from it, they were vexingly uncomfortable – but now she had to walk barefoot on a chilly stone floor with only a fine carpeting of dust for protection.

Good riddance, I suppose. The cursed things almost caused me to break my neck running around this bloody palace, Yilonia thought.

Tossing aside her useless footwear, she stepped cautiously into the room. Concealing shadow seemed part of its furnishings. The ramshackle door groaned shut behind her, plunging the space into darkness, save for two streams of light. One shone through a wide crack in the door, the other through the damaged keyhole. The room was insufferably stuffy, the air thick and acrid with dust. Feeling her way further into the room, Yilonia stubbed her toe against something heavy, sending her tumbling across the floor.

'Ouch! By the Uniter's sword, that smarts!' she swore loudly, before remembering where she was and what she was doing.

Well, at least no one saw that, she thought, switching back to the safer course of keeping quiet. She reached out and felt around for what had tripped her. Her hand darted around the floor, grasping blindly at swaths of nothingness, until she felt something large and bulky enough to be the offending item.

Ah, just a book. A damn solid volume, too.

Rising unsteadily to her feet, Yilonia opened the door, letting a wave of light flood into the room, and placed the hefty book against it as a stop. With any luck, the bloody thing wouldn't close on her again. Now, she could take in the bounty of secrets hidden behind what had appeared a humble door.

Books. Books everywhere. Piles and piles of them, as far as the eye could see. Dusty old tomes bundled high in precarious stacks, others strewn about the floor, tossed aside like a whole orphanage of neglected children, left to rot with their upturned pages open wide as if pleading for help.

The number of books needed to cover this room was too mind-boggling to estimate. Yet covered it was. The size of her own father's library – although Yilonia hesitated to bestow a room this disorganised with the name *library* – had astounded her when she was a small child. She'd spent many an hour engulfed by her father's voluminous chair, effectively teaching herself to read, happy in her little sanctuary away from the other, meaner children of the household. The seemingly boundless knowledge confined within this one room was truly wonderous to behold. Yet Yilonia's bibliomania raged within her at the sight of such flagrant negligence, a crime tantamount to treason in her mind.

In the centre of the room, a large desk sat alone, gathering dust. It must've once been ornate, yet through years of poor care, its carvings had worn to a pale comparison of their former selves. It sat neglected under a cairn of books, some neatly stacked, others piled haphazardly. Squeezed between the piles stood a single candlestick, which appeared to have seen recent use. Cursing her lack of flame, Yilonia rifled through the books, squinting as she tried to make out the titles: *Wigtree Hefindoren's Hystories of the Beasts of the Nourf; Diets of the Various Reptiles of the Lande, Including Drakons; Holding a Flame – A Theory on the Reproductive Cycle of Dragons; Howl to Extinqish Accidental Fyres, Revised Edishion; Dealing with Drakon Fyre …*

A select and rather specialist collection of books. Only, to what end? Her mind racing with possibilities, Yilonia tided everything she'd touched as best she could and made her way out. She most definitely hadn't studied the craftsmanship of fixing doors, so the damn thing would just have to stay as it was.

Wandering blindly around the corridors, she tried to work out the way back to the main hallways of the palace. What she'd do when she got there, though, she couldn't say. Running away for good would be too tricky, too dangerous. She'd never make it out without being spotted. Eventually, she concluded that, for now, it would be best for her to return compliantly to her room. From there, she could focus on uncovering more about her role in whatever bubbling plot of menace she'd found herself stewing.

With the odd wrong turn and a little backtracking, she made it back to more familiar corridors. *From here, it shouldn't be too hard to find my way ba—*

Yilonia's heart stopped as the familiar icy grasp of a gauntleted hand fell upon her shoulder.

Ah, fuck.

'Good morn to you,' she said, innocently. 'I don't suppose you could point me in the direction of the highest room in the tallest tower?'

CHAPTER SEVENTEEN

LET THE PUPPETS DANCE

'Giving the girl freedom to roam the palace unguarded? A bold move, if I may say so, Your Eminence.'

A grim silence fell over the room. Consumed within the abyss of his black robes, High-Keeper Relfread slouched in his chair. It was an uncomfortable beast, one that appeared to have grown from some hellish plant, rather than being crafted by hand. It was entwined in a crumpled mass of twisted vines, some spouting malicious buds, others razor-sharp ebon thorns.

Rather than crush the Inquisitor like the irritating spider he was, Relfread cracked a smile. Casually, he licked the ends of his thumb and forefinger, pulling a long string of saliva to trail across the table with them, as he snuffed out the flame of the candle that had been slowly burning beside him.

'Naturally, I'll be having her watched. However, as things stand, we can presume she knows nothing of any real significance,' he croaked, his voice haggard and strained, as if he'd just finished choking on a mouthful of rusty nails. 'Keeping her happy with the illusion of freedom will be enough to quell any further disruptions ... until the time comes when we decide what to do with her.'

'Why not just let me kill her while she sleeps?' asked the Inquisitor, rather too eagerly.

'Because martyring her within the hearts of the faithful could topple my plans. To leave us solely in control of the narrative, you were tasked with disposing of the officers who found her. Thanks to your efforts, the story of the girl who witnessed a live dragon for the first time since Byrnegona bestowed her final gift unto Arnheld has flooded the kingdom.' His talon-like nails rattled on the table. 'Therefore, if she were to suddenly die or vanish into smoke without us having a tangible alibi, too many people would start asking questions.'

The Inquisitor stiffened in his seat. He sat mute for a few moments, rubbing perspiration from his brow with the back of his leather-gloved hand.

'Then why not work her position to your advantage?' he asked. 'Give the people what they want, and parade her before them like a prize ewe at market. Surely a glorious display of their new prophet would bring them flocking to the Cathedral of Fire.'

'Such a wheel is already in motion. However, using her to attract peasants to our cause, while undoubtedly beneficial, would also run the risk of her gaining too much power. If she were to stop dancing to our tune and divulge too much of the destruction she witnessed, then disposing of her would become much harder than before. Keeping her alive, but well within the confines of the palace, will bring us converts without the danger of her full story becoming public.'

'Far be it from me to question you, Your Eminence, but—'

'Yes, far be it from you, indeed!'

Regardless of Relfread's tone, the Inquisitor carried on without so much as a stutter of fear.

This one reaches too far, Relfread mused, carefully storing the thought for later.

'Despite how little information our interrogations have drawn out, I still believe she is lying about something. You know what soldiers are like – boastful, arrogant pricks, the lot of them. What if she overheard something on the journey to the city? What if the men failed to keep their mouths shut about their duties in the north, while they drunk their fill of wine on a dreary night? What if she overheard, High-Keeper, and she manages to ruin all your plans? If you'd let me interrogate her properly ... a few smacks across the mush with a gauntleted hand, and she'll be singing, I promise. It's not like you'd want to save her comely face for any—'

'For the last time, no, you cannot torture her! I want her unharmed, damn it. If I see so much as a graze on that girl's knee until I've ordered otherwise, I'll have you strapped to a table and personally slash every tendon in your body. I hope I've made myself clear.'

The Inquisitor winced briefly at the threat but met Relfread's stern gaze with a viperous stare of his own.

'Yes, Your Eminence. Quite clear, I would say,' he hissed, reaching for a goblet. 'I'll have to try your technique out myself sometime. Presiding over *that* particular method of questioning must be most delightful.' Gracefully, he took a sip of his wine. 'But, as you say, I shall have to wait,' he said, as he dabbed at his chin with a handkerchief.

'Indeed,' said Relfread. 'Every man who brought her here stated she was in a state of complete delirium while journeying south. I believe you witnessed her arrive yourself. There is no chance she remembers anything from her trip. Therefore, enough talk of her for now; we have bigger issues with which to contend. What is the latest news on the health of my dear brother? I do hope that Petyier is well enough to attend the meeting of his Privy Council this afternoon.'

'Rumours tell me the king has seen off the worst of his flu, yet is still considerably weakened. Solid food is a while off, and he soils his bed regularly. I would wager his presence will once again be sorely missed at the meeting.' The Inquisitor bowed his head, careful to avoid any words that could be taken as treasonous.

At least he isn't completely stupid, thought Relfread.

'Good, good. My brother's period of ill health, while obviously regretful,' he said, as a broad smile splintered his face, 'couldn't have come at a more opportune time. While the petty little lords of Uprynenos scramble like cockroaches to secure whatever meagre foothold they can on the throne, we are left to our own devices.'

'But the king passing now would leave our plans unfinished. Surely, we would have to scuttle our efforts, lest we risk their exposure?' asked the Inquisitor, his tone doing little to hide the reality that he merely cared for his own hide.

'Oh, there's no need to worry, my loyal servant. I have considered every situation and planned accordingly. While I pray that the Great Fires of Byrnegona will fan Petyier's life-flame so it won't extinguish just yet, the continued distraction his declining health provides is certainly a divine blessing upon our noble cause. If he were to pass tomorrow, the inevitable squabble for succession would conceal our mounting power until it became too late for anyone to impede it. No matter whom they choose to be king.'

Rising from his mangled chair, Relfread stretched out his arm, his every joint cracking as he did so. Regardless, his hand hung in front of the Inquisitor's face without a quiver of frailty, waiting for him to kiss the murky grey crystal on its finger. After a few moments, he relented and did as was expected of him.

How I enjoy watching the puppets dance, thought Relfread. The Inquisitor, however, appeared less than amused.

'I accepted this position,' he said, 'because you needed a man who could break the silences of those who opposed you by breaking their bodies, while maintaining an air of sophistication around court. I don't mind playing the humble servant in a public setting, but when it's just you and me, try to remember that I'm a crust-sword and not a zealous follower of the Flame.'

Relfread fixed the Inquisitor with a crooked smile, marked by the fragmented ruins of the few rotten teeth remaining in his mouth.

'Come, we have less delicate matters to discuss, and I'm beginning to tire of this squalid place. Have a guard fetch my carriage. We can continue our talk on our way back to the Cathedral of Fire.'

Upon leaving the room, Relfread pulled up his hood, shrouding his withered face in a mask of shadows. Not to hide his identity, as his eldritch figure was a familiar sight around both the palace grounds and the city. Nor was he concerned by the rumour that every fool he passed would whisper: that he wore his robes to hide his fragile shuffling, akin to a scorpion that had lost a limb – weakened, but still fatally venomous. No, Relfread wore his hood to hide the movement of his lips from prying eyes.

Like a carousel, we go around and around, twirling to the same tune as we have done for years. Thankfully, I learnt how the song goes my first time around, and I know whose eyes belong to whom in this little circus of deception.

The High-Keeper, the Inquisitor and their pursuing guards strolled through the corridors of the Palace of the United, unconcerned by the hordes of servants busying themselves with trivial tasks. They had no choice but to duck and dive out of Relfread's way as he sailed through like a pugnacious swan drifting along a river of ducks.

'The pilgrims,' he began, 'they are still entering the city in the numbers we'd hoped for?'

'Yes, in their droves, Your Eminence. The faithful flock to Spyrata like dwarfs to the last tavern open after midnight. If this continues, the Dragona shall outnumber the Circle for the first time in almost two centuries. A resounding success, considering we haven't even begun to calculate the converts within the city.'

'Good, good. Keep sending your men out into the countryside. Spread the word of the glorious return of dragons to every country bumpkin and village idiot. Tell them of the world long before the Uniting of the Kingdoms, where dragons ruled a peaceful land and made men rich with lavish treasures of gold and silver, in return for farming simple sustenance. Be sure to keep the details firmly within the boundaries of what has been written and passed down as Dragonian legend.' Relfread glared out at the Inquisitor from within his shadowy hood.

'It shall be done as you've instructed. I'm fully aware of what effect the truth would have on your plans,' the Inquisitor replied curtly. 'I do feel I should inform you about the growing civil unrest within the city. Mounting conflict between the new converts and the Circle faithful has already resulted in the burning of three taverns, the desecration of two Circle temples and the subsequent attacks on their priests, along with countless arrests of followers on both sides. Sooner or later, the King's Council will have to take notice of the threat right under their noses.'

'And by that time, the Dragona will outnumber the Royal Guard quite considerably,' finished Relfread.

The Inquisitor remained silent for an uncharacteristically long spell as they wandered along narrow corridors, which in all probability were brimming with listening ears behind every expensive tapestry and painting.

'I hadn't realised you planned to be so direct,' he said, finally.

'Oh, me? No! I'm not going to be direct in anything whatsoever,' said Relfread. 'What will be, will be. If the loyal followers of the Flame and those Circle filth want to lock horns, then who am I to interfere? I am but a humble priest, after all. Nonetheless, if the Inquisition were to become involved ...' He let his words soak into the wet sponge that he assumed formed the Inquisitor's brain.

'I don't see how imprisoning a few Circle followers and putting them to the Flame will cause Dragona faithful to riot.'

'Don't be so naive!' Relfread snapped, almost coughing up a lung in the process. 'You shall arrest members of the Flame. Although founded as a branch of the Dragonian church, the Inquisition falls under direct command of the Crown. As sure as I am that your personal loyalty is mine, a newly reformed Inquisition displaying a soft hand to Circle followers, while violently seizing loyal members of the Flame, would be sure to cause an uproar. Torture them as you will. Fabricate a plot to kill the king and other immediate members of the royal family. Once you're done having your fun with them – and be sure to be thorough – dump their bodies upon the steps of the Cathedral of Fire. The other followers will make martyrs of them and rise in revolt. In their fury, the palace will be attacked, the king most likely killed, and you and I shall watch it all unfold from within the safety of the cathedral. Once the dust has settled, the Royal Court shall pardon you for acting in the best interest of the king and the other lords of Uprynenos – who we all know truly follow the Circle – and the throne will have your part in offending the Flame wiped from the minds of its followers.'

'This seems to rely on a significant degree of danger being hung over my head instead of yours, Your Eminence. I expect due payment for such a risk.'

As the Inquisitor's hint dropped harder than an arrow-stricken soldier, they arrived at the palace courtyard, where a humble carriage of chipped black wood waited.

'Indubitably, my son, don't you worry. Lands, titles, gold ... the works,' said Relfread, climbing into his carriage with a flippant wave. However, when the Inquisitor moved to join him, he held out a hand. 'Remember – I *made* you, Inquisitor Siskin. I brought back an ancient institution to give you a title and standing in court. Your money, your future, your life and everything you stand to gain all comes from my hand. Therefore, when I ask you to show some courtesy, you get down on your knees and grovel! Now act like the good dog you are and walk yourself back to the cathedral.'

With a crack of the whip to send the horse into motion, Relfread set off, a grin curling across his withered face as he pictured Siskin gawking helplessly while the carriage rolled through the palace gates without him.

Chapter Eighteen

A Long Night

Lights from distant farmhouses speckled the hills for miles around, mirroring the faint twinkle of the budding stars in the sky. The crescent moon sat grumpily in the heavens, waiting for the glow of daylight to dwindle further as Arbour Vale drifted into the seductive lull of twilight. Soft plumes of chimney smoke rose into the gathering darkness as hardworking farmers and their families settled in for a cosy night. The world seemed at peace, without a cloud in the sky, yet Brolo had spent enough time working under nature's mercy to know it could end up being a wet night regardless – and spirits were damp enough around here for a brisk shower to make little difference. Everyone was already tired and sore. Being wet would be the icing on an incredibly shit bun.

In the fields, cows and sheep had huddled together in preparation for the night ahead. The party's horses ambled lethargically along the Qhondik Road, signalling that they too yearned for the rest enjoyed by their farmyard friends. As far as the eye could see, they were the only folks traversing the rolling countryside. However, the tell-tale rustling in the thickets – the whimpers of prey darting cautiously between hidey-holes, followed by ominous hooting from the trees – signalled that the creatures of the night were equally as active as they. And once again, a certain rodent was testing the patience of the group, steadily decreasing his own chances of making it through the night.

'I just don't see why I ... sorry, *we,* need to camp outside! It is utterly ridiculous to suggest that the son of a great and noble lord of the realm sleep under a filthy hedge like some rustic. That village we passed a while back seemed a pleasant enough place to stay for the night,' Wilkhelm said for no less than the sixth time, despite knowing the answer damn well. Nevertheless, Stánwilte again explained why they couldn't afford the luxury of a roof over their heads this night, although he was becoming increasingly incomprehensible through the gnashing of his teeth.

'Because it wasn't *a while back* – we passed that bloody village eight hours ago!' he spat. Brolo caught a glimpse of his right eye twitching un-controllably underneath the hood of his brown cloak and stifled a chuckle. Stánwilte took a deep breath to compose himself. 'An hour wasted because you want to kick back by the fireplace of every inn we pass is an hour gifted to those ahead of us. You'd be remiss to believe that we are alone in our goal.' He feigned a cough to shield the last two words from prying ears, proving to be as evasive as ever, even out in this remote part of the country. 'Lords from all over the sodding kingdom may have sent their best men on the same quest as—'

'Who, who?' came an inquisitive outburst from a branch up above. Stánwilte swung around in his saddle, fixing the offending tree with such a cold, dead stare that the owl he held culpable dared to look around irreproachably, hoping to avoid eye contact. However, after a few moments under his steely gaze, the owl proved to have a backbone of custard and flew away. Turning back, apparently satisfied, Stánwilte carried on.

'Some of the most loyal knights in all the land have been given the same task by our good king, and many live far further north than we. So, not only do we have their head start to contend with, but if we stumble across any of the bastards ... they'll cast down anyone and anything in their way.'

'If we are in such a rush, then why, pray tell, are we riding towards the capital?' asked Wilkhelm.

'As I've told you a hundred times before, all you need to know is that we're paying a visit to an old friend of mine,' said Stánwilte evasively.

Blimey, the idea he actually managed to maintain a cordial relationship with an acquaintance for long enough to describe this clearly disturbed individual as an 'old friend' boggles the mind, thought Brolo. *Three of Wilkhelm's pinched coins says they can't stand each other.*

'My ma, she always used to say to me and my siblings, *Do what you're told by those above you. Don't expect reasons – reasons are for those who are capable of reasoning,*' said Smiggly, clearly mistaking the rather harsh insult to his mental faculties for sage advice. If they rode as His Majesty's fist, tasked with recklessly pummelling the ferocious dragon of the north, Smiggly was surely the sore thumb of said disfigured hand, sticking out as he did in his vibrant red tunic.

'Your mother is a creepy imbecile with some serious issues in regard to cutting the cord and letting you get on with your life,' said Wilkhelm snidely.

'Wilkhelm!' barked Stánwilte, sending a cluster of birds flapping wildly from the trees. 'Leave the boy alone, for fuck's sake!' Dropping back to ride next to Smiggly, he patted the boy on the shoulder. 'Wise words, Jenkins, wise words. Maybe if these two simply got on and did as required of them without bitching and complaining every second breath, they wouldn't feel so bloody tired.'

Brolo and Wilkhelm gave each other a doubtful look.

'Smiggly?'

'Yes, Captain?'

'Maybe you should wear this over your tunic,' said Stánwilte, taking off his thick woollen clock.

'Oh, yes. Thank you, sir,' Smiggly said nervously, as he struggled to put it on. 'It's a bit big. You won't be able to see me under it!' He gave a chuckle that died away as quickly as it had begun.

'Yes, that's the point,' was all Stánwilte said, as he rode back to the front of the group.

***

After the rain began to descend, falling in a fine mist that dampened rather than soaked, they rode on for what must've been three hours. Irritatingly, the deluge soon increased to a steady shower, shattering Brolo's hope they'd get away with an easy ride. The rain made for a few sore, tedious miles, during which night hungrily swallowed the word around them. The landscape that had appeared to sweep endlessly beyond the horizon now seemed dreary and inhospitable.

Despite his unquenchable thirst to be better – or, failing that, to be comparatively less of a pain in the rump – than Wilkhelm, Brolo couldn't help but agree when he again began to protest that they'd travelled far enough for one day. Regardless, Stánwilte failed to stop his mount. He seemed to care just enough to occasionally look back and check whether any of his men had fallen asleep in their saddles. Presumably, letting their horses wander off into the night and getting themselves lost in the process would cause delay, something that at least appeared to concern him.

Smiggly still followed him dutifully. The poor young mite rode along with a glassy stare, one shared by cows who found themselves woken up in the wee hours of the morning by a cold-handed farmer clasping a bucket and a stool.

Eventually, after much tag-team nagging, Brolo and Wilkhelm were able to coerce Stánwilte into muttering a brief *'Almost there'* before they resigned themselves to silence for the best part of another hour.

Brolo's eyes ached with the continued strain of staying open, each eyelid drooping asynchronously to a close for a gnat's heartbeat of rest, before fluttering open to let the other take its own moment of respite. Frazzled as he was, it wasn't until his geriatric horse plodded straight into the rump of Stánwilte's stallion that he realised they'd finally come to a stop.

Stánwilte had already slipped down from his mount and taken its reins. Through the murky darkness, it was tricky to perceive where exactly they were, but Stánwilte had begun to lead his horse off the road and up a hill much like the dozens they'd already passed this evening.

'Right, lads, we'll be making camp here tonight, although I'd not spend too much time making yourselves at home. We ride out at dawn.'

Brolo didn't want to think about how few hours remained until then, but he was at least glad that the day's travel was at an end. Some gits, however, could never be pleased.

'Here? We're stopping here?' said Wilkhelm. 'Please say you aren't honestly telling me we're sleeping on some bleak hill in the arse-end of nowhere! What makes this one any better of a campsite than any of the others we've passed? All of us have been beyond shattered for leagues now. We could've stopped at any old peak hours ago!'

Brolo had to concede it was a valid point, but he was well past caring. Stumbling along with all the vigour of shuffling ghouls, he and his weary horse followed Stánwilte blindly through the darkness, until he almost broke an ankle tripping into a sudden drop. Cursing and dusting himself off as he got back to his feet, Brolo squinted so he could focus through the gloom, allowing him to distinguish a shallow dip encircling the hill.

'Mind the ditch,' he heard Stánwilte mutter from somewhere out front. Mostly from exhaustion, but also due to his lack of hoots left to give, Brolo decided against repeating the warning back to Wilkhelm and Smiggly.

They can make their own mistakes. It's the only way to learn, he thought, conceivably mirroring Stánwilte's own view.

The climb was exhausting. When he reached the top of the hill, Brolo came incredibly close to falling asleep on the spot, too knackered to care about finding a more comfortable place to lie down – until he properly took in his surroundings.

Crumbling walls were strewn around the length of the hill, marking the outline of some ruin long since abandoned. Remnants of the ancient stonework still stood in places, as tall and imposing as they had ever been, untouched by the centuries. Less fortunate walls only reached Brolo's chest, while others came no higher than his ankles. However, all of it protruded from the ground like the remains of some ancient stone giant, hastily buried in a shallow grave, unearthed by time and the sweeping winds that blew across the hilltop. However, as he struggled in the darkness to appreciate the full scale of the ruins, Brolo soon realised that time hadn't been the only thing to conquer them.

Ivy had claimed them as its own. It had smothered every stone like a rash, standing or not, forming an imposing green mass.

Trundling up from behind, Smiggly and Wilkhelm reached the crest of the hill, practically clawing their way up on their hands and knees with their respective mounts in tow.

'Ah,' said Stánwilte, 'so you've finally decided to join us. Let me welcome you boys to the castle of the great King Onyur. You've never heard of him? I didn't think you would have. This place was built long before the Unification, and has seen its fair share of bloodshed, war and death over the years. Anyway, enough of the history lesson. Sleep well, everyone.' Without skipping a beat, Stánwilte turned to make his bed for the night.

'Wait!' called Wilkhelm, panting as he recovered from the climb. 'You never answered my question. Why in the far-flung fuck are we staying in this forsaken place? We've passed plenty of farmsteads and abandoned shacks that offered far better cover than here. This looks a terrible place to spend the night!'

Stánwilte rubbed his temples. 'Because common folk don't tend to like visiting abandoned castles. They're a superstitious lot. A great deal believe that old ruins such as these harbour ill omens, evil goblins, dark fancies and the spirits of the dead. Therefore, with a bit of luck, nobody should come stumbling across us. Onyur's Tod is as secluded a place for a safe, late-night rest as we could've hoped to find. Now, unless you need me to talk you through undoing your sodding bootlaces, I bid you all goodnight.'

Stánwilte wandered off without a second glance, leaving Brolo, Wilkhelm, and Smiggly alone. The three stood around, unsure about where to set up camp. All agreed they were either far too tired to build a fire, or too worried that by the time they did so, the sun would creep up from the horizon and outshine their efforts. Therefore, each in turn found a spot of grass not too damp from the rain and not too close to the derelict walls – on the off-chance the country folk had it right about Onyur's Tod being haunted – and made what would have to pass for their bed for the night.

Being as exhausted as he was, Brolo had fully expected sleep's warm embrace to take him as soon as his head hit the saddlebag he was using as a piss-poor replacement for a pillow. Alas, try as he might, it wouldn't come.

It was rare for sleep to elude him. When it did, downing a few horns of wine normally worked a treat. Now that he thought of it, however, it was always after a few days of not touching a drop of booze that he'd find himself struggling to drift off.

No, stop it! That's the kind of thought that drives a man to sobriety! Stop thinking and go to sleep, you bastard!

Arguing with himself did nothing but fuel his frustration, which was close to a raging inferno as it was, due to the gravelly snores roaring from his travelling companions as they slept soundly nearby. Twisting and turning on his makeshift bed of wet grass and dead ivy, he fought to quell the deluge of nonsensical thoughts threatening to overwhelm him.

I wish that bloody breeze didn't sound so much like breathing. I miss my bed. I hope Mrs Dwimm hasn't fallen down those crooked steps and snapped her chicken neck. There's that bloody rustling noise again. I hope we get a few days' respite in Spyrata; there must be time enough for a few games of cards. I must be hallucinating, because why does the wind sound so much like voices? I hope I didn't leave the hearth on when I left home ... wait, hold the signal fire!

Brolo bolted upright. Caught in a wash of panic, he stupidly took a deep breath to shout a warning to the others – something sure to also alert whomever the voices belonged to. A bubble of sense rising to the surface, he clamped his own mouth shut with one hand. All previous tiredness leaked from his body. In its stead coursed a wave of adrenaline.

It's probably just farmers, he thought, in a feeble attempt to comfort himself.

Trying to remember some of the combat training he'd received from Bæwylm, then recalling that he hadn't paid attention to any of it, Brolo scrunched himself as low as he could get into the soggy grass and peered out into the darkness.

'I'm telling ya, their track leads here,' came a hushed whinge from somewhere worryingly close by. 'Them hoofprints lead right up this bloody hill.'

A moment of silence went by, before another, even whinier voice whispered a reply. 'As you keep sayin', Hürkyot, but I don't like the looks of this place one bit. It's giving me the heebie-jeebies. Four days we've been tracking these idiots, without a glimpse of a fresh turd to say if we're even close. How d'you know you're following the right tracks?'

''Cause I do, ya ruddy imbe … limber … limberseal!' yapped the first voice, stumbling over the evidently unfamiliar word. 'Now shut that big flapping mouth of yours and keep your eyes peeled.'

Masters of stealth, these boys are not, mused Brolo, somewhat relieved by the fact, if still a teensy bit worried by the prospect of death. *Why and who would bother with following us? Especially for four bloody days!* But for now, such information could wait. He needed to warn the others.

Keeping low, he crawled towards where Wilkhelm and Smiggly spluttered like hogs choking on a pinecone. How that piss-awful noise hadn't got them all discovered already was beyond him.

'Oi, Doht! I've found their horses!' called the one known as Hürkyot, barely lowering his voice. 'I told you they'd be here!'

'Shit,' Brolo muttered, as he picked up his pace. He swore a swarm of curses as he dragged himself blindly through ivy and wet grass, until he reached two feckless lumps, who snoozed on under the faint shimmer of moonlight, blissfully unaware of the shitstorm brewing around them.

'Wake up!' Brolo hissed into the ear of the mound he thought the most Wilkhelm-shaped, giving it a good old shake and a slap or two.

'*Whumphf!*' mumbled Wilkhelm, as Brolo clasped a hand firmly over his mouth, keeping him from waking half the kingdom and giving their presence away.

'Shh! Shut up, it's me! *Ouch* – stop biting my fingers, you arsehole. It's me!'

Wilkhelm struggled to break free from Brolo's grasp for a few more moments. Gradually coming to his senses, he calmed down enough that Brolo could safely remove his hand. Still breathing heavily from the shock, and looking more than a little confused, Wilkhelm opened his mouth. Brolo put a finger to his own lips.

'I need you to stay quiet and keep sodding calm, alright? For once in your life, listen and shut up. We're not alone. Someone is here and looking for us. Two men, I think.'

'What? Looking for us? How can you be sure it's us they're looking for?' Wilkhelm whispered, wearing a grim expression that suggested he felt far less sceptical than he sounded.

'Because I overheard one of them say they're tracking down the biggest twat in all the land and his band of merry chums. Despite the insinuation that I, or any of us for that matter, are in some small way your friends, I'm willing to consider it an apt enough description.'

'Oh, ha bloody ha! How very amusing. I almost lost control of my bowels due to the unrelenting hilarity,' whispered Wilkhelm.

'Stupid answers for stupid questions,' Brolo retorted. 'Look, we don't have time to piss about bickering. Wake Smiggly up, grab your belongings, then we'll try and find—'

'Well, look what we have here!' came Hürkyot's reedy voice. 'Just the lads we've been looking for. Doht, get your hefty arse over here!'

'Oh, bollocks,' said Brolo, all previous attempts to keep quiet now forgotten.

As he rolled over and put his hands up in surrender, his mind flashed through a million and one ways he could try and worm their way out of the situation. Regrettably, no viable options came up. Given the circumstances, most ended with all their deaths at worst, or a limb or two going missing at best.

'Now, boys,' he said, 'I'm sure this is all some big misunderstanding ... hang on. I recognise you! You're those two louts from the breakfast table back at Ryoksham! Why in the deepest Pit of the Flames have you two followed us all the way out here?'

Brolo thought it a fair question, but Hürkyot and Doht simply stood cracking their knuckles, coming across considerably more fearsome than they had while stuffing their faces with eggs. Especially now the moonlight reflected off the bared steel of their swords.

'Wilkhelm, I told you your big bastard mouth would get us in trouble!'

'That it has, lads. That. It. Has,' said Doht, in his distinctively childlike voice. 'Why don't you make this easier for everyone involved and hand over that fat purse of gold we know you've got, all nice-like, eh? Me and my brother here got all four of your horses, so if you just pay up, we'll be on our way. We may even let you live if you've got enough Swans to make all this hassle worth it.'

'Yeah.' Hürkyot leered at them with his one heavily bloodshot eye, as a grin formed across Doht's face like a splinter in a sheet of ice, reaching from the corner of his blistered lips and up to the patch covering his own missing eye. The two brigands obviously wouldn't let them walk away from this encounter alive, but Hürkyot's gaze bounced between them, as he presumably weighed which of the three might be worth keeping alive for the slave market. He'd probably been enjoying the thought of the riches to come for a moment too long when a realisation flashed across his face.

'Doht, there's three of them! We found *four* fucking horses. Where's the other one?'

No gasp of panic or shock came in reply. Only the gurgle of blood. Doht's eye bulged as he scratched futilely at the bright shard of steel sticking out where his Adam's apple had once sat. His blood showered them all as Stánwilte yanked his sword out as effortlessly as it had gone in, Doht's bulk falling to the floor like a puppet with its strings snipped.

'If there's one thing I can't stand,' growled Stánwilte, 'it's bad table manners.' He looked down at the twitching corpse by his feet, still spurting blood from the wound in its throat, then back up to the slowly retreating Hürkyot. 'I don't think he'll be scoffing down more eggs anytime soon, do you?'

Brolo sat in the grass next to his companions, mouth hanging open as he watched on, dumbfounded by the turn of events. In contrast, Stánwilte stood a malignant figure in his full armour, the dull steel gleaming despite the spray of crimson across its breastplate. He swirled his blade in a flowing arc. If performed by another, the motion would've seemed flashy and pointless. Yet, executed by Stánwilte, standing amid ominous ruins on a rainswept hill in the black of night, it was a brutally impressive display. The hairs on the back of Brolo's neck stood on end.

Retribution now blazed in Stánwilte's dark blue eyes. His sword shimmered in the moonlight, dripping a small pool of Doht's blood onto the grass as it hung in a deceptively open guard. A stance inviting attack, but even Brolo knew only a blithering fool would accept the chance to do so.

'Whoa, now, let's not be doing anything hasty,' said Hürkyot, raising his hands slowly. However, Brolo noticed he had yet to drop his blade. 'It was all his idea anyway.' He nodded down at Doht's corpse. 'I just did as I were told, is all. Didn't wanna anger him and the likes.'

From there on, Brolo watched the best production of bullshit story spinning he'd ever had the good fortune to witness. Hürkyot painted a tale of a younger sibling coerced into a life of despicable deeds and horrific violence. Made to steal from passing travellers, forced to torture others into revealing the location of hidden treasures, else risking a savage beating at the hands of his brother. The overwhelming pong of the dung spouting from his mouth was enough to bring tears to Brolo's eyes, which stung so much he had to dab them away with the sleeve of his tunic. The dedication Hürkyot poured into his performance almost roused Brolo to give a standing ovation, yet he thought better of making himself the centre of attention in the middle of this much bared steel, electing instead to stay huddled on the ground.

Regardless of this stirring portrayal of a young man led astray, it soon became clear that Stánwilte was not a fan of the performing arts.

'I'm going to give you one chance and one chance only,' he said. 'Throw down your weapons and take off your boots. Afterwards, I will watch you walk down this hill with your hands firmly behind your head, keeping a keen eye as you stumble back along the road the way you came. If I catch you so much as fancying a glance back in this direction, I will have Smiggly here put an arrow through your other eye before you can turn back again. Do I make myself clear?'

Hürkyot seemed to consider the offer, mulling it over as he twirled his sword nimbly.

'Can't leave my brother up on a hill alone,' he muttered.

'You can join him if you wish,' Stánwilte replied coldly.

That remark brought a grin to Hürkyot's scarred face. His odd golden tooth clashed horribly with his few remaining real ones, which were stained blackish-green with decay.

'Nah.' He spat on his brother's corpse. 'A much bigger share for me with him gone.'

Without skipping a beat, he swung his blade through the air in a cleaving stroke aimed to take Stánwilte's head clean off. Stánwilte calmly dropped to one knee, raising his sword like a pike as Hürkyot's momentum carried him forward. The big man sank down as he skewered himself through the chest on the waiting blade.

No screams of agony marred the peaceful night. Just a flatulent pop of breath from Hürkyot's yawning mouth as his life drained away.

Rising to his feet, Stánwilte gently lowered Hürkyot's body, put his boot upon the dead man's shoulder and wrenched his sword free of the flapping corpse, kicking it backwards onto the dirt.

'As you're all up, we may as well make ready to ride out. No point staying here anyway,' he said, as if he hadn't just killed two men before breakfast. He frowned down at the bodies on the ground before him. 'From here on out, we take turns keeping watch during the night. Now, find your horses, and let's go.'

Sitting in the grass, covered in blood that thankfully was not his own, Brolo scoured through all the times he'd witnessed fights, wrangles and late-night scuffles in taverns, which had ended with a fair share of blood being spilt. Fortuitously, never in all those numerous brawls had he seen a man die. Now, this morning, he had seen two.

Well, you know what they say about waiting around for something, he thought, discovering he had less heart for his own poor humour this morning than normal.

CHAPTER NINETEEN

A QUAINT LITTLE TOWN

I would've whipped out the old sword and impaled a few men sooner, if I'd known it would cause such a drastic effect, thought Stánwilte.

It was a sinister thing to pass through his mind, and he hated himself a little for thinking it, but the pure, unadulterated peace he enjoyed as they continued their ride towards Spyrata fanned his dark wish that they'd been attacked a tiny bit sooner.

With the blessing of a long spell of clear weather, they trundled along many tiring leagues east, crossing over rolling hills and passing through dense woodlands, under the watchful gaze of ancient trees that'd grown to what the boys whispered to be unnatural heights. Whispers Stánwilte didn't find hard to believe as they huddled, resting, against one of the mighty obligers. From a distance, they would've seemed like specks against the enormous girth of its trunk, let alone from atop the dizzying heights it had managed to stretch to. A labour easier to accomplish this far from the danger of a woodsman's axe.

During the night, by a feeble fire of twigs and dried moss, Smiggly recounted a story his father had told him as a child, of the forest wizards who'd grown these impossibly large trees to build great warships for the kings of old. Tales of wizards weren't exactly Stánwilte's favourites, but he nonetheless enjoyed it.

Most bitter for the group were the cold and lonely nights they spent yomping across a countryside devoid of life, which had probably remained untouched by man, elf or dwarf for thousands of years. The dull landscape offered almost as few conversation topics as it did fresh meat or rivers to fish.

Days drifted by without a peep of excitement, but as they gradually left the wilderness behind them and stumbled across further signs of habitation, they happened upon other travellers passing on the Qhondik road. Farmers on their way to market, singers drifting from town to village, even a wandering crust-sword seeking any passing adventure to pay for his next meal. Stánwilte briefly considered his services but dismissed the idea.

No one seemed to eye them suspiciously. In fact, some folk carting sacks of grain waved merry greetings, complete with broad smiles, as the four of them trotted past. Although he waved back, going by his experience with small folk, Stánwilte held little doubt their fervent greetings were intended to ensure the group would ride on by and leave them unmolested.

Occasionally, small children walked alongside them to trade news for a few coins. Stánwilte heard the same stories at least six times over by the time they approached the outlying villages of the capital, yet he paid the little ones with a smile on his face all the same. It was amazing the generosity a little peace and quiet could bring. Besides, it was Wilkhelm's coin anyway.

Ever since the bloody night amid the ruins of Onyur's Tod, the constant arguing had all but stopped. Smiggly carried on as whimsically carefree as he'd ever done. Wilkhelm generally complained less about each trivial issue they came across, but still found time for the occasional snide remark. Brolo troubled Stánwilte, however. His eyes were always watching, his gaze constantly burning a hole in Stánwilte's back as they rode. Stánwilte suspected he still harboured a minor grudge for whatever reasons he chose, but most of the issues they'd had with each other had been hammered out back at The Stoned Wizard. At least, so Stánwilte hoped.

He had to admit, Brolo had taken the events back at Onyur's Tod a little harder than he would've expected. For all Brolo's arrogance, Stánwilte had always presumed him to be made of sterner stuff. Death did tend to affect people in different ways. However, the thought had crossed his mind once or twice that it was *what* had caused the deaths that truly troubled Brolo.

It's not like he didn't know who and what I was before I got shipped off to Peplyshaw. Half the bloody Watch – nay, most of the sodding kingdom – has never let me forget my past! Stánwilte thought. Still, it was one thing to hear about a man's martial prowess, and another to see them enacted before your very eyes.

Stánwilte sometimes found it too easy to forget that the three lads had led relatively sheltered lives back in Peplyshaw. Guilt ravaged his thoughts harder than ever. To all intents and purposes, he'd abused his position to conscript these young, tiresome, ill-prepared men into embarking on a foolish escapade, which as a seasoned veteran, he didn't really believe they had a goat's-arse chance of surviving. He couldn't exactly take all the blame, however.

Lord Cormorant had freely and frivolously offered up his own son for the quest, knowing full well what its most probable outcome was. At least what he stood to lose was, in his eyes, more trifling than the prize of his ambitions – the chance to be the King of Uprynenos. What did Stánwilte want? Forgiveness from King Petyier, who, if the persistent rumours of his health proved true, was losing his faculties rapidly enough that he likely wouldn't remember who Stánwilte was. It was becoming harder to believe it was worth endangering his life, let alone anyone else's.

No matter how many hours they'd put in at the training yard, none of the men had ever seen any real action, other than the odd scrap in The Crone's Wimple. Demanding that they take the harsh realities of the world in their stride was perhaps too much to ask. Why it had taken so many leagues for Stánwilte to consider how his selfish folly would affect the others joining him, he was ashamed to contemplate. The inability to admit his faults had caused him grief in the past; he loathed to let the shame trudging alongside him each day grow heavier by letting others suffer for his mistakes.

Alas, no matter how circumstances have changed, for better or for worse, it's far too late to go back.

As promised, when the group reached the first decent-sized town after Onyur's Tod, Stánwilte – so, by extension, Wilkhelm and his father – paid for properly-fitted and significantly more comfortable saddles. Brolo opted to trade his wheezy gelding for a marginally younger and hardier beast of burden. A vast improvement over the waste of oats he'd been putting up with, though a shame for P'va, who hadn't tried to bond with Brolo. Now the unfortunate bugger had been condemned to the knacker's yard, where he'd make a firm bond, whether he liked it or not.

As they drew closer to the capital, they spent more nights resting in the relative comfort of local inns. At first, Stánwilte held to his stance against taking such creature comforts in lieu of progress on their journey, but the significant boost in morale – and resulting decrease in bickering and complaining – caused him to change his mind. Although he ensured a few stipulations were in place first, of course.

There was to be no mention of their real names, especially for Wilkhelm. Some fool might recognise his family name and take him hostage, under the ridiculous notion that his father would value his life enough to offer anything significant in exchange for it. Stánwilte also banned excessive drinking – tongues tended to flap, namely Brolo's, after too many brews were poured down the hatch, and the last thing they needed was to be kicked out without their gear or coins after a fight they'd probably lose. Most important, as always, was the rule about not even giving off a whiff about where they were heading, or what they intended to do once they arrived.

Stánwilte couldn't have stressed this enough if they'd travelled during times of peace. Under the delicate circumstances the kingdom found itself in, however, he oft had the dreaded feeling that it'd take the cold reality of a serious string of fuck-ups to really hammer the message home.

***

Life tended to be a fickle prick, noticeably when all seemed to be pleasant – such was a given. Unexpectedly, then, upon their arrival in the market town of Alisgate, a mere three-day ride from the walls of Spyrata, everything appeared as boring and ordinary as it should be in any place more than a trebuchet shot from the nearest city.

The sun had long passed its zenith, settling into another slow afternoon. However, it was tricky to pinpoint exactly how long ago that had taken place, for despite the superb string of weather as of late, murky grey clouds now stained the sky, sweeping in to cover the landscape for miles around, casting the world into shadow. As a strong gust of wind blew in from the east, Stánwilte decided it was chilly enough to suggest an early stop to warm the cockles.

Encircled by what Stánwilte would deem a shamefully maintained palisade, Alisgate bore a resemblance to Peplyshaw, despite being of a much greater size. It screamed of a town left to its own devices by its local lord.

Plainly, he was content to let it grow lazy and fat with trade, so it could pay generous taxes to fill his coffers, sparing few thoughts for defence in the case of a raid or war.

Even as the western gate swarmed with activity, the lack of stern authority was woefully clear. The party waited amongst a stream of baying merchants, cart-pulling farmers and shady pedlars. Due to the late time of day, the flow of people should've been heading away from Alisgate. Nevertheless, the two hapless guards manning the gate were apparently collecting a new tax imposed on those wishing to trade within the town, while also trying to catch those on the way out. This resulted in a long delay, as each trader spent a significant amount of time arguing, complaining, pleading and bribing their way out of the tax.

Regrettably, not everyone had deep pockets – and, in the cases of the extremely poor farmers, some had no pockets whatsoever. Consequently, the anger at a double dose of taxation was in imminent danger of boiling over into outright chaos by the time the four had waded their way through the rabble of merchants and pig shit to the front of the line. Before entering Alisgate, however, they had to pass under the crooked – presumably from suffering its fair share of fist-induced breakages – nose of the weaselly guard who stood collecting the extortionate taxes.

He watched Stánwilte approach with a glare thick with disdain. Clearly, he'd already assumed, from their lack of goods, that they offered him little in the way of opportunities for coin to be made and thus were a waste of his precious time. He closed one nostril with a scrawny finger and blew hard from the other, so a blast of snot shot like a sticky comet to land squarely at Stánwilte's feet. He took a long pause to wipe his finger across his tatty and disconcertingly green-stained gambeson before finally bothering to address them.

'State your purpose. Business or pleasure?' he asked. 'Doubt you'll find much of the second, mind.'

Not wishing to hold up the line prattling around with thinly-shrouded threats, Stánwilte produced a small pouch containing a few Silver Geese and lesser Ducks, tossing it at the guard's feet. He promptly snatched it up and began to count its contents. It contained change left over from several petty purchases they'd had to break Swans up for, and therefore wasn't a significant stash to them, but it was still probably more than the guard was going to bleed out from these miserable farmers all day. However, he still found the nerve to scoff while he passed the coins from one hand to the other, eyeing Stánwilte with suspicion as he counted them for the third time.

'Aye … well, too bloody generous with your coin to be a bunch of fanatics. Too flashy by half to just be common folk, either. We've got enough trouble in town as it is, so I don't wanna hear about you lot stirring the chamber pot, understand?'

Stánwilte held his hands up innocently. 'Not here for trouble, just beds and a feed. We're passing through on our way to the capital and thought we'd take the opportunity to enjoy the comfort of a half-decent tavern.'

'Hark! *Half-decent*, he says! *Comfort*, he wants! By the wings of Iros, are you thick in the head? This place has gone to pot! Started as trickle of 'em, at first. One or two preachy bastards, standing in the town square, whipping up a storm about this and that, setting fire to statues of false idols and all the usual rubbish. Next thing ya know' —the guard snapped his fingers loudly in Smiggly's face, startling the boy— 'people started tossing about accusations of heresy for naught reason at all – more often than not, at their own blasted friends. Now you can't walk the streets without hearing some religious git condemning all sorts of fun. Worst of all, the taverns have emptied out their grog! It all just got tipped into the gutter by the mad sods, bleating about how drinking be a sin in the eyes of the dragons.' Sniffling, the guard wiped his cheek as if to dab away a tear that hadn't quite managed to seep from his eye. 'Poor Mr Fumff was bundled out of his own cellar by those bleeding fools and torched alive after being doused in brandy! Most folks drank at The Barrel o' Laughs all their lives, and not one raised a finger to help the fellow. One or two even tossed bottles at him to boost the flames! Alisgate's been overrun by the Dragona ever since. Not a chance for an innocent man to make it out of the town less crispy than when he went in, I can tell you.'

Stánwilte raised an eyebrow. 'And all this is innocent, is it?' he asked, nodding at the numerous sacks of coin that had been accumulated by fleecing honest and dishonest traders alike.

'Never said it was,' the guard said, with a wolfish smile. 'Restoring the old Dragonian church must be paid for somehow, and it's only fair we get a little commission on the side. Anyone who has a problem with us taking a cut … let me tell you, I'm a crack shot with a bottle of spirits, if you get my drift.'

'Oh, I get the gist of it, thank you. Don't you worry, we intend to spend one night here and be on our way.'

'See that you do. Keep to yourselves, and if anyone asks you questions, be sure to keep your beaks shut. No need to go getting your rumps toasted. Especially when there's a fee to collect on the way out, too.'

With that, he stuck his finger into the gaping crevice of his nostril and sought out a long string of snot, which he hung in front of his eyes, appreciating the sheer size of the nugget he'd unearthed. When he'd finished admiring his handiwork, he once again wiped it across his front, as casually as someone stifling a yawn, or dropping their breeches in the middle of the street and emptying their bowels in full view of passers-by.

***

Rain began to fall as they worked their way down the main thoroughfare leading into the centre of town. It was a mere speckle of what the grey clouds had in store, yet already, the streets were sloppy with a tantalising cocktail of trampled mud, urine, straw and dung. Stánwilte had no doubt the muck would swallow his boots whole if he was unfortunate enough to step into a deep enough patch of the sticky brown-green goo.

After the wide-open vastness of the countryside, it took a few short minutes within Alisgate, cramped between the smelly, grimy, incessantly bellowing locals, for Stánwilte's patience to snap. He resorted to barging through any momentary fracture in the crowd before someone else slipped in to seal it shut again. Cries rang out from all directions, as desperate pedlars attempted to strike last-minute bargains before the rain began to fall properly and ended their business for the day. The air was pungent, which was usual for a settlement with such congestion. Yet there was another acrid ingredient to the back-alley broth that held the faintest whiff of familiarity.

Burning. Not merely of wood. Something had been roasted – something of flesh. From the potent stench of the smoke, the fire had been large and relatively recent. None of the stalls they passed seemed to be selling much in the way of meat, let alone cooking it. Stánwilte racked his brains for where he recognised the smell from. Then his eyes caught the faint plume of smog drifting up from the square ahead, and he was struck by a stray arrow of remembrance, delivering a bitter memory into his skull without remorse.

Green droplets fell like a widow's tears from the clouds looming in the sky, illuminating the marshlands, landing in blinding explosions of arcane fire.

The wails of dying men pierced my eardrums as I charged back towards safety, kicking away the outstretched arms of my fellow soldiers, engulfed in emerald fire as they were, pleading for help I could not give. I could only stare in horror as their bodies blackened and contorted, consumed by searing blasts of pure magic. Their mail melted into their bubbling flesh as they lay in the murky brown sludge, spared no final dignity, many trampled under the hooves of their own flailing horses ...

Stánwilte shivered. Usually, he swiftly banished such thoughts to the dark, foggy caverns of his mind, before they found a nerve to latch onto and took hold of him once more. Now, though, he let his past awaken to the scent in the air, and the realisation of its source stole his breath like a punch to the throat.

They're burning someone. More than just someone; there's far too much smoke for it to be from one poor soul.

'You lot, don't say a word to anyone,' he told his companions. 'I'm beginning to get the sense that pissing off the wrong person here will result in us pleading for someone to piss on *us* to douse the flames.'

Tension rose all around them. As they squeezed through the packed streets, Stánwilte hoped they'd remain a band of nondescript fish in a nameless and unremarkable sea. Disquietingly, alas, paranoia pulsated deep within his brain, whispering that everyone's eyes were watching them as they slipped towards the square.

Above the calamitous hollering of the coin-hungry stallholders packed into every conceivable crevice of Alisgate began a soothing chant. It drifted in a dreamy cloud, drowning out the merchants' bellows, swallowing the attention of the populace as it rang soulfully down the streets.

The flow of the crowd shifted. No longer did Stánwilte and his men need struggle against the townsfolk to make their way into the market square. They were caught in a determined surge as the entire populace appeared to target the same destination. They could but follow the raging course of the herd, the three boys gazing around anxiously for some sign of reassurance. Stánwilte met their stares with a calming nod, despite his own nerves being equally on edge. While a majority of the crowd shuffled blankly along, as if entranced by the wailing chant, a scattering of sombre faces within the crowd implied the watchmen were not alone in their fears. Many had tears rolling down their cheeks as they strode on, but none made any effort to slink away.

Stalls had been packed up and carried away with miraculous speed by the pedlars willing to cut their losses. Shutters slammed as the stream of people passed by. Step by eerie step, they drew closer to the market square. By now, the air was thick with choking smog. Each wheezing breath took immense strain, as if Stánwilte were trying to fill his lungs with stodgy gravy. It rendered speech and sight nigh on impossible, yet out from the grey haze, he could hear the beckoning chant still being sung unhindered.

'Captain, I ... I don't want—' Wilkhelm looked close to hacking up a lung. His eyes were bloodshot and streaming with tears, but to his credit, he still fought to finish his sentence. 'I suggest we shouldn't proceed along within this parade of madness, sir. We could still weave our way out and be on the road in no time. A little rain never killed anyone. I, for one, believe a nice hedge would be more than ample shelter for tonight.'

Stánwilte didn't doubt that what was unfolding around them was indeed a display of mass insanity, nor that a swift retreat would in all probability be the smart move to make. However, his curiosity had been tickled by the bizarre behaviour of the occupants of Alisgate, so despite what he hoped was simply fear grumbling in his bowels, he shook his head, resolved to see this through.

Wilkhelm's shoulders sank as his hopes of flight were crushed by the stampeding horde. Stánwilte's conscience began stabbing at him like an overenthusiastic fencing student getting his hands on a sabre for the first time.

Once again, he was ignoring the obvious fears of his own men.

Guiltily, he looked back at them. Smiggly's chubby, innocent little face darted around as he held tightly onto a tense-looking Brolo's arm, seeming set to flee at the first sign of danger. Before Stánwilte could make amends for his error and lead his men on the fight back through the town, the crowd surged forward, spilling like a burst abscess from the narrow streets and into the wide expanse of the square. Townsfolk piled through fervently, scrambling to get closer to the front, pulling those in their way to the ground and stumbling over fallen bodies without a care. Stánwilte barked as loudly as his ash-filled lungs would allow, ordering his men to hold on to each other. Despite his best efforts, he still lost sight of them in the cavalcade of faces.

The miasma was now rising into the gloomy sky in soft billows, finally allowing Stánwilte to see what waited before the assembled mass. At the furthest end of the square stood the town hall and the office of the Mayor of Alisgate. The half-dozen shallow steps before it had been fashioned exorbitantly from marble, which had probably once gleamed the purest white, yet was now charred black by fire. Standing either side of the steps were twelve people. From the oversized hoods of their heavy dark robes came the deep, sombre chant that had drawn in the people of Alisgate.

Atop the centre of the staircase stood a lone figure, dressed in a similar fashion to the choir, though his robes were trimmed in crimson and his hood was down. His long, arching nose and trowel-like chin gave him the appearance of a malnourished bird of prey, plucked of all its feathers. Bald except for long, patchy straggles of ghost-white hair, which clung to his face in the light drizzle, he held his hands up to the heavens and screamed into the wind with impressive vehemence for one so advanced in years, leading

Stánwilte to conclude he was a priest of some kind. Men like him always were.

At the base of the dainty steps were the remnants of eight smouldering pyres.

Well, I suppose this explains the smell, thought Stánwilte, wincing. Ash rose like specks of deathly snow, carried by the wind from the fiercely sizzling embers and skeletal remains. Along with the captivated crowd, he watched as the priest howled a fervid deluge of damnations upon the people he'd purged within the righteous fires of the Dragona.

Just as Stánwilte noticed the prolific number of well-armed men lining the square, decked out in striking black armour with flowing capes of fire, an all-too-familiar voice shattered the silence of the crowd. It interrupted proceedings, seizing attention in a manner as ill-advised as smothering your genitals in bacon grease and dipping them into shark-infested waters.

'Please tell me you gormless nincompoops don't truly believe all this hullabaloo,' echoed Brolo's voice around the square.

The crowd turned as one in his direction, as if connected by a hive mind. A ripple of gasps passed through the spectators, but mostly, the quiet held.

'By my ears, I know we bumpkins have a reputation to maintain, but this goes above and beyond what rustic simplicity can excuse! Look around you, for all that's sane! Surely your families have been in this town for generations. You can't think it's worth burning your kinsmen for wearing rings of the Circle, just to appease this puckering donkey's arse? A *sin*, he claims! Call me cynical, but I find the idea of a flying lizard grasping the concept of religious sanctity a mite fishy. We'd be nought but meat to one of them, and you'd better soon come to your senses, or you'll all end up on the hot end of a spit roast before too long!'

Stánwilte cursed. He was sure Brolo must've been feeling exceedingly minute – more so than usual – under the sheer scorn of all the searing gazes atop of him. Astoundingly, however, his face remained stony, even as the robed priest lowered his arms, sunken eyes flashing wide as if to swallow him whole.

Stánwilte squeezed through the crowd in a desperate attempt to reach Brolo before he said anything more to widen the rift between them and the rest of the town.

'Lo!' bellowed the wizened priest, pointing a skeletal finger in Brolo's direction. 'Spawn of elven and dwarfish blood, disowned by both and true to neither! Your kin lived amongst the almighty dragons in peace for thousands of years as their proud and honoured vassals, mining and working the land to provide sustenance for our most splendorous winged gods – until the time of man came and brought that glorious era to a shameful end. You spit poison, but you more than most should rejoice in the divine return of a dragon to these lands. Do you shun what your ancestors held so true to their hearts and proclaim it mere hogwash? Your forefathers would be ashamed by such dishonest treachery!'

By the time the priest had finished spitting out this venomous dressing-down, Stánwilte had pushed his way to the front. Judging by the redness of his face, Brolo couldn't have been angrier at those words … until Wilkhelm and Smiggly slid in through the crowd beside him.

'Gosh! Getting burnt by the Flame, eh? Now that must've stung something fierce,' said Wilkhelm, a grin stamped on his face from ear to ear.

Brolo's hand darted to snatch the collar of Wilkhelm's tunic, pulling him in to match his rapidly fading smile with a furious snarl.

'Keep your mouth shut, you snivelling puddle of stoat's piss!' Brolo snapped. '*Dishonest treachery?* The daft old prat doesn't even make sense! What, is he opposed to the *honest* kind of treachery we all know so well? That fired-up git has been sniffing far too much sulphur for my liking.' He transferred his glare back up to the priest, who had a look on his face that suggested he was considering how many logs he'd need to roast one insolent dwelf.

'Anything can be honest and true if done for the right reasons,' the priest said bitterly.

'Ha! Thought so! Trust the Dragona to spew up *that* sort of limp-cocked rationality to argue its incredibly flawed dogma.'

This bloody situation is getting out of hand, thought Stánwilte nervously. As he scanned the crowded square for any available exit, his eyes fell back onto the armed men guarding the priest and the charred ground where the fiery executions had taken place. For the first time, he noticed the badge adorning their chests: a pure white question mark crossed with a flaming pair of pincers. *That's the badge of the Ministers of Sin within the Dragona Inquisition! They've not existed for centuries. Why in the blazes are they here now?*

Stánwilte needed to shut Brolo up as soon as physically possible and escape from town before it transformed into a slaughterhouse. He cursed himself again for not predicting that the dwelf would get himself involved in some sort of conflict.

'The Circle deceives you into forfeiting all of your possessions and hard-earned money, under the false ideal that sharing your worldly goods with those around you brings you greater joy in the next life. Nonsense, I say!' the priest proclaimed, not just to Brolo, but the whole crowd – most of whom nodded in agreement. 'Your contributions pad the pockets of the rich, and nothing trickles down unto the poor. All the dragons would ask of you is a sheep or two a week in tribute!'

'I don't care for the Circle either,' said Brolo. 'You're both as twisted as the other, but at least they don't forcibly extend their reach into the governance of the realm!'

Oh, shit, that's gone and done it, thought Stánwilte, though he couldn't help conceding that Brolo had walloped the nail on the head. *Bæwylm has the truth of it ... the boy has a spark of intellect kicking about in his noggin. Bastard needs to learn when to use it, though.*

The priest shrieked as if Brolo had taken on the form of a vast slug and rolled around in a dish of salt. Like every other priest in the kingdom, he was poised to exploit any chink in a disbeliever's armour with the cold, merciless hammer of misinterpreting their words and throwing them back with a completely different meaning.

'This blasphemy has gone too far!' he screamed, pointing his accusing finger once again at Brolo. 'He spits on our gospel and seeks to kill the dragon! Ministers of Sin, have him taken away to be burnt at the stake!'

Brolo turned to face Stánwilte, expression baring the idea they should probably consider leaving at this stage. However, before he could even attempt to verbalise this, Stánwilte had already unsheathed his sword in a lightning-slick movement. He lunged over Brolo's shoulder – the blade narrowly missing his cheek – and buried it deeply into the throat of the first Sinister who'd made a grab for the dwelf, sending him keeling over backwards in a shower of blood.

Stánwilte shouted for his men to move out, swinging his sword in a bloody arc above the crowd. It came down in a thunderous clash against the raised shield of another Sinister, who'd leant down from the steps and begun to grapple with Wilkhelm in a rabid struggle to reach Brolo. Using the Sinister's supposed height advantage against him, Stánwilte grabbed at his feet and swept his legs out from underneath him. He crashed unceremoniously to the ground, whereupon Stánwilte made good use of his crosspiece, caving in the Sinister's skull with repeated strikes to the face. During this process of transforming a head into a bloody pulp, Stánwilte found himself jerked violently from behind. Thanks to years of being meticulously trained to respond instinctively during battle, he spun around in one fluid motion, ramming the blade into his would-be attacker's eye socket.

There was a gooey pop and a spurt of blood as a lanky elf – who wore the drabs of a beggar, rather than the flashy garb Stánwilte was accustomed to seeing elves dressed in – went to his knees with a high-pitched scream, clutching at the hole where his ruined eye once sat. To shut him up, Stánwilte kicked him backwards to the muddy ground with as much force as he could muster. Sure enough, the elf soon fell suitably silent.

Looking up to gauge his bearings, breathing a lot harder than he would've done a decade ago, Stánwilte saw that the rest of the watchmen were having some trouble of their own. While many of the townsfolk had backed away to avoid danger, a large proportion had been riled up enough to take an active part in their apprehension.

Brolo was swinging his hammer around wildly. He caught a Sinister across the back of the head, creating a large dent of splinted bone as his skull caved in. Carried by his momentum, Brolo conveniently smashed in the face of another attacker, all in the same rotation. His attack snapped the aggressor's head around in the best impersonation of an owl Stánwilte had ever seen.

Wilkhelm and Smiggly were huddled together amid the press of the crowd, Wilkhelm flailing a hatchet to-and-fro, temporarily proving successful in keeping the Sinisters and townsfolk at bay. To his credit, he was doing a stellar job of protecting the terror-stricken Smiggly.

Stánwilte needed to lead them away from the square, preferably without killing any more locals. He didn't mind killing officials armed and charged to harm them, but soft-minded townsfolk who'd been brainwashed by whacky priests were generally innocent in the grand scheme of things. Unless they attacked him first, of course.

Due to the packed conditions of the brawl, using his sword as nature intended was at present an unavailable option. Making the most of what he had, Stánwilte clutched his blade like the haft of a mighty war hammer and smashed his way through the wave of oncoming Sinisters, thwacking at any citizens of Alisgate who posed a threat. He reached Smiggly and Wilkhelm after the latter had finished performing a mild dental procedure on an overexcited dwarf, delicately removing most of his teeth by thumping him in the mouth with the haft of his hatchet. Wilkhelm appeared more surprised than the dwarf by the accomplishment. Both he and Smiggly were marked by the odd cut and scrape, but were relatively unharmed, for now. Brolo, regrettably, seemed a bit worse for wear. He'd lost his hammer in the scuffle, and the crowd seemed to have decided they wouldn't let such vulnerability go unpunished.

'You two,' barked Stánwilte, motioning his sword towards Smiggly and Wilkhelm, 'head towards the eastern gate and get the fuck out of town. We'll catch you up on the road. Just go! Run!'

Being inclined towards cowardice, Wilkhelm immediately made to flee the crowd, whose attention was now fully on the captured Brolo. Smiggly, dutiful as ever, at least gave a few wide-eyed glances back, as if wishing to stay and help.

Stánwilte briefly watched them fight their way out, relieved they no longer had to witness more death. To that effect, he knew what he had to do – delaying it wasn't going to spill any less blood. He just wished there were some other way around it. After taking a few deep breaths, he charged like a bull through the throng, focusing his attention on those circled around Brolo.

Sweeping into the press of angry men, Stánwilte swung his weapon with all his might, catching a local around the neck with the cross-guard as if it were a shepherd's crook. Stánwilte pulled him, flapping, away from Brolo.

He went down hard, choking on his crushed throat. Before anyone else could react to the intrusion, Stánwilte stepped over him and grabbed a fistful of an unsuspecting Sinister's hair, who'd been launching a series of kicks into Brolo's sternum. Stánwilte pulled the Sinister's head back to expose his neck and effortlessly slid the sword across it, opening a gaping wound that instantly gushed with a tide of warm, sticky blood.

Tossing the lifeless body aside, Stánwilte shifted one hand back along his sword, holding firmly onto the centre of the blade. Keeping the other hand on its hilt, he spun and rammed it up into the chin of another Sinister with all the force he could muster. The ridiculous gurgling sound he emitted served only to make his death all the more undignified, given his surprised expression as he found six inches of steel piercing through his face.

Catching him off-guard, a brutish mountain of a man grabbed Stánwilte by the shoulders and threw him like a rag doll. He flew backwards into an awaiting gang of townsfolk, dislodging his sword from the skull of the dead Sinister. Disoriented, he lost his footing and fell arse-over-tit. An Alisgateian thumped him round the noggin with a cosh, while another shoved him down with such force his head almost snapped clean off his shoulders.

Stánwilte panted for breath with his cheek pressed against the cold stone paving of the square. The light grew dimmer, and his eyelids grew heavier, as the smoke-hazed silhouettes of the townsfolk and Sinisters edged in, ever so slowly, to surround him.

Chapter Twenty

Get Out of Town

Brolo shivered, groaning in the foetal position at the foot of the blood-stained steps of the town hall. Lawgismirin sat just a few short inches away, yet the tight-packed throttling he was currently on the receiving end of had rendered his chances of reaching it negligible.

Once again, letting his tongue flap unchecked had resulted in a steaming heap of trouble, and he held a strong suspicion it could very well be the last time it ever did so. As close to death as he supposed he was, he couldn't help rolling his tongue around his gums to check what teeth – if any – remained. He spat out a mouthful of saliva, thick with the salty, metallic taste of blood and dirt. Miraculously, his pearly whites all seemed to be intact.

Not much of a mercy, come the crunch, he thought. *And oh, what a crunch it's going to be.*

Hazily, he watched with swollen eyes as a boot rose before him, promising to turn his intestines into pâté. He braced himself again by scrunching up into what he hoped was a tight protective ball. Sadly, all he accomplished was a feeble parody of a spineless – in both senses of the word – hedgehog. Hopefully, sooner or later, someone would get bored of using their hands, feet, or blunted implements to beat him into a helpless pulp and go for something with a bit more edge to it. At least that would get things over and done with. Frustratingly, being the stickler for self-preservation he was, the inevitability of such an outcome caused Brolo to piss his breeches, drenching him in a shamefully warm pool.

Teeth gritted and breath held, he waited what seemed like millennia for the heavy boot to come crashing down into his stomach. Yet the blow did not come. Exhausted from tensing up his body for so long, and a little bored, Brolo dared to relax from his huddle, opening one bruised eye as far as he could to see what was causing the hold up. It took a while to focus on what was going on around him. What became evident, once his sight recovered, was how the foot that had been swooping in to connect with his belly was now twitching in a puddle of blood, along with the rest of its associated body.

Brolo's first response was relief that he may not have pissed himself and had instead been showered in another man's blood. Secondly, he realised that his attackers' focus had shifted away from him and onto someone else.

By King Arnheld's bejewelled nutsack, things just keep getting better! Brolo thought. Cursing the pain racking every joint and muscle in his body, he shuffled through the dirt and gore to where Lawgismirin sat abandoned, hoping not to draw any attention to himself. *Always your speciality, that. Idiot ...*

After the beating he'd taken, he could scarcely cling on to Lawgismirin's haft, yet a soothing wave washed over him upon feeling its weight once again. Breathing heavily, he made a gruelling attempt to stand, using the hammer to support him. He made it back on to his feet, but he had little time for taking it easy, his brief respite whipped away by the realisation of what had distracted the Sinisters and townsfolk from rearranging his internal organs into external ones.

Stánwilte was down and in serious trouble.

He seemed to have put in a last-ditch attempt to save Brolo's arse. Unluckily, he'd been left bloodied for his efforts, looking awfully dazed and shaky as he struggled to rise from his knees, sword out of reach. A menacing behemoth of a man loomed over him, steadily raising his fist to sky, winding up like a siege engine. Enemies flanked him, egging him on, shouting abuse and taunting Stánwilte's feeble efforts to stand, shaking their weapons in the air.

Things appeared dire for Stánwilte, but after a brief assessment of his state, Brolo decided one more blow from the muscle-bound beast wouldn't be sufficient to finish him off. Two, on the other hand, would do the job nicely, so that was Brolo's window of opportunity. He had to do *something*, but he also knew he had time to wait. Rushing in to intervene now would almost certainly result in Brolo himself taking the meaty strike. As sure as he was that Stánwilte would object to his logic, letting the captain take one for the team might get them both out of Alisgate alive.

Gripping the haft of his father's great war hammer tightly, Brolo prayed he wouldn't screw this all up and get them both killed in an altogether more brutal fashion than the one already lined up for them. This didn't help him feel much more optimistic. Therefore, he instead concentrated on the giant thug's hand, which hung in the air like a scorpion's tail, waiting for the faintest indication that it was about to lash out.

A splinter of a smile dared to form at the edge of Brolo's swollen lips. The two possible outcomes of his next move were painfully clear – either he would find the strength of nerve to do battle, or he'd be killed as a helpless fool no one would ever care to remember. Yet as he stood fingering the ancient glyphs carved upon the Nimudian sproak haft of Lawgismirin, blooded and bruised in the middle of a hostile town, for the first time in his whole life, Brolo truly *felt* dwarfish. The sensation of blood pumping through his veins as he spoilt for a fight against unlikely odds was something out of a dwarfish hearth-tale. Precisely the sort of thing Brolo imagined would've made his father proud.

Even as his fanciful thoughts worked him up into a lather, an overwhelming wave of power crashed through the hand gripping Lawgismirin. Surging up his arm, it coursed through his body in a flow of raw strength, screaming through his muscles like green fire and scouring the weakness from his body.

The world around Brolo juddered to a halt. He could sense his own heart beating, thudding slumberous in his ear. His vision stretched, each grain of time falling through the hourglass of reality into vast swaths of boundless possible moments, events appearing in his mind's eye before they'd taken place. Stranger still, he sensed it all in the subtle breath of the wind – in the gentle fluttering of a fly's wings as it hovered around the corpse of a fallen Sinister, in the caress of the giant's fingertips as his hand began its descent towards Stánwilte's face.

The moment had come. Letting himself be taken by the raging torrent of whatever power now dwelt within him, Bolo ran, hefting up Lawgismirin, cutting through time as a whispered blur, the world fighting to catch up with him.

***

Blink, and you would've missed the whole fight. Brolo himself wasn't fully aware of everything that had happened. When the dust settled, the events played out in his memories as if he'd witnessed everything from above, looming over the brawl like a spectre watching a cockpit matchup between Boris 'The Berserking' Bantam and a pack of woodlice with strongly held pacifist beliefs.

What parts of the brawl Brolo did remember played back with an unhelpful emerald distortion, splattered by lashings of crimson blood.

Through it all, the consummate ease with which the Brolo-shaped figure below dispatched his helpless victims stood out in his mind most vividly. He stood dumb as he played back the memory of lifting Lawgismirin with nary a wince of effort and bringing it around in a swirling arc, obliterating the skull of the big townsman in a burst of splinted bone and gore. The hammer had connected a mere heartbeat after the townsman had delivered his own devastating blow to Stánwilte.

The deadly impact should've exhausted all his strength. Yet power had flowed from his father's war hammer, engulfing his entire body in a shimmering green glow, rejuvenating him with a strength and speed he'd never dared to dream of.

Making good use of his speed, before so much as a splinter of the cracked shell of the giant's head had fallen to the ground, Brolo had taken out the next aggressor with a sweeping sidestep. Parrying the Sinister's half-hearted slash, Brolo had brought down Lawgismirin upon his head like a gruesome game of splat-the-rat. He'd crushed his victim's skull so utterly that it had left the distasteful impression of the Sinister's head having disappeared into his own shoulders. A neat trick, if the massive spurt of blood and flying brain tissue hadn't betrayed the illusion.

As the Sinister's headless corpse had hit the ground, an odd tingling sensation at the back of his mind had warned Brolo of danger coming at him from behind. Providing him with ample time to gracefully dance out of the path of a charging dwarfish townsman wielding a rusty pike. For his trouble, the dwarf had earned himself a pulverised spine, after Brolo had swung Lawgismirin with the full force his newfound strength could muster, smashing it into the dwarf's back. Brolo had felt the moment the dwarf's spine turned to jelly through the vibrations in Lawgismirin's haft, sensing the added crunch of ribs and the squelch of imploding internal organs.

A handful more of either bravely stupid or stupidly brave townsfolk and Ministers of Sin had made flaccid attempts to strike Brolo down in one way or another. Any who'd dared come close had been put down with swift, violent efficiency. Brolo had sent the remaining attackers screaming down the nearest street, fleeing the murky green spectre wreaking havoc amongst them. Many had fallen to the ground and begun pleading for mercy, up to their knees in the coagulating blood of their own dead kin.

To Brolo, the whole fight seemed to have lasted for approximately a dozen minutes, but the cold reality was that the last man to die had hit the ground only forty seconds after Brolo had smashed the big man's skull, spreading his cerebrum about the square like wedding confetti caught in the wind.

Brolo howled, summoning his inner beast, daring someone to challenge him. Never had he felt so alive. Never had he so yearned for blood. He stood triumphantly amid the shattered bodies of those who'd been foolish enough to stand in his way, and now not a soul willing to test their mettle against him remained. For the time being, at least, the fight was over. A hollow tingle crept down his spine. A shudder of loss, as if Lawgismirin had sensed the cessation of combat, draining the ecstasy of battle from his body, rendering him a pale shadow of the formidable warrior he had been before.

With the emerald fire leaving him, Brolo began to sense his old self returning. Young, sly, suitably arrogant, yet ever so afraid. The vague recollections of the last few minutes whirled nauseatingly around in his head, causing him to drop Lawgismirin to the ground in growing horror at his actions.

His body ached all over. His clothes bore stains of blood from head to toe. He fell to his knees to throw up, finding himself vomiting onto a squashed eyeball still attached to the hammer-crushed skull of a Sinister.

As he added the contents of his stomach to the unpleasant soup of bodily fluids amassed upon the stones of Alisgate Square, a heavy hand fell on his right shoulder, another reaching under his left armpit to lift him to his feet.

'We need to go, now!' coughed Stánwilte into Brolo's ear, leading him the first few steps along the street, heading towards the eastern side of town.

Brolo's head rolled around like a spinning wheel when Stánwilte left him to walk by his own will – not an easy task, as he struggled to make out which way was up, let alone follow the captain out of Alisgate.

What exactly had overcome him back in the town square eluded Brolo beyond all the rational explanations he could fathom, which in the state he was currently in, wasn't exceptionally challenging. Still, as he staggered down the blurry street, occasionally he caught Stánwilte looking back to fix him with a grim stare – not one of care, but fear.

As his senses began clicking back into place, Brolo was able to gather that in their haste, they were abandoning their four horses back at the stables. Although the townsfolk had been quelled within the square, fighting their way back to the western gate was likely to bring them face to face with a larger group of fresh opposition. Whatever power had engulfed him certainly couldn't be trusted to save their hides a second time from being tanned and turned into new leather shoes, replacing the ones used to kick them to death. Thankfully, Stánwilte made a habit of keeping their supply of coins about his person, so once they hit another town or village, they should be able to resupply with fresh mounts and gear. If not, what should've been a couple days of gentle riding to the capital would become a tedious slog on foot.

Nightfall was fast approaching by the time they made it to Alisgate's east gate and the continuation of the ancient road to Spyrata. They had fortunately been able to make their escape down crooked side streets and grubby, unlit alleyways without any further challenge to their persons. Oddly enough, the eastern side of Alisgate had been eerily devoid of life – until they reached the two gruff-looking guards leaning against the wooden gate, barring their way to freedom. The guards' shadows shivered in the gathering gloom, meagrely dished out by the solitary torch aflame between them.

By a miraculous stroke of luck, the gate itself stood open. Brolo could tell this was a big relief to Stánwilte, as he huddled behind a conveniently placed stack of empty ale casks, waiting in awkward silence for the captain to finish planning their next move.

'I'm going to assume casually strolling out through the gate isn't an option? Maybe it would help if we fluttered our lashes at them as we passed,' Brolo ventured, hoping he could ease the tension with humour and maybe help Stánwilte stop looking as if he were sucking on a lemon while having a grapefruit shoved up his arse. Naturally, of course, he was mistaken.

'Shut up,' whispered Stánwilte through a grit-toothed snarl. 'You got us into this fucking mess, let me deal with getting us out.'

Brolo was about to argue that he'd already dealt with getting them out of trouble back in town, but in his current state, Stánwilte could apparently smell incoming sarcasm fifty leagues away. He fixed Brolo with one of his hallmark *'Speak, and I'll wear your intestines as a lovely new scarf to keep me warm at night, and maybe even turn your kidneys into a fashionable pair of earrings'* looks. Thus, Brolo prudently kept his mouth shut.

That *not* said, whatever plan Stánwilte was hoping to pull out of his arse, Brolo wished he would come up with it damn quickly. He must be aware that the closer it crept towards total darkness, the more likely it became that the town gates would close for the night, making escape a tad trickier.

'Wait here, be still, and be fucking silent,' Stánwilte said. Drawing a small dagger from his sword-belt, he slithered stealthily into the shadows of the oncoming night without so much as a syllable of further explanation.

Oh, great. I'll sit here all nice and snug with my thumb up my arse then, shall I? brooded Brolo, peering out through the thin gaps between the casks in a futile attempt to view what Stánwilte was up to.

A brisk wind blew through the town, carrying a wave of dead leaves and soggy straw, sending the rusted sign of a burnt-out tavern swinging with the horrible screech of someone buggering a pig with a mace. A lung-tearing cough echoed out from one of the guards, who swiftly took a hearty swig from the wineskin hanging loosely around his neck. It took a few mouthfuls for him to get his breath back, before he proceeded to hawk up enough phlegm to form a small bloody-green puddle at his feet.

Time trickled by tediously without a peep of action. Brolo, fed up of waiting for Stánwilte to act, was rapidly approaching giving him up as captured or incapacitated elsewhere. As he considered trying his own luck with waltzing out the gate, the wind blew a second and drastically more violent time.

From behind his makeshift fort of empty casks, Brolo saw sod all and heard little more above the rustling swell of the breeze. Sighing, he brushed aside his hair to reveal his ears. Sure enough, once he concentrated as hard as he could, he could hear a muffled gurgling sound seeping beneath the dying wind. Even as he winced, the gurgling was abruptly stilled, quickly followed by the tell-tale thud of something heavy hitting the ground.

A moment of utter stillness passed as Brolo prayed to avert the bad omen the sound of one death implied. Thankfully, the thud was swiftly followed by another strain of someone choking for air. Then came the stomach-churning sound of a bucket of used washing water splashing to the ground from a high window, implying that a jugular had sprung something more than a tiny leak. Another ominous thud rang out through the night.

Brolo sat, frozen. Heavy footsteps drew closer to the gutted-out inn, splashing through a deep puddle along their way, all notions of stealth forgotten as they stopped short of the mound of empty casks.

'You still coming with me, or what?' asked Stánwilte, in a snappy yet nervous tone. Standing from behind the casks, Brolo pointedly dusted himself off. If Stánwilte wanted to act like a puckered arsehole, Brolo would enjoy fishing around for his sensitive new nerve, hoping to snag it on his hook.

'Look, I understand you're more than a little disgruntled by today's events, and I apologise for my part in the minor scuffle in the square, but don't be ashamed for needing a little help back there. You're only huma—'

'Sometimes, being *only human* is better than the alternative!' Stánwilte shouted. He took a deep breath, slowly releasing his grip on the hilt of his sword. 'Now, if you wouldn't mind finding it within yourself to shut up for a moment, let's leave this bloody place, shall we? Don't you worry – we'll discuss this further once we're out of this shithole and we've caught up with Smiggly and Wilkhelm ... if they haven't managed to get themselves killed.'

Mouth flapping open at this insult against his heritage by his previously supportive captain, Brolo watched Stánwilte stride back towards the gate without waiting to see if he followed, stomping heavily through the sludge and shit, muttering curses into the night.

For a moment, Brolo seriously considered telling Stánwilte to go pickle his tiny gherkin in a vat of spiced vinegar, before packing in this whole bloody journey and returning to Peplyshaw without a second's thought about the fate of his former companions. However, he decided he was above throwing his cards on the table in surrender. Confronting Stánwilte's ignorance would only serve to irk the git more, therefore providing grater entertainment. Smiling vindictively, Brolo grabbed Lawgismirin and followed his captain out of Alisgate.

His nerve faltered briefly as he passed the corpses of the two guards. Their throats had been … well, not *slit* – that would imply a delicate yet fatal cut drawn smoothly across the width of the throat. This, however, looked like the hack-and-slash handiwork of someone who'd attempted to portion out a few scraggly ends of lamb on their first day of a butchery apprenticeship, but had made the classic rookie mistake of practicing on a live specimen.

'I thought I'd help cure him of his cough,' said Stánwilte, as he stood outside the gate, watching Brolo warily.

'Remind me to never ask you for medical advice,' Brolo muttered with perfunctory sarcasm, still seething too much to enjoy his own wit.

Remembering that the bulk of their possessions had been left behind at the stables, undoubtedly forfeit to the people of Alisgate, Brolo decided to quickly rummage through the corpses of the guards to rid them of their unnecessary earthly belongings. He found a few coins, a small Dragonian pendant and a rusty dagger. Meagre offerings, but with no horses or supplies, anything that could be sold might prove useful down the road.

Dreading the long night ahead, Brolo pocketed the paltry items and followed Stánwilte out through the gate. He kicked loose stones, cursing the Dragona, as they went to find Smiggly and Wilkhelm, leaving the chaos of Alisgate behind.

CHAPTER TWENTY-ONE

A CAPITAL IDEA

'I've had enough of your excuses, Brolo. After everything we've been through, you still seem to have this deeply-ingrained hankering to let your tongue get us all killed!'

Perhaps, upon reflection, exploding at the dwelf while stomping down the road away from Alisgate's murderous inhabitants hadn't been a sage move, but the urge to vent had proven too great for Stánwilte to resist.

'This isn't the first time your impulsive actions have brought our violent deaths a hair's breadth away – and you can take that fucking look off your face, I don't care if you *do* always somehow manage to worm your way out of these situations!' Stánwilte had wagged a condemnatory finger at Brolo. 'Look, I despise religious fanatics as much as the next casual sinner, but you can't expect to burst into every crud-encrusted town of yokels and slander their beliefs without facing some extreme ramifications. You'd get a better outcome if you smothered yourself in honey and broke into a beehive with the intention of whipping all the workers into open revolt, exposing the injustices they suffer at the mandibles of an absolute monarchy! It's not just unrealistic, it's dangerous. Peasants are comfortable and safe in their little worlds of fancy. Piss on whatever helps them sleep at night and you risk them spilling out like cheesed-off ants whose hill has been knocked over.'

Looking back on it, Stánwilte's scornful barrage hadn't come out sounding quite as tactful as it had done in his head. In fact, now his rage had subsided a touch, Stánwilte kicked himself at how much of a condescending arsehole he'd been, especially when resorting to insect-laden language.

'That's your problem right there,' Brolo had hissed. 'How long has it been since you first arrived in Peplyshaw? Five, maybe six years? All that time you've lived and worked with us, yet you still believe that you're better than us all, don't you? Go on, you bastard, try to deny it!'

Damningly, Stánwilte had been unable to refrain from dropping his eyes to the ground.

'I've seen it on your face a hundred times. Your superior glare as you step cautiously through the shit-laden streets, afraid a splat of mud may soil your pricey city-made boots! The way you eat your meals alone, as if our measly gruel isn't refined enough for your sophisticated palate! You're all airs and haughty graces! Well, I have news for you, Stánwilte Stángefeall – you're stuck with us!' As if to punctuate the finality of this statement, Brolo had spat a gobful of saliva onto the dirt. 'Once ... *if* this is ever over, and we somehow make it home, I dare say that before too long you'll be back to wasting away in your dingy solar, all alone, pondering what could've been. You may as well come to terms with the fact your precious king has abandoned you to your fate. You're now as lowly as the rest of us. Accept it before it's too late, or you may discover the people you scoffed at when they welcomed you with open arms will no longer wish to accept *you!*'

After ten minutes of fraught silence, they found their two travelling companions waiting for them a mile or so up the dirt road, with young Smiggly sleeping soundly in a grassy patch beside the Qhondik as if all was as normal. Wilkhelm was pacing up and down beside him, furiously biting at the skin around his fingernails. When he clapped eyes upon Stánwilte and Brolo trudging along the road, he gasped a dramatic sigh of relief and kicked Smiggly awake with a touch too much force. Clearly, the prospect of leading Smiggly along the path back to Peplyshaw without Stánwilte's guardianship had troubled him. On the other hand, the fat purse of gold Stánwilte had safely tucked away, which Wilkhelm was ignorant of rightfully being his, could very well have been his primary concern.

Wilkhelm's ecstatic smile slipped from his face like steaming cow muck flung at a freshly cleaned window as soon as Stánwilte barged past him, knocking him out of the way with a shove of the shoulder. Nevertheless, unable to resist temptation, Wilkhelm opened his cavernous trap.

'So, you made it out—'

'Oh, just shit off,' Brolo snapped from behind Stánwilte.

'Once again, the Wit of the West has come to dazzle us all with the sharpness of his mind and tongue!' Wilkhelm said. 'I'd seriously consider seeking a refund for the whetstones you use to hone your deadly retorts. They're obviously so soft they could very well be sponges.'

'By Arnheld's regal arse ... why did I receive exile instead of execution?' Stánwilte groaned to himself, before raising his voice. 'Wilkhelm, shut up. Smiggly, get up off the sodding floor. You're going to follow me in utter silence to Alisgate Tor, which, before you ask, is approximately another a league northeast of here. Once we arrive, we're going to patch ourselves up and make our beds for the night. I don't care to hear your petty bickering – all that needs to be said has been spoken. So, and may the Flame strengthen my resolve otherwise, can we please peacefully put today's events behind us?'

'Oh, and I'm not welcome, am I?' spat Brolo, obviously spoiling for a fight.

Stánwilte, racked with anxieties over what he'd recently borne witness to, suffering from rapidly waning patience, came teeteringly close to obliging him.

'Your presence was implied,' he said curtly, before turning his back on Brolo and storming off into the night, the soupy Qhondik road slurping at his feet. Brolo, however, squelched after him.

'Implied? I have no doubt you're trying to imply *something*, but if you headed back into Alisgate, rifled through the corpses and hunted down the testicles you've so obviously lost, maybe you'd be able to say it to my face!'

This insult proved to be the straw that not only broke the camel's back, but trampled upon it, pissed on its twitching remains and laughed as it died in a crippled heap.

Survival instincts seemingly kicking in, Wilkhelm muttered a string of excuses and made off quickly down the Qhondik. Smiggly – following the precedent set during previous altercations, which was one of simple obliviousness to the impending danger – stood gawking, his eyes wide and glassy, akin to a fluffy rabbit caught short amid a pack of wolves. Stánwilte was sure his ears would've flopped down if they'd been as pointy as Brolo's, which Stánwilte was imagining ripping off and shoving up that bulbous dwarfish nose.

As could be expected, the night spent atop Alisgate Tor was a turbulent one. Vicious, rabid arguments had prolonged their journey to the isolated hill. The most deeply cutting home-truths had come spilling out in hateful splurges, as the pair sought to disembowel each other with their words. Neither Stánwilte nor Brolo had been able to resist scooping through the bloody organs of the other's emotions, flinging their steaming offal back and forth. After they climbed the perilously steep peak, through the utter darkness of a moonless night, Stánwilte could discern the murky glow of torchlight from Alisgate a short distance behind, which somehow seemed more peaceful than the windswept outcrop.

The next morning, Stánwilte was as furious with himself as he had been with Brolo a few sleepless hours previously. How had he allowed himself to become enraged by such infantile goading? He sat in a brooding silence as the sun climbed up from behind the horizon, creeping into the orange-tinged sky like a young ward sneaking back from a night spent smooching a pretty girl in the village tavern, hoping to have his lord's breakfast ready before he woke up. Stánwilte paid little attention as the sun scattered its rays of glistening light upon the dew-kissed fields surrounding Alisgate Tor. Instead, he stared at Brolo's hammer with an anxious rumbling in the pit of his stomach, forcing vivid flashbacks from that long-ago morning down to the darkest corner of his mind, locking them away in the shadows.

Once the sun had risen proper, and the three lads had woken, they wordlessly fought their way through a chewy breakfast of dried meat. After collecting what paltry scraps of their gear remained, they marched off without a peep, treading sluggishly through the damp grass on the final stretch to Spyrata.

Four gruelling days of endless road followed. Four long, awkward, drizzly, foot-blistering days of traipsing through village upon gloomy village, hill upon knackering hill, puddle upon sodding puddle, before they finally caught their first real glimpse of the capital. The milky-white walls of Spyrata loomed over the surrounding countryside, Gizzards Bay nestled at their feet, the five dizzying Towers of the Crown emerging like stalagmites from behind them. It was a view Stánwilte had beheld many times before. One, deep within his heart of hearts, he'd wished to see again every day since his unjust exile.

The road they were following led directly to the main gate in the west of the city – the Toll Gate, named for the large bell hanging above it, rather than the tolls collected there for entering the city to trade. Most traffic flowed through the Toll Gate, so it was heavily guarded. Hoping to avoid attention, and the slim risk of an old soldier recognising him, Stánwilte took a right turn onto the dusty track sweeping down towards the smaller Dock Gate to the south.

Wilkhelm grumbled over the delay caused by taking a longer route, boasting of his eagerness to chat up some fancy city girls. Smiggly waffled on about the awe-inspiring sight of the capital. Brolo kept his head down, kicking up dust as he walked.

As predicted, they were able to enter through the Dock Gate without stirring up any interest from the two fresh-faced boys Stánwilte supposed passed for guards these days. They wasted no time blending into the hive of activity congesting the wharfs by Gizzards Bay, slipping between dockhands and merchants peddling molluscs doused in vinegar. The salty cocktail of the Lepra Sea, blended with the sweat of the men who laboured under the glaring sun, the pong of rotten fish guts left in open-top vats to ferment, and the eye-stinging smoke wafting from the tall huts in which the disembowelled fish were being cured, made it a thoroughly unpleasant environment. Never mind the general hubbub of the dockyard, the level of crime in the area, or the intimate proximity to the No-Lights District, named as a piece of advice for anyone who considered spending their coin there. Regardless, lodge by Gizzards Bay they would. It happened to be its closeness to the whore-dens that made it a desirable place to reside – though not for the obvious reasons.

'I've made arrangements for us to stay at The Slimy Haddock, on the left down Shuck Street,' said Stánwilte, pointing through the bustling crowd to the entrance of a narrow alleyway. 'Ask for Vyvwym Cu'Mal. Tell him you're with the old First – he'll know what you mean.' Pausing, Stánwilte studied the expressions of his party. 'Why do you look so worried? Vyvwym and I go way back. The chap used to be a tracker in the army, a friend from before I earned my promotion to the Royal Guard. Elves were always best for the role, especially in the marshes down south ...' He cleared his throat. 'Look, that doesn't matter. Just do as I say and trust him. I'll be joining you soon enough. I simply need to seek out a couple of old contacts and arrange an important meeting.'

Brolo fixed him with a suspicious glare. 'Contacts? What bloody contacts? You can't seriously abandon us to our own devices straight away! Who's going to look after Smiggly? Who's going to stop Wilkhelm from getting himself mugged? Me, I presume. How should we provide for ourselves? Have the fabulous duo of Lord Bottom-Smooch and the Phantom Nostril-Picker dance on a street corner for Silver Geese? We can't simply sit in the corner of an inn, nursing a cup of water between the three of us, until you grace us with your mug again. We'll need at least some money to tide us over.'

Stánwilte had wasted enough of his time on petty arguments with Brolo. His plans needed hammering out before nightfall. Adding to his problems, Smiggly had wandered off to gawk at dockworkers going about their chores. An innocent enough activity, up until he'd been approached by a lady of ... *conspicuous occupation*, who he was now chirpily conversing with.

'Here's a few Duckies. Get yourselves some grub and a round of drinks,' he said, shoving a handful of coins into Brolo's palm. 'Don't worry, you'll all be at this meeting. I'll need you there for – oh, let's call it *dramatic effect*. Understood? I'll be back in two shakes of a thistle. In the meantime, would you be a lamb and explain the birds and the bees to Smiggly? Thanks. Bye!'

Having swiftly discharged his problems, Stánwilte rushed off towards the No-Lights District to call in several favours he'd been saving for a plan exactly like the one he now had in mind.

Chapter Twenty-Two

And into the Garden Comes the Spider

Yilonia had worked out the maths. If her next fifteen immediate descendants gave up on cutting their hair for the entirety of their lives, assuming they all survived to a ripe old age of eighty, then the sixteenth in line could twist their collective hair together into a rope. If things went well, it would be strong enough for them to use to climb out of the window and make it far enough down the tower that they wouldn't make too much of a mess when they inevitably ran out of rope and splattered over the street below.

It had been another tedious afternoon stuck in her room, locked away in one of the Towers of the Crown, with nothing to do other than entertain herself with ideas of escape, ridiculous as they were. Frustratingly, Yilonia couldn't even blame anyone other than herself for having her freedom withdrawn immediately after it had been granted.

The guard whom she'd had the unfortunate pleasure of bumping into had at least let her walk unshackled as he'd marched her silently back to captivity. However, he'd clutched the pommel of his sword, as if daring her to test his leniency. Yilonia had considered making a second dash for freedom, but she'd noticed the badge of the Inquisition upon her captor's breast and decided one of Relfread's cronies wasn't worth trifling with.

Yilonia had no doubt she'd be dragged before him again before too long. She'd certainly have plenty to ask him. More so once she'd puzzled out the mystery behind the collection of books she'd found during her little escapade. They must've belonged to Relfread, which would certainly go towards explaining his fascination with the trivial details of her … northern expedition.

It seemed so long ago now. Yet each time her thoughts slipped back to those events, when searing dragon's fire had burnt her dreams to ashes, Yilonia was powerless to prevent tears from welling in her eyes.

Relfread had implied the people knew about her brush with the beast, so why was he keeping her hidden? What else could he want from her? His library implied he had a vested interest in the topic, yet her experiences certainly didn't qualify her as an expert in the mysteries of dragon-lore. *I only ran away from the flaming thing,* she thought, frustrated. *I don't know anything important!*

Yilonia slumped down onto her bed before the whirlwind of questions gathered enough force to knock her into delirium. She stared up at the ceiling, rubbing her forehead, as she tried to force her mind to sift through the cryptic answers.

Why had the Dragonian Inquisition been revived? Centuries had passed since its disbanding. Surely a live dragon sighting alone wouldn't have been cause enough. If anything, mustering an army to march north and deal with the threat to the kingdom and its ruling classes would've been the rational solution. But then, her father had been grumbling for years about the king's illness and ineffectualness at court.

Tiny pieces of a vast puzzle began to fit into place. Judging by the number of guards bearing the Inquisition's badge, they hadn't found it hard to fill the ranks of the outdated religious institution. Which was an odd situation on its own, as the Dragonian church had been floundering for a long, long time.

A single explanation hit Yilonia slap-bang in the face, hard enough to send her teeth chattering. *That slithering bastard has milked my suffering to convert the public from the Circle to the Dragona! It would explain why I'm being kept alive yet hidden away. I'm a figurehead for his little conversion rallies. Worse, I'm being treated like a snot-nosed child – better seen alive occasionally, but not heard!*

It was precisely how her toad of a father had treated her back at home. She'd tossed aside a privileged life as an earl's daughter to escape his clutches. She wasn't about to let herself be taken for the same kind of pony ride by some jumped-up, prune-faced bishop!

Yet ... there had to be something deeper going on. Some game Relfread was lining up his pieces for. A rejuvenated Dragonian faith would provide a bountiful source of pawns. The only important question was: why?

As if summoned by thought alone, the hefty door to her room groaned open to admit a disturbingly sanguine Relfread. Yilonia rose from her bed and stood before him, striking what she hoped was a defiant pose.

'My! I hadn't realised we'd been so generous when we found you a chamber,' he wheezed. 'That must be why you were so eager to waste all your time and effort and get yourself confined here.' A smile as thin as fractured glass splintered his shadowy face, shrouded as it was by the hood of his black robes.

'I'd hardly call myself a voluntary hermit,' Yilonia replied, her voice sweet with mockery, her words a spoonful of honey coating the angry wasp hidden within. She spread the skirts of her garish dress in a flashy curtsy, maintaining fierce eye contact with Relfread while doing so.

'Oh, I would, so-called Yilonia Risúe of Stunheath.'

Yilonia's heart dropped to her bowels.

He knows! But how?

'Don't look at me like that, you petulant bitch!' Relfread shrieked. 'Did you honestly believe we wouldn't investigate every detail you revealed to us? Girl, I control the Inquisition! This is exactly the kind of work we do – rooting out truths from the vast midden of falsehoods. My Sinisters have eyes and ears spread like weeds throughout the whole of Uprynenos. Therefore, the name of any craftsman in any town I care to ask for is quite within my reach.' He drew himself up, eyes flashing like the lightning-torn sky of a cataclysmic storm. 'I'm sure you could imagine my surprise when I heard that there is no blacksmith in Stunheath, nay, anywhere in Trisindall, with the family name of Risúe!' He removed his shrivelled hands from the murky confines of his robes and tapped his chin with a bony finger, as if in deep contemplation. 'Oh, there was a Master Ulof and a Master Witsudor, who'd been blacksmiths in Stunheath for seven and twelve years respectively. But you would already know that, wouldn't you?'

Yilonia sat on the edge of her bed, fisting her hands so tightly her long nails started to draw blood from her palms. Relfread wandered over to the balcony, pondering the view of dusk peacefully descending upon the capital. She eyed him coldly.

A nudge is all it would take…

'Alas,' he began, not showing the slightest awareness of what was running through Yilonia's mind, 'despite my search for a Master Risúe proving futile, I did happen upon an interesting story drifting from Stunheath. A tale of a young woman – a lord's daughter, no less! Rumour has it, this scamp fled from her father's castle over a minor … *moral* disagreement quite some time ago. Sadly, she hasn't been seen nor heard from since.'

Resting both hands on the balustrade, he sagged visibly as he gazed out over Spyrata. His usual glass-gargling crackle of a voice took on an earnest tone, which complimented him as poorly as Yilonia assumed her revoltingly flowery dress suited her.

'In front of such delicate innocence, I couldn't bring myself to repeat some of the utterances the girl's father used to express his anger towards his errant bratling. *Absolutely fuming with blood-filled rage!* Yes. I think such a phrase conveys the point well enough. Which is a distressing thought, as it's the tamest description in a gallery of so many colourful portraits of fury painted for me. I certainly wouldn't want to be there when she eventually returns. No, by the Flame, I would not!'

Before Yilonia could gather her wits enough to seek escape, Relfread scurried over to her and gripped her cheeks tightly in his hand. Squeezing with a strength no man so frail should possess, he forced her to stare into the smoky eyes lurking beneath his hood.

'Now, come to think of it, the description given to me of this particular young woman would paint her with, oh ... your height, your age, your eye colour, your juvenile insolence, and perhaps most condemning of all, your name, Yilonia Essiun!'

Yilonia yanked her face from Relfread's grasp and bolted up from her bed. Her position was precarious at best, yet having already figured out her importance to Relfread's plans – whatever they may be – she could at least consider herself safe from being dragged back to her father, as the king or any noble would be obliged to do if they were to discover her. Relfread hadn't gone through all the effort of confirming her identity just to have her sent home. No. She could smell blackmail coming from a league away.

The way Yilonia saw it, there were only a handful of options available to her, with the majority of those involving violence – which would lead to a rather unsavoury outcome if she made a mess of her escape. It would be dangerous to poke the metaphorical bear, especially when this particular bear had some deeply personal information that he could choose to drop like a vast post-hibernation turd on her head at any moment. Sadly, maintaining an air of belligerence was the only choice that would keep her from dancing along to Relfread's tune long enough to either escape or unravel his plans. Meekness, feigned or otherwise, would see her jigging at the pull of a string in short order.

'Pardon my impertinence,' she said, folding her arms, 'but can you blame me for withholding certain personal information? After almost dying in the wastelands of Ánad, I awoke to find myself locked away in the Palace of the United of all places, with no explanation as to the reasoning behind my confinement, other than repeated questions by your minions. Excuse me if I find it a tad rich to be scolded for concealing details by a man so extraordinarily shady that he must have to discourage people from lounging under his shadow on a summer's day!'

'You should be counting your sweet blessings, child, for you never caught a whiff of a thorough Inquisition questioning. If you would like for that to change, then pray, carry on as you are.' Relfread's joints cracked like roasted pork rind as he took a seat by the cold fireplace with a sweep of his robes. 'I fear we've been too lenient with your complete disregard for gratitude. Have you not been kept well? Food, clothes and freshly drawn baths have all been at your disposal. Not a hair on your head has been harmed. You ought to realise these are all simple privileges that can be withdrawn at any time I command.'

A tinge of annoyance wriggled in Relfread's voice, but otherwise, he remained composed. If Yilonia was going to crack answers out of him, she'd have to settle into her own stone-faced composure before calling his bluff.

'Ha! You can shove your so-called *privileges* where your precious Flame doesn't burn,' she said, tossing her hair over her shoulder. 'This little parley has gone on for far too long. Go on, you know who I am now. I demand you notify my father of my whereabouts and return me to him forthwith. While you're at it, have a gaggle of serving girls sent to me. I require help preparing for the trip home. It's about time I had a few capable maids see to my needs, as befits my station, wouldn't you agree?' Tilting her head, she bared her teeth in a grin. 'I'm sure the king would. In fact, I'm sure my father would be interested in having an audience with His Majesty once his rage eases enough to hear my story. We've had our *moral disagreements* in the past, but knowing my father, he would take any offence against me as if you'd come into his home and relieved yourself upon his supper.'

In truth, her father likely saw her as nothing other than damaged property. The knowledge stung, as it always did, even after the many years Yilonia had endured her father's callous disposition. Still, the truth of it remained – if anyone was going to cause Yilonia Essiun pain and suffering, it had better be Lord Essiun holding the whip.

Unnervingly, in lieu of flapping his mouth like a trout, positively frothing at the gills at the sheer brazenness of her demands, Relfread merely clapped his hands together, cackling. 'I admire your spirit, girl, I really do. However, I'm afraid you are not in a position to make demands. Nor can you be trusted to stay within the palace. Alternative arrangements for your accommodation have already been made.'

A gentle tap on the door preceded the entrance of the serpentine Inquisitor, followed by four burly guards in plate armour, the Dragonian badge taking pride of place on their shields. The Inquisitor brushed a hand through his slick black hair, delicately working any stray strands back into place, as he strolled over to Yilonia. Quite ridiculously, he bowed stiffly before her, reaching out his hand as if seriously expecting she would take it. Yilonia expected that if she were to do so, his fingers would wrap tightly around hers, squeezing like a python coiling around its victim.

'My lady, the advice I give to you shall only be offered this once,' he said, his greasy hand still suspended in the air. 'Come with us now without struggle or argument, and you shall be led from here without restraint. As much as your freshly exposed nobility entitles you to certain comforts once you're safely within your new rooms, I must inform you that any attempt to escape while we make our way through the palace will be met with a gauntleted fist loosening your teeth. A second attempt shall be followed by the tendons at the back of your chicken-like ankles being cut. I will personally take care of this punishment if needs be.' He raised his head, pale blue eyes boring into her own. 'Make no mistake, it truly is a nasty little injury. After suffering such a cut, I've seen men buckle into weeping babes, howling themselves hoarse for their mothers. Therefore, I'm afraid any vocal display of pain shall have to result in your jaw being broken. It's the most efficient way to stop the screaming, you understand. I hope I've made myself clear.'

'Crystal,' said Yilonia curtly.

The failure of her briefly held plans had left her caught between a barnacle-encrusted hull and the harbour wall. Yet she might salvage some small good from a change in location. Now the prospect of being forgotten about in some dingy cell wasn't up for consideration, she had ample time to free herself, and perhaps even worm her way into discovering the details behind Relfread's machinations.

'Considering my imminent departure, should I tidy my things, or will you have someone take care of it for me?' she asked. 'Although I wouldn't choose the maid charged with cleaning up your study, Relfread. I'd be loath to call it a library, such as it was – dusty old books strewn about the place, without a care in the world for their spines. I must confess, however, you have an extremely interesting collection. Very informative, if I may say so.'

In the corner of her eye, Yilonia caught a wisp of a nod from within Relfread's hood. Before she could consider its meaning, she was flat on her arse, warm, metallic liquid trickling from her nose and into her gaping mouth, leaving blotchy red stains as it dripped over her dress. Yilonia couldn't say she would lament the loss.

'Consider this a warning that our dear Inquisitor will follow through with his threats, my child,' said Relfread, as he shook his head ruefully. He turned to leave but stopped at the door. 'Just get her to the cathedral without a fuss. We don't want any unfortunate scenes. Now, I have an appointment I'm very keen to keep, so I expect not to hear any stories of this while I'm out. Inquisitor Siskin, she's yours until I return.'

With those parting words, Relfread disappeared.

Dizzy from the punch, Yilonia tried to spit at Siskin while he and a guardsman dragged her off the floor. In her present state, it only resulted in her dribbling bloody phlegm. Her nose burnt as if she'd fallen face-first into a bed of glowing embers.

She would make them pay. She didn't know how, but she was more determined than ever to cause Relfread's downfall. So much the better they intended to keep a closer eye on her. She'd make damn well sure she kept Relfread occupied with petty arguments and whimsical requests each day, granting her the time to wreak havoc on his plans.

Time was all she needed.

CHAPTER TWENTY-THREE

INNUENDO

'I want to ride her horse!' groaned Smiggly for the fourteenth time. 'She told me it would be the most pleasurable Chick I'd ever spend!'

'No!' barked Brolo.

'But why not?' Smiggly pouted, folding his arms.

'Because your mother would crack my skull with a rolling pin if she found out, that's why,' said Brolo, steering Smiggly through the bustling dockyard. Wilkhelm, who was snickering like a snake peddling rotten apples at premium prices, certainly wasn't helping.

'How could you deny me this? The kindly lady guaranteed me the ride of my life!' Smiggly cried. 'My father taught me how to handle a pony, so maybe I could show her a thing or two. Can't say she looked like she spent much time in the saddle, anyways.'

'Depends on what kind of establishment she works at,' Wilkhelm whispered into Brolo's ear. 'And I bet they charge extra for *that* particular service, too!' He howled with laughter, slapping his thigh, as if he'd witnessed the king's own jester perform his infamous *Hide-the-Sausage* trick – a stunt supposedly so funny and outright scandalous that at least one spectator died during each performance. Brolo pondered whether the remarkably uncouth tastes of the kingdom's nobles said all you needed to know about those born to positions of power, but nonetheless wished Wilkhelm would choke to death on his own glee.

Leaving the nostril-offending smells and coarse language behind them, they followed Stánwilte's directions and headed down the shady, unwelcoming Shuck Street. It was scarcely wide enough for two wee carts to pass each other without grinding against one of the foul-smelling oyster stalls or faded, grimy shops, which, despite the lack of trade wandering by, appeared to be open. The merest specks of daylight pierced through their jettied upper floors, plunging the generously titled *street* into a dreary gloom. Gradually, the aroma of fish guts dissipated, replaced by the pong of soured wine and the rotting filth of carelessly dumped chamber pots. When caught in the sparse light, the cobblestones glistened with the slime of decaying bodily waste.

The whole street seemed to leer at Brolo, eyeing him up like one of the brooding, scar-faced thugs who surely waited in the shadows. Through the silence, Brolo sensed he wasn't the only member of the group finding the suffocating confines close to snipping his last claustrophobia-ridden nerve.

Finally, backtracking from a junction that split off into three unappealing, rat-infested backstreets, Wilkhelm caught the creaking of The Slimy Haddock's rust-crusted sign. It was sequestered between a butcher's shop, which displayed a disproportionate amount of greenish offal in its window, and a closed store called Phwoarmongers that appeared to sell various paintings of a risqué nature.

Hesitant as he was to go inside, Brolo found himself seduced by the thought of some much-needed wine and the knowledge Stánwilte shared some history with the proprietor. Nonetheless, he still feigned a loud cough, before shoving Wilkhelm over the threshold.

Brolo and Smiggly waited for Wilkhelm's surprised cursing to die down, listening for the sound of a good old-fashioned tavern kick-in enacted by upset regulars. When, regretfully, the squeal of a horrifically injured Wilkhelm never came, Brolo led Smiggly into a musty, squat common room populated only by a lanky elven fellow with squinty eyes and lumps of scar tissue where his ears should've been. He stood glaring at them as he polished a tankard behind the bar. Wilkhelm sat in a heap on the floor, rubbing his chin and scowling at Brolo.

'Afternoon, good sir,' Brolo said. If there was one thing he'd learnt over the last few years of his life, it was to always start things off on the best foot possible when commencing a new relationship with a barkeep. They'd more than likely be seeing the very worst of you at some point. Being openly rude to those working within a rough establishment such as this one would characteristically end with your purse being nicked. Unless you were monumentally offensive, in which case your throat could end up with a worse nick, moments before your still-twitching corpse was tossed into the nearest river. 'A drink of your finest wine for me, whichever ale you empty your slops into for my chum on the floor, and a small cup of something brown and frothy for the young lad.'

The elf gave them a soul-searing eyeing up, as if weighing the hassle of their custom, then shrugged and began to prepare some drinks without a single utterance. Undeterred by his silence, Brolo attempted to revive their swiftly dwindling rapport.

'Nice little place you have here. Very ... very ...'

'Sticky,' snapped Wilkhelm, rubbing his cheek. He'd lost a layer of skin to the floor, which had gained the almost glue-like quality only attained through years of dedicated resistance to cleaning.

'Oh, shush,' said Brolo, nudging him sternly in the ribs. 'I was going to say quaint. Yes, this is a quaint, homely place you have— what's this?' Brolo stared down at the three identical servings of questionable black liquid that had been plonked down onto the bar, which appeared to ooze rather than foam over the rims of their tankards.

'Three Chicks, please,' said the barkeep.

'What? No, I mean, what are these? I ordered a small mug of ale, one cup of whatever piss you have going cheap and a wine for myself. Not three of ... whatever this stuff is.'

The elf squinted at Brolo, then shook his head.

'Nope, I'm pretty sure you said three tankards of Huntsman's Bane.'

'Huntsman's Bane? Why in the entire kingdom is it called that?' asked Wilkhelm, sounding suitably concerned.

After peering at him for a short while, the barkeep seemed to work out the question posed to him.

'Oh, because right now, you'd detect a prize stag from fifty paces,' he chirped, sounding as if it was a droll slogan he spieled out at least once an hour. 'After sinking a skinful of that stuff, you wouldn't notice if a Hedge Hog came and plopped its bristly balls in your pint.'

Hedge Hogs – grotesque swine of a thorny nature, possessing a gruesome set of gnashers hidden behind a cutesy cone-shaped snout. Owning to their powerful jaws, a Hedge Hog could chomp through bone with ease, devouring an unfortunate lumberjack in mere minutes, leaving nothing but a scattering of bloodstains to identify the savagery that had taken place. Yet, cured right, Hedge Hogs made for some of the most exquisitely scrumptious flitches of bacon in the kingdom. Hence why they'd been hunted to the brink of extinction.

'Never mind that, I wanted a wine,' Brolo insisted, in as friendly a manner as was possible.

'Sounds like you're having one, lad,' said the elf. 'Anyway, that young one of yours has already finished half his drink, so you'll have to pay up now.'

Alarm bells ringing, Brolo spun around and snatched the tankard from Smiggly's lips.

'Whoa! That's enough for you. Your mother would tan our hides if she caught wind of us getting you drunk.'

'We ... *hic* ... we're already ... *hic* ... gonna be fightin' one dragon. What's wrong with fighting ... *hic* ... another one?'

Wilkhelm flung Brolo a panicked glare. Frantically, Brolo began spewing out excuses. 'Ignore him! The beer's gone straight to his head. Little drunkard doesn't know what he's talking about.'

The elf watched Brolo intensely as he spoke. Smiggly had gotten so sloshed in such a remarkably short span of time that Brolo could do nothing but hold him up by his armpits to stop him from crashing to the floor.

'No, the privy's out back,' said the elf. 'Through the door there, take a left and head outside. You can't miss it.'

Brolo stared back with glazed eyes, absolutely dumbfounded.

Oh, for ... well, at least the deaf bastard didn't hear anything he shouldn't have, he thought, relieved.

'Still, that's three coins, please,' the barkeep said, extending his hand. 'Chicks.'

Stánwilte had provided Brolo with a good fistful of Ducks. However, money had been tight since Alisgate – and Stánwilte's behaviour towards him had gone from grudging captain to owner of a vicious hound that would have to be put down one day. Pocketing the money for his own keeping would be a prudent measure. And it would be interesting to see how favourably Stánwilte was regarded around these parts.

Rolling the dice, Brolo pulled up a stool and plonked Smiggly on it, who promptly flopped to the side and fell asleep against his shoulder. Tutting, he wiped drool from his arm and grabbed his drink.

'Tell me,' he said, taking a sip of ale. Such was its almighty concentration of alcohol that his lips briefly and involuntarily pulled back over his gums. 'You wouldn't happen to be Vyvwym Cu'Mal, would you?'

The fleshy stumps where the elf's ears had once sat appeared to twitch as he fixed Brolo with a wary eye.

'That depends, half-breed,' he said, placing down the tankard he'd been polishing and resting both of his tightly closed fists on the bar top. 'Who wants to know?'

Brolo ignored the offensive comment and calmly put his hands up, causing Smiggly to drop to the floor like a sack of spuds.

'We happen to be very close associates with the old commander of the First,' he said.

The elf gazed at him in mild puzzlement.

'Well, you've come to the right place to quench your thirst, but I don't see why you need to start sticking that bulbous, dwarfish nose of yours into my business. Asking too many questions is a sure way to end up in a chum bucket around these parts. Especially with how jumpy folk are these days.'

'No! By my ears, not *thirst*. I mean the *First*. We've travelled all the way across Uprynenos with your old pal, Stánwilte!' Brolo clasped his hands together. 'By golly, he didn't stop talking about you. I didn't realise how much praise could be heaped upon an elf. *Always the keenest eye in the army*, he'd say. *Not an elf to let danger get in the way of his duty*. How could I, a steadfast devotee of his, fail to be engrossed by the stories he would tell? My personal favourites being about how your generosity is second-to-none … speaking of which, we arrived in Spyrata a short time ago, and life on the road is surprisingly expensive—'

The elf shot over the bar, whipped his wet polishing towel around Brolo's throat and pulled it tight. Wilkhelm gallantly dived to the floor next to a soundly snoozing Smiggly.

'You'd better stop them lips of yours from flapping,' growled Vyvwym into Brolo's ear. 'Are you trying to tell me Stánwilte Yoakilor is back in

Spyrata? If you're not careful, I'll be forced to stuff your head up your arse and truss you up for a good roasting over a spit.'

Didn't the bastard say he'd made living arrangements? Brolo thought, as he gasped for air. He hadn't expected the news of an old comrade being back in town would be met by an aggressive garrotting with a grubby cloth. As his eyes began to bulge, threatening to pop from their sockets, Vyvwym realised him and slipped out from behind the bar. Cautiously, he peeked out through the Haddock's door, then bolted it shut.

'Now, I think that three obviously mistaken young lads such as your-selves had better get your facts straight before you go around making such bleeding stupid claims. Being in the slightest way associated with Stánwilte, if he dared enter a city that every peasant and their fleas know he's banished from, would assuredly result in being hanged.'

'Well,' Brolo began, as Vyvwym poured himself a large tankard of ale, 'it's quite a tedious story, really. Certainly not a page-turner. Besides, we're not at liberty to divulge his reasons for sneaking into anywhere.'

'Especially not after the last time we opened our gobs,' said Wilkhelm, dusting himself off as he rose from closely admiring the floorboards.

There was a sudden rattle at the door as a prospective patron tried to enter.

'Come back later!' Vyvwym snapped, then gulped down his ale. 'Right, so you aren't going to tell me any details, or give me anything at all to back up the piss-weak tale of you being chummy with Commander Stánwilte.' He scoffed into his drink. 'I mean, why would he risk his hide by doing something as idiotic as ignoring a royal decree? And why, if what you say is true, would he drop you three whelps on my doorstep without word? I can't believe he'd risk sending me anyone foolish enough to have helped him enter the city unnoticed.'

'Because, old friend, I want you to help me make it out again unnoticed if my plans all fall to pieces,' groaned Stánwilte, as he climbed up through a hatch behind the bar. 'And I see you still forget to lock the street access to your cellar. Fortunately for me, as the front door seems to be bolted tight.'

Vyvwym glared from Stánwilte to Brolo and back a few times, before raising his tankard and giving the dregs a sniff, as if searching for any drugs or poisons that could account for the sight before him. Seemingly satisfied, he drained the last of his ale and grew a broad, sweeping smile.

'By the Serpent's fiery breath, it really is you!' he said, as he took Stánwilte's hand and shook it firmly.

'Ss ... shh ... see?' spluttered Smiggly. 'We told you he was—' There was a thud as he slumped back to the ground, followed by the distinctive sound of vomiting.

Shaking his head, Vyvwym went on. 'I'm not sure what's harder to believe – that these three *aren't* talking utter badger shite, or that you came back to Spyrata by your own accord! Either way, it sure is wonderful to see you again, especially after all this time.' His face turned grim. 'And with everything that happened after ... ah, you know.'

'Let me put your mind at ease. Brolo here is rather prone to spouting dung from a whole variety of woodland creatures, so don't be too hasty to distrust your instincts.' Stánwilte ran a suspicious eye over Brolo, pausing at the foaming drink in his hand.

Oh, here we go, Brolo groaned to himself, savouring another mouthful of ale before Stánwilte kicked off.

'And I trust those drinks were paid for in good coin, lad,' Stánwilte said, as he walked around the bar to inspect the crumpled mass that was Smiggly Jenkins snoring loudly in a puddle of his own vomit.

'No, sir,' said Wilkhelm, tossing Brolo under a passing horse and cart, right as the metaphorical animal decided to empty its bowels. 'Apparently, you left us as destitute as a two-bit rotten scoundrel of a father walking out on his sweetheart and their ill-formed bastard love child.'

Brolo slammed his tankard down onto the bar top, spilling ale everywhere in the process. He kicked himself up from his stool, ready to lunge at Wilkhelm, whose smarmy grin was barely concealed by his own cup. Unfortunately, his attack came to a halt as Stánwilte's hand thwacked against the wine-stained wood of the bar, leaving a significant crack in its surface.

Blimey, thought Brolo.

'I thought we were over this petty squabbling!' Stánwilte roared.

Brolo flopped back onto his stool, decelerating from a seething rage to mild abashment as abruptly as a myopic eagle crashing into a mountainside.

'I see my trust in leaving you two alone to look after this one,' Stánwilte said, nudging Smiggly in the back with his boot, 'was, once again, terribly misguided. Thankfully, I require you all to accompany me on a little errand later this evening, otherwise you'd be in the midden heap. At least I'll be able to keep a proper eye on you.'

Well, this is all deliciously vague, thought Brolo. *The sneaky bugger must have some other chum whom he's hoping to drag into our little motley gathering of fools.* If his theory proved to be correct, he couldn't fathom why Stánwilte thought such secrecy necessary, but it was the best guess he could summon.

'Brolo,' snapped Stánwilte, bringing him back into the moment, 'pay Vyvwym whatever you owe him for these drinks, plus a tip for the mess you let Smiggly get himself into. And then give me the rest of that blasted money back. We don't have enough coins for you to line your own damn pockets.'

Wilkhelm sat quietly, his smug grin sprouting unhindered.

If that bastard gets away without punishment again ...

Bringing his voice back down to a reasonable level, Stánwilte turned to Vyvwym.

'I'm sorry about all the shouting, Vyvwym. It's like smashing your head against a rock with these three.'

'What shouting?' asked Vyvwym, looking slightly puzzled.

Of course, thought Brolo with a sigh.

'Don't worry,' said Stánwilte. 'Anyway, right now I need your help, old friend.'

'Anything ... within reason.'

'Do you perchance have a room we could stay in for a short while? No more than two nights, I promise you. We'll make sure to keep away from the common room or anywhere we may bump into your patrons – no one would even notice we were here.'

Vyvwym scratched the stump of his right ear for a few moments.

'I don't want any trouble coming back here, Stánwilte. The city's in a delicate state as it is, with the king being ill and all. Never mind the fanatics flooding the place.'

'And there'll be none. On the memory of all those tiresome years spent serving together, you have my word,' said Stánwilte, extending his hand.

Vyvwym shook his head but took Stánwilte's hand, with noticeably less vigour than he had previously.

'I have a room you can use, but I'm afraid it only has two beds. I'll admit they aren't the comfiest of things. In saying that, two of you will have to make do with the floor and a patch of itchy, damp straw.'

Wilkhelm's smirk dropped. 'Who exactly do you think we are?' he protested. 'I'm not some blasted goat to be housed in a stable! Patch of straw, indeed!'

Brolo caught Stánwilte's right eye twitching.

Ah, he thought, *thanks for taking the arrow for me, you stupid prat.*

'Cancel the town crier, because we have ourselves a volunteer,' hissed Stánwilte. 'How very decent of you to put the needs of others before your own, offering up a bed to Brolo. Most charitable of you, indeed. Now, with your sleeping arrangements decided, I will take the other bed. Smiggly here can take the second patch of straw – probably for the best, considering his present state.'

Stánwilte strode over to Wilkhelm, bent down, and patted his cheek just gently enough for it to not count as a slap. 'I'd ensure you make your bed tonight with more consideration than you did this one, lad. This building isn't level, and if young Smiggly decides to leak violently from any orifice, you wouldn't want it to seep down to you as you sleep, would you?'

Wilkhelm gulped audibly, and Brolo smiled to himself. Despite their differences, he'd readily acknowledge that Stánwilte sure knew how to hammer home his authority.

'Well,' Brolo said, stifling a yawn as he rose from his stool, 'with all those years to catch up on, I'm sure you two would like to be left alone to trade war stories and drivel on endlessly about your mighty deeds. Don't let me keep you. I'm going to head on out and—'

'Hold your bloody horses,' snapped Stánwilte. 'Both times you've been given freedom to scarper around without supervision, you've proven yourself to have an utter lack of restraint, causing us no end of trouble.'

It was a reasonable point, yet Stánwilte's inability to let the glowing embers of Alisgate fade gnawed at him. He and Lawgismirin had seen them right in the end, so why in all the flaming kingdom did Stánwilte have to keep bringing it up?

Nonetheless, Brolo obediently sat back down on his stool. The grouchy old prick was peevish enough as it was, and there'd be plenty of time for playing cards and eyeing up city lasses later.

Stánwilte eyed Brolo dubiously, before turning back to the elven bar-keep.

'Vyvwym, we'll have to catch up over some wine before I leave the city, but for now, I'd appreciate it if you would be kind enough to show us to our room. Our journey has been wearisome and immediate rest would be welcome. We'll all need to be refreshed for our appointment this evening.'

The sun would be up for a few more hours yet, but Brolo knew complaining would be of no use. Besides, he was a little sleepy from the potent ale he'd consumed – and eager to unravel what exactly Stánwilte was up to. He helped Wilkhelm drag Smiggly up the crooked stairs to their dingy room without complaint, then crashed down onto his creaky, fart-reeking mattress and spent an hour mulling over some viable answers. All the while, Wilkhelm grumbled under his breath, muttering about how unfair life was while he fashioned a crude bed from straw in the far corner of the room, as far as he could get from Smiggly's ocean-churning snores.

CHAPTER TWENTY-FOUR

A MIDNIGHT STROLL

Darkness had hungrily devoured the last glimmer of daylight by the time Brolo woke to Stánwilte shaking him in his bed. With unfocused eyes fresh from slumber, he gazed out through the room's only window. He failed to spot a single star through the thick grey clouds hanging like plums in the sky, smothering all but a silvery sliver of the moon.

There was a distressed groan beside Brolo's bed as Stánwilte struggled to wake Smiggly, who fought a gallant yet futile battle to remain in his mound of straw. Wilkhelm was already up, slumping against the doorframe.

By the state of these floorboards, I hope he spent the evening rolling around in a meadow of splinters, Brolo thought. It was a little infantile, but the image of a sleepless Wilkhelm constantly having to yank tiny pricks from his rump certainly brightened Brolo's mood.

Once everyone, including Smiggly, had dressed, Stánwilte led them out of the room and down the shadow-cloaked corridor, which appeared to have been constructed solely from floorboards that creaked and groaned under the lightest of footsteps, descending the stairwell at the rear of the building. They tiptoed out through an old door at the rear of the Haddock, which Vyvwym had left unlocked for the night.

The alleyway they came out in was murky, empty and disconcertingly devoid of noise. The utter lack of so much as a scurrying rat left Brolo with the unwelcome understanding that the alleyways surrounding the dockyard were even more murderous at night than they had been during the day.

If ever there was a time we needed weapons, now is ruddy it, thought Brolo, trailing behind Stánwilte, who strolled through the fetid backstreets as if enjoying a leisurely afternoon finding his way around a maze in some lord's estate. Stánwilte had banned them from bringing along any sort of weaponry to prevent '*accidents if tensions run a little too high*'. Stánwilte's explanation had raised more questions than it answered regarding where he was leading them, but even Brolo didn't believe he'd willingly deliver them into a dangerous situation without the means to defend themselves. Perhaps he was catching up with another old associate – some other wretch from his days in the army. Perhaps their relationship wasn't the best, but he'd like to patch it up, hence all the drivel about tensions. Nothing to be concerned about ... surely.

He followed Stánwilte blindly down numerous twists and turns, slinking down the labyrinth of cramped alleyways, grappling with a lingering sense of anxiety. His cockiness was somewhat weakened without having Lawgismirin to hand. The reassurance of the power it lent him would've calmed his nerves no end. Instead, he suffered the embarrassing tingle of goosebumps rising like molehills on his arms. A small voice of reason in the back of his mind whispered that Stánwilte's nerves about that very power might be the reason he forbade weapons in the first place.

After all, Lawgismirin was in some shape or form enchanted, so it was an itsy-bitsy bit illegal to possess, let alone fight with. But Brolo still couldn't see why Stánwilte had to give him such scandalised looks every time he carried the thing. As watchmen, they were supposed to uphold the King's Peace, which meant suppressing sorcery, witchcraft, enchantments and all that sorcerous balderdash, but it wasn't like he was going to start summoning the dead or making rabbits hop out of Wilkhelm's arsehole, now, was he? Never mind that Stánwilte was currently breaking a lifetime banishment laid upon him by the king himself.

Brolo was so busy lathering himself up into a teeth-grinding fury that he failed to notice how the rest of group had come to a dead stop. He crashed straight into Wilkhelm, who spilled to the muddy floor like the innards of a sacrificial cow, landing on his face with a cry and a crunch. Stánwilte swung round swiftly, drawing a small blade from somewhere about his person. Looking up at Stánwilte with eyes glazed in terror, Smiggly appeared to have been so shocked by the sudden calamity that he'd wet himself.

'For the love of all things divine, what sodding part of keeping inconspicuous do you three bumpkins fail to understand?' groaned Stánwilte, slipping away his knife. He bent down, lifted the profusely-bleeding Wilkhelm by the collar of his shirt and pushed him over to where Smiggly was quivering in his urine-filled boots. 'Bloody children, that's what you are. We're undertaking a very delicate operation tonight, and I'm forced to spend most of my time playing nanny to a pack of pups still fresh from their mothers' teats!'

Smiggly whimpered and began to shed a few pitiful tears. Wilkhelm, the memory of his earlier punishment clearly fresh in his mind, at least looked abashed as he began to complain.

'It was Brolo's fault I fell over in the first place. I—'

'I don't want to hear it,' Stánwilte said, putting up a gloved hand. 'I've had more than enough for one day. You two, go back to The Slimy Haddock and get yourselves cleaned up. Where we're going, it's important for me not to look weak. I can't do that with one of you covered in blood and the other drenched in piss. Brolo and I will head off on our own.'

There were no arguments. Wilkhelm drifted away, pinching the bridge of his nose as he shot Brolo a venomous glare. Smiggly trailed behind him, crying and wiping his nose with his sleeve.

Stánwilte's right, Brolo thought. *We are just children. We're not suited for gallivanting across the country on mindless adventures or traipsing through the dangerously unfamiliar underbelly of the capital.*

'So, no weapons, eh?' he whispered to Stánwilte, as they watched the others fade into the night.

'Precautionary measure. I at least trust myself to not do anything stupid,' Stánwilte replied gruffly.

'You brought us along, didn't you?'

'Humph,' was all Stánwilte gave in reply. 'We're almost where we need to go. Now there are only two of us, we'd better bloody well hope my friend has kept her word.'

'And, pray tell, what happens if she hasn't?'

'Then I'd become approximately a head shorter in the near future, while you'd have to get used to confined spaces and gruel for the rest of your significantly reduced lifetime.' Stánwilte paused. 'Well, at least you'd have an easier time than Wilkhelm and Smiggly.'

'Oh, height jokes, is it? Who's being childish now?' Brolo asked, folding his arms peevishly.

'Give over. You're always first to crack a joke at the expense of every unfortunate wretch to cross your path, so stop being so ruddy sensitive. I had no idea Bæwylm was letting you grow into such a sop. Now come on.'

I am not fucking sensitive, you puckering arsehole. I simply get pissed off with idiots like you making jokes as worn as an infantryman's boot! Brolo thought, as he followed behind Stánwilte, flexing his hands with the overwhelming urge to choke his captain in the darkness.

After worming their way through countless more alleyways, Stánwilte halted their stealthy creep at the mouth of a street that seemed to be of some significance. The area was oddly alive with the sound of laughter, drifting from numerous taverns and the swarms of folk crisscrossing from building to building. Brolo wondered what amusements could be taking place to stir up such revelry and sighed irritably at not being able to join in on them.

Putting a finger to his lips, Stánwilte pointed to a rundown, three-storey building across the street, which had a good deal fewer visitors than most of the other establishments. Other than being relatively well-lit behind its overabundant curtains, it didn't seem to have any symbol of distinction or obvious sign as to what function it served, but it did boast a hulking ogre of a man standing beside what Brolo assumed to be the main entrance.

If Stánwilte thinks I'm going to help him take on that big brute without a weapon, he can jolly well go sit on a maypole!

Stánwilte, however, just hugged the lip of the corner, occasionally glancing up to the hazy image of the moon, watching and waiting in silence.

Inevitably, Brolo soon became bored. He'd never witnessed so many taverns in one place, populating the area like fungus growing on a fallen trunk. Although he did his best to resist, he could almost sense himself drifting away to a barstool in some tavern where the ale-slops weren't added back the barrel, the dice rolled like cheese down a hill and the barmaids were bustier than a room full of sculpted kings' heads.

A tap on his shoulder from Stánwilte snapped Brolo back to reality. An elderly woman in fine silk clothing had shuffled out of the door and begun calling to the burly guard, waving for him to come inside. He appeared to hesitate, but nevertheless saluted her and slid in through the door without further question. Rather than following, the woman crossed her arms, peering straight at the mouth of alleyway Brolo and Stánwilte inhabited.

Brolo suffered a moment of panic, but she simply nodded once, slowly, and turned to go inside, leaving the door open a fraction behind her.

'Aelia, you utter treasure. I knew you wouldn't rat me out,' Stánwilte whispered. 'Alright then, let's not waste any more time out here.'

Boldly, Stánwilte marched across the street towards the gaping door, shouldering past any drunken stragglers who got in his way. With a little more caution, Brolo followed, taking in the sights of the area around him. Finally, he cottoned on to something he should've deduced far sooner.

Poach my boots and serve them with gravy, we must be in the sodding No-Lights District! He's taking me to a brothel, the saucy git!

Before Brolo had a chance to wonder over their present location, Stánwilte reached the open door and barged in without waiting for him to catch up. Not wishing to fall behind, he quickened his pace and slipped inside, just in time to see Stánwilte bounding up a flight of stairs.

'Bloody slow down, you great ox,' Brolo groaned, as he tackled a second set of stairs, wheezing heavily. When he trundled up the third and final flight of stairs to where Stánwilte crouched in wait, he was sure he could hear the pained groans of some poor chap being viciously tortured nearby.

Wait, did I just hear him scream for them to go ... harder?

'Right, on the count of three, we're going to charge in through that door,' whispered Stánwilte. 'Don't say anything – just stand behind me and look menacing. Understood?'

Brolo nodded, even though he wasn't exactly sure how a young, un-armed, four-foot-eleven-inch dwelf was supposed to appear menacing to anyone. Nonetheless, he was sure he could improvise something when the moment came, providing there wasn't anyone he would actually be required to menace.

'Ready? One ... two ... now!' Stánwilte launched himself forward, kicked the locked door with stupendous force – enough to splinter the wood

around the lock and leave the whole thing hanging limply by its hinges –
and stepped casually over the threshold.

'What in all the fiery breath of Byrnegona is the meaning of this?' Brolo
heard screech out from inside the room, in a voice he imagined would resemble a sword swallower with emphysema who'd recently been garrotted.

Brolo crept in behind Stánwilte. Immediately, he regretted doing so, and
quite urgently wished he could stab out his eyes.

On a large oval bed adorned with bountiful purple velvet sheets and
pillows sat a skeletal man, absolutely stark-dangly-bollock naked. A grisly
sight enough, but the additional horror of the brittle-boned fellow being
straddled and surrounded by a dozen or so equally nude women, all of
whom must've been pushing their late eighties, if not their early nineties,
was enough to make Brolo deathly giddy. The amount of wrinkly, flapping
skin on display made the scene resemble an unqualified tanner's latest work
drying on a clothesline during a windy day.

'You!' growled the man, wide nostrils flaring as he pushed off the geriatric prostitute who'd been servicing him. 'What in the Flame are you
doing here?'

'Ah, Your Eminence, fancy bumping into you,' Stánwilte managed
without throwing up, much to Brolo's amazement. 'I was wondering if we
could have your help with something. Now, don't get up too quickly, or
you could break a hip.' Stánwilte grinned. 'Of course, not necessarily your
own ...'

CHAPTER TWENTY-FIVE

AN OPPORTUNITY PRESENTS ITSELF

I swear that someone – no, many souls will pay dearly for this brutal assassination of my sacred authority as High-Keeper! The humiliation I endure this night shall fan the seething fires of my desire for vengeance, or may my skin bubble and blister for all time in the flesh-searing torrents of the Flame!

Relfread, High-Keeper of the Dragona, younger brother to the King of Uprynenos, sat upon his dragon-bone cathedra, nestled within the apse of the Cathedral of Fire. His pulse thumped behind his eyes as he tapped a baleful drumbeat upon the armrest – the bone polished to a gleaming white over the long years – and glowered at the two figures standing before him. One, a forgotten thorn in Spyrata's past, whose very presence threatened to pierce the bubble of his carefully laid plans. The other, some young abomination of bastard blood, born from the sin of an elf and a dwarf.

Ordinarily, the presence of such a lowly creature wouldn't be worth a furrow of his brow, yet with how tonight had developed and with whom he kept company, Relfread decided it would be prudent not to underestimate him. A tatty sheath could still hold the sharpest of blades. And, cursedly, Stánwilte Yoakilor and his little half-breed follower had seen him in all his lustful shame. Stánwilte must've orchestrated events to surprise him at his most vulnerable. He knew not to what end his degradation was to be used against him, but what appeared flawlessly crystal was how they would both inevitably pay for their actions. So would any of those found to have helped them.

Of course, he would have to deal with Aelia. After so many years of catering to his … unique tastes … supposedly with the utmost secrecy, it truly was a shame that she'd erred by betraying him now. Unfortunately, he couldn't take risks when so close to unleashing his scheme. He wouldn't have her tortured by his Inquisitors. He would simply make sure she and all her whores wallowed in the Pit of Iros after falling to the Flame. Once his plans finally came to fruition and bore the nightshade that would bring Spyrata to its eternal sleep, she would sample the first taste of his wrath.

For now, Relfread would order Inquisitor Siskin to spread amongst the faithful that the glory of the Dragonian Flame would scour the sins of the flesh occurring within the No-Lights District, eradicating lustfulness from Spyrata in a blaze of righteousness. After tonight's affair, Relfread would need to bring his plans forward. *Such a pity,* he thought, *but as they say, whores spread stories faster than venereal diseases – even those without any teeth.*

Deciding he could finalise the details of his vengeance at a more opportune time, Relfread cast his mind back to more pressing matters. 'So,' he said, 'what is it you have such urgent need of my assistance with, Former Commander Yoakilor? I do sincerely hope it's of deathly importance.'

Stánwilte raised an eyebrow ever so slightly.

For him to go to the trouble of catching Relfread in a compromising position, he must have had a momentous reason to blackmail him. Not simply so Relfread didn't have him arrested on sight, which he most definitely would've done, but to ensure his assistance. Otherwise, Stánwilte would've spewed his demands with sword drawn, back when Relfread had been exposed at the brothel, rather than letting him dress himself and escorting him back to his own domain with his final shred of dignity intact.

If he intends to coerce me into helping him return to the good graces of my dear brother, then he should brace himself for a very sizeable boulder of disappointment to roll over his efforts, thought Relfread. He revelled in the comfort of having Stánwilte's feasible motives all stacked up in a nice little pile of ammunition to use against him when the negotiations began. *Those years spent bumbling around in some slum in Arbour Vale, dealing with nothing but farmers' disputes over grazing rights, have left him with as much intelligence as a rotten cabbage.*

'Your assistance ... yes, I suppose you could say I require your assistance, Relfread,' said Stánwilte cautiously.

As I suspected, thought Relfread, his self-assurance growing.

'Then you should remember common courtesy when addressing those from whom you require succour,' he said. 'You shall henceforth address me as Your Eminence or High-Keeper.'

'Oh, I think we've witnessed more than enough *succour* for one evening,' said Stánwilte, looking pleased with his remark. 'However, there are a few pressing issues I need ask your assistance with, Your Eminence.'

Relfread ignored the insincerity in Stánwilte's tone as he spoke his title, considering it victory enough he had used it at all.

And, step by step, superiority is re-established.

'Out with it, man. I imagine we can both agree that as things stand, you have nothing to be coy about.'

Devalue your weaknesses before your enemy. Remove the heads from the arrows they draw against you, and they shall prove worthless, no matter how true their flight.

'Dragons,' said Stánwilte, as he began to pace, feet clacking like clock-work against the stone floor of the cathedral. 'I presume you to be an expert on them.'

Ah, so he was aware of the three ravens. Lord Cormorant must truly want rid of him. The other Lords of Uprynenos had merely fashioned the illusion of sending their best men on such a suicidal charge – simply another mistake by the king's advisors that would be publicly lamented, along with the other parts they played in his downfall.

Relfread ensured that his features remained smooth as a slate tile. *There is no need to pounce on the mouse and go straight for the jugular. Let us play for a little while.*

'They are my life, Yoakilor. You see, when my dear father saw fit to dispose of his *spare* by sending me off to become a novice in this very cathedral, he could not have foreseen how mesmerising I would find my studies. I have touched scriptures as ancient as the dragons themselves, records from the great cities of the past detailing the lineage of Byrnegona. I have read countless pages recounting how the lands flourished under the governance of dragons, how intricate law codes dictated the people of the kingdoms that became Uprynenos, how vast tributes were paid to the dragons for the honour of their guardianship. Tell me, do you even know where the name Uprynenos comes from?'

'Can't say I do,' said Stánwilte, sounding markedly disinterested.

'No, of course you don't. It means *Under the Prosperous Reign of Iros.* It was beneath Iros's wings that these lands reached their zenith, more than four thousand years ago. Alas, the only remnant of him remaining in modern times is when heathens use his name in a blasphemous curse. The ignominy of this drove my learning through my formative years. Painstaking study and faithful dedication forged my early life, bestowing me with increasing renown until I became the youngest High-Keeper of the Dragona since its foundation. I have since brought the faith's smouldering embers back to a raging inferno, bringing followers in their droves to bask in its warmth. So, I hope I have quelled your doubts regarding my expertise, Stánwilte.'

'Now you mention it,' said Stánwilte, as he strolled over to Relfread's cathedra, 'that was one aspect I wished to grill you about. How exactly have you whisked up this fervour across the kingdom in such a short amount of time? And I don't suppose the re-establishment of the Dragonian Inquisition is merely a coincidence.' He rested both hands on the seat's dragon-bone armrests, bending down to stare into Relfread's eyes.

'My humble message merely strove to unravel the oppressive constraints lashing those cowed by the Circle filth to the falsehoods of their doctrine,' Relfread said. 'What was so easily forgotten by the nobility of Uprynenos had been kept alive by ancient traditions, passed down for generations by the common folk, begging to be reawakened. The lore of this land is not simply a dreary stream of myths to be told around a fire in the gloom of a winter's eve. Instead, they're memories from an age gone by. A time when being a peasant did not mean extreme poverty, meagre food and nothing but a bed of sodden straw to sleep upon. The Age of Dragons was a utopia, before the rebellion of magic-wielding elves and dwarfs that scorched the earth ... and man, with their newfound airs of nobility and petty houses that squabbled over strips of land like wolves at a carcass.' Relfread looked past Stánwilte to lock eyes with the dwelf, fixing him with cold, mirthless smile. 'That is why the pilgrims have been rejoicing, Yoakilor. The common folk are dissatisfied with the lies of the gentry, with being penned up by the nobles' precious Circle while they're farmed for their sweat and blood. They sense the time for change has arrived. I deliver nothing other than my sermons. It matters not the size of the congregation, be it fifty or fifty thousand – only that the message is spoken and heard.

The flock are perceiving the call of destiny, heralding them forth to a new age. It is only what has been promised to them for hundreds of years.'

'The return of the dragons,' muttered Stánwilte, as he pushed himself away from Relfread. 'A fanciful story, Your Eminence, but I'm afraid we're here to ruin the ending for you.'

'Is that so?' Relfread asked, with a yawn, laying bait to the prize carp of Stánwilte's ego. However, he seemed undeterred.

'I want you to disclose any weaknesses that dragons possess, as we have cause to slay one,' he said.

'And why, pray, would I betray my faith, my followers and my office for the likes of you? I hope you are not relying on my compliance simply because you caught me partaking in an unsavoury act. If I weren't already the High-Keeper, I'm also, in case you have forgotten, a member of the royal family. I can make witnesses disappear before you ever reach another ear to splurge your filthy lies upon!' Relfread sat back in his seat and broke into a thin, victorious smile.

Stánwilte had nothing. By the dejected fracture on his face, it was obvious he'd gambled on blackmail alone being enough to secure Relfread's help. However, an insatiable idea gnawed its way into Relfread's mind, planting a parasitic seed that rapidly grew into an ingenious solution to various potential complications.

'Of course, I do very much enjoy the status quo of being High-Keeper,' he said, slowly. 'There's no telling what would happen to my position if a second Age of Dragons dawned. While dozens of the scrolls I've read portray dragons as wise, they oft appeared whimsical to us mere mortals.' He rested a bony finger against his lips and began tapping gently. 'The miraculous reappearance of a single dragon has already served the Dragona by encouraging this surge in fresh devotees, but I would be inclined to admit that any change to the old ways would be drastic one, considering we have no idea of the beast's mental state. Is it the last of its kind, perhaps? If so, then its considerable time in isolation may have caused a deterioration in sagacity, mayhap to a degree where only its most ferocious, animalistic characteristics remain. It would require an awful amount of faith to allow the creature a wing of governance in this kingdom's affairs. I can assure you, dragons did not rule a dictatorship, but kept a council of sorts.'

Stánwilte eyed him suspiciously. He'd intentionally wrapped his hints within slivers of the finest winter ham – enough to rouse a few questions, but not so tightly that Stánwilte wouldn't take the bait. Relfread was High-Keeper and brother to the king, unable to inherit due to his place in the church, but wealthy and blessed with a position at the pinnacle of society. What more was there to gain?

Everything, fool, thought Relfread. *Everything.*

'So, are you going to help us or not, Your Vagueness?' asked the young bastard-blood testily.

Relfread stifled an urge to cackle. After the boy had basked in his humiliation a short while ago, he thoroughly enjoyed seeing that galling smugness chip away. Inclined to continue provoking the dwelf's fury, Relfread directed his reply to Stánwilte.

'Help you personally? Bah! Utterly out of the question, I'm afraid.' Relfread raised himself from his cathedra, his joints cracking like rusted gears in desperate need of grease. 'If you're fortunate enough to survive what you propose, I cannot risk any association with you from this day onwards. If suspicions began to arise about my involvement in the slaughter of the last known dragon, I dare say my position of High-Keeper would suddenly and violently become vacant.'

Relfread crossed to a font of ebony stone adorned with intricately crafted dragons and leant upon it as if looking over a tactician's map. In a way, he was. In the past, the font's function had been to bless high-status converts with the Baptism of Fire, but since the faith had fallen out of favour with the monarchy, the contents of its basin had gradually evaporated until it sat gathering dust. Relfread would see it filled again with the tears of all who dared stand in his way.

'Incredible as it may be, I'm starting to agree with Brolo.' Stánwilte stepped to the other side of the baptismal font, facing Relfread. When he spoke again, his voice had lowered enough that only the two of them could hear it. 'I've had enough of your elusiveness, Relfread. It has been a long night for us all, and I'm not in the mood to deal with games. Obviously, you're implying we can come to some arrangement, but do not believe for one second that if I detect a wisp of deception, I won't break your brittle spine.'

'And I've had enough threats in my own cathedral for one night, too.'

From beneath his hood, Relfread stared up into Stánwilte's piercing yet weary eyes. While his irises were the deep shaded blue of an ocean under a full moon's light, the whites of his eyes were heavily bloodshot. Dozens of little crimson splinters revealed the stresses, the pressures and the sheer desperation Stánwilte otherwise hid so well. Whatever scraps of hope Relfread offered him, he would certainly lap up. And Relfread was throwing a far bigger bone than Stánwilte deserved, even if he was tossing it off a cliff.

'As I've already told you, I cannot personally aid your task. Nevertheless, I could gift you somebody who may.'

'I don't want one of your snivelling underlings following us about, feeding you information about where we are and what we're up to,' answered Stánwilte.

Relfread put his hands up innocently, with a haggard cough of a laugh. 'To even suggest I'd orchestrate something quite so blatant betrays your ignorance of my capabilities, Stánwilte. But you're within your rights to be suspicious, so let me ease your concern by assuring you that your conscript is not affiliated with myself or the Dragona in any official capacity.'

'Subtle wording,' Stánwilte said. 'How about tied to you *unofficially*? I can't see anyone agreeing to tag along on an expedition as dangerous as this without expressly having to.'

'That's precisely what you and your dwelf companion are doing,' replied Relfread.

'Touché.'

'And regarding their motivation to join you – leave that little matter to me. I can be rather convincing when I must.'

'But who exactly are they?' Stánwilte asked.

'I presume, when Lord Cormorant detailed the events leading up to this journey north of yours, he was informative enough to mention a survivor of an attack by the dragon?'

'In passing, yes. I've heard little else in the way of fact since. Every settlement we've passed has been teeming with various rumours, but as far as I can tell, no one has seen or heard from this alleged survivor since they found their way to capital. So,' Stánwilte said, eyes narrowing, 'what of them?'

'To begin with, I can quell any doubts you have about their existence. Since investigating their account was of paramount importance, they were painstakingly nursed back to health, having fallen into a coma before coming into my care. They have since enjoyed my continued protection from the scrutiny of Circle worshipping courtiers. Furthermore, now they have been restored to full health, I cannot fathom anyone better suited to assist in slaying a dragon than the only known person alive to have seen it. Can you?'

Rather than jump at the idea as Relfread had anticipated, Stánwilte appeared to consider the vaguely rotten root vegetable hanging before him for quite some time. Judging by the vein pulsing in his neck, he was reluctant to display his apprehension before Relfread, his gaze drifting over to his comrade as if the runt would somehow provide answers.

'And why would they, after suffering so greatly in their previous encounter with the dragon, elect to go and face it a second time? They'd have to be a few slices short of a loaf to voluntarily endure such a nightmare again.'

'Believe me,' wheezed Relfread, 'they will have their reasons.' All had gone according to plan thus far. However, it was time for element number two to be introduced, and if this didn't play out exactly as Relfread hoped, everything could be ruined. 'Now, regarding how you proceed from here, I have a few stipulations for you to adhere to.'

With a sound like dry twigs crunching underfoot, Relfread snapped his fingers. Drifting from the shadows, a figure adorned with the flaming crown and golden wings of the Inquisition slipped into place beside him.

'This is Siskin, head of the Dragonian Inquisition and my right-hand man. He will make sure your departure tomorrow goes without a hitch.' It was a command, not a request.

'Tomorrow? We've only just arrived. We're in dire need of supplies and horses, let alone rest. We have two more in our party, and thanks to a run-in with your damned Sinisters, very little money between us. One night simply isn't enough time—'

'Everything will be sourced and gifted to you by the Dragona,' interrupted Relfread, with a wave of his hand. 'Although in a highly secret, unofficial capacity, you are undertaking my will. Therefore, I shall see to it you are properly provisioned. You and your band of cretins will meet the Inquisitor at the foot of the cathedral steps at noon. He will be waiting with your equipment, horses and new party member.'

Stánwilte still seemed wary, but Relfread was confident he couldn't afford to look a gift horse in the mouth. Not one for each of his party, anyway.

'Being brutally honest,' Stánwilte said, 'I only came to you for information. I'm sure you can understand why I'm having a hard time believing that, as reward for us barging in on your evening of geriatric lust, you're going to send us on our merry way with everything we need and no negative consequences. Even if I could trust you, noon tomorrow is still too soon. We're tired from the last stretch of our journey – we need a few more days of rest.'

'It's tomorrow or not at all. I should stress that the *not at all* refers to ever leaving this city again, too. You know too much, so I'm afraid I'd have to instruct my associate here to have his way with you if you refused ... and let me tell you, there are things he can do with a red-hot poker that would make your eyes pop.'

Subtle, Relfread thought gleefully.

'Cast your suspicions aside,' he continued. 'My offer is generous because it's beneficial for us both if you accept. Yet your departure must be tomorrow. I cannot have you hanging around the city, risking your presence being uncovered by some other authority.'

With his options so plainly laid out before him, Stánwilte visibly sagged before nodding assent to the terms.

'So be it, then,' he said, pushing himself away from the font. 'But mercy find you if this is some sort of trick.'

'Yes, yes. Painful retribution shall be delivered by your sword,' rasped Relfread.

As Stánwilte and his abominable friend retreated down the vast nave of the Cathedral of Fire, Relfread muttered after him, 'You are a very untrusting man, Yoakilor ...'

And oh, by the Flame, you should be.

Without turning to face Inquisitor Siskin, Relfread dismissed him with a set of gesticulations that fiendish minions could inherently interpret.

Once they leave the city gates, spread word of their intentions far and wide. See if your Sinisters in the countryside can rouse some of the faithful to put together a little parting gift for them somewhere down the road.

The Inquisitor nodded and withdrew from Relfread's side, leaving him alone to watch as the great doors of the cathedral thudded shut behind the disgraced commander and his mongrel.

CHAPTER TWENTY-SIX

UNCEREMONIOUS DEPARTURE

The merciless gleam of daylight stabbing through Stánwilte's eyelids thwarted his best efforts to ignore it any longer. Rolling over on his grubby mattress, he grumbled at the selfishness of the night that had already been waning upon his arrival at the Haddock an hour or so ago.

Smiggly and Wilkhelm had both been snoring calamitously as he and Brolo snuck back into their dingy room. The rumbling duet had turned into a trio of thunderous growls as soon as the dwelf's head hit his own pillow, uniting with his fellow Peplyshans in the world of dreams. Their cataclysmic screeching had been the chief cause of Stánwilte's struggle to slip into a restful slumber, right up until the sun had decided to aim its piercing shards of light through the bedroom window and into his eyes.

In a huff, he rolled over and sat at the edge of his bed, caressing the pounding ache behind his left temple in a weak attempt to ease the pain. He sat there in silence for a long time, pondering over the preceding night's events.

Things hadn't exactly gone down as he'd envisioned. Astonishingly, however, the outcome had seemed favourable – though Stánwilte found it impossible to shake the looming suspicion that at some point down the line, Relfread was going to orchestrate a situation that would leave him nothing more than a mound of dog excrement lying helplessly on the road. A disheartening thought that continued to bother him as he woke the boys and led them downstairs to breakfast.

The four of them sat silently in the kitchen, steaming in a vat of their own weariness. Master Roux di'Day could've generously seasoned breakfast with the salty aura floating around the room. Unfortunately, as Stánwilte gagged on a waft of the meal being prepared, he deemed it unlikely that The Slimy Haddock's portly cook possessed any keen knowledge of seasonings.

'Your mother,' Stánwilte said, as Roux slid over a bowl of gelatinous gruel, which looked to have been cultivated in some hellish realm of existence, 'she didn't abandon you to begin a misguided career as a witch, by any chance?'

Roux took a moment to mull over the question. Scooping wax out of his left ear with his little finger, he flicked his bountiful harvest in the direction of the table and various uncovered breakfast items.

'Guess it's possible, but I couldn't say for sure-like. My ma left me and my old man before I were conceived, she did. Never found out what happened to her. Why?'

'No reason,' said Stánwilte, fearing that rummaging for answers could ruin his chances of keeping breakfast down. All the same, he made a mental note to discuss Mistress Roslyn's potential offspring with her if they should ever make it home to Peplyshaw.

Awkward silence, interrupted only by the occasional *gloop* of a spoon cautiously probing oaty goo, swiftly reclaimed the dining table. Smiggly kept scooping his porridge around in his bowl, as if hoping a morsel of edible food would reveal itself somewhere within its depths. Brolo had his cheek buried in his breakfast, snoring gently as he snatched a few more minutes of sleep. Wilkhelm sat in his chair, arms folded, steaming away like the bowl of porridge before him. Both of his eyes had swollen practically shut. He looked as if somebody had shoved a whole punnet of blueberries up his nostrils, which had all burst around his eye sockets, leaving his face a puffy purplish mess. He'd likely broken his nose in the fall last night, with the blame resting at Brolo's feet.

The lack of punishment Stánwilte had issued unto Brolo, whether the injury had been intentional or no, paralleled with the action of sending both Wilkhelm and Smiggly back to The Slimy Haddock, had undeniably stoked the flames of animosity between the pair. A shame, as their bickering had finally begun to ease off, but it couldn't be helped. Stánwilte had required *someone* to act as muscle when confronting Relfread. Half of intimidation was theatrics – showing up with some prat pissing blood from his nose and another with piss-sodden trousers would've somewhat spoilt his demonstration of supremacy. Granted, a dwelf with a scraggly beard worn in a ridiculous braid wasn't exactly going to install fear into the hearts of most men, but he made the best of the tools to hand.

Stánwilte tossed his utensils down in defeat, unable to conquer so much as a spoonful of breakfast, just as Vyvwym came into the kitchen carrying a basket full of revoltingly limp vegetables.

'I made a killing in the markets this morn, Roux. I may have retired as a tracker a long time ago, but I can still sniff out a bargain from a mile away! Bought all this lot for a brace of Chicks from old Jhol. Some of the veg that aren't supposed to be green are turning it in a few spots, but it'll be ideal for soups and the like.' Vyvwym passed the basket over to di'Day, who promptly waddled over to the larder.

'Are potatoes supposed to weep like that?' asked Smiggly innocently.

'Not strictly, no,' Vyvwym replied. 'But Roux is just going to mash the living shit out of 'em, so buying spuds already nice and soft removes the need to boil them for so long. Firewood is very expensive, lad.'

Vyvwym yanked out a chair opposite Stánwilte, filled himself a bowl of porridge and began to scoff it down. Plainly, he'd grown more accustomed to the kind of poor-quality meals served in the army than Stánwilte ever had.

'I hope you didn't get up to anything too stupid last night,' he said, stabbing his porridge-caked spoon in Wilkhelm's direction. 'Anything I need to know?'

'Lad fell over trying to find the chamber pot in the dark, is all,' said Stánwilte with well-rehearsed conviction.

Vyvwym gave him a look that clearly expressed how he would've heard someone crashing around in his own tavern during the dead of night, yet took the hint to press no further.

'Well, if you're going to be staying here for a while, you'll wanna be a trifle more careful. Typically, when some tit looks like that 'round here, it's because they've taken a short trip through my front window. I don't want anyone asking why I've got a lad with a face like a trodden-on plum moping around when I haven't needed to get the glaziers in.'

There was a groan as Brolo, awoken from his slumber, pulled his face out from his breakfast, straining as if tugging a trapped boot out of an exceptionally gloopy riverbank.

'Don't you worry. We'll be leaving this city by lunch, thank fuck,' said Brolo, as he stifled a yawn.

'Eh?' asked Vyvwym, cupping one of his stumps. 'Don't cover your sodding mouth when speaking to me, lad.'

'He hopes the food will be just as good here at lunch,' said Stánwilte, raising his voice for Brolo's sake as much as Vyvwym's. Brolo shot him a puzzled look but didn't broach the topic again, wisely sensing this was a time to shut up and move on.

'Coincidentally, we have to head on out for a while today,' continued Stánwilte. 'I want to track down another old acquaintance from my time in the First. He was there ... on *that* day, so he knows the truth of events. Besides, he owes me a favour, and with any luck, he won't try to worm out of it by turning me in. Can't imagine having another chance to call in these debts, so I may as well do it now.'

Vyvwym's ear-stumps twitched. 'Seeing as you need someone found, Stánwilte, I'll come along with you,' he said, with a nostalgic glint in his eyes. 'It's been a many a year since I last had to track a man down, and I've got nothing else planned around the Haddock this morning. It'll be just like the old days, eh?'

'No, that's fine, Vyvwym. You've done enough by taking us in – I can't distract you from your work, too.'

Vyvwym waved his spoon around in protest, but Stánwilte raised a hand to cut him off before he could speak. 'I can't burden you with all my problems, my friend. We may not return until late, so try not to worry if we're not back in time for supper. I promise we'll catch up properly this evening.'

This buffered the disappointment on Vyvwym's face, yet it pained Stánwilte to deceive someone who'd shown him nothing but loyalty. Justifying his lies by telling himself they were for the greater good came as little comfort. Brolo could gawk at him all he liked; the less Vyvwym knew, the lower the chance he'd be dragged off by the Dragonian Inquisition. Stánwilte at least owed Vyvwym that courtesy, whether he'd appreciate it or not.

After thanking him for providing a delicious spread and bidding him a fine day as normal, Stánwilte led the boys back to their room to ready themselves for the journey ahead. He glanced longingly at the bed he'd spent only an hour or so sleeping on, rueing the haste with which they were leaving the creature comforts only a city could provide.

Once they were ready, they exited the inn via the same backdoor they'd used last night. Stánwilte had decided it was best to avoid the front door, minimising the chance of bumping in to Vyvwym and evading further awkward conversations – specifically about why they needed to take all their belongings out with them. The elf was a tracker, after all. He'd pick up such minor details.

After a short period of time trudging through the slums by Gizzards Bay, Stánwilte took a sharp right down a nondescript alley. It led to a gap between two houses, wide enough for them to slip through sideways if they sucked their stomachs in. Wriggling from the gloom of Spyrata's snaking backstreets like maggots from a festering wound, the four watchmen immediately found themselves caught in a surge of activity. The capital crashed into them in a swell of rude, impoverished, self-important city people who made the hustle back in Alisgate seem like market day in Bumfuck-Nowhere during the midst of a plague, sweeping them down the main thoroughfare leading to the Square of Purification.

Stánwilte was accustomed to city life. Wilkhelm, he presumed, had been to Spyrata on official visits with his father. Brolo and Smiggly, however, appeared a smidge overawed by the mad rush of the capital's citizenry, befuddled by the overpowering smells and horrendous noises accompanying it. Smiggly's eyes practically popped out in their struggle to take in the hundreds of towers piercing the skyline in every direction.

It was always the same with country bumpkins making their first trip to the big city. Even the smallest of districts within Spyrata dwarfed Peplyshaw in terms of area, let alone the sheer number of buildings stuffed into each available square inch of space. Spyrata would've been beyond anything the humble Peplyshans could ever have imagined. Stánwilte watched with a nervous eye as Brolo walked through the capital, caressing the hammer hanging from a loop on his belt. The last thing Stánwilte wanted to deal with was a re-enactment of the frenzy back in Alisgate. He hoped the lad had learnt to keep his foolish mouth shut.

Trundling along through the horde of Spyratans, Stánwilte let his gaze drift over to the Palace of the United sitting upon Arnheld's Hill, way off in the distance. The five golden Towers of the Crown shimmered in the morning sun like vast candles sitting atop a richly decorated cake, the same way they had when Stánwilte first witnessed them as a small boy. It warmed his heart to see that even after all these years, the proud symbol of this kingdom's power stood steadfast and resilient, even as the current monarch faded into the Eternal Shuffler's embrace without an heir to follow him. Alas, a palpable decay crept amongst the poorer quarters of the city.

To the untrained eye, Spyrata ticked along with a semblance of normality. Merchants plugged their wares from stalls lining the street as far as the eye could see. Hundreds of grizzled sailors hunted for strong drink and a bed, preferably one also occupied by something without fins. Great swaths of children played in the filthy streets, picking the pockets of anyone not keeping a close eye on their valuables. All good old-fashioned scenes that would've been recognisable to anyone who'd spent significant time in Spyrata. Yet behind the shroud of the everyday humdrum sat a restrained hostility Stánwilte caught while glimpsing the distrustful eyes of the greater population – an unsettling, tense atmosphere he'd not felt since Alisgate.

Observing the citizens of the capital as they flowed around him, Stánwilte noticed a sizable number of religious pendants hanging around their necks. A troubling discovery, as Spyratans were traditionally a sceptical, agnostic bunch who only observed spiritual practices that involved at least two kinds of distilled spirits and a slice of exotic lime. It wouldn't have been strange to witness the odd noble or well-to-do merchant wearing the ring of the Circle for the sake of appearances. It was, however, quite unusual to behold thousands of Flame pendants flagrantly adorning the necks of the populace.

Having the hearts and minds of so many people held by the throat was exactly the kind of symbolism Relfread would revel in cultivating.

As they drew closer to the square, Stánwilte grew aware of the zealous babble of Dragonian preachers spouting from various street corners, spreading their filth over the captivated crowds like farmers liberally mucking their fields. The overwhelming stench of manure was enough to curl Stánwilte's toes, yet much to his disdain, the people of Spyrata were lapping it up. He struggled to ascertain the gist of the closest preacher's prattling through the general hubbub of the city. Judging by the vehemence of the wrathful cries erupting from various pockets of his listeners, Stánwilte deduced his proclamations contained the same hateful, devout self-righteousness that had whipped the crowd in Alisgate to such a violent frenzy.

Here and there, scuffles broke out between the Dragonian preachers' spectators and committed adherents of the Circle. By their furious hollering, the Circle faithful took offence at what they deemed a concoction of old wives' tales, delusional fancies and convenient prophecies – the irony of which wasn't lost on Stánwilte. Mercifully, the fights were broken up swiftly by city guardsmen.

Stánwilte was now far more relieved to be departing the capital than he had been this morning over breakfast. After all he'd witnessed, it seemed inevitable that the friction between the Circle and the Dragona would soon send a spark flying into the tinderbox of hostility. He had no intention of being around when the resulting inferno raged.

We're going to have fires aplenty to douse when we come face to face with this infernal dragon, he thought, strolling into the wide expanse of the Square of Purification.

At the other side of the square, the Cathedral of Fire hunched above a short flight of marble steps. The insectile construct of ebon stone dwarfed all surrounding buildings in both size and architectural scope, glaring at the group with hundreds of stained-glass eyes. Stánwilte shook off a mental image of the whole building rising and scurrying across the busy square to devour them all. Oddly enough, he hadn't been as put-off by the cathedral the night before, but light could play funny tricks on the mind.

Thousands of followers had amassed before the cathedral steps, shouting pleas for guidance from the wisdom of the dragons. Hundreds of furious proclamations about the crimes of the ruling classes were tossed about in the general hubbub, condemning their mistreatment of the common people in the dragons' absence. Most disturbingly of all, several threats were being chanted by the crowd, promising retribution upon the offenders if any of the returning dragons came to harm. Those cries sat particularly poorly in Stánwilte's gut, with only his strict policy of secrecy giving him some relief. A policy he was even more grateful for when they passed a wide, empty space barricaded off within the centre of the square.

'Why, exactly,' Smiggly asked nervously, 'is this place called the Square of Purification?'

It was a valid question for one who didn't grow up in Spyrata, and therefore wasn't aware of its long history and traditions. Now wasn't the most reassuring time to discuss such matters, but Wilkhelm was obviously in the mood to frighten the young lad for his own amusement.

'My father used to tell me that the Square of Purification earned its name from the years following the unification, when Arnheld of Schwartz would have all those who'd stood against him during the struggles of the Ohmen

War burnt alive in Byrnegona's searing breath. Only after forcing them to watch their wives, sons and daughters all suffer the same fate first, of course. Thus purifying their treacherous lines for the newly-formed Kingdom of Uprynenos.'

'That's quite enough of that, thank you,' snapped Stánwilte. 'I don't know if you ever paid much attention to your history lessons, as your father was obviously trying to upset you with grim tales – much like you're presently attempting to do to Smiggly – but Byrnegona was dead long before the kingdom was forged. If you must know, this square was where the Dragonian Inquisition used to burn heretics before they were disbanded.'

'Then ... why is that section closed off?' Smiggly asked, once again prob-ing around in areas Stánwilte really wished he wouldn't.

'If you hadn't noticed,' said Brolo, 'the Inquisition isn't disbanded anymore. So, when it comes time to roast up some good old-fashioned heretics-on-a-stick, where else would they set up shop?'

The colour drained from Smiggly's face, and he stepped closer to Stán-wilte's side.

While they pressed towards the centre of the Square of Purification, through the gaps in the crowd, Stánwilte could distinguish a host of ar-moured men waiting by the foot of the cathedral steps. They stood guard over some trunks, several sacks and five saddled horses. Standing by those horses was the menacing, ivory-skinned minion who'd emerged from thin air by the High-Keeper's side last night.

The Inquisitor, Stánwilte remembered.

As they drew closer, he noticed the retinue of men all wore the white question mark and red-hot pincers of Inquisition Sinisters. A small force: simply enough to ensure his party left the city as instructed, or to make swift work of them if they didn't.

Speaking of my party, where's the tag-along we're supposed to be dragging off with us? he wondered, studying the group. *The only other person I can see with the Inquisition is that young girl— oh, Relfread, you utter bastard! As if I didn't have enough bloody problems!*

Stánwilte groaned audibly at the sight of the woman with lustreless brown hair, which wasn't so much cut short as on the cusp of growing back, stroking the mane of one of the tethered horses. Her emaciated frame gave the impression she was recovering from a severe illness, but her posture held a hint of steel. The eagerness in her eyes implied she at least had the pluck for adventure.

Or the desire to be away from that sneaky Inquisitor and his leash-holder, thought Stánwilte with sympathy.

He mulled over the issue of how three immature, contentious boys were going to react to a girl who'd passed the monstrous hurdle into womanhood. It was an added stress he could picture littering the road ahead with battered prides and the bloody drips of broken noses.

'Captain Yoakilor,' hissed the Inquisitor, cold eyes catching on Stánwilte as he approached the steps. 'I was beginning to believe ... nay, *hope* that you'd decided to reject the High-Keeper's offer and play a little game of hide-and-seek with my Sinisters. Such a pity.' The Inquisitor casually stretched his back, revealing a hint of the muscular frame hidden under the finery of his position. 'The Inquisition has become quite deft at smoking out rats, and I personally enjoy the hunt.'

'Sorry to deprive you of your satisfaction, but I'm afraid we woke up a little sluggish this morning. Late night, you see.' Stánwilte cracked a smirk at the thought of Relfread's bare and suspiciously red arse bouncing down the stairs of Aelia's brothel.

The Inquisitor expelled the faintest wisp of a laugh.

'Relf— the High-Keeper has elected to leave me in the dark over the finer details of what took place before my arrival last night. I can assure you, though, after your departure ... well, His Eminence was in something of a savage fury. I fully expected him to void your arrangement and command me to bring you to him in chains. Alas, all remains as agreed upon, despite the frustrations you have caused.'

'Oh, I bet he's frustrated, alright,' said Brolo, stifling a chuckle.

The Inquisitor's eyes narrowed. 'I would learn to keep your mouth shut, boy. Unless you would like me to reach in there and rip out your humorous tongue? His Eminence has commanded that you leave this city alive, but he spoke nothing of being whole. I suggest you let the human-folk do the talking, eh?' His voice snapped with an icy draught that cracked the curve from the spine and froze it into a solid rod of terror. A remarkable impact, considering he hadn't raised his voice further than the shush of a stern librarian.

'Brolo, by Arnheld's beard, can you rein in your damn tongue before it once again gets us all in the shit?' barked Stánwilte. Lowering his tone, he turned back to the Inquisitor. 'If Relfread hasn't bothered to tell you anything, then you shan't be hearing of it from me. I want to depart this place before he does change his mind.'

'Everything you need has been provided, have no fears there. Fresh horses, weapons, food, wineskins, coin – all as the High-Keeper generously promised. You can be on your way as soon as you're sitting in your saddle. Of course, we do have one more matter to address. Girl, come here!'

The young woman who'd been tending to the horses grudgingly strode over to the Inquisitor, brandishing a murderous countenance that could break a rock. Preferably, Stánwilte got the impression, over the Inquisitor's head.

'This insolent bitch is called Yilonia. She is to travel north with you, as discussed. I've instructed her to give you no trouble, but I would advise you to tie her to her horse now and save yourself from future inconvenience. Much like you, Stánwilte, this one is a nut I will rue not being able to—'

A rush of frantic screams interrupted him. The tell-tale ripple of a commotion in the far corner of the square caused a surge in the horde, as the amassed citizens of Spyrata rushed over in the excitable way crowds do at the first sign of a brawl. A group of armoured men formed in a defensive wedge were gradually forcing their way through the crowd, hacking and stabbing with halberds at any unarmed peasant who dared try to grapple with them. Which, despite the sheer suicidal idiocy, was being attempted by a fair number of people. Anything and everything close to hand was being launched at the force, bouncing pathetically off their large shields. This futility did nothing to quell the waves of items pelting them.

'At least they ain't pissed at us this time,' said Brolo.

After glaring his annoyance at such a daft remark, Stánwilte secretly admitted to himself that he concurred.

Narrowing his eyes to slits, trying to focus on the cause of all the hub-bub, Stánwilte glimpsed an old hag of a woman dressed in shoddy black robes between the mass of armed men. A stack of old wooden crates, where one of the plethora of street preachers had previously stood, was now vacant of its righteous fanatic. Instead, a small group of citizens attempted to mount the heap, striving to gain a better shot at the shielded men slowly fighting a path away from them.

As far as Stánwilte could deduce, the woman was a Dragonian preacher who, in one way or another, had caused enough offence that the City Guard had felt the need to take matters into their own hands. A simple enough reason for the uproar of the Dragonian population. Neverthe-less, some minor detail seemed wrong. Something Stánwilte had missed.

His suspicions stirred like a hibernating bear waking in need of a snack, discovering it now shared its cave with a group of unsuspecting travellers sheltering from the rain.

When did the Guard change the colour of its livery? he thought, trying to remember his years in Spyrata, struggling to recall any time when the guard hadn't worn the royal gold and blue. He glanced about the Square of Purification as if the answer were a fly buzzing annoyingly around his face that he couldn't swat away. As the fighting amongst the crowd grew fiercer and citizens of Spyrata fell in their dozens to the blades of the armoured men, Stánwilte caught a flash of a badge of flaming pincers and realised the answer had been staring him in the face all along.

'Those are your men!' said Stánwilte, as he turned to the Inquisitor. 'Why in all of Arnheld's balls are you arresting your own supporters?'

The Inquisitor casually removed his leather gloves and tucked them into his sword belt, declining to glance over to the violent brawl. He slipped out a small knife from within his left sleeve, which he proceeded to whirl about menacingly for a few moments, before using the blade to casually scrape the sleep away from his eyes.

This bastard is a few plump raisins short of a fruitcake, thought Stánwilte.

'Melvanna Burkus. Although a vocal advocate for the Dragonian faith, it pains me – which I can assure you will eventually pain her more – to say I was recently informed she'd been inexcusably misconstruing the dogma of the church in her preaching to the masses.' The knife disappeared with a flash back up his left sleeve, only for another blade to be drawn from his right, which he subsequently used to pick the grime from his fingernails. 'And that is something the High-Keeper takes an extremely grim view on.'

Every muscle in Stánwilte's body tensed as he stomached the unpleasant visualisation of the Inquisitor being a despicable snake, preying on anyone he could sink his fangs into.

'I suspect you mean *dim* view on,' said Wilkhelm, his voice rich with smugness.

'Trust me, you nauseatingly pompous turd, I know when to use the word *grim*,' said the Inquisitor, flashing a grisly smile. 'Generally, it is at a time when most other people would be using words like *absolutely, stomach-churningly, bile-swallowingly, flesh-tearingly horrific.* I hope you catch my drift?'

Wilkhelm appeared to catch enough of the Inquisitor's drift that he could've flown away like a kite. In fact, judging by the glaze of terror on his face, Stánwilte guessed he rather wished he could.

'How far could someone deviate from Relfread's *return of the dragons to rule us all* nonsense when he's clearly scribbling out his vision for this utopia as he goes along?' asked Stánwilte, fully expecting a justification as ridiculously fatuous as the need to ask for it.

'Because,' said the Inquisitor, 'Melvanna was sharing her radical views on how her kind are being treated by the church.'

'What do you mean? Is she elven or something? I suppose she does look kind of elven if you squint a bit,' said Brolo, trying his best to look over the crowd.

The Inquisitor shook his head, in a manner that made it tricky to ascertain whether he was answering the question or just trying to shake the stupidity of that statement out of his skull.

'You truly are out of your depth, dwelf. I of course mean that she was slandering the Dragonian position on the role of women in the times to come. The church cannot tolerate such wild and dangerous ideas, let alone allow them to spread amongst the faithful. Melvanna was fortunate she'd been allowed to preach to begin with.'

Growing weary of the tripe spewing from this vindictive dullard's mouth, Stánwilte decided it was time to depart from his presence and leave the city.

'Well, I would say it's been a pleasure making your acquaintance, Inquisitor Siskin, but believe me when I say that I hope you never, ever slither into my path again,' said Stánwilte. 'Thank your master for all these gifts, though, won't you?'

'Never fear, Stánwilte. I do believe I shan't be seeing any of you alive again once you pass through those city gates.'

True to Relfread's word, the Inquisitor stood back and watched as the party of five climbed atop their fresh mounts and headed off, escorted by a small guard. Stánwilte sensed the Inquisitor's burning gaze as they traipsed toward the vast walls of Spyrata, suffering from the uncomfortable itch of his presence long after they'd passed through the gate. Not for the first time, Stánwilte could only wonder what sort of city he would be returning to if he miraculously managed to survive and come home in glory to his king.

CHAPTER TWENTY-SEVEN

THE ROAD HOME

The distinctive bouquet of the countryside wafted up Yilonia's nostrils, swarming her brain with a blend of unique fragrances. Not all of them would be considered traditionally pleasant, but she was equally overjoyed to catch a wisp of horse manure on the gentle breeze as she was the aromas of wildflowers and wheat. Oft-overlooked pleasures, such as the soothing trickle of a stream running below as her horse crossed its waters, or the pleasing clip-clop his shoes made upon the planking of the wooden bridge, had been denied to her for so long that she was unable to resist hungrily sucking them all in.

After her time spent following Ánad's endless horizon of bleak sand, comatose after the attack on Val's caravan, imprisoned in the palace and confined within the Cathedral of Fire, Yilonia was eager to take in all of nature's beauty. Her mood failed to sour even when it started to bucket down with rain.

Despite enjoying the pleasures of freedom, Yilonia knew something was still amiss about her sudden change of fortune. Less than a week ago, she'd been moved to the Cathedral of Fire under threat of meticulously described violence. She'd prepared herself for a protracted incarceration, along with the perilous escape attempt such a scenario would necessitate. Therefore, when she'd been suddenly woken in the small hours of the morning and commanded to prepare for imminent departure from the capital, she'd been utterly perplexed. Her probing the elderly Dragonian priest who'd been sent to wake her had promptly unearthed that she was to be escorted back to her father in Stunheath and would be leaving the city by noon.

Possibly, Relfread had resorted to corresponding with her father, extorting money from him by employing the shame her alleged sordidness would bring to his court if made common knowledge. Yilonia imagined her lordly father would've tried his best to haggle the High-Keeper down to the lowest possible price for her release. The idea he would've paid anything at all was astounding.

The fury and disgust in his eyes the last time she'd seen him had been ferocious enough she'd feared for her life, leaving her no recourse but to flee beyond the borders of the kingdom. The only reason he'd cough up coin in exchange for her return would likely be so he could inflict some form of punishment on her himself. However, she was confident a method of flight would present itself. She'd escaped her father's retribution once before and thus could easily do it again. At least, she hoped she could.

Yilonia took comfort in watching the dominating figure of Spyrata's walls reduce to a mere speck. *If I ever step foot in the capital again, I'd better be on my way to make harp strings of Relfread's guts,* she thought, as she spat on the ground, drawing a curious glance from the small boy riding alongside her. He offered her a gap-toothed grin, then retreated shyly into the confines of his thick red cloak.

Unquestionably, they were an odd group of misfits. Far too young for a mercenary band, but maybe not for a group of marauding brigands. Although, the greying fellow who'd been exchanging pleasantries with Siskin seemed too haughty for a bandit. *I suppose it's possible he could be father to the boys, if he'd been very busy between the sheets,* Yilonia thought. *What did that turd call him? Stán something or other?*

Whatever his name happened to be, there was no ignoring he rode a Dragonian-gifted steed, while draped in gleaming mail no wretched bandit could afford. Further patronage was visible by the fat purse of coins hanging from his belt that Siskin had handed over. He'd obviously been indifferent towards the Inquisitor, but how strongly were he and his rabble bonded to the High-Keeper? By the sheer wealth of provisions provided, her escort were either graciously paid due to the complicated nature of her identity or a crack unit who'd donned a scruffy disguise.

Due to the months Relfread had spent squirreling her away from prying eyes, it seemed unlikely that he'd lump her in with the first ragtag band he found in need of coin. Maintaining her wellbeing increased her value as a hostage, which would be beneficial to most parties involved. Yet it was well-established that folk who worked for coin couldn't be trusted. Particularly considering the way the elder boy with two fresh black eyes kept gazing at her, as if he were attending a banquet and she happened to be the last prawn left on the platter.

The boy attempted what could only be described as a seductive wink and smile. Unfortunately for him, his swollen, purple visage and missing teeth revealed a leer more likely to put a raven off feasting upon a fallen soldier's eyeball than attract Yilonia's attention. *Boys will be boys*, as her father used to say when her brothers hassled the maids. Well, this one was going to have a tougher time of it than her siblings.

Regardless of their oddities, her escort's lax demeanours at least implied they wouldn't be a direct threat to her person. They seemed content to silently ride to their destination without placing her under too heavy a guard. Perhaps they could spend a pleasant week or so trekking through the charming hamlets scattered around the craggy countryside of Atrinoc, leading up to Trisindall. Afterwards, they'd cut through the region's sizeable mines, quarries and forests until they reached home. It certainly wasn't a terrible trail, allowing for ample opportunity to appreciate this picturesque slice of Uprynenos. Yilonia's nerves would benefit from a period of tranquillity before dealing with her monstrous father.

After their reunion was safely out of the way, Yilonia would escape. Maybe she'd head north again. Obviously not so far as before, but perchance she'd be able to find a place in Lundinia. She'd always dreamed of seeing the Circle City. It would be a sanctuary away from Relfread and his followers, if nothing else – although she'd rather give anywhere with such large pockets of religious fanatics a wide berth. Followers of the Circle tended to be less inclined to violence but far more likely to bore a girl to death.

Still, Yilonia had dozens of leagues ahead until Stunheath would appear on the horizon, with only a band of strangers with dubious intentions to accompany her. To stave off her fears, she might as well undertake a wee probing of her chaperones.

They travelled on what gradually became less of a road and more of a muddy snail trail, left by years of merchants dragging their carts between the various settlements dotted around the countryside. Pale grey clouds lingered sheepishly behind the distant hills, not yet daring to drift on over and continue the efforts of their more ominous brothers, who'd earlier spent a considerable amount of time pissing upon the land. Without warning, a stunning gleam of sunshine burst from one of the fragile puffs of vapour, which swiftly scattered themselves to the wind, leaving the sun to beam in an untarnished sky.

Sensing the change, the youngest boy dared peek out from his cloak with all the cautiousness of a timid mole coming to surface. Yilonia rode alongside him, pondering how a lad attached to a shoddy mercenary band could develop such a jittery disposition. He'd have his reasons, whether due to his experiences on the road or mollycoddling by his parents. Shrugging,

Yilonia heeled her horse into a brisk trot, deciding it would be best to leave him alone for now. She'd try her luck with one of her other travelling companions.

Further up the road, Yilonia caught up to the two elder boys. Despite riding in line with each other, both appeared to be pointedly keeping to opposite sides of the path, as if each greatly offended by the other's pong. She hoped that her presence wasn't adding fuel to the fire of their petty feud, understanding comprehensively how boys of their age tended to act around a woman. However, it was none of her concern if two eager, imbecilic bucks wished to butt heads over the first female to pass by ... even if they happen to be horribly misguided about the doe's yearning for antlers.

Rolling her eyes, Yilonia passed the pair without so much as a glance, riding to catch up to the leader of their little troupe. As she approached him, beams of blistering noon sunshine glistened off his mail and sweat dripped from his brow.

He must be tremendously uncomfortable in all that armour, Yilonia thought, glad her simple grey shirt and riding breeches were breathable.

He barely registered Yilonia as she pulled her horse up alongside his. She rode beside him for a few minutes in an anxious wait for acknowledgment, anticipating he would demand she go away or something along those lines. Anything, really.

As they passed by a field of flax, Yilonia dabbed at the salty dew forming on her brow with her sleeve, hoping the movement would snap him from his daydreaming so he might acknowledge her presence. When it failed to have the desired effect, Yilonia attempted the only other tried-and-true method she knew.

'So … this weather, eh? Freezing cold and rainy one second, positively sweltering the next! At least we'll all dry out soon enough if it stays like this.'

'The rain at least was refreshing,' the man said, tugging at the collar of his hauberk as if to release the steam building up pressure within. 'This blasted heat is verging on ridiculous, and it's only going to get worse the further north we go.' He gave a rueful sigh.

Odd, Yilonia thought. *Stunheath isn't too much further north of here.* Presumably, the band were travelling to somewhere in Lundinia after they deposited her back into her father's care. If they didn't turn out to be a band of thuggish mercenaries, perhaps she could convince them to forget taking her home and allow her to follow them northwards for a while. If that didn't work, maybe she could simply lie and tell them she could pay double what Relfread had offered to take her to a wealthy uncle in the Isle of Jadiea instead of to her father.

Having broken the ice, Yilonia strove to unearth a cosy method of worming her way into the group's trust. Building up a rapport with this old crust-sword and sustaining a passive demeanour would be a prudent start.

'Would you not be more comfortable in this sweltering heat if you didn't ride as if primed for battle, good sir?' Yilonia asked. She spoke in the elegant manner her father had always expected her to use during formal occasions, rather than the haughty over-the-top voice she had typically used to irk him. 'No other of your noble men seems concerned enough to don his war-gear, and surely no bandits would be foolish enough to risk attacking a formidable group such as yours this close to the King's Justice.'

The man turned his head slightly, enough to peer at Yilonia out of the corner of his eye, and scoffed.

'Those *noble* lads wouldn't know a coif from a codpiece, so I wouldn't feel quite so comforted by their ability to deter brigands,' he said, turning back to face the road ahead. 'So, despite your concern, I think I will be remaining in my mail. What's more, feel free to drop the *tender-hearted dame* act. I saw the way you impaled Inquisitor Siskin with your gaze – you've got far too much fire in your belly to play the placid little maiden.'

No point carrying on with this little charade, I suppose, thought Yilonia.

'Alright, fine. I was merely trying to play nicely. As such, can I rest your anxieties regarding the need to wear such armament on my account? Despite what the Inquisitor would lead you to believe, I won't cause you any hassle.'

'Don't worry, I already take anything he spits out with such a large pinch of salt that one conversation is enough to leave me with a kidney stone the size of a fist,' he said. 'And I'm used to riding in armour much heavier than this. Mail makes a refreshing change. I'd forgotten how much more freely it allows me to move, which may prove vital down the line. In steel-plate, I'd probably get roasted alive like a pig on a spit.'

This one doesn't seem too bad, she thought. *For one of Relfread's followers, he seems courteous enough, if a little rough around the edges ... especially his sense of humour. Gosh, surely even the Eternal Shuffler has a more sophisticated funny bone.*

However, Yilonia wasn't entirely ready to throw in her lot and risk being held under tighter restrictions solely because this mercenary could churn out several japes. She needed to scratch a little further to see how deep his loyalty to the Dragona ran.

'Well, I'm sure for a crust-sword such as yourself, being endowed with some shiny new armour and a cart full of provisions isn't too bad a payment for such a simple task, eh? It is surprising to see Relfread chucking a bone to those who do his bidding.'

'Ha!' the man huffed. 'A crust-sword, indeed! Girl, I didn't serve in His Majesty's army for fourteen long and bitterly cold years, and as Commander of the King's First for seven more, merely to be addressed as a sodding *crust-sword*.'

He went silent for a moment. A pained grimace sank his jowls like an old hound's as his shoulders sagged. If what he said about being in The King's First – being its commander, no less – was true, it was clear he had since fallen from grace, with his pride still nursing the wound.

'Forgive me,' he said. 'It's all in the past, and that's where it should remain. I am not a crust-sword, but the humble captain of a town watch plopped at the arse-end of Arbour Vale. Nothing more, nothing less. I am Stánwilte Yoakilor, at your service.'

For a moment, Yilonia considered lying about who she was. Then she twigged that Relfread had likely informed this Stánwilte of his captive's identity. Trouble was – why, precisely, was a small-fry watchman leagues away from his town of jurisdiction the one tasked with returning her home? More importantly, from where did she recognise his name? Something wasn't adding up.

'Lady Yilonia of House Essiun of Stunheath, daughter of Feldspar, Earl of Stunheath. It is a pleasure to be in your custody, Captain Stánwilte.'

Shock quivered through the muscles of Stánwilte's right cheek. Running against her assumption, he'd obviously not been told whom he was transporting to Stunheath. Maybe he'd thought he was earning a tidy little sum to take some delinquent back to face trial, and, not wishing to lose pay over poking his nose in, had never questioned it further. Perhaps he was a mite too trusting of Relfread, the poor fool.

Yet when Stánwilte spoke again, he didn't seem angry about this sudden change in circumstance.

'You're Feldspar Essiun's daughter?' he asked, as if something had clicked into place in his mind. 'I thought you had the air of a strong will about you. I don't think I've ever known anyone quite as contentious as your lordly father.'

Yilonia was the one now caught by surprise. 'Am I to presume you've met my father, then?'

'Met him, angered him and spent the next week cleaning rust from my armour. Never had a summons to the King's Court over a land dispute been so furiously refused, nor with such a bottomless ocean of spittle. The man does tend to salivate when shouting.'

Yilonia found she was absentmindedly nodding along, caught in one of the countless memories of being drenched by her father's violent deluges.

'He slobbers because he is enjoying himself far too much. And I'm afraid to inform you that his temper hasn't yet been cooled by the passage of time,' Yilonia said grimly.

'Then I, for one, am glad not to be likely to cross his path any time soon. I mean no offence to your home, of course. Stunheath is a reasonably charming place, most certainly boasting a greater array of merits than damn Peplyshaw can claim. Why, when I last passed through, there was this one tavern ... well, let us not discuss such things now. Regardless of my enjoyment of prior visits, I don't believe I'll be returning in the foreseeable future.'

Yilonia stopped her mount dead in its tracks. Foolish as she'd been for believing the noose Relfread had tied around her throat had been cut loose, the meaning of Stánwilte's speech was not lost on her. Now the rope had been pulled taut, constricting enough to choke the hope out of her.

Again, Yilonia had been lied to. She wasn't going home.

Chapter Twenty-Eight

A Choice to Make

Intestines writhing around as if she'd taken a punch to the gut, Yilonia spat onto the road, battling with a vile concoction of confusion, relief and anger. In her heart of hearts, she'd sensed the freedom gifted to her by Relfread was a mere guise. Yet she failed to fathom his motivations. Why cast her away after months of confinement? She'd undoubtedly been a minor thorn in his side, but his sinister demeanour had dripped with the implication that she'd be imprisoned under his supervision indefinitely. Her worth to him couldn't have been so quickly exhausted, so why toss her aside now? Why with this curious assemblage of oddities? And this Stánwilte had clearly also been lied to about what her presence in his party entailed. She began to wonder how privy he was to the framework of Relfread's scheming, if at all. Most likely, he was complicit only to the extent that he'd been manipulated into getting rid of her.

Stánwilte had trotted on a few yards. After a time, it appeared he noticed Yilonia had fallen silent and no longer rode beside him. He turned back to where she sat on her mount in the middle of the road.

'I'm sorry,' he said. 'I hope you haven't taken my words as a slight against your home or father. Alas, we have no pressing need to visit Stunheath on our path north, as it would be a tad out of our way, though we will ride through some of your father's lands. My apologies if you're suffering a bout of homesickness, but haste is of the essence if we are to succeed. No offence was intended, I promise.'

'Shut up,' Yilonia said suddenly. 'You ... you said *out of our way*. Where in Uprynenos does *our way* lead?'

Stánwilte gave a subdued chuckle, as if unsure whether a joke had been told or not. 'Where precisely on a map? I haven't the foggiest clue, but that's why you've been lumped with us – to help us plot our course once across the border. Isn't it?'

A light breeze blew through the air, rustling the encompassing trees and startling a small kit of wood pigeons into flight. Somewhere, way up in the furthest reaches of the desolate north, a lone tumbleweed had detached itself from its roots, drifting aimlessly across the scorched landscape to fulfil an obligation it could not understand but could only satisfy in death.

'Isn't it?' Stánwilte asked again, succumbing to the discomfort stifling the air.

'Would I be asking if it was?' Yilonia snapped.

Stánwilte gazed into her soul, subjecting her to intense scrutiny, before his right eye began to twitch. He must've realised that Relfread had played them both for fools. Kicking his horse harder than strictly necessary, he shuffled closer to her. By now, the rest of the party had caught up, and they gathered around the pair cautiously.

'You haven't been told a single sliver of information about where this road takes us, have you?' asked Stánwilte.

Yilonia shook her head and ran a hand over her knotted hair, unsure where to instruct he begin digging through the mound of lies she'd been buried in. 'Only that I was to be returned to my father. I assumed we'd be taking a leisurely journey to Stunheath, which would end with a swift exchange of money and you all riding off again without a second glance. Would I be correct in assuming my release comes with no financial benefit to Relfread, but that I am to serve some ulterior purpose in his devious games?'

She began to clench and unclench her fists, fighting to rein in her fury before it gained control. Stánwilte, on the other hand, appeared to be the kind of man who, if offered a golden platter garnished with candid fruits to sweeten the taste, would still find swallowing his own rage not the least bit palatable and would most likely hurl it back at the head of the servant who'd gingerly placed it before him.

'Bastard!' he barked, as he threw the conical helmet that had been nestled between his legs onto the road with enough force to leave a sizeable dent in the metal. 'That conniving, crone-gobbling bastard!'

Yilonia sat there nervously as Stánwilte bombarded the peaceful countryside with enough filth for a pig to roll in happily for a month, painfully aware her presence must be of some complication to his plans. Yet something bemusing tickled her inquisitive nature.

'What exactly is a crone-gobbler?' she asked herself out loud. Swiftly, she heard another horse riding up next to hers and turned to see the lad with two black eyes leaning over to whisper in her ear.

'The High-Keeper,' he said softy, as if this covered all she needed to know in the utmost detail.

Unsure whether he held some interesting dirt on Relfread or she was being set up for an immature joke, as he was plainly attempting to hold back a grin, Yilonia nonetheless resolved to humour him.

'What about the High-Keeper, exactly?' she asked, with an irritated sigh.

'Let's just say this – rather than enjoying a nice, juicy, rare piece of steak, he would prefer a whopping great chunk of over-boiled mutton.'

He sat back in his saddle with an exaggerated gasp of disgust, as if to let Yilonia absorb the scandalous nature of what he'd divulged. She wasn't entirely sure why Relfread's eating habits held any relevance to the question ... unless he was partaking in cannibalism.

'I don't get what you mean,' she said.

The boy groaned. 'Ah, okay. How to explain this without offending a lady's sensibilities?' he asked, his lecherous smirk revealing a couple of gaps where teeth had been knocked free. 'I know! How about this – my father's lands have several immense cave systems that are most assuredly both smaller and younger than most of the vaginas the High-Keeper has stuck his cock into. And probably hold fewer bats, now that I think of it.'

He leered at Yilonia with what he likely believed to be a cheekily playful grin, but to her was slimy as a bowlful of fermented slugs.

'I assume you weren't to Relfread's particular tastes, hence why you've been tossed aside like yesterday's scraps. Though fret not, I'm certain you would be welcome to—'

Yilonia's hand, much to the detriment of the boy's swollen face, was in the clenching stage of her anger control when they connected. The blow popped his bottom lip like the yolk of a poached egg, sending him tumbling off his horse and into a puddle, where his gelding had unfortunately decided to empty its bladder. As the boy dropped to the piss-soaked dirt in a bloodied heap, Yilonia tingled with warmth, as if she'd slipped into a bath scented with rose petals and fragrant oils, washing away months of tension and hardship in its steamy embrace. She hoped the boy's own bathing experience wasn't as pleasant as her imagined one.

At least he can't complain that the water isn't warm, she thought, with a smile.

'Wilkhelm!' shouted Stánwilte. 'What in Arnheld's nadgers are you doing, boy?'

The vile shit named Wilkhelm wiped his bloody face with his sleeve and pointed up at Yilonia. 'That crazy bitch struck me!' he exclaimed. 'Do you have any idea who my father is? By the Pit, I think I've lost another tooth!'

Stánwilte looked up from the whingeing Wilkhelm. Yilonia assumed she was about to be lambasted for attacking one of his men, regardless of her justification, but he simply shook his head wearily.

'I don't think your father's station will be of much help in this case,' he said. 'Now pick your sorry hide up and apologise for whatever the fuck you did to earn yourself a bollocking this time.'

Wilkhelm's jaw dropped. 'Me? Apologise? I'm the one bleeding here, remember?'

'Yes, and don't you forget it. Yilonia has only been with us a few damn hours, and already she's been forced to knock you off your bloody high horse!'

The marginally younger half-dwarfish, half-elven boy let off a snort of laughter.

'Did I say something funny, Brolo?' snapped Stánwilte.

'Well, Captain ... she *did* punch him off his ho—'

'I don't want to hear it! I need you three to try and act like adults for a while, as Yilonia and I have a delicate matter to address. Wait here with the horses. We're going for a walk in private.'

Stánwilte dismounted his horse and gestured for Yilonia to do the same. Apprehensively, she climbed down, all the while being scowled at by Wilkhelm as he removed his filthy, urine-sodden tunic. She also found herself on the receiving end of a nod of approval from the one called Brolo. He raised a thumb in her direction while watching with glee as Wilkhelm struggled to pull off his clothing without any of the soiled items touching his skin.

Stánwilte waited for her by the patch of road where he'd cast his helmet, surveying the damage he'd caused.

'Not so bad that it can't be fixed by a smith in the next town we pass,' he muttered, 'but if the sodding thing dented so easily from a toss to the mud, it would be utterly useless in combat. Shoddy craftsmanship, pure and simple.' He looked up and acknowledged Yilonia's presence. 'Of course, knowing where it came from, that may have always been the plan. Never mind that now – walk with me.'

He started off back down the road with such a determined pace that Yilonia had trouble keeping up. Before long, they'd marched far enough that the rest of the group looked like mere fleas in the lush countryside of Atrinoc.

'Unless you intend to march me all the way back to Spyrata on your own, I'd say we've strolled a safe enough distance for the sake of privacy,' she huffed, more out of breath than she would've expected.

Stánwilte slowed to a halt and turned to face her with his hand resting on the pommel of his sword. Not in a threatening manner, but in that of a man bone-weary and in need of support.

'Before I start, I should let you know that you're free to leave here and now, or at any point in the future, if you do choose to remain with us once you've heard our intentions. At no point were you intended to be our prisoner. To my mind, your services – as I understood you to be providing them – were offered willingly. Having said that, if what Relfread told me regarding your experiences was also a complete fabrication, I shall forbid you from accompanying us any further. The going will be tough. Therefore, anyone coming simply for the thrill of adventure would eventually become a liability. With this in mind, should you opt to leave us, I would request you kindly keep what I'm about to tell you to yourself.'

Yilonia stood in silence, considering Stánwilte's words. The day was stinking hot, yet she shuddered as if a biting chill had swept across the rolling landscape, unsettled by the gravity with which Stánwilte spoke to her.

'Forbid all you like, but I feel I've earned the right to decide how I will proceed down the path ahead,' she said, displaying a bold front to mask the way her legs wobbled like the jellied eels her father was so fond of. 'Your intentions may be honourable, but I am no delicate flower you need to protect against the forces of nature. In fact, I can be quite forceful myself when the need arises. So, pray tell, what expertise did Relfread dupe you into believing I possessed? How exactly would it have been useful to you?'

'Firstly,' Stánwilte began, 'I hoped you would know of a shorter route north than the one I currently plan on taking.'

'You need a guide? Not exactly what I would deem an overly complicated task, although I can't think why I'd be seen as a prime candidate for the role, considering hundreds of merchants within Spyrata alone would possess a knowledge of the country profoundly superior to my own.'

'That's the point – where we're heading isn't technically within the confines of the kingdom. We'll be taking a long march north, avoiding most major settlements if possible, and crossing into Ánad. That is where you were expected to fit in. I was told you'd spent some time across the border?'

Yilonia's heart skipped more beats than a peasant with an aversion to purple root vegetables. Relfread, that sadistic fiend, knew exactly what she'd endured. The endless stretches of sand dunes, the complete lack of food and drink for leagues on end. The intolerable anguish of the unceasing sun sucking the moisture from her eyes. The helplessness of being alone in a parched, featureless void as her flesh withered away and her skin blistered and shrivelled until it turned as brittle as an ancient piece of parchment. And he dared send her back there?

Yilonia struggled to grasp whether she was more furious or terrified at the thought of going back to Ánad. She began to sweat profusely. Not the sticky and uncomfortable sweat one would normally feel on a stinking hot day, but countless beads of icy dew that leaked from her skin and ran down her body like blades slicing into her flesh.

Taking subtle yet laboured breaths, she wrestled to steel her nerves. Stánwilte was eyeballing her, waiting for a reply to his question. Behind his weariness, beyond his confusion at her sudden silence, she could've sworn she saw a glimmer of sincere, sympathetic understanding.

'I ... I have indeed been north in the past,' she said, as she wiped what she chose to believe was sweat from her eye. 'That much, at least, Relfread was truthful about.'

Stánwilte scratched at his chin. 'Not to give that steaming pile of goat turds any kind of credit, but I believe something else he mentioned is likely to be true – you are the so-called *survivor* of that dragon attack, are you not?'

With a looming sense of dread, Yilonia nodded, words lost in a torrent of painful memories.

'Then your company would indeed be invaluable,' said Stánwilte softly. Walking over to her, he placed a hand upon her shoulder. It sat awkwardly, as if he was replicating a gesture he'd only recently seen performed. 'No matter what minor truths Relfread divulged about your past, you're still burdened by his lies, which I can only apologise for. The truth is that my men and I are on a ... delicate mission. We wish to ride deep into Ánad and hunt down the dragon residing there. The dragon that – I bloody hope, because I don't plan on fighting two of the bastards – attacked you.'

Yilonia's eyes clenched shut. Her heart had pumped through all her reserves of anger and fear, leaving precious little emotional strength to soothe her. She'd had a sense of what was coming, but that hadn't made hearing it aloud any easier. Nor had it made Stánwilte's intentions sound any less ludicrous. As always, solving one question had led to several more arising.

After what seemed an age of being lost deep in the murky grove of her own consciousness, Yilonia began to hear muffled voices. They gradually grew louder, closer and more distinct through the dense shroud of fog swamping her thoughts. However, before she could untangle their words, they increased in volume so rapidly that what had begun as a mere hush in the wind grew to a hurricane of raging screams battering against her skull. She fought to banish the shrieking from her head, yet she felt utterly weak against it. The almighty clamour threatened to engulf all that stood before it, until she could withstand it no longer ...

Yilonia's whole body convulsed, her eyes snapping open. She looked up at Stánwilte, who'd apparently continued talking without noticing she'd switched off. Abruptly, she brushed his hand away from her shoulder, renewing her resolve to forge her own path.

'As I wouldn't like to have missed any smear of shit that has led us to this point in time,' she said, voice sharp with sarcasm, 'let me summarise the deceit that has brought us together. Relfread, the High-Keeper of the Dragona, has heralded the return of a benevolent dragon to Uprynenos. While trying to revive his ailing church, he has found a former commander of the royal bodyguard and three boys at least behaviourally on the wrong side of manhood, kitted them all up with bright, shiny armour, and commanded them to travel into the harsh and unforgiving north. All that to kill the very dragon he parades about as being the kingdom's saviour, presumably with no knowledge about how to execute such a gargantuan task. How can you be sure he's not paying you to be a delicious offering to his little pet?'

Stánwilte gawped at her incredulously. Yet he was quick to recover his composure, taking a step back and crossing his arms.

'This has nothing to do with Relfread!' he barked, then breathed in deeply. 'Sorry, but don't be so naive as to believe I haven't attempted to pick through his motives. It's an extraordinarily complicated matter, alright? Suffice to say, our suicidal jaunt northwards germinated as a personal endeavour, for reasons that shall remain my own until we decide where you fit into this mess.'

Stánwilte uncrossed his arms, let out a great huff of a sigh and flopped down on the grassy bank at the side of the road. Yilonia joined him. They sat in silence for a few moments, Yilonia wishing she'd picked her spot more wisely, as she now dealt with the awkwardness of a muddy and damp rump.

Eventually, Stánwilte broke the silence.

'You're right, of course. We don't have a sodding clue how to kill a dragon,' he said. 'I'm clutching to the hope that a well-placed strike with a sword will do the job, like it does with most things. In all honesty, my utter lack of familiarity with dragon-lore was the reason I decided to involve Relfread, stupid as it was. I hoped he would be aware of some ancient secret or forgotten fable from times of yore that told of a weakness inherent to dragonkind we could exploit. How very wrong I was! We would've been better off staying well away from Spyrata. At worst, I'd expected we would get our hands on some tome full of blasted magic that we could unleash if the situation became dire enough.' Yilonia noticed that Stánwilte began nervously stroking the pommel of his sword as he spoke of magic, clenching his other hand into a fist she suspected she couldn't pry open with a crowbar. 'But instead, we got you. No offence intended, of course. I simply didn't want to involve anyone else in this mess.'

'None taken,' said Yilonia, though his account possessed several missing pieces in need of explanation before she could believe he spoke the truth. 'Surely seeking Relfread's help wasn't a completely fruitless endeavour, though? When you arrived at the steps before the cathedral, you had almost nothing with you. Now you've all been provided with armour, weapons, food, horses and that sizeable pouch of coins chinking away on your belt. Never mind having me as your token dragon-hunter extraordinaire. Something must've been given or promised in return, surely?'

Stánwilte shrugged. 'Such is the barrel of pickled turnips I've been trying to open. Other than stipulating that we leave Spyrata today, Relfread asked nothing in return for showering us with everything we required. Don't misunderstand me,' he said, holding up his hands, 'I'm fully aware such a conniving spider will have some way to extract compensation in mind ... particularly as our negotiations didn't exactly begin on the right foot.'

'He wasn't expecting you?' asked Yilonia, intrigued.

'Let's just say that our dear High-Keeper was preoccupied with his charitable work ensuring that the aged of the capital have the means to put bread on their tables,' said Stánwilte, a slight grin forming on his lips. Yilonia suddenly remembered something Wilkhelm had mentioned to her earlier and decided to not pursue the subject any further. Thankfully, Stánwilte also returned to the original topic. 'Regardless of all his material gifts, I'm still no closer to forming a feasible strategy for killing this blasted dragon. He refused to offer any tangible help in that respect, claiming he couldn't aid us in any official manner. Whether he's bluffing, and there's truly no method to bring down a dragon, I couldn't say.'

A whipcrack of realisation snapped within Yilonia's mind. Ever since her first genuine escape attempt, a minor conundrum had puzzled her. Now, perhaps, she'd figured out its significance.

'A short while ago, I found myself in a disused section of the Palace of the United,' she said. 'Disused, I suspect, by everyone except Relfread. I discovered what seemed to be a library, which held a plethora of ancient books, all early sources on dragon-lore. Now, I'm not saying he must've discovered a way to slay a dragon and withheld it from you, but knowing the devious little weasel, I suspect he was investigating something he certainly wouldn't reveal to you or me.'

Stánwilte rose to his feet and began pacing back and forth along the road, kicking up a cloud of dust. 'Undoubtedly, he's up to something,' he said. 'Our endeavour will have consequences upon his position. Alas, as it stands, I can't do anything about it – my road lies ahead, not behind. Therefore, whatever he's plotting will have to wait until I return. I'm assuming he can't act until then, so that's when I will untangle his web.' Stánwilte stopped directly in front of Yilonia and stood in silent consideration for a few moments before speaking again. 'For now, the only issue you need concern yourself with is your intentions from here. In spite of your inexperience in slaughtering colossal, fire-breathing reptiles, I'd be more comfortable keeping you with us and dealing with Relfread together than leaving you behind, but the decision is yours alone to make.'

Stánwilte extended a hand. Yilonia stared at it blankly, conflicted. A difficult choice stood before her. She could follow her brain and flee in the hopes of forging a peaceful life alone, away from the painful memories of the past. Or, she could listen to her heart and confront the darkness head-on: go back to the place all her nightmares began, walking willingly into a realm of hardship and misery, all for the miniscule possibility that she'd someday relish a sliver of revenge against Relfread.

In the end, there was only one choice. Ignoring the voice wailing in terror at the back of her mind, Yilonia took Stánwilte's hand.

CHAPTER TWENTY-NINE

THE SHADOW GROWS

As the bundle before him burst into a bright orange flame, thin tendrils of smoke drifting from the firewood Smiggly and Brolo had gathered without need of strenuous encouragement, Stánwilte smiled. He relished the rare satisfaction of a task being promptly and efficiently fulfilled, forgoing the customary whining, fighting and bitching for a change. This kind of rewarding moment had been too few and far between on the road.

Skewering pieces of rabbit that had hopped around everywhere in the woods – right up until Yilonia had proven her worth with a bow and snagged a few for supper – Stánwilte sat and pondered over the last four days. Obviously, he didn't give two shakes of a pissing goat's member about Relfread, or his own misjudgements during their confrontation at the Cathedral of Fire. Any regrets over the matter had long since been pushed to the very back of his mind. Nevertheless, the renewed belligerence Brolo displayed towards him was immensely frustrating, particularly with how hard Stánwilte had worked to win him over. Oddly, he'd even taken to ignoring Yilonia. Stánwilte had been anticipating that he would follow Wilkhelm's ill-judged example and make an attempt at courting her. Instead, over the last few days, he'd been riding at the very back of the group, alone.

Judging by her penchant for riding at the fore with him, Stánwilte trusted Yilonia didn't take this shunning personally. Wilkhelm, naturally, had avoided her like the plague since she knocked him from one side of Uprynenos to the other. With Brolo throwing some sort of petulant protest, other than Stánwilte himself, Yilonia only had Smiggly to talk to. However, all the lad could manage was a nervous babble, a clumsy smile and a whispered statement that he was feeling unwell and needed to ride at the back for a while. It was as if he was worried his mother would jump out from the trees, waving her rolling pin, at the mere idea he would speak to a woman other than herself.

I will never cease to be amazed by how utterly sheltered these county bumpkins can be, Stánwilte thought, shaking his head. Not that boys born and raised in the cities were any superior in their approach to women. If these were city boys travelling with him, Stánwilte would've probably had to have chopped off at least one wandering hand by now.

As it appeared that no one else was capable, Stánwilte had spent a good deal of the last four days engrossed in conversation with Yilonia. It was, admittedly, a satisfying change of pace to have a travelling companion unaccustomed to the trivial bickering smalltown folk championed as a local pastime.

During the first two days, Yilonia had been hesitant to speak on her time in Ánad. Once she'd relented and begun discussing her horrifying experience with the dragon, she'd still left out specific details, like why she'd been going north in the first place. There were evidently things she wanted to keep to herself. After everything she'd been through, Stánwilte believed she was entitled to that. He wasn't going to push the subject.

As the miles slipped by, Yilonia had delved deeper into her time within one of the Towers of the Crown, painting a startlingly accurate image of the main chamber within Slyvista's Tower. Then, she'd detailed her confinement away from the King's Law, within the Cathedral of Fire itself. Listening to her tale, Stánwilte had occasionally found himself clenching a fist, scandalised by how frivolously the palace guards had treated the kingdom's laws, even if it was a member of the royal family flouting them. A grim symptom of the king's illness. Even more dire was the idea that the Dragona and their Inquisition had been granted legal permission to waltz around Uprynenos seizing and holding whomever they saw fit.

Bile crept up Stánwilte's gullet, almost discouraging him from the smell of roasting rabbit as it sizzled over the flames. *The barons and earls must truly fear a peasant uprising under the Dragonian banner to cede Relfread such powers,* he thought.

Stánwilte wished nothing more than to see King Petyier restored to full health, unshackling him to undo the blatant power-grabbing of his crooked sibling with a snap of his fingers. Finding fresh vitality with each squalid detail of Relfread's machinations that Yilonia disclosed, Stánwilte resolved to undertake whatever deeds necessary to regain His Majesty's favour, even if *whatever deeds necessary* was a petrifying thought. He peered into the ravenous campfire before him, reaching his hand into the flames until the hairs on his fingers began to singe and the searing pain became unbearable. Snapping his hand away, he opened and closed it to shake out the pain, grumbling.

All we need to do is slay a dragon, he thought, optimistically hoping Yilonia's portrayal of the serpent's fiery rain of devastation had been exaggerated.

Huddled in a circle around the sparse warmth of the campfire, the five ate their woeful meal in near silence. Near, other than the sound of pointedly exaggerated chewing, with the associated grumbling from stomachs waking up to the discovery that this bland, charred meat was all the nourishment they were due to receive.

Stánwilte tried heroically to ignore the disparaging glares of four sets of eyes. He'd never said he *could* cook, simply that he *would*. As there was an outsider in the group, he'd thought it would be beneficial if they started taking turns fulfilling certain duties while making camp. He'd intended to ease frustrations, bring in a sense of solidarity and instil some semblance of military order. All he'd likely accomplished was a mild bout of food poisoning. At least he could take a newfound respect for Mistress Roslyn's efforts away from his own culinarily attempt. Nevertheless, when it was next his turn to prepare the evening meal, Stánwilte decided he'd pay for them all to dine at the nearest inn.

As long as we can find a town not touched by the shadow of the Dragona, he thought.

***

Willowford, the place had been called, named after the ancient trees lining the banks of the river Aight, which flowed placidly through the town. Despite its charming name, Stánwilte had been ill at ease as they'd ridden into the severely-dilapidated settlement that morning. He'd been forced to cover his nose with one hand to stop himself from gagging on the acrid stench that hung in the stagnant air. The pong, along with the haunting aura of unseen eyes watching them from the shadows, had almost caused Stánwilte to order the group to turn around and find another spot to cross the river. However, he'd shaken off his unease as childish nerves and let curiosity get the better of him, leading the band through the murky decay of Willowford.

As they'd ridden past a host of burnt-out dwellings, memories of his time in the army, when he'd rummaged through the smouldering wreckage of fishing villages fallen to raiders or towns taken by drawn-out sieges, had plagued Stánwilte's mind. Several carts and old market stalls had been over-turned and left to rot, their former contents strewn about them. The only life had been a handful of malnourished pigs and scraggly hens wandering about in the dirt, snuffling and scratching in a futile search for sustenance. Stánwilte would've been sure the town had long since been abandoned if it hadn't been for the scattered plumes of grey smoke drifting from several chimneys at its centre.

As they'd drawn nearer to the town square, Stánwilte had heard the high-pitched wails of a baby in distress, ripping through the thin blanket of silence that had engulfed the rest of Willowford. Then it had cut off in a way Stánwilte had never heard any child silenced before. So suddenly. So permanently.

With a fretful look in her eyes, Yilonia had urged Stánwilte to either charge through the town and be done with it or lead them back the way they'd come. Smiggly had also voiced a wish to leave as he'd sat wrapped within the imagined safety of his cloak, eyes zipping around in search of a threat. Determined, however, to solve the mystery of Willowford, Stánwilte had waved their objections aside and urged his mount forward.

Before long, further signs of habitation had begun to appear. An elderly dwarfish woman in tatty garments had whimpered in her sleep, slumped upon a filthy bed of straw beneath a rusted seamstress's sign. When Stán-wilte had peeked into the shop through a broken window, he'd seen that it had been devoid of any furnishings, bare and decrepit as the woman outside it. Stánwilte had guessed her to be the seamstress, who'd been forced to close shop due to some form of hardship.

Amongst a handful of other rough-sleeping beggars, a smattering of grim-faced townsfolk had shuffled about the square, eyeing Stánwilte and his group with distrust. In contrast, several chirpy children had run around in scant rags, playing games, ignorant to the state of their home. In the very centre of the square had stood the stump of what must've once been an obligger tree of considerable size. After starting to count the rings and giving up, Stánwilte had proclaimed it to have been a very ancient tree indeed, perhaps older than the Unification. Now, after all those centuries of growth, it was gone. A symbolic elder of the town brought down in an act that surely had enraged the citizens of Willowford.

Intriguingly, to either side of the stump had been two large circles burnt into the paved surface of the square. From those markings, Stánwilte had formed a reasonable theory as to what use the wood from the fallen tree had been put to, as flickers of the lunacy whipped up by the nimble wrist of the Dragona at Alisgate played back in his mind.

After stilling the sense of impending dread in his heart, Stánwilte had led the group across the square to the building that held claim to being the closest thing in Willowford to a hive of activity. A place that, if the iron sign rusting in a puddle by the front door had been anything to go by, had at some point been known by the rather tongue-in-cheek name The Obligatory Half.

Leaving the others to look after the horses, Stánwilte had taken Brolo with him to pick the scab of his curiosity by nosing around inside the inn. Brolo hadn't been pleased by the prospect, but Stánwilte had wanted to keep an eye on him in case he inadvertently started another riot. Also, if a scuffle broke out, his damned hammer might've been required to save their metaphorical bacon.

When Stánwilte had opened the door to the inn, the hinges had squeaked like a mouse having its tail torn off, drawing the glares of everyone in the room. Ignoring the few dozen sets of eyes stabbing Brolo and him repeatedly in the necks, Stánwilte had strode over to what he'd taken for the bar. He hadn't been able to see any innkeeper around to serve drinks, so while he'd waited, he'd taken the time to soak in the aura of The Obligatory Half.

The common room had been spacious but barren of decoration, dotted with a mishmash of old tables and crooked chairs that had given the impression they'd be far better as firewood than functional furniture. Which was why, Stánwilte had assumed, everyone occupying a seat had looked so bloody miserable. Another reason he'd deduced for all the inn's patrons scowling as if they'd been slapped across the face with freshly laid cow pats was the fact nobody had appeared to have any form of fermented beverage before them. In fact, no one had had a drink of any kind at their table. The final confirmation Stánwilte had needed to prove something very worrying indeed was afoot came when Brolo had pointed out the bar itself was devoid of any bottles or barrels.

After a few minutes of tense smiling and nodding to the locals, who'd returned the gestures with scowls so pissy you could've soaked a cow's hide in a vat of the stuff to transform it into a fine piece of leather, a small hatch at the far end of the bar had burst open with a crash. Out of it had climbed a furiously mumbling dwarfish fellow. Cursing to himself, he'd dusted himself off, kicked the hatch closed and made to storm out a doorway behind the bar, but he'd stopped upon looking over at Stánwilte and Brolo.

'I hope you ain't here for ale, lads, 'cause we don't got none of that filth here no more,' he'd said. 'We've been cleansed-like by the flaming glory of the dragons, as the priest told us.'

He'd stumped over to stand in front of Stánwilte, scratching at his scraggly beard as if trying to retrieve an item lost within the dense forest of blond hair. His pox-scarred face had had more chunks missing than a city wall after an extended siege.

'No, no. None of that toxic bile for us, thank you, kind sir,' Stánwilte had said. 'We are merely humble followers of the Dragona who happened to be passing through when we heard news of this … charming place … being a bastion of faith to the Flame. As devoted friends of His Eminence, the High-Keeper Relfread, my companion and I simply had to pop in and commend you all on your stellar work in scourging the Circle from this town.'

Stánwilte had raised his voice enough for everyone in the room to hear his little performance, hoping to bring a trickle of goodwill their way. Unfortunately, the dwarf had been one of those sceptical bastards who questioned absolutely everything put to them. It wasn't a bad trait – it was merely incredibly tedious if you happened to be the dishonest party. Stánwilte would've needed a whole flock's worth of wool to pull one over that dwarf's eyes. As it stood, he hadn't had enough to knit a child's sock.

'Hark to this one, youse lot,' the dwarf had exclaimed to the room. 'He be best chums with the High-Keeper, don't ya know?'

A few coughs had bounced around the room. As mirthless as the response had been, the dwarf had crossed his arms and fixed Stánwilte with a smug grin.

'Look, I never said we were best friends,' Stánwilte had begun, before being abruptly interrupted.

'We've had all sorts of folk coming here and claiming shit about what bigwigs they know and what their business in these parts be,' the dwarf had snapped. 'Frankly, like, we've had enough of strangers like you causing mischief and such. We got enough to deal with by sorting out our own folk. We don't need outsiders sticking their noses in, too.'

The conversation had gone downhill faster than a yokel chasing a wheel of cheese. Stánwilte had been cautious about unnecessarily provoking the locals to anger, but he hadn't wanted to leave Willowford without finding out what had happened there before they'd arrived.

'I assure you, good innkeeper, we have no intention to meddle with your affairs,' Stánwilte had said.

'Bah! I ain't no darn innkeep. I'm just the sod who collects any trinkets left by sinful buggers who refuse to see the Flame till they're purified in it.'

Oh, here we go, Stánwilte had thought, knowing full well what had been coming next.

'So, the actual innkeeper is …'

'Not a pile of ashes. Not once we all pissed on 'em, anyway,' the dwarf had said. 'He were more of a sludge by then.'

It had taken a supreme reserve of self-restraint for Stánwilte to resist knocking the few remaining teeth out from the dwarf's triumphant smile. Through gritted teeth, he'd hissed out a commendation for how well they'd fulfilled the will of the dragons. Regretfully, his praise had only induced the dwarf into further barbaric detail.

'Aye, you think we did good work that day? You should've seen when the tanner's wife caught him wearing a ring of the Circle under his tunic. Staunchly unrepentant, he were. The dragon-priest told us we'd best make an example of him, like. Only thing to be done was give him his own set of wings, right here in the square. Bless his pious wife. She plucked the lungs from his gaping back herself, she did. Didn't even flinch when told to rub salt into his open wounds, which is more than can be said for the tanner.'

As much as he'd fought against it, Stánwilte's imagination had painted the grisly scene in his mind in vivid detail. The cold, merciless brutality the Dragonian priests were able to instil in their followers had churned his stomach, regardless of his own violent years serving in the army. How blind religious zeal could bring family members to savagely put each other to death over minor indiscretions had unnerved him greatly.

'Of course,' the dwarf had gone on, 'the most glorious day was when we held a mass.'

Stánwilte had been ignorantly relieved at this seemingly innocent religious celebration.

'Coming together for a celebration of faith must've been a pleasant experience for the community,' he'd said.

'No, no, no. Not that kinda mass,' the dwarf had said, as he'd rubbed his hands together. 'A mass burning, we had. And what a spectacle it was! We had such a need of wood, we resorted to hacking down our giant tree. Such was the scale of sin in this place.'

After such a casual recitation of mass murder being unleashed upon an otherwise innocent population, Stánwilte had decided he'd heard enough.

'Right, well. I think my friends and I should be moving along now. Many leagues to ride, not enough hours in the day, and so on. Sorry to have bothered you, sir.'

Stánwilte had turned to lead Brolo out through the door when the dwarf had snapped out after him. 'Friends? I thought you said it were just youse two.'

Bollocks, Stánwilte had thought, kicking himself.

'Er, we have three more companions with us, but they're simply tending to our horses before we continue along the next stretch of our journey,' he'd said.

The dwarf had begun to scratch at his beard, apparently unconcerned by this new information, but Stánwilte had noticed how his eyes sat fixed on Brolo, studying him intensely.

'Five of ya, eh? And one of youse be a bastard-breed to boot …'

He'd trailed off into an almost hypnotic daze of chin scratching, yet his eyes had taken on a hungry sheen that had had the pair of them slowly backing out through the door, followed by a hasty jog to their horses.

Electing not to discuss the details with Yilonia and Wilkhelm until they'd crossed the ford – and to leave Smiggly safer in his ignorance – Stánwilte had pushed the group to ride hard even after they'd been a considerable distance away from Willowford. Yilonia had voiced her horror at the description of the events that had taken place in Relfread's name. Yet her eyes had not been drawn to tears or touched by sadness. Instead, they'd hardened with steely determination.

***

Dwelling upon this morning's gory details while attempting to chew dinner would've put Stánwilte off his supper, if the foul taste hadn't already beaten the memories to the punch. Sighing, he cast the remaining portion of his rabbit into the campfire and took a deep gulp of wine to wash away the ashen flavour in his mouth.

The wine Relfread had supplied them with wasn't particularly bad, although endless weeks of swilling what Stánwilte assumed could've only been vinegar diluted with cat's urine may have dulled his taste somewhat. In fact, this stuff was the finest red that'd trickled past his lips in quite some time. Tart cherries and a subtle hint of peppercorns, with a sumptuous oaky finish. Truly splendid stuff. If he was honest, he'd been enjoying its delightful flavour with such abandon that it hadn't been so much trickling past his lips as surging down his throat in the manner of furious rapids spilling over the precipice of a cliff.

For the first time in many a moon, Stánwilte was having what some might dare to call a delightful evening, enjoying sitting around a campfire again, sharing the night with a few good friends – or, at a pinch, three underlings and a near-stranger. The stars glistened spectacularly, twinkling in time with the singing of various forest creatures. The conversation was poor … well, almost non-existent, but with wine flowing in his veins and warming his heart, Stánwilte summoned a brilliant idea to bring the group closer together.

'So – so—' Stánwilte burped. 'Sorry, excuse me. Anyone got good stories to tell?'

Like most seemingly brilliant ideas conceived under the influence of strong wine, Stánwilte was sure he'd come to regret this one soon enough. Nevertheless, like an owl who'd taken a vow of silence, he didn't give a hoot.

CHAPTER THIRTY

A RAIN OF EMERALD FIRE

With the meal on offer about as appealing as spending six hours tied to a chair while Old Wee Pete spewed out his repertoire of war stories – which tended to be the same one told on an endless loop – Brolo slipped his portion of rabbit meat into his pocket for safekeeping, in case they needed to poison someone in the future. He didn't try to conceal the act from anyone. He'd observed each member of the group in turn discard their supper in various subtle and unintentionally humorous ways, presumably to avoid offending Stánwilte and his cooking ability, or lack thereof. Fortunately, Brolo bore no such qualms about bruising his ego.

Tired, fed up, stomach rumbling, Brolo was pushing himself up to leave for an early night when Stánwilte slurred his way through some comment about telling stories. A suspiciously out-of-character suggestion. It therefore came as little shock when Brolo caught a glimpse of his glazed, bloodshot eyes and realised he'd been hogging the wineskin for most of the evening.

Oh, sodding great, thought Brolo. *The captain's gotten himself pickled as a jar of onions! Can't say that's a spectacle I've missed having to clean up after…*

Although Stánwilte had curtailed his drinking in more recent times, memories of his burdensome dependency during his first months in Peplyshaw came rushing back to Brolo like a man darting off to the privy to expel an entire evening's worth of whisky.

Stánwilte's contempt for his circumstances had been obvious by the glower nailed onto his face during his first tour around Peplyshaw. Rumour had it that the newly installed captain had ridden in such a fury that there had been genuine concern amongst the citizens that his scowl would set the town's thatched buildings ablaze. Anyone who'd mustered the audacity to greet him with a courteous doff of the hat had been looked down upon with such disdain that many had fled homewards for a thorough wash, assuming they'd been mysteriously caked in shit. Not long after Stánwilte had completed his circuit of the town, he'd settled himself in the Watch house, and very promptly, the drinking had begun.

Day in, day out, Stánwilte had whittled away the hours by brooding alone in his solar, swigging his way through the Watch's store of whisky. During that particularly dark period, the distinct shatter of a glass of potent alcohol being cast into the fireplace, followed by a sudden surge in the flames, had been heard echoing through the halls of the Watch house at least three times a night. The Watch's expenditure on glass had become unsustainable within a matter of months. However, no one had been bold enough to broach the subject with Stánwilte ... not after the first time. Poor old Nige, who oversaw the Watch's finances, had been picking glass shards out of his forehead for a week.

If any official duties had needed performing, Stánwilte had usually been in such a stupor his workload had fallen into the lap of an already duty-laden Bæwylm, who'd picked up his slack with characteristic stoicism. After several tempestuous demonstrations of cock-swinging, during which Stánwilte had attempted to stamp his authority over the man who should've had his position, he'd begun to rely heavily on Bæwylm. Eventually, he'd become the only member of the Watch who Stánwilte would speak to. A few months of wallowing in booze and bitterness later, it had been Bæwylm who'd finally coaxed Stánwilte into climbing out from the immense hole he'd dug for himself and standing up to his responsibilities. Unfortunately, it had come far too late to salvage even a sliver of Stánwilte's reputation. His intolerable attitude, booze-exacerbated rage and callous treatment of everyone he'd dealt with during those first months in Peplyshaw had cemented Stánwilte as the shining beacon of what an arsehole could make of itself if it really tried.

'Perhaps we should all hit the hay for the night,' said Brolo, rising to his feet. 'No offence, but I have no desire to listen to the string of dreary anecdotes I could expect from you lot. Certainly not within proximity to such a wide selection of trees from which I could be tempted to hang myself.'

'Oh, don't be such a wet rag, Brolo!' snapped Stánwilte, taking another swig from the wineskin. 'Can't you drop that *agonised recluse* act and have some fun for a change? We're not in bloody Peplyshaw, so you don't have anyone but us and a few owls to impress.'

Stánwilte's snide remark caught Brolo off guard, cutting a touch too close to the bone. He'd seemed blissfully cheerful a few moments ago, but now he glowered at Brolo like he'd just been informed the wine he'd been enjoying so much had been freshly squirted from Brolo's bladder. It was strikingly reminiscent of his drunken mood swings from times past. Brolo noticed how Yilonia was eyeballing both him and Stánwilte anxiously, plainly unaware of their previous tensions.

'Tossing out a compromise,' she said, 'why not stay awhile and tell a tale about yourself, if you don't feel up to hearing any of ours? I, for one, would be eager to listen to the fuckups and near-misses with the Eternal Shuffler that led you to this forest, as I still know so little about you all. Six Silver Geese says your storytelling can't be as frighteningly boring as the Palace of the United.'

It appeared she was trying to defuse the situation. Noble, but Brolo knew it to be naught but a fool's errand, especially after Wilkhelm chirped in with his two Chicks.

'Ha! Maybe Brolo could regale us with the story of where his father obtained his magical hammer ... if only he'd stuck around long enough to tell it,' he said, nudging Smiggly in the ribs.

'How about I regale everyone with the story of how we caught you in one of the old storage rooms, spreading butter over an impressively large marrow with your undergarments dropped down to your ankles?' snapped Brolo.

'Slander!' yapped Wilkhelm, bolting to his feet. 'That's nothing but a filthy lie, and you know it! He's lying, he's lying!' He turned to each member of the party, pleading his case.

Of course, Brolo had indeed made the whole thing up, but he didn't see any reason to admit so.

'If it's not true, then why did you keep volunteering to take cellar duty late last year, eh?' asked Brolo.

'Because it's fucking freezing outside in winter, you pus-brained igno-ramus!' said Wilkhelm. 'Why in all the turnings of the Circle would I elect to trudge through the sleet and shit of a frostbitten Peplyshaw if I could remain inside?'

'Why indeed?' asked Brolo.

'What? That doesn't even make—'

'Boys!' barked Stánwilte. 'Cease this now, or I will personally rip your tongues out! And I can promise one thing – it won't be through the orifice you'd expect! Was it overly unseasonable ... unreasonable of me to ask for one peaceful evening together? Sodding forget the idea. I have little dessert ... *hic* ... desire to hear anything about magic fucking hammers tonight, thank you very much. How about we let Smiggly tell us a tale?'

At this, Smiggly sat up ramrod-straight with a look of pure wonder in his eyes. 'Me, sir? Cor! Where do I begin? Well, my old Ma used to say to me, *Smiggly, my boy*—'

'Let me stop you right there,' cut in Stánwilte, much to Brolo's relief.

Smiggly deflated like a puffed-up frog slipping under a cart's wheel. Nevertheless, Brolo noticed he soon cheered up again after Yilonia put a sympathetic arm around his shoulders.

No longer quite ready for bed after all the hullabaloo, Brolo sat mulling over Stánwilte's actions these last few weeks, particularly surrounding Lawgismirin and the topic of magic in general. Stewing in a pot of vindictiveness, he decided to press Stánwilte for some answers.

'If you're so insistent that we bond tonight by waffling about our experiences, Captain, how about you enlighten us on why you grow so uptight any time a mention of sorcery slips into our banter? It couldn't possibly have anything to do with you inflicting a minor case of *death* upon the heir to the throne, could it?' Brolo sat back down by the fire, crossing his legs in mock eagerness to hear Stánwilte's reply.

Over the crackle of Smiggly feeding moss-coated branches into the heart of the campfire, the hush of trees swaying in the late-night breeze cut through the sound of Stánwilte's deep, fastidiously-controlled breathing. In and out. In and out. Each exhalation resonating as if through the ghostly, claustrophobic press of a forest, enlightening the unfortunate soul lost within to the fact that somewhere behind the low-lying mist waited a wolf with a remarkably keen sense of smell.

'No,' said Stánwilte, his refusal falling like an executioner's axe. Unfortunately for him, Brolo's interest resembled an earthworm – even cut in half, it would simply keep on wiggling. Sometimes in two different directions.

'Come now, don't be so salty,' said Brolo. Since Stánwilte's arrival in Peplyshaw, there had been an abundance of delicious morsels of gossip to feed the town rumourmongers, yet he'd always remained resolutely silent about why he'd truly been sent there. As such, Brolo had resolved to extract the marrow of the story. Its bones had to be easy to crack after so long simmering away in a broth of trauma. 'All the lads back at the Watch have theories on why you got royally shafted after Hoghamny. Some sympathetic, mind. Most absurd. A few of the more imaginative boys think the whole mess was a botched attempt to rush in the end of the Schwartz dynasty. One theory I heard figured Prince Auldalin's disgruntled guardian had found the most opportune moment to slip a blade into his—'

'Stop this utter gobshite now!' roared Stánwilte. 'I was charged with protecting the prince, and with tooth and nail, I did just that!' He rose to his feet and paced around the campfire, spurting out his account of events like a cask of too-lively ale being tapped.

'As commanded by the prince, our forces rose early. Many had spent the night in their mail, so they might delay waking to a head sore from wine, or from the thought of coin lost to games of cards and dice.' Stánwilte gave a wistful smile. 'The atmosphere the previous evening had been jovial, confident, and, as fate would prove, horrifically ignorant of the sheer power the wizards we would ride against could unleash upon us.

'I'd wasted my opportunity to catch a few precious hours of rest by imploring the prince, or anyone who still retained rational thought, to reconsider our hastily cobbled strategy ... although *strategy* may be too generous a word. I vividly remember how Auldalin dismissed my concerns with smug, impertinent ease, waving away the rebellion as a trifling matter we could clean up before returning to camp for lunch.' Stánwilte spat into the fire, crimson spittle creeping down his chin. 'I was in court before the brat learnt to wield a spoon, let alone a sword! Alas, sage though it was, my advice may as well have been the broccoli he'd despised as an infant, with the way he turned his nose up at it!

'I knew each of the wizards to a varying extent due to their prior standing within the Palace of the United. I'd witnessed numerous demonstrations of their power over the years, oft innocently wielded. They'd exulted in unleashing astounding displays of illumination, lighting the sky with dazzling colours for various festivities. Each time, I'd marvelled at how their sorcery could be used to conjure howls of pain as easily as the oohs and aahs of common folk, especially if several came together to combine the might of their magic. One might be overcome by sheer numbers, but five,' said Stánwilte, clumsily raising four fingers, 'could summon a power verging on godlike. Nevertheless, my pleas were tossed from the prince's tent only slightly sooner than myself.

'As I readied myself for what inevitably lay ahead, I dwelt on what could've been if Deguro Flay had remained. The man possessed a sheer force of will I've never myself mastered. Together, we may have been able to convince Auldalin to take a more sensible course. Alas,' Stánwilte said, with a groan, 'Auldalin had sent a message back to the capital to have him reprimanded for dissent. Dissent, I say! The ignominy of it!'

Silence fell for several minutes as he regained his composure.

'Even after all these years,' he began again, 'I still have no clue what happened to him.' He cleared his throat. 'Before long, our cavalry troops were mounted, headed by the prince himself, ready to make the charge into the marshland of Hoghamny. Following in their wake, our infantrymen were to march in tight formation, cutting through the reeds and tall grass to sweep out any rebels eluding our horsemen. We sought to strike the wizards while they were presumably at their most inattentive.

'As Commander of the King's First, I was at Auldalin's right, waiting nervously for him to give the signal to charge. The waning night still cast its shadow upon us, leaving it difficult to see beyond the rider positioned either immediately in front or behind. Regardless, the whispers of the troops eager to spill traitorous blood echoed around the hill, betraying the size of our force.

'After a short time, the prince rose his fist into the air, immediately stirring our front rank into motion. Moments after we'd begun stampeding down the hill, our mounts shifting from a rhythmic canter into a wild gallop, I could distinguish the first signs of our impending doom through the visor of my helm. Green clouds swept in to snuff out the moonlight, flashing with forked bolts of lightning. An indication of our failure to catch the wizards by surprise. As we charged heedlessly with swords held aloft, hollering a war-cry to rival the calamitous pounding of the clouds, they countered our assault by unleashing a deluge of disaster.

'Under a rain of emerald fire, we rode in terror. Tiny droplets cascaded from the pre-dawn gloom and burst into unquenchable infernos upon contact, sending our army instantly into disarray. Within seconds, the marshland began to ring with a horrific choir of screaming men and horses. Hundreds upon hundreds of cavalrymen lit up like candles. Terror-stricken mounts charged uncontrollably. Many fell in the mire and snapped their legs, tossing their riders to be crushed under the hooves of another stampeding horse. Men flailed all around me, roasting alive in their armour. Some dashed for the pools of the swamp, but the wizard's fire could not be extinguished by mere water.'

Stánwilte shook his head, tears glistening in his eyes. 'The only small mercy was that the rain had fallen like a volley of arrows, rather than a persistent downpour. By sheer luck, I, Prince Auldalin, and several other officers had remained untouched, although we could only watch in horror as Sir Nuthain Haynes was engulfed in a ghostly blaze. In his panic, he fell from his charging horse, yet his foot caught in his stirrup. He was dragged like a flaming rag doll through the chaos surrounding us, never to be seen again.

'Despite the prince's plan falling to ruin, he bellowed for the assault to press on. I pleaded with him to order the retreat. Shouted above the howls of the thousands dying around us until my voice grew hoarse, yet he ignored me once again. He roared some claptrap about all the deaths being in vain if we fell back, completely disregarding those he consigned to similar fates by pushing on.' Stánwilte sighed weakly before taking a deep draught of wine. 'However, he was my prince, and I was duty-bound to obey him, so I followed his command.

'Once we renewed our charge, many of the surviving men rallied to the scorched remains of the prince's banner, appearing like phantoms through the choking veil of smoke. Two further bombardments stole hundreds more lives. At last, in what seemed a blessed relief, the emerald rain ceased falling upon us. A half-hearted cry of triumph went up through the ranks of men. I suppose they believed the wizards had exhausted their power.

'Then the first of the corpses exploded. One by one, the charred carcasses that lay scattered in every direction became weapons against us. Each body erupted in a devastating burst of fire, flinging shards of armour and burnt chunks of flesh and bone. Scores of our remaining men were caught in the blasts. Dozens more suffered vicious wounds from the shrapnel. The smouldering bodies of the horses caused the worst devastation – their detonations had a far greater radius than those of the men. Any poor bastard unfortunate enough to be found within proximity of the blasts was torn apart into unidentifiable hunks.

'All zeal for the assault was thus cast into the emerald flames. Survivors fled in droves from the marshland, rendered now a maze of thick smoke and vast craters. Finally seeing that the day was lost, Auldalin called for an official retreat. However, somewhere to my left, the remains of a fallen soldier went off, throwing me from my horse. I landed awkwardly on my right leg. Nothing was broken, but the shock from the blast had shattered my hearing. I was left utterly disoriented.

'It happened as I rose to my feet. Auldalin was riding away in haste, closely tailed by a few survivors, though his standard-bearer was nowhere to be seen. As he rode, he appeared to be beckoning men to follow his lead out of the maelstrom of eruptions and death. Most continued to flee blindly in all directions. Seeing this, the prince made his mistake. He lifted the visor of his helm to reveal his face. I can only assume he did it to let the men know it was their noble prince who wished to lead them to safety. The foolish whelp!

'Time slowed to a dying man's crawl. A corpse exploded close to where Auldalin was standing up in his stirrups, waving and hollering at the survivors. He was at a safe enough distance to be untouched by the initial blast, but a large piece of plate armour shot through the air and pierced his left eye like a well-placed arrow. It must've sunk all the way to the brain, for he fell from his horse instantly. And with him fell my career and reputation.

'For a time, I rejected the truth of events, certain I had merely been witness to a sorcerous illusion created to dismay the men. Knowing what I now do, I should've remained in that damn marsh and died with Auldalin, yet I eventually made it out of the chaos on foot. That day has been a fixture in my nightmares ever since. Nevertheless, despite claims to the contrary, guilt has never been at the root of those dreams.

'As soon as news of the death of the king's only son and heir reached the capital, the blame fell upon my shoulders. The handful of nobles and commanders who'd survived the havoc had darted for Spyrata while the marsh still burnt, all claiming the attack had been my idea. Some claimed I hadn't even charged onto the field of battle, declaring I was nowhere to be seen when Auldalin fell. I ultimately made it to the capital to plead my case, yet the king refused to see me. *Me!* The Lord Commander of his personal guard!'

Standing, Yilonia attempted to place a hand upon Stánwilte's shoulder. He shoved it off, then weakly nodded an apology to her.

'Before long,' he continued, 'the decree came that I was to be executed for treason and desertion. Soon after, perhaps owing to my past services, the order was reduced to exile from Spyrata. I tried to fight for my restoration and clear my name, but my efforts proved fruitless. No one cared that I advised against the charge. No one remembered that I mounted my horse and rode into that ghastly marsh regardless. In the end, I was a scapegoat, thrown to the midden heap to cover other people's standing in court. There was nothing I could've done to change what took place. How, I ask, can a mere man protect a prince from his own folly?'

Brolo looked away as Stánwilte's eyes bulged in painful memory. His tale left the impression it had been spoken a thousand times in his head, but never out loud. Having achieved what he'd desired, having dumped a cumbersome bale of straw onto the shattered spine of Stánwilte's emotional camel, Brolo suffered a pang of shame. Shame and embarrassment. For himself, and for his captain.

He watched as Stánwilte drained the rest of the wineskin in a succession of deep gulps, in what was the only suitable course of action after publicly expunging years of bottled-up agony. From across the campfire, Yilonia was staring at Stánwilte with a sympathetic shimmer to her eyes.

'You're *that* Stánwilte. I thought your name sounded familiar, but I couldn't quite place it,' she said softly, as if afraid to stir up further emotion. 'I'd heard the story of how Prince Auldalin died some time ago, though only the … official side of things. It was all my father could talk about for a month.'

'Ha! And I bet you've never heard why I returned to Spyrata much later than the other commanders, which gave them all time to spin the yarn of blame so freely. I happened to be the only bastard to stay behind and recover Auldalin's body from the marsh. A mistake born of devotion, a foolish act of loyalty! A deed many claimed to indicate my guilt!'

Stánwilte chuckled bitterly. He shook his head, wiping away a tear that only extortionately priced hindsight could draw from a man, and threw the drained wineskin to the ground.

'And you know the worst thing?' he asked the group, who sat in silence, waiting. 'Those rebellious wizards were never caught! Nobody found even the slightest whiff of their whereabouts. They simply vanished into the marshland without a trace. So, I became the only person to face punishment for that debacle. That is the cause of my hatred for magic, Brolo. That is why the blood drains from my face at the thought of you wielding your father's hammer. The best thing to come out of the whole affair was King Petyier outlawing sorcery – magic wielders were far too powerful for their tomfoolery to go on unrestrained. Lamentable as it was for the various schools of magic, they were notoriously resistant to the idea of limits being placed on their abilities. The need to purge their kind from society became unavoidable. Now, if you'll excuse me, I think I need to go vomit behind a bush and pass out.'

With that, Stánwilte staggered away into the forest, stopping to pinch another skin of wine from their bags of supplies. Doubtless, Brolo thought, to stop the picked scabs of his memories from bleeding into his dreams during the night.

No one said much after Stánwilte left. One by one, the group drifted off to their blankets, dwindling until Brolo alone sat awake by the fire. His eyes fixed on Lawgismirin as she sat against the trunk of a spruce tree, along with a heap of other supplies.

Maybe fear of prosecution is why my mother never told me about Pa's hammer being enchanted, he thought. *Maybe she didn't want it to be seized by the Crown, or maybe she didn't know of its magical properties at all. Either way, it was sodding irresponsible of Father to leave something so dangerous lying around.*

Illegally enchanted or not, one thing Brolo knew for sure was that he wouldn't be surrendering Lawgismirin to anybody. He'd like to see somebody try to prise it from his fingers without their brain leaking onto the floor like scrambled eggs.

After the abnormally violent images subsided from his mind, Brolo pondered Stánwilte's words about sorcery and the atrocious devastation it had dealt to the realm. A pang of regret for the forcefulness of his previous thoughts thumped him in the kidneys. He was a smidge sympathetic to Stánwilte's prejudices, if not wholly in agreement with them. Perhaps he had point – to a degree – about magic, but Brolo would simply show him that Lawgismirin was different. She would only be used when necessary for defence.

Magic can be a force for good, too, Brolo thought. *I'll prove it.*

He even, bearing in mind the events of Alisgate, found a glimmer of understanding for Stánwilte's recent attitude towards him. Considering the trauma of what Stánwilte had gone through, it was clear why he'd come out of it all with quite the psychological chip on his shoulder. He was still a cavernous arsehole of a man, but an arsehole with a whiff of justification. If the thought didn't make Brolo as nauseous as a sea-sick acrophobic climbing a ship's mast on a stormy day, he might've said he and Stánwilte had more in common than either of them cared to admit. The

Eternal Shuffler knew he wouldn't be the first to acknowledge it ... though maybe he could cut Stánwilte some slack. Maybe.

Brolo was mulling over the value of empathy when the crackle of twigs snapping underfoot indicated Stánwilte's return from expelling the contents of his stomach over the undergrowth of the forest. *By all the dwarfish gold, the soused git must've stumbled around a full loop of the forest,* Brolo thought. *I could've sworn he staggered off behind that big elm.*

He spun round casually to face the sound.

'Look, Captain. I'm sorry about—'

In the faint glow of the dying fire, Brolo caught the slightest glimpse of a blunt instrument swinging towards him, followed by the distinct sensation of a direct hit across the temple, before the world fell dark.

EPILOGUE

'I must admit, dear brother, it truly is a most beautiful city ... in the right light, of course,' said Relfread, gazing out the window of the King's Chamber, up high within the Palace of the United.

The king himself shivered gently in his bed, drifting in and out of consciousness. Down below, beneath the darkness of nightfall, the streets of Spyrata shimmered with a bright orange glow. Flames tore indiscriminately through residential and commercial districts, through slums and affluent neighbourhoods. The distant roars of the riotous hordes hummed through the glass, bringing a smile to Relfread's face.

How many dead already, I wonder? he mused, tapping his nails against the windowsill. *Many would be trapped in their homes by fear of the mob, with nothing left to do except huddle together as suffocating wafts of pitch-black smoke cradle them gently to sleep and their shoddy dwellings become both their funeral pyre and their tomb. The figures must surely run into the thousands already. Never mind all those fighting out in the streets!*

Relfread was sure some would say he was insane, to revel in such chaos. A monster, even. Yet, watching on as the swarm of rioters destroyed, looted and murdered with insatiable brutality, he swelled with nothing but pride at a job well done. He'd deftly woven the string of events that had served as the fuse to ignite the populace of the capital. Now, in the smog of confusion billowing from a city purged through incineration, he could move ahead with the next stage of his plan.

Relfread slipped away from the window and the carnage of the world beyond. Gliding past the dim candles glittering like distant stars around the room, he lowered himself into the sumptuous violet chair beside King Petyier's bed.

'You always did have a taste for the gaudy things in life,' he said, taking his older brother's skeletal hand in his own.

For a while, Relfread sat in silence, watching from beneath the hood of his robes as Petyier's chest gently rose and fell. Typically, the chamber would've also been occupied by a member of the King's First, but Inquisition men had slowly taken over the role of guards within the Palace of the United. Therefore, the guard stationed outside the door had humbly complied with Relfread's request that he be left alone with his beloved brother. Simply another privilege of his newly secured influence.

The delicate consolidation of his power within the capital, right under the stuck-up noses of the nobles of the Royal Court, had been almost laughably simple. A domino effect that appeared to have been set into motion by one girl's sensational account of the first dragon to be witnessed since Byrnegona's demise.

Of course, no one is to know that I was the first in centuries to gaze upon the majesty of a dragon. No one, other than our former Grand Mage, of course, thought Relfread, as he patted Petyier's hand. *Oh, how it would freeze the blood of the lords and ladies of Uprynenos to know how far my influence stretches!*

Relfread gently placed Petyier's trembling hand back down and sank into the comfort of his chair, content. For decades, he'd been deprived of such luxury, instead obligated to live a life of utter abstinence as he dedicated himself to the warming embrace of the Dragonian Flame. Seated at the precipice of glory, relishing in the sheer cunning of his own schemes, he allowed himself to soak in the extravagance of utter power. Not for too long, however. There was still more to be done.

I suppose I've wasted enough time with the sickbed pleasantries. I dare not delay what needs to be done any longer, thought Relfread, as he pushed himself up from his seat, clutching one of its plump cushions.

Sombrely, he drifted to the other side of the opulent bed and hung over Petyier's sleeping form like a spectre waiting to strike. In most circumstances, he despised taking care of his own dirty work. However, the chafing binds of family ties obligated him to deal with Petyier personally.

Conquering a surge of trepidation, Relfread lowered the cushion onto the face of His Majesty Petyier the Third of the House Schwartz, King of the Five, Guardian of the Isles and Beacon of the Flame. He summoned all his years of resentment and jealousy, giving him the strength to push down and smother Petyier with all the force he could muster. Despite this – despite all their differences – his chest thumped with the weighty blows of regret as his older brother's pitiful fight against the inevitable gradually withered away into stillness.

Relfread held the cushion against Petyier's face long after he'd stopped thrashing. It would be beyond foolish to get sloppy now. Nothing could be left to chance. Only after his arms began to tremble from the prolonged strain did Relfread ease his pressure on the cushion and throw it back onto the chair. With how Petyier used to tease him when they were children, effortlessly besting him each time their infantile squabbles came to blows, it was marginally disappointing that he'd died by his younger brother's hand with so pathetic a struggle.

I do hope Inquisitor Siskin at least puts up a show of resistance once the rabble hunts him down, he mused. *In all likelihood, it shall be a delightfully bloody demise.*

Inquisitor Siskin was the other loose end that had to be dealt with during the evening's chaos. An irritating thread that Relfread had no qualms in letting the rampaging hordes of Dragonian zealots snip for him. Siskin's head had become a prized target after Relfread issued a declaration claiming he'd acted without permission to incarcerate an innocent Dragonian preacher. He'd been excommunicated from the Dragonian Church, with the followers of the Flame whom he'd brutally tortured and killed declared as martyrs.

Each step had been part of their original plan, so for a time, Siskin would expect that he'd be cleared and free to come out of hiding in a day or two. What wasn't part of their original plan, however, was the fact that all the locks to the various safe houses at Siskin's disposal had been changed, or the rooms themselves had been filled with Dragonian faithful, who'd been supplied with astonishingly detailed descriptions of the man who'd violently murdered their brethren.

It was always a shame to lose such a ruthless killer. However, as Siskin had alluded to himself, he wasn't a fanatical follower who would do as commanded without question or hesitation. No, he was an unreliable, argumentative crust-sword who would only follow Relfread's directions while the gold was worth the risk. A crust-sword with an undeniably useful set of skills ... but, regrettably, an unpredictable element who would best suit Relfread's upcoming schemes if he was simply removed from the equation.

Once the dust and ash of the riots have settled, I'm sure a suitably devoted replacement can be found, Relfread thought, casting the issue from his mind.

He tucked his brother's corpse snugly into bed. Petyier looked quite at peace, blissfully unaware that the world beyond his chamber was far from harmonious. After dusting off his final goodbye to his brother, Relfread crossed the room to a woodworm-riddled desk. It bowed under the weight of numerous documents, much as it had done in the days when the chamber had belonged to his father, King Triard the Second.

With a heave, Relfread shifted the desk a couple of feet to the side, revealing an inconspicuous wooden panel in the wall behind it – a secret entrance to the maze of passages that snaked throughout the palace and under the city streets, leading to various landmarks within the capital. It was admittedly an overly dramatic exit route, especially when the guard already knew of his presence in the chamber. However, considering the ferocity of the riots raging outside, he deemed it a sage choice to leave through the back door, so to speak.

Relfread had left the guard explicit instructions to enter the room after an hour had passed, tidy any disturbances and leave to update the Royal Physician on the king's condition. If he managed his task without betraying Relfread's presence, he could see himself in the running for replacing Siskin. Or, more likely, he'd have to die for knowing far too much.

I'll mull over his fate during supper, thought Relfread, as he removed the panel and slipped like a spider into the web of passageways. After crawling several claustrophobic miles under the burning city, he emerged deep within the bowels of the Cathedral of Fire, sodden from head to toe with the decades of filth that had accumulated upon the walls of the dank tunnels. He could've taken a different path and climbed out from a trapdoor within the cathedral's vestry, which would be conveniently devoid of witnesses this time of night. Yet his anticipation had gotten the better of him.

Relfread scuttled through the extensive cellar network beneath the Cathedral of Fire, taking turn after turn with the absolute certainty of an insect working its way through its nest. Much like his mind, his eyes had adjusted to the darkness a long time ago. His belief in the Flame was the only light he needed to guide him now.

Finally, Relfread burst forth into a cavernous chamber. Through the faintest of cracks in the ancient rock ceiling, hundreds of feet above, a single beam of dazzling light shone into the centre of the room. Steeling his nerves for what he was about to unleash, Relfread crept towards the large chest illuminated by the light. He took out a key from the depths of his filthy robes, unlocked the chest and lifted its lid. Inside, nestled on a thick bed of straw, were two scaled eggs. One crimson, the other indigo.

Shivering with exhilaration, Relfread began to recite the incantation he'd manipulated the court wizards into discovering for him. The same incantation that had woken the sister of these two eggs, after it had been stolen from the Royal Collection. While his harsh, flame-scorched voice echoed around the chamber, speaking the words of forbidden sorcery, Relfread watched on as both eggs began to emit an emerald hue, quivering with increasing vigour in their nest.

Their shells began to crack.

THE END